東西学術研究所研究叢書第11号
西洋文学における信仰とフィクション研究班

Trends in Eastern and Western Literature, Medieval and Modern.

Edited by Yoko Wada

関西大学
東西学術研究所

FOREWORD

It is a pleasure to introduce this book which represents the results of research conducted by the Western Literature Group of the Institute for Oriental and Occidental Studies. The period of their research covered the three years between April 2016 and March 2019, and the theme they assigned themselves was "Cultural Exchanges in Western Literature." With this broad rubric in mind the eight members represented here worked individually in their areas of specialization, while at the same time endeavoring, where possible, to collaborate by crossing the conventional boundaries between academic fields and engaging in comparative research — in keeping with our Institute's cherished principle of encouraging a comparative approach to the study of eastern and western cultures. Overall, the present book covers a wide range of topics, demonstrating the rich variety of both eastern and western literature over a period of thirteen centuries.

It is my sincere wish that the Western Group will continue to advance the mission of the Institute and Kansai University as a center of research on eastern and western cultures. And I hope that readers will find much to learn from this book.

Shen Guowei

SHEN, Guowei
Director

EDITOR'S FOREWORD

This book brings together the work of a very diverse group of eight scholars
with interests and areas of specialization spread across three continents and
spanning more than thirteen centuries. Their investigations involve a variety
of languages, eastern and western, ancient and modern, each one studied as a
literary phenomenon within a well-defined cultural context. Thus, Latin in
early medieval Ireland and England (O'Neill and Whitman); Japanese in the
early and later medieval periods (Whitman and Wittkamp); Middle English
in 14th century Anglo-Norman Ireland (Wada); Russian in the 19th century
(Kondo); French in late 20th century philosophical exchanges (Kawakami);
and Modern Spanish in both its European and Latin American expressions
(Shu and Hirata). Collectively, these articles cover a multiplicity of literary
genres and modes, such as poetry, fiction, religious texts, philosophical tracts,
and parody. What ties them together, however tenuously, is that they address
texts which bear witness to change, either induced by external influences or,
having been generated internally, carried over to other cultures. Not
surprisingly, many of these articles reflect a willingness to cross linguistic
and cultural boundaries.

We thank the former director, Professor Keiichi Uchida, and the present
director, Professor Guowei Shen, for giving us the opportunity to publish the
results of our research. We also acknowledge the constant help of Ms Satoko
Nasu, who assisted at every stage of the book's preparation.

Lastly, this book is dedicated to Professors Kazuyoshi Yamanouchi and Yoshihiro Yoshino, both eminent philologists of medieval English, on the occasion of their retirement. *Wesað hale!*

Yoko WADA
Editor

Trends in Eastern and Western Literature, Medieval and Modern.

目 次

The Earliest Evidence for Construing in the West:

the *Codex Usserianus Primus* Gospels and the Cambridge, Trinity College, Pauline Epistles

Patrick P O'Neill

The present paper has its origins in a collaborative project begun with Professor John Whitman who some years ago broached the idea of a comparative study between the Japanese system of *kunten* and the Western tradition of construe marks, especially as represented by evidence from early medieval Ireland. On both sides there was a clear-eyed awareness that any kind of direct contact was out of the question and that at best one could talk about significant parallels. Nevertheless, the circumstances in which both systems developed shared remarkable similarities. An insular culture endeavors to master the reading of texts in a foreign language which for cultural reasons it regards as superior to its own vernacular. The superiority derives from the fact that the language in each case came as part of the intellectual baggage of a new religion introduced from outside. Ireland received Christianity in the fifth century from the neighboring island of Britain, a province of the Roman empire. The conversion was evidently a gradual and bloodless process which (as far as we know) was completed by the mid-sixth century. But our interest here lies not in the system of beliefs and observances of the new religion but rather in its intense culture of literacy in Latin, the language required both for reading the Bible and conducting Christian liturgy. Coincidentally, at about this time Japan was also playing host to Buddhism, a

1

new religion introduced from neighboring China, while also grappling with the linguistic challenges of reading its sacred texts in Chinese. In the words of Japanologist Ivan Morris, "State activities in Heian as in Nara were modelled on those of T'ang and this continued long after the dynasty itself had disappeared. All official and semi-official documents were written in Chinese or, more usually, in a hybrid form of Sino-Japanese. This too was the principal language that men used for scholarly and literary work, corresponding to the rather debased version of Latin that was current in the West."[1]

Both cultures emphasized the training of a literate priestly caste within a monastic setting, a process which began with acquiring literacy in the language of the new religion, followed by mastering of its grammar and syntax, in preparation for the reading and interpreting of sacred texts. And since the reading of the manuscripts which enshrined these texts posed considerable challenges, both cultures devised various techniques to facilitate comprehension, mostly in the form of glossing, an activity which I define broadly as lexical and/or symbolic cues inserted adjacent to the main text[2] to facilitate the reading, understanding, and interpretation of its words. In Irish manuscripts, the two types of glosses are often found together, sometimes even working in a complementary relationship. However, the present study will confine itself to the symbols, which are variously called 'construe marks' or 'syntactical glosses.'

The focus of the present paper is two Irish manuscripts which provide the earliest known evidence in the West for construing. While scholars of Japanese *kunten* have established a reasonably accurate chronology of the system, with origins in the eighth century, such is not the case for its Western

---

1) *The World of the Shining Prince: Court Life in Ancient Japan* (London, 1985), p. 24.

2) Old Irish *corp*, literally 'body.'

counterpart. The early-twentieth century paleographers of Irish manuscripts, such as W. M. Lindsay and R. I. Best, noted the existence of this phenomenon, referring to it as "syntax marks" and "signes de grammaire," but they did not engage the subject systematically. The pioneer in this field was Maartje Draak who plausibly reconstructed from early-ninth century manuscripts how Irish scribes went about clarifying the syntax of a Latin text, using construe marks.[3] More recently M. Korhammer has provided the most comprehensive investigation (to date) of Western manuscripts containing construe marks. He proposes a tripartite classification based on function: (a) those providing a comprehensive syntactical overview of a whole passage; (b) those establishing a connection between two or more words in a passage; and (c) those making a 'logical' connection between two words.[1]

All of these studies are based on the evidence of manuscripts dating from after 800AD, with an understandable bias towards those cultural areas that offered the most evidence, that is, mainland Europe and Anglo-Saxon England. In the present paper I would like to shift the geographical focus further westwards to the periphery of Europe, to Ireland where the earliest manuscript witnesses to construing are to be found. At least two manuscripts of Irish provenance have survived which were written, and construed a century or so before 800AD, raising the possibility that they represent the earliest evidence of construing, not just in Ireland but arguably in the West. The claim, as far as I know, has never been addressed before.

---

3) M. Draak, "A Leyden Boethius-Fragment with Old-Irish Glosses," *Mededelingen der Koninklijke Nederlandsche Akademie van Wetenschappen, afd. Letterkunde,*11.3 (1948), pp. 115–27; "Construe Marks in Hiberno-Latin Manuscripts," ibid. 20.10 (1957), pp. 261–82; and "The Higher Teaching of Latin Grammar in Ireland during the Ninth Century," ibid. 30.4 (1967), pp. 109–44.

4) M. Korhammer, 'Mittelalterliche Konstruktionshilfen und altenglische Wortstellung,' *Scriptorium* 35.1 (1980), pp. 18–58.

We begin with the obvious question of why construe marks were devised. As already noted, for Irish monastic students Latin was a foreign language whose grammar and syntax had to be mastered *ab ovo* before they could read the Christian Latin texts which formed the core of their study. During the seventh century Ireland seems to have been especially receptive to continental influences (perhaps connected to closer ties with Italy as a result of the Easter controversy) and evidence of Late Antique works arriving at that time has survived. Examples are the Late Latin grammarians such as Charisius, the commentary of Pelagius on the Pauline Epistles, and of Julian of Eclanum on the Psalms, and no doubt copies of biblical texts. These would probably have been transmitted in manuscripts written in the *scriptio continua* which was prevalent at that time. So, in addition to the predictable problems of comprehension associated with Latin grammar and syntax, there was the visual problem of reading *scriptio continua*, a style of writing in which individual words, periods and sentences were not separated by spacing. The so-called 'Boniface Gospels' (Fulda, Landesbibliothek, MS Bonifatius 1), a sixth-century Italian manuscript written in this style, shows an eighth-century Anglo-Saxon reader addressing this problem by entering thin vertical lines between letters so as to delimit individual words.[5] No such example has survived from early Ireland, not necessarily because the Irish were better readers, but rather because they devised a more effective system of remediation. Malcolm Parkes called it the "Grammar of Legibility," which he defined as

> a complex of graphic conventions by which the written manifestations of language operates to facilitate access to the information it conveys. These conventions did not spring up all at once, they developed over time as readers demanded greater clarity from the written medium itself. And

5) See Plate I(a).

they operate at all levels of that medium: the letter, the word, the sentence, the paragraph and the page.[6]

For example, among the innovations they adopted were the *littera notabilior* (where the first letter stands out by virtue of its size or shape) to give visual emphasis to the beginning of a text or section; and the marking of a pause for a sentence, clause or phrase by means of a sequence of dots and comma at the mid-point level in an ascending order of importance; thus ·, ··, ···. To Parkes' list of graphic conventions to aid 'legibility' should now be added the technique of construing, with its concomitant symbols. We can justify their inclusion because like the other conventions described by Parkes, the construe symbols function visually; they "signal directly to the mind through the eye."[7] At the same time their incorporation into the complex of graphic conventions posed a challenge. Just as the conventions used to identify words had to be visually distinguished from those used to identify sentences, clauses and phrases, so too the conventions which addressed syntactical issues would need to stand out in such a way that they could not be confused with any other set of conventions, notably those dealing with punctuation. The solution was simple: whereas punctuation symbols were present on the line of writing, the construe symbols were entered directly above or below the word(s) of syntactical interest.

The conventions identified by Parkes were already beginning to appear in Irish manuscripts dating as early as the first half of the seventh century. One such manuscript, the Ussher Gospels (Trinity College, Dublin, MS 55),

---

6) M. B. Parkes, "The Contribution of Insular Scribes in the seventh and eighth centuries to the 'Grammar of Legibility'" in *Scribes, Scripts and Readers* (London, 1991), pp. 1–18 at p. 6.

7) M. B. Parkes, *Pause and Effect: Punctuation in the West* (Burlington VT, 1992), p. 21.

seems to bear witness to a very early stage of the process. While maintaining the old-fashioned Late Antique practice of *scriptio continuata* (though in much less uncompromising form than the Boniface Gospels), it does contain evidence of punctuation in accord with Parkes' graphic conventions.[8] Despite its damaged condition, the Ussher Gospels (hereafter 'Uss') is remarkable on several counts. It contains a copy of the Old Latin Gospels, a type of text which harkens back to the earliest Christian period before St Jerome's Vulgate Gospels became dominant in Europe during the sixth and seventh century. Furthermore, the manuscript itself is very old; some would date it to the fifth century, though most scholars agree on a date in the early-seventh century. Finally, it is the earliest witness to dry-point glossing in Ireland, a technique whereby notes or comments on the main text were entered between the lines or on the margins, but without ink (hence the name dry-point), literally carved into the page with a metal stylus. This dry-point glossing happened sometime after the copying of the main text, though probably within the seventh century, as suggested by its semi-uncial script; the presence of an Old Irish word with the archaic spelling, *focrici* (later OIr *fochraici*, 'payments, rewards') consonant with a pre-700 date; and the fact that the most recent of the Latin sources used by the glossator probably belongs to that period.[9] Among these glosses are found some twenty-two occurrences of symbols, in contradistinction to letters or words. Since all of the dry-point glosses appear to be the work of the same scribe, the symbols are presumably also of seventh-century date.

---

8) Parkes, *Pause and Effect*, observes that the two scribes of the manuscript indicate the end of a section of text by a series of 'comma-' or small 7-shaped marks, though he also suggests the influence of sixth-century Italian models.

9) P. P. Ó Néill, 'The earliest dry-point glosses in Codex Usserianus Primus,' in T. Barnard *et al.*, *A Miracle of Learning: studies in manuscripts and Irish learning* (Aldershot, 1998), pp. 1–28 at pp. 9–10.

They take the following forms:

·|	(*alogus*)[10]
—	(*obelos, above or below*)
∸ ∹	(*obelos, dotted, above or below*)
:	(*double* punctus)
ʘ	(*oculus*)
··	(*distigme*)
∴ ∵	(*trigon*)

Most of these signs have technical names, pointing to the fact that they had an earlier existence as textual annotations in manuscripts from the Late Antique period or even earlier. Some of them originally formed part of an elaborate set of signs (*nota*) used in the ancient classical world to annotate well-known texts of poetry and history such as Homer's *Iliad.* So, for example, the *alogus*, written beside a word, indicated some kind of error; the *obelos* that a word or sentence was spurious, superfluous or erroneous. These marks were originally entered by readers trained in textual criticism, working in their native Greek or Latin language. How Irish scribes acquired them is unclear. Isidore of Seville's *De notis sententiarum* (*Etymologiae* I.xxi–xxiv) treats of twenty six such signs, including three found in Uss: the *obelos*, the *obelos* with a point above, and the *alogus*. A more immediate source may have been the so-called 'technical/critical signs,' a group of symbols often found on the margins of early medieval manuscripts, serving to correct, draw attention to, or identify words or passages in the main text. These symbols are found in Latin manuscripts of Late Antiquity, including biblical texts such the Codex Vaticanus 1209 (fourth century), which employed the *obelos* and the *distigme*,

10) Strictly speaking the dot is not found in Isidore's description of the symbol, so it is possible that the form in Uss represents a vertical *obelos* with dot.

the former to mark spurious text, the latter to mark textual variants.[11] Three such symbols commonly occur in Irish manuscripts, including Uss, the *distigme*, *trigon* and the *oculus*.[12] However, in their function as construe marks these symbols must be distinguished from the technical signs on which they were probably modelled. Such technical signs are found on the margins, but the construe marks occur within the main text, above or below individual words; and whereas the technical signs signify a word or at least a meaning (e.g. 'ask' 'correct' etc.), these same signs when used as construe marks are mere symbols lacking semantic force, as evident from the fact that they can be used indiscriminately throughout a text. Construe marks, whatever their origin, have no intrinsic meaning; they are essentially visual cues.

For the symbols found in Uss, the frequencies are as follows: *oculus* (2x); *distigme* (2x); *alogus* (3x); *double punctus* (3x); *triga* (3x); and various forms of the *obelos* (8x). Why so many *obeloi*? The simple answer might be that they were the easiest sign to scratch into Uss with a stylus, since they involved a straight line and dots. But the same advantage could have been better gained by using dots by themselves, so we are forced to look for a more convincing explanation. The *obelos* had become a common symbol in Irish biblical manuscripts (borrowed from continental biblical texts), where it served to mark words or passages in the biblical text at hand (the Septuagint-based Vulgate) not found in the Hebrew Bible. It was St Jerome who popularized this use of the *obelos* in his version of the psalms known as the Gallican (though it had been used by earlier biblical translators such as Origen), by marking the beginning of a collocation of superfluous word(s)

---

11) See, for example, P. B. Payne, "Vaticanus *Distigme-obelos* Symbols Marking Added Text, Including 1Corinthians 14. 34–5," *New Testament Studies* 63.4 (2017), pp. 604–25.
12) The term used by E. Steinová, "Technical Signs in Early Irish Medieval Manuscripts Copied in Irish Minuscule," in M. J. Teeuwen and I. VanRenswoude (edd.), *Utrecht Studies in Medieval Literacy* 38 (Turnhout, 2017), pp. 37–85.

with the *obelos* (plus dot above and below) and the end with two points like a modern colon. Commenting on his use of the *obelos*, Jerome remarked that "whenever you see a preceding *obelos*, from there to the double points (=colon), you should know that the Greek (Septuagint) version contains an addition by comparison with the Hebrew text." For example, Psalm 1:4 reads in his Gallican version as "NON SIC IMPII÷NON SIC:" where the *obelos* and the two dots delimit words not found in the Hebrew version, which has "NON SIC IMPII." The same usage is employed in an Irish copy of the psalms, known as the *Cathach*, dating to the first half of the seventh century, which suggests that use of the *obelos* and the double *punctus* would have been familiar to Irish monastic scribes.[13] Arguably, the precedent of Jerome's usage, and possibly also Isidore's discussion of the *nota*, gave the *obelos* an advantage over the other symbols.

The following examples show the construe marks at work in Uss:[14]

(1) fol. 37ᵛ (Jn. 3:14–16):

EXALTARI **OPORTET** FILIUM HOMINUM UT OMNIS QUI CREDIT

IN EO...HABEAT UITAM AETERNAM SIC **ENIM** DILEXIT DEUS

HUN<C MUND>UM UT FILIUM SUUM UNICUM DARET

("it is only right that the son of mankind [Jesus] be exalted so that everyone who believes in him may possess eternal life....seeing that God so loved this world that he gave it his only son").

Under OPORTET stands an *obelos* with upper dot, while above ENIM an

---

13) See Plate I(b).

14) For ease of reference, here and throughout, words that have construe marks are printed in bold letters. A digital version of Uss is available at https://www.tcd.ie/library/early-irish-mss, in which some of the construe marks are visible, e.g. those of (2), below.

obelos with lower dot (hardly visible). This complementarity both in the location of the symbol (below and above the respective lemma) and the position of the dot (above and below the *obelos*), is a recognized technique of later Irish construers to indicate the interdependence of two symbols and their associated lemmata.[15] But while the visual connection between them is clear, the reason for linking them is not so easy to figure out, especially since a whole verse of two clauses intervenes between them. Moreover, the second lemma ENIM is an uninflected particle, thus ruling out any kind of grammatical relationship between them. And yet one finds ENIM very frequently glossed with construe marks in 8th and 9th century Irish manuscripts.[16] Evidently, for Irish construers the particle in certain contexts served some significant syntactical purpose — as indeed it can in Latin usage, establishing, for example, a confirmatory or causal connection with a previous clause. In the present context ENIM could be read as introducing a causal clause ('seeing that...son') which explains why Jesus is worthy of being exalted (OPORTET EXALTARI),[17] a relationship to which readers are directed by the complementary construe marks.

(2) fol. 36ᵛ (Jn 2:19–22):

ET IN TRIDUO **RESUSCITAB<O** ILLUD>....RECORDATI SUNT

DISCIPULI EIUS QUONIAM HOC DIC<EBAT ET> **CREDIDERUNT**

SCRIBTURAE ET **UERBO**

---

15) See Draak, "Construe Marks," 14: "The construe mark group comes to an end... when the signs change over...as to position (the identical sign, but over instead of under the (connected) word, or the other way round)."

16) Discussed below, in section C. v. (p. 29).

17) The intervening verse mentions the rewards intended for those who believe in the son of God.

("And on the third day I will restore it....His disciples recalled that he said that, and they believed the Scriptures and the utterance").

Here two different symbols are being used, the *oculus* and the *distigme*, and again they seem to form complementary pairs, as indicated by the above-and-below principle. The link between RESUSCITABO and UERBO is potentially difficult to follow, not least because the two signs are so far apart — two verses and six clauses between them — a feature which suggests that their relationship is not grammatical or even strictly syntactical, since even the most attentive reader would find it difficult to retain the association between them. The first lemma marks the end of Christ's shocking statement to the Jews that if the Temple were destroyed he could restore it in three days (RESUSCITABO); the second lemma belongs to a statement that after Christ had risen from the dead his disciples remembered and believed these words (UERBO) — the words in question refer to Christ's earlier statement which ended with the keyword RESUSCITABO. Thus, by using the *oculus* symbol, the construer linked the statement with its subsequent recollection by the disciples, thereby emphasizing Christ's prophetic powers about his own death.

The second pair of marks, the double (horizontal) dots under DISCIPULI and above CREDIDERUNT seems to link a plural subject with its correspondingly plural verb. But the explanation is facile since such basic grammar hardly justified a symbolic prompt. Rather the answer may lie in the word after CREDIDERUNT, the noun SCRIBTURAE. At first glance it looks like a plural noun and therefore a potential subject for the plural verb CREDIDERUNT. In reality, it is a dative singular, the indirect object of that verb. Evidently, to head off this misreading and to avoid any ambiguity the construer directly linked the verb CREDIDERUNT with its true subject.

(3) fol. 97ᵛ (Lc 7:26–27): [18]

SED QUID EXISTIS UIDERE PROFETAM DICO UOBIS **AMPLIUS**
.

QUAM PROPHETAM HIC EST DE QUO SCRIBTUM EST ECCE
.

MITTO **ANGELUM** MEUM ANTE FACIEM TUAM

("But what did you go out to see? A prophet? I tell you, something
more than a prophet. This is the one of whom it is written, 'See, I send
my angel into your presence…'")

Here AMPLIUS and ANGELUM are linked by a double *punctus*, one under
AMPLIUS and the other above ANGELUM. Since syntax is hardly a problem
here, we might look at grammar: *amplius* (originally a comparative adjective/
adverb) is being used (somewhat out of the ordinary) as a substantival neuter
noun ("something more"), whose meaning, moreover, is rather vague. Both
of these issues are clarified by connecting it through the double punctus with
ANGELUM, so that the vague "something greater than a prophet" is identified
as an angel, in this context a personal messenger of God, John the Baptist.
The two symbols serve both as grammatical clarification and as identification.

(4) fol. 118ʳ (Lc 12:51):

PUTATIS QUONIAM PACEM UENI MITTERE IN TERRAM

("Do you really think that I have come to give peace on earth?")

Here we have a singleton, a symbol without a complementary partner; in this

---

18) The digital image shows the two *distigmai*, the first directly under the M of
AMPLIUS, the second (above) between the N and G of ANGELUM.

case a subscript *obelos*. The verb is familiar and there are no obvious syntactical problems. But a Modern English translation would surely supply a punctuation mark not available to the seventh-century glossator, the mark of interrogation.[19] Without this visual clue PUTATIS could be misread as declarative "You think" instead of interrogative "Do you think?" Evidently, the glossator inserted the *obelos* under the verb to draw attention to its interrogative character.

(5) fol. 78ʳ (Jn 21:21–22):

CUM UIDISSET PET<RUS> DIXIT AD IESUM DOMINE AUTEM

QUID **DICIT** EI IESUS SIC EUM UO<LO>

("When Peter observed that person he said to Jesus, 'Lord, and what will this person do?'" Jesus said to him, 'so I will" etc.)

Again, a singleton, the *obelos* above the word DICIT. As with the preceding example, there appears to be no obvious issue of grammar or syntax. However, there is potential for syntactical confusion in that the cryptic interrogative QUID has no verb — a form of *facere* ('to do') is understood — and so could be mistakenly run together with the following DICIT. The *obelos* over DICIT probably served as a syntactical warning, while also marking the beginning of a new sentence and verse, a precaution made all the more necessary because the *scriptio continuata* did not provide clear word division.

Altogether, Uss has 11 singleton symbols and 6 complementary pairs of symbols, performing a variety of functions: disambiguating, clarifying grammar, and making connections between clauses, including ones far removed from each other.

*　　*　　*　　*　　*

---

19) Later Irish construers adverted to the interrogative by inserting a lexical gloss, an abbreviated form of Lat. *interrogatio*, above the initial verb.

The second Irish manuscript of interest for the present study is a heavily glossed copy of the Pauline Epistles, dating to the second quarter of the eighth century, Cambridge, Trinity College, MS B.10.5 (hereafter referred to as the 'Trinity Epistles'). Its script, punctuation, decoration and mis-en-page, suggest Irish origins. Yet certain features point to Northumbria, notably the distinctive abbreviation at the end of verbs ending in *(t)-ur*, a usage peculiar to scribes of that kingdom. It appears that the scribe was either Irish, working in Northumbria and influenced by local scribal practices, or a local Northumbrian trained in the Irish tradition. The former hypothesis seems more likely given the frequent citations in the glosses of Pelagius's commentary on the Pauline Epistles, a work well known in Ireland but likely to have been shunned as heretical in Northumbria. Also, the close relationship between this manuscript and another copy of the Pauline Epistles copied in Ireland in the late-eighth century (Würzburg, Universitätsbibliothek, MS. M.P.th. f.12) in the content of their glosses and their techniques of construing points to ultimate Irish origins for the Trinity manuscript.

In contrast to Uss, the Trinity Epistles offers an abundance of evidence, with almost every page containing some form of construing. Interestingly, it appears that the construing preceded the lexical glossing, as suggested by a number of instances where a gloss had to be split up or written around a prominent construe mark.[20] Since this stratum of glossing is contemporaneous with the writing of the main text and may have been done by the main scribe, that suggests the construe marks belong to the same date. Pending a

---

20) See Plate I(c), where the penultimate word of the first gloss, *traditus* (above ET QUIA) is split, with *tradi-* on one side and *-tus* on the other side of a protruding *obelos* construe symbol; likewise with the second gloss on the same line (above EST ET QUIA), where *gloriorum* is awkwardly split into *glo-* and *-riorum* on either side of a second *obelos* symbol. For other examples, see fol. 7ᵛ, lines 17–18; and fol. 10aᵛ, line 20. A digital version of the Trinity manuscript is available at https://www.trin.cam.ac.uk/library/wren-digital.library

more thorough investigation than the present paper can provide, three main categories of construe marks are identified here, based on form: (a) matching pairs of marks; (b) multiple occurrences of the same mark within a large syntactical unit; and (c) singletons, single marks without a partner.

A. Matching pairs of marks

These serve various functions:

1. Relating clauses (result, consecutive, purpose and noun clauses) to each other

(i) For example, IICor 1:4 (fol. 10aʳ):

DEUS...QUI **CONSULATUR** NOS IN OMNI TRIBULATIONE
NOSTRA **UT** POSSIMUS ET IPSI CONSOLARI EOS...

("the God who comforts us in all our tribulation, so that we may be able to comfort them...")

The double *punctus* under CONSULATUR (which introduces a relative clause) and above UT (which introduces a consecutive clause) could be read as indicating that the latter clause is the result of the former. By virtue of being consoled by Christ, the Corinthians are now able, in turn, to offer consolation to others.

(ii) Likewise, IICor 1:9 (fol. 10aʳ):

SED IPSI IN NOBIS METIPSIS **RESPONSUM** MORTIS **HABUIMUS**
UT NON SIMUS FIDENTES IN NOBIS SED IN DEO QUI SUSCITAT
MORTUOS

("But we had the sentence of death within ourselves, so that we should not trust in ourselves but in God who raises the dead")

The first pair of symbols (*distigme*) seems clear enough, connecting HABUIMUS with a consecutive UT clause denoting a result. Indeed, the connection is so obvious that one might well ask why the construer expressly made it. The answer may be that the cause which produced the UT clause is not simply HABUIMUS but the collocation HABUIMUS RESPONSUM MORTIS, hence perhaps the single *obelos* above RESPONSUM.

(iii) IICor 1:11 (fols. 10a^r–10a^v):

ADIUUANTIBUS ET UOBIS IN ORATIONEM PRO NOBIS ŪT EX
MULTARUM FACIERUM EIUS QUAE IN NOBIS EST DONATIONIS...

("You also assisting by prayer for us, so that for the gift bestowed on us by the means of many persons...")

A cause-and result-construction linked by *oboloi*: the supportive prayers of the Corinthians (ADIUUANTIBUS), has brought about that (UT) God has shown favor to Paul.

(iv) ICor 12:15 (fol. 5^v):

SI **DIXERIT** PES **QUONIAM** NON SUM MANUS NON SUM DE
CORPORE

("As if the foot should say 'because I am not the hand, I am not of the body'").

DIXERIT of the first clause has a dependent noun clause introduced by QUONIAM, a relationship marked by the *distigmai*. That above QUONIAM may have also served to alert readers to the switch to direct speech.

(v) IITim 4:17 (fol. 52^r):

DOMINUS AUTEM ADSTETIT ET **CONFORTAUIT** ME **UT** PER ME

PRAEDICATIO INPLEATUR

("Nevertheless, the Lord stood with and comforted me, that by me the preaching might be fulfilled").

Here the two *distigmai* frame a purpose construction (final clause): God comforted Timothy in order that through him the preaching of the divine message might be accomplished.

(vi) ICor 11:18–19 (fol. 5^r):[21]

PRIMUM QUIDEM CONUENIENTIBUS UOBIS IN AECLESIA **AUDIO**
+
SCISURAS ESSE ET EX PARTE **CREDO NAM** OPORTET HERESES

ESSE **UT** ET QUI PROBATI SUNT MANIFESTI FIANT IN UOBIS

("First of all, when you come together in church, I hear that there are divisions among you, and I partly believe it. For there must be heresies among you, so that they who are approved may be made manifest among you")

Here a triplet of *distigmai* links CREDO with the NAM...ESSE clause which

21) See Plate II(a).

serves as a qualifier of EX PARTE CREDO, the latter, in turn, linking with the following UT...UOBIS, which functions as a result clause. The singleton under AUDIO probably serves to highlight that it, rather than CREDO, is the primary verb, to be repositioned at the very beginning of the verse, an arrangement which would accord with the normal verb initial of Old Irish syntax.

2. Clarifying grammatical or syntactical relationships between words

(i) For example, IICor 1:19 (fol. 10aᵛ):

DEI **ENIM** FILIUS IESUS **CHRISTUS** QUI IN UOBIS PER NOS

PREDICATUS EST PER ME ET SILUANUM ET THIMOTHEUM NON

FUIT IN **ILLO** 'EST' ET 'NON'

("For the Son of God, Jesus Christ, who was preached by us among you, by me and Silvanus and Timotheus, was not 'YES' and 'NO.'")

Here an obelus with two vertical dots below connects CHRISTUS with ILLO, which has the same symbol, but inverted. Evidently, its purpose was to mark that ILLO referred to Christ, rather than any of the three persons mentioned immediately before it.

3. supplying an unexpressed word

(i) ICor 14:5 (fol. 7ʳ):

UOLO AUTEM UOS LOQUI LINGUIS MAGIS **AUTEM** PROFETARE...

("I wish indeed that you all spoke with tongues, but would prefer that you prophesied...")

The paired symbol of four dots in a square above UOLO and again above AUTEM indicates that UOLO should be supplied before the latter.

(ii) Likewise, ICor 11:23–25 (fol. 5^r):[22]

...**ACCIPIT** PANEM ET GRATIAS AGENS FREGIT ET DIXIT HOC

EST CORPUS MEUM QUOD PRO UOBIS TRADETUR HOC FACITE

IN MEAM COMMEMORATIONEM **SIMILITER** ET CALICEM...

("He took bread, and giving thanks he broke it and said 'This is my body which is handed over for you; do this in memory of me.' Likewise, with the chalice...")

The ⁓ mark above SIMILITER linking it with ACCIPIT (below) indicates that the latter verb should be supplied before SIMILITER. Theologically, the linking may suggest the complementarity of the blessing of both bread and wine.

(iii) ITh 4:4–5 (fol. 37^r):

UT SCIAT UNUSQUISQUE UESTRUM SUUM UAS **POSSIDERE** IN

SANCTIFICATIONE ET HONORE **NON** IN PASSIONE DESIDERII

("...that everyone of you should know how to possess his vessel in sanctification and honor, not in the lust of concupiscence.")

The mark above NON is a cue to supply the previous verb having the same mark, POSSIDERE.

---

22) See Plate II(b).

4. Connecting two noun phrases in apposition

(i) IICor 1:12 (fol. 10aᵛ):

NAM GLORIA NOSTRA **HAEC** EST. **TESTIMONIUM**

CONSCIENTIAE NOSTRAE **QUOD** IN SEMPLICITATE ET IN

SINCERITATE DEI ET NON EST IN SAPIENTIA CARNALI SED IN

GRATIA DEI **CONUERSATI SUMUS** IN HOC MUNDO

("For our rejoicing is this, the testimony of our conscience, that in
simplicity and godly sincerity, not with carnal wisdom, but by the grace
of God we have engaged with this world")

Here the *distigmai* correlate HAEC with TESTIMONIUM. Even though they
do not concord grammatically, since the first is feminine and the second
neuter, it appears that the construer sought to highlight TESTIMONIUM
CONSCIENTIAE NOSTRAE as a gloss on HAEC GLORIA. Another pair
of marks (double *punctus*) also links TESTIMONIUM with QUOD, presumably
as antecedent and relative pronoun. If so, the linking is probably wrong, since
QUOD here is a conjunction, an explicative 'that.' Two 'free' marks remain
to be explained. The cross over NAM may highlight its primacy (in Old
Irish terms) as the opening word of its clause, while also serving to introduce
an explanation of the spiritual power implied in the previous verse; while the
trigon under CONUERSATI (SUMUS) may have served to identify it as the
main verb of the passage.

(ii) Likewise, ITh 4:3 (fol. 37ʳ):

HAEC EST ENIM **UOLUNTAS** DEI **SANCTIFICATIO** UESTRA

("For this is the will of God, your sanctification").

Here SANTIFICATIO is in apposition to UOLUNTAS, both qualifying HAEC EST ENIM.

5. Disambiguating

(i) IICor 1:6 (fol. 10aʳ):

SIUE EXORTAMUR PRO UESTRA EXORTATIONE ET **SALUTE**

QUAE OPERATUR IN TOLLERANTIA EARUMDEM PASSIONUM…

("whether we be afflicted, it is for your consolation and salvation which works by the enduring of the same sufferings…").

Here relative QUAE is linked to SALUTE by the same *distigme*. While this seems like a rather obvious connection to make, the construer may have wanted to emphasize that SALUTE, rather than its coordinate EXORTATIONE, was the antecedent of QUAE and thus the subject of the relative clause introduced by the latter. The purpose of the singletons under EXORTAMUR and SALUTE is unclear.

(ii) Tit 1:2 (Fol. 52ᵛ):

IN SPE **UITAE** AETERNAE **QUAM** PROMISSIT

("In the hope of eternal life which [God] has promised")

Here the pair of *distigmai* seem to serve a dual purpose: highlighting that QUAM is a relative pronoun (rather than an adverb) with UITAE as antecedent, while also obviating the risk of misreading SPE, which is also feminine, as the antecedent. The *obelos* with single dots above and below (Isidore's *leminiscus*) is not a construe mark, but was meant to alert the reader to a lengthy adjacent gloss on SPE.

(iii) IICor 1:11 (fols. 10a^r–10a^v):

ADIUUANTIBUS ET UOBIS IN ORATIONEM PRO NOBIS UT

EX MULTARUM FACIERUM **EIUS** QUAE IN NOBIS EST

DONATIONIS...

("With you also assisting by praying for us, so that for the gift bestowed on us by the means of many persons...").

The first related pair of *obeloi* has been discussed above in 1.iii. Because EIUS is separated from its complementary genitive DONATIONIS (God's gift to Paul) by a relative clause, the matching pair of *distigmai* evidently served to link them; that over EIUS may also have obviated any erroneous linking with the preceding genitive FACIERUM.

(iv) Hebr 12:17 (fol. 66^r):

SCITOTE **ENIM** QUONIAM ET POSTEA CUPIENS HEREDITARE

BENEDICTIONEM REPROBATUS EST NON ENIM INUENIT

POENITENTIAE LOCUM QUANQUAM CUM LACRIMIS

INQUISSISET **EAM**

("For you know how afterward, when he desired to inherit the blessing, he was rejected because he did not find the place of repentance, though he sought it carefully with tears").

The double *punctus* linking POENITENTIAE and EAM suggests that the latter is a personal pronoun standing for POENITENTIA, not the earlier noun BENEDICTIONEM which, as a feminine singular noun, is also in grammatical concord with EAM. Curiously, the main scribe adopted the opposite view and glossed EAM with 'benedictionem.' For a possible explanation of the mark above ENIM, see pp. 29–36, below.

B. Multiple occurrences of the same mark within a period

This phenomenon involves a series of parallel clauses or phrases or words whose close relationship is marked by assigning the same symbol to each member.

(i) The most striking example is Paul's famous discourse on charity (ICor 13) which begins with an exhortation to his audience "to be zealous for the better gifts," the CARISMATA, underneath which word the construer has attached a pennant-shaped symbol ▸ (containing a dot). Eight lines further on, where Paul expounds in detail on the nature of Christian love (*caritas*) these pennants appear, one for each attribute, positive or negative:[23]

CARITAS PATIENS **BENIGNA** EST CARITAS **NON** EMULATUR

NON **AGIT** PERPERAM **NON** INFLATUS **NON** EST AMBITIOSA

NON **QUERIT** QUAE SUA SUNT **NON INRITATUR NON** COGITAT

MALUM **NON** GAUDIT SUPER INIQUITATEM

---

23) See Plate II(c).

("Charity is long-suffering and kind; charity is not envious; charity does no wrong; is not puffed up; is not conceited; does not seek her own advantage; does not provoke; does not plan evil; does not rejoice in iniquity").

(ii) IICor 1:15-16 (fol. 10aᵛ):

ET HAC CONFIDENTIA **UOLUI** PRIUS UENIRE AD UOS UT

SAECUNDAM GRATIAM HABERETIS **ET** PER UOS TRANSIRE IN

MACEDONIAM **ET** ITERUM A MACEDONIA UENIRE AD UOS **ET**

A UOBIS DEDUCI IN IUDEUM

("And in this confidence I desired to come to you before, that you might have a double benefit; and to pass from you to Macedonia; and again to come to you from Macedonia; and by you to be led on my way to Judea").

What holds these *oculus* marks together is the verb UOLUI which governs a series of clauses containing infinitive verbs, each clause listing a stage in Paul's proposed itinerary.

(iii) IITim 3:10 (fol. 51ʳ):

TU **AUTEM ADSAECUTUS** ES MEAM **DOCTRINAM**

INSTITUTIONEM **PROPOSITUM FIDEM LONGANIMITATEM**

DILECTIONEM PATIENTIAM PERSAECUTIONES PASSIONES

QUALIA MIHI FACTA SUNT ANTIOCHIAE

("But you have fully followed my doctrine, manner of life, purpose, faith, long-suffering, patience, persecutions, sufferings — such as were inflicted on me at Antioch").

Paul's catalogue of the guiding principles, virtues and sufferings involved in his evangelical mission are connected by means of *distigme*. In identifying the individual items of this list, the construer seems to distinguish between the theoretical (*distigme* underneath) and the practical (*distigme* above).[24] As the verb ADSAECUTUS ES governs all of these items in the accusative, it is also marked with the *distigme* below.

(iv) Hebr 12:22–23 (fol. 66ʳ):

SED **ACCESSISTIS** AD SION MONTEM **ET** CIUITATEM DEI

UIUENTIS HIERUSALEM **ET** MULTORUM MILIUM ANGELORUM

FREQUENTIAM ET AECLESIAM PRIMITIUORUM QUI CONSCRIPTI

SUNT IN CAELIS **ET** IUDICEM OMNIUM DEUM **ET SPIRITUS**

IUSTORUM PERFECTORUM ET TESTAMENTI NOUI **MEDIATOREM**

IESUM

("But you have come to Mount Zion and to the city of the living God, the heavenly Jerusalem, and to the company of many thousands of angels, and to the church of the firstborn who are inscribed in the heavens, and to God the judge of all, and to the spirits of the just made perfect...").

---

24) See also ICor 11:30 (fol. 5ʳ).

Here two sets of multiple occurrences of the same symbol are at work. The first begins with the symbol ⊦ under ACCESSISTIS, which thereafter occurs six times above ET to mark that they introduce clauses coordinate with the main ACCESSISTIS clause. At the same time this symbol could also be read as a cue to mentally supply ACCESSISTIS after ET. The second repeated symbol (four points in a squarish shape) above FREQUENTIAM and SPIRITUS harkens back to the same symbol under ACCESSISTIS, presumably to indicate that they are the direct objects of that verb.

C. Singletons:

These occur with considerable frequency, often side by side with the paired construe marks of category A.[25] Perhaps because of their isolated character they are often marked by visually bold symbols. Some seem to admit of ready explanation.

(i) For example, IICor 10:7 (fol. 16ʳ):

QUAE SAECUNDUM FACIEM SUNT **UIDETE**

("Take a look at things according to outward appearance").

In normal syntax, UIDETE as an imperative verb would head the sentence, followed by its object (here a noun clause). The solitary *oculus* over UIDETE

---

25) The phenomenon of the singleton symbol is quite common elsewhere in Irish manuscripts. See R. I. Best, *The Commentary on the Psalms with Glosses in Old-Irish preserved in the Ambrosian Library (MS. C 301 inf.) collotype facsimile* etc. (Dublin and London, 1936), fols. 2b27, *autem*; 14a3, *uoluerunt*; 14a8, *sed*; 14a31, *misit*. At 14b6, in the long sentence beginning "*Huic ergo....*," *ergo* has a subscript "**a**" with no alphabetical congeners; presumably it was intended to mark *ergo*, rather than *Huic*, as the first word of a syntactically rearranged sentence.

highlights its abnormal position at the end of the sentence and perhaps cues the reader to reposition it first.

(ii) ICor 11:32 (fol. 5'):

$$\overset{...}{}$$

DUM IUDICAMUR AUTEM A DOMINO **CORRIPIMUR** UT NON

CUM HOC MUNDO DAMPNE<M>UR

("But when we are judged, we are corrected by the Lord, so that we should not be condemned with this world").

The symbol of triple dots over CORRIPIMUR was probably meant to identify it as the main verb among three sharing the same passive inflection.

(iii) Likewise, Hebr 12:18-19 (fol. 66'):

ET TURBIDINEM ET CALIGINEM AD PROCELLAM ET TUBAE

SONUM ET UOCEM UERBORUM QUAM QUI AUDIERUNT

EXCUSAUERUNT SE NE EIS FIERET UERBUM

("you are not come to...the blackness and darkness and tempest and the sound of the trumpet and the voice of words, which those who heard begged that the word should not be spoken to them").

The isolated *distigme* was probably intended to mark EXCUSAUERUNT as the main verb, in contradistinction to the adjacent AUDIERUNT which, because of its shared subject and form, might mistakenly have been assigned that role.

However, the function of other singletons is not so readily explained.

(iv) For example, ICor 12:4 (fol. 5ᵛ):

‹various diacritical symbols over text›

DIUISSIONES UERO GRATIARUM SUNT IDEM **AUTEM** SPIRITUS

("Indeed, there is a diversity of gifts, but the same Spirit.")

Two singletons are present. (The symbol ⁒ can be eliminated since it is a *signe de renvoi* to a marginal gloss.) Those above UERO and AUTEM belong to a special category of particles which is discussed below. The one above DIUISSIONES is puzzling — perhaps a topic marker rather than a construe mark, highlighting a new subject, the different types of spiritual gifts.

(v) Tit 1:1 (fol. 52ᵛ): [26]

PAULUS…**APOSTOLUS** IESU CHRISTI **SAECUNDUM** FIDEM
ELECTORUM DEI **ET AGNITIONEM** UERITATIS **QUAE**
SAECUNDUM **PIETATEM** EST IN SPE **UITAE** AETERNAE **QUAM**
PROMISSIT

("Paul…an apostle of Jesus Christ with respect to the faith of the elect of God and the acknowledging of the truth which is in accord with religion, in the hope of the eternal life which he has promised").

Here we have four sets of symbols at work. (1) The *obelos* with single dot under SAECUNDUM has its counterpart above AGNITIONEM, presumably to mark a preposition and its governed accusative object. (2) Under FIDEM the *obelos* with dot above and below (Isidore's *leminiscus*) correlates with the same symbol above SPE further on, presumably to link them as two of

26) See Plate II(d).

the three theological virtues. (3) The *distigme* underneath AGNITIONEM correlates with the same mark above the following QUAE in an antecedent-relative pronoun relationship; likewise, with UITAE and QUAM. (4) That leaves the four triga, one attached below APOSTOLUS, and the other three above SAECUNDUM, AGNITIONEM AND PIETATEM, respectively. To read these latter three as a grammatical unit (preposition governing accusative nouns) seems an unlikely option, since the same grammatical function is served by the symbols of (1). Rather than being a singleton, the first trigon under APOSTOLUS belongs with the other three, as the head of a concatenation of key words (APOSTOLUS...SECUNDUM...AGNITIONEM ...PIETATEM) which serve to define Paul's apostolate to the elect in terms of teaching them an awareness of truth consonant with Christianity. Note that the marginal gloss also focuses on this aspect of the Pauline role, defining AGNITIONEM as a rejection of the literalism ('relica litera') of the Old Testament.

The most common occurrence of the singleton is above the particles *autem, enim, nam, ergo, uero,* and *igitur,* the first two of which are frequently so marked in the Trinity manuscript. Since this type of single symbol has no associated partner within the syntactical period and since it highlights particles which are conventionally treated as mere connective fillers — at least by readers of the Latin Vulgate — it is difficult to determine what purpose it serves. Nor can this usage be ignored: it occurs so frequently in the Trinity manuscript as to suggest that the construer saw it as having semantic and even rhetorical import. Viewed pragmatically, these Latin particles can be read as polysemous, their meaning very much depending on the immediate context, so that they can have causal, explanatory, contrastive, or adversative functions. A few examples of marked AUTEM will help to explain.

(vi) IICor 10:1 (fol. 16ʳ):

IPSE **AUTEM** EGO PAULUS OBSAECRO UOS…

("Now, I Paul myself beseech you…").

Here the tau symbol (with two dots underneath each arm) stands out as an outlier, its purpose evidently being to highlight that in the present context AUTEM introduces a fresh idea ("now"), a shift from the pastoral exhortation of the previous verse to a personal appeal. Note that in the modern printed text of the Vulgate, this verse begins a new chapter, so the change of subject would be obvious — but not so in the Trinity manuscript.

(vii) IICor 10:2 (fol. 16ʳ):

ROGO **AUTEM** NE PRESENS AUDEAM…

("But I appeal to you that I may not have to be bold when I am present…").

Here AUTEM is adversative: in the previous verse Paul declared that normally he was bold towards the Corinthians only when away from them, and mild while among them, but now because of changing circumstances he may have to switch tactics. The construer highlights the contextual force of AUTEM with a single trigon.

(viii) Likewise, IITim 3:10 (fol. 51ʳ):

TU **AUTEM** ADSAECUTUS ES MEAM DOCTRINAM…

("You, on the other hand, have followed my teaching…"),

where AUTEM serves to mark the sharp contrast of Timothy's behaviour with that of recent heretics, described in the preceding verses, and consequently is highlighted in this function by the symbol above it.

Turning to the particle *enim*, it also can be read in different ways depending on the immediate context. One of its most common uses is causal, to introduce the reason or explanation for a preceding sentence.

(ix) For example, Hebr 11:16 (fol. 64^v):

IDEO NON CONFUNDITUR DEUS UOCARI DEUS EORUM

PARAUIT **ENIM** ILLIS CIUITATEM

("So, God is not ashamed to be called their God, since he has prepared a city for them").

Here the second clause vindicates the statement of the first by asserting that God confirmed his association with the patriarchs by building a city for them. The marking of ENIM ('since') seems to suggest a causal connection with the previous clause.

(x) In Col. 4:13 (fol. 44^r), *enim* serves a different purpose:

TESTIMONIUM **ENIM** ILLI PERHIBEO

("Indeed, I will bear witness to him").

Here ENIM is not causal but rather confirmatory of Paul's previous statement that the subject (Epaphras) has worked hard as a missionary.

(xi) Yet another function of *enim* is evidenced in ITh 2:19 (fol. 36ʳ):

ʰ
QUAE EST **ENIM** NOSTRA SPES AUT GAUDIUM AUT CORONA

GLORIAE NONNE UOS...

("What then is our hope or joy or crown of glory? Is it not you?"),

In the previous verses, Paul talked of Jewish plots against him, but now he changes the subject, addressing the Thessalonians directly, so that ENIM functions as "a consensus particle which indicates an appeal to the involvement...of the addressee."[27]

A few anomalous cases where the symbol accompanying ENIM has a matching symbol within the same syntactical unit may offer possible clues as to its different functions:

(xii) ICor 14:1-3 (fol 6ᵛ):

SECTAMINI CARITATEM EMULAMINI SPIRITALIA MAGIS UT

PROFETETIS QUI **ENIM** LOQUITUR LINGUA NON HOMINIBUS
⋰
LOQUITUR SED DEO NEMO **ENIM** AUDIT

("Pursue charity; be eager for spiritual gifts, but rather that you may prophesy. He, however, who speaks a tongue speaks not to people but to God, for no one understands him").

---

27) See C. Kroon, Latin Particles and the Grammar of Discourse," in J. Clackton (ed.), *A Companion to the Latin Language* (Wiley-Blackwell, 2011), pp. 176–95 at p. 192. Korhammer does not advert to these particles (and their singleton symbols) as independent markers, instead referring only to their associative role with other words ("Der logische Anschluß von Konjunktionen wie *nam, enim, igitur, ergo, autem...*;" "Mittelalterliche Konstruktionshilfen," 33).

In the case of the first ENIM, one naturally looks back to the previous clause(s), to surmise its function; in this case, however, it does not seem to have its normal confirmatory or causal function in relation to what immediately preceded. Quite the opposite. Paul desires in the first verse that his congregation should have the gift of prophecy, but he then hastens to add in the next verse (QUI ENIM) that prophecy in the form of speaking in a tongue was anything but useful, since only God could understand it. It appears that the first ENIM has an adversative function.[28] The second occurrence of ENIM, by contrast, seems to have a causal function. But how to explain the fact that the two ENIMs are apparently linked, since they share complementary symbols (the trigon below and above, with corresponding inversion of the three dots) and belong within the same period, as suggested by the absence of any major punctuation at this point in the manuscript. Evidently, the construer treated them as syntactically related since they shared the same subject: "he, however, who speaks in a tongue does not speak to humans, but to God, since no one understands him."

(xiii) Again, IICor 1:13 (fol. 10aˇ):

NON **ENIM** ALIA **SCRIPSIMUS** UOBIS QUAMQUAE LEGISTIS ET

COGNOSCITIS

("For we write no other things to you than what you read or acknowledge").

ENIM has a symbol above, as is commonly the case with these particles. Its function is suggested by the context. In the preceding verse Paul talked of

28) Adversative *enim* is found in Late Latin usage; see B. Löfstedt (ed.), *Der Hibernolateinische Grammatiker Malsachanus* (Uppsala, 1965), p. 32, n. 1.

the simplicity and sincerity of his dealings with the world, but especially with the Corinthians. In the present verse, introduced by ENIM, he declares that his letters to them contain nothing but what they could easily read and understand. In other words, viewed in context, ENIM introduces the grounds for his previous statement of why he favoured them, perhaps best translated by 'seeing that.' The presence of a similar trigon in inverted form under SCRIPSIMUS suggests a complementary relationship with ENIM, the most likely possibility being that they were intended to form the collocation ENIM SCRIPSIMUS as the opening phrase of the sentence. This seems odd since one might have expected the introductory negative NON to collocate with SCRIPSIMUS in this role. Instead, as a result of the construer's collocating of ENIM with SCRIPSIMUS, the remaining words of the opening clause are by default conjoined, hence NON ALIA ("nothing other"), a combination which works better syntactically with the comparative clause following. Thus, the rearranged first clause would notionally read as follows: ENIM SCRIPSIMUS NON ALIA (QUAMQUE... ("Seeing that we have written nothing other than...").

(xiv) ICor 11:22 (fol. 5^r), offers further support for the syntactical priority of *enim*:[29]

proponit   adsumit   confirmat

QUID DICAM UOBIS **LAUDABO** UOS IN HOC NON LAUDABO:-

concludit

EGO **ENIM** ACCIPI A DOMINO QUOD ET TRADIDIT UOBIS...

("What shall I say to you people? Shall I praise you in this matter? I will not! For I received a message from the Lord which I have passed on to you...").

---

29) See Plate II(e).

Although the double dot under the first LAUDABO corresponds to the same symbol above ENIM, the possibility of a direct link between them seems unlikely, not only because ENIM as a singleton is commonly marked by a *distigme*, but also because a major syntactical break after the second LAUDABO (indicated by the punctuation mark :-) would seem to preclude a direct connection. More likely the mark under the first LAUDABO is to signal that it is a question ("shall I praise you in this matter?"). Some light on the syntax of ENIM may be offered by the four glosses accompanying the verse, all rhetorical terms, in particular the final gloss 'concludit' which, unlike the other three, sits directly above the particle ENIM rather than the adjacent verb, ACCIPI, as if to indicate that the sentence which gives Paul's resolution of the question begins with ENIM. Its singular role as an introductory conjunction is reflected in the fact that it has no matching construe mark within its sentence.

From examples C. (xiii) and (xiv) above, it also appears that the construer pointed his readers to a word order of PARTICLE + VERB to introduce a clause or sentence. Based on such examples we can push a step further the observation that the construe system guided readers to a Verb-initial order, to argue that where particles such as ENIM and AUTEM occurred, the same system dictated the order PARTICLE + VERB. And just as the Verb-initial order had its origins in Old Irish usage, so too the PARTICLE + VERB order could be read in the same way, since it agrees in this matter with Irish syntax. Indeed, looking ahead chronologically to the next Irish witness to construing, another glossed copy of the Pauline Epistles from the late eighth century, Würzburg M.P.th.f. 12 (Wb), we actually find examples of *enim*-clauses being paraphrased in concomitant Old Irish glosses with this word order of PARTICLE + VERB. Thus, Wb 5b40, 'POTENS EST ENIM DEUS' is glossed '.i. ar codicc dia' ('for God can do it'), where the Irish gloss has the word-order of conjunction *ar* + (infixed object pronoun) + verb + subject. Likewise, Wb 5c13, CONCLUSIT ENIM DEUS: *.i. ar duetarrid* ('for he seized it'); and 2a5 QUID ENIM...: *ar ciaricc...* ('for why...?').[30] Because ENIM (and AUTEM) normally occurs in second position in a Latin context, it would be understandable for an Irish construer to begin by relocating it to first position by means of a prominent, isolated construe mark, with the verb presumably following. Even particles which occur initially in Latin such as *nam* and *igitur*, also often receive the same treatment from the Trinity construer.

To conclude: despite the paucity of evidence in Uss, both in the variety of symbols and the frequency of their occurrence, it shows construe marks being used for essentially the same purposes as in the Trinity manuscript: to relate words and clauses to each other; to clarify grammatical and syntactical issues; and to disambiguate. Both also highlight the particles AUTEM and ENIM, positioning them as the headword of their clause, often with a causal meaning in relation to the previous clause, as in the example above from Trinity and the single one in Uss (no. 1). As discussed earlier, both Uss and the Trinity manuscript employ other patterns of construe marks besides the binary, notably the singleton, and (in the case of the latter) multiple occurrences of the same mark within the period.[31] Also noticeably absent in both, in

30) For other examples see S. Kavanagh, *A Lexicon of the Old Irish Glosses in the Würzburg Manuscript of the Epistles of St. Paul*, ed. D.S. Wodtko (Vienna, 2001), pp. 89–94. The text of the Trinity Epistles, with glosses, has been edited by J. L. de Paor, *The Earliest Irish Glosses on the Pauline Epistles* (Freiburg, 2015).

31) The approach to reading construe systems as essentially binary works quite well for many of the post-800 manuscripts, such as the Milan Commentary on the Psalms (early ninth century; see n. 25), as shown by Korhammer who frequently refers in his analysis to "paarweise" and "zwei Zeichen miteinander korrespondieren" ("Mittelalterliche Konstruktionshilfen," 32 and 25, respectively). However, the evidence present in the Trinity Epistles presents a more complex mixture of binaries, singletons, and multiples.

contrast with the post-800 construe systems, are the so-called linking construe marks (*das verbindende System*) designed to provide a comprehensive syntactical overview of a whole passage.[32] It is possible that the absence of this type of system in Uss and Trinity may simply reflect the fact that as biblical texts their syntax is relatively simple compared, say, with that of Julian of Eclanum in the Milan commentary on the psalms,[33] with the result that the focus of construing was within, rather than between, clauses.

With their late-seventh-century date the Uss symbols mark the earliest witness to the practice of construing in western Europe, followed chronologically by the Trinity Epistles from the second quarter of the eighth century, and later again by the late-eighth century Würzburg Pauline Epistles. It can hardly be mere co-incidence that these Irish witnesses predate all other attested construed manuscripts from the West, and that the earliest of the three does so by more than a century. Collectively, their evidence suggests that they derive from a tradition of construing which developed in seventh-century Ireland.

---

32) Korhammer, "Mittelalterliche Konstruktionshilfen," pp. 23–32.
33) See n. 25.

APPENDIX

CAMBRIDGE, TRINITY COLLEGE, MS B.10.5: A HARMONIZATION OF FOLIO AND PAULINE TEXT

The present foliation, beginning with fol. 2r, follows that of the online copy of the manuscript (https://www.trin.cam.ac.uk/library/wren-digital-library), itself based on sixteenth-century pagination. Note, however, that the page number lacking for the folio after '10' has now been renumbered as "10a."

Fol.			Fol.	
2^r	ICor 7:32		15^v	IICor 8:23
2^v	ICor 8:6		16^r	IICor 9:11
3^r	ICor 9:9		16^v	IICor 10:9
3^v	ICor 9:22		17^r	IICor 11:7
4^r	ICor 10:12		17^v	IICor 11:22
4^v	ICor 10:29		18^r	IICor 12:4
5^r	ICor 11:16		18^v	IICor 12:17
5^v	ICor 11:32		19^r	IICor 13:7
6^r	ICor 12:15		19^v	Prologomena to Galatians
6^v	ICor 12:31		20^r	Gal 1:1
7^r	ICor 14:4		20^v	Gal 1:16
7^v	ICor 14:21		21^r	Gal 2:6
8^r	ICor 14:37		21^v	Gal 2:20
8^v	ICor 15:16		22^r	Gal 3:15
9^r	ICor 15:34		22^v	Gal 4:3
9^v	ICor 15:52		23^r	Gal 4:21
10^r	ICor 16:12		23^v	Gal 5:7
10^v	Headings to IICor		24^r	Gal 5:24
10a^r	IICor 1:1		24^v	Gal 6:15
10a^v	IICor 1:11		25^r	Prologue to Ephesians
11^r	IICor 2:2		25^v	Eph 1:8
11^v	IICor 2:17		26^r	Eph 1:21
12^r	IICor 3:15		26^v	Eph 2:11
12^v	IICor 4:11		27^r	Eph 3:3
13^r	IICor 5:7		27^v	Eph 3:17
13^v	IICor 5:21		28^r	Eph 4:11
14^r	IICor 6:16		28^v	Eph 4:22
14^v	IICor 7:11		29^r	Eph 5:3
15^r	IICor 8:8		29^v	Eph 5:19

Fol. 30ʳ Eph 6:3	Fol. 49ʳ *tituli* and *argumenta* to IITim
30ᵛ Eph 6:16	49ᵛ *argumenta* to IITim, IITim 1:1-
31ʳ Headings to Philippians	50ʳ IITim 1:13
31ᵛ Phil 1:7	50ᵛ IITim 2:11
32ʳ Phil 1:24	51ʳ IITim 2:24
32ᵛ Phil 2:10	51ᵛ IITim 3:14
33ʳ Phil 2:25	52ʳ IITim 4:11-; *tituli* to Titus
33ᵛ Phil 3:8	52ᵛ *argumenta* to Titus; Tit 1:1-
34ʳ Phil 4:1	53ʳ Tit 1:8
34ᵛ Phil 4:14; headings IThessalonians	53ᵛ Tit 2:8
35ʳ headings, *argumenta* IThessalonians	54ʳ Tit 3:17; *tituli/argumenta* to Philemon
35ᵛ ITh 1:1	54ᵛ Phil 1:1
36ʳ ITh 2:2	55ʳ Phil 1:16-; *tituli* to Hebrews
36ᵛ ITh 2:14	55ᵛ *tituli, argumenta* to Hebrews
37ʳ ITh 3:6	56ʳ *argumenta* to Hebrews; Hebr 1:1-
37ᵛ ITh 4:9	56ᵛ Hebr 1:8
38ʳ ITh 5:6	57ʳ Hebr 2:8
38ᵛ ITh 5:27; headings and IITh	57ᵛ Hebr 3:4
39ʳ IITh 1:5	58ʳ Hebr 3:19
39ᵛ IITh 2:7	58ᵛ Hebr 4:13
40ʳ IITh 3:3	59ʳ Hebr 5:11
40ᵛ Prologue, headings to Colossians	59ᵛ Hebr 6:11
41ʳ headings to Colossians, 1:1-	60ʳ Hebr 7:5
41ᵛ Col 1:12	60ᵛ Hebr 7:19
42ʳ Col 1:25	61ʳ Hebr 8:5
42ᵛ Col 2:10	61ᵛ Hebr 9:3
43ʳ Col 3:1	62ʳ Hebr 9:13
43ᵛ Col 3:16	62ᵛ Hebr 9:24
44ʳ Col 4:18-; Prologue to ITimothy	63ʳ Hebr 10:9
44ᵛ Prologue to ITimothy	63ᵛ Hebr 10:25
45ʳ Prologue to ITimothy, ITim 1:1-	64ʳ Hebr 10:38
45ᵛ ITim 1:13	64ᵛ Hebr 11:11
46ʳ ITim 2:8	65ʳ Hebr 11:24
46ᵛ ITim 3:11	65ᵛ Hebr 11:36
47ʳ ITim 4:11	66ʳ Hebr 12:8
47ᵛ ITim 5:11	66ᵛ Hebr 12:20
48ʳ ITim 5:24	67ʳ Hebr 13:4
48ᵛ ITim 6:12-; *tituli* to IITim	67ᵛ Hebr 13:17-25

(a) Fulda, Landesbibliothek, MS Bonifatius 1, fol. 2^r

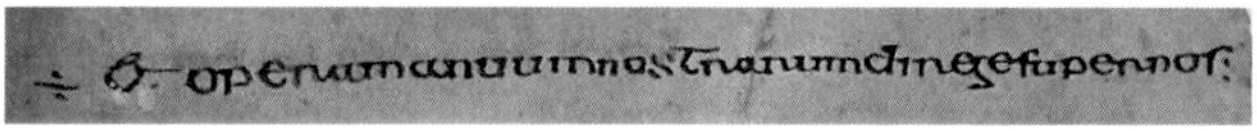

(b) Dublin, Royal Irish Academy, MS 12 R 33, fol. 48^r

(c) Cambridge, Trinity College, MS B.10.5, fol. 8^r

Plate I

(a) Cambridge, Trinity College, B.10.5, fol. 5^r

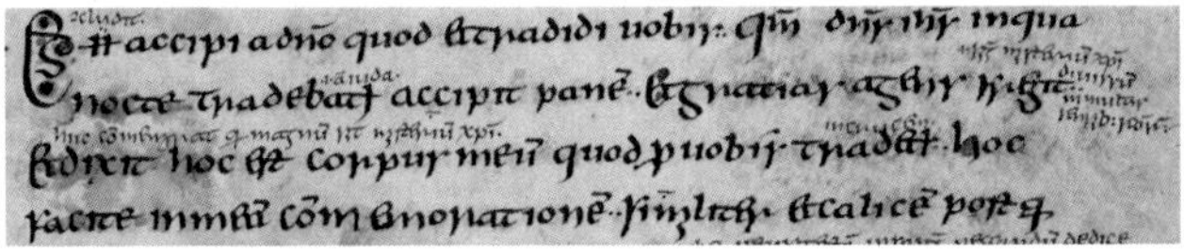

(b) Cambridge, Trinity College, B.10.5, fol. 5^r

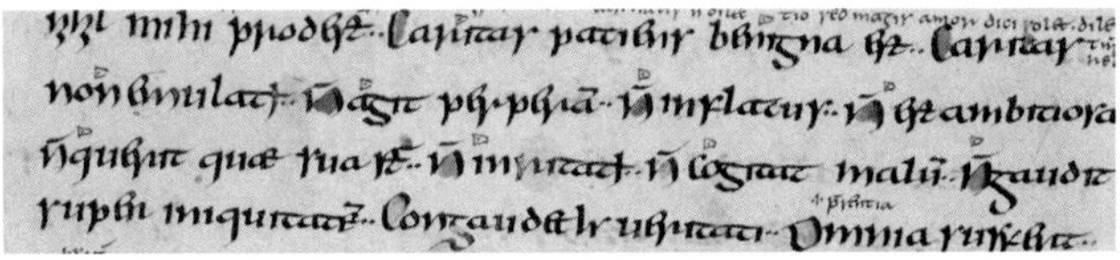

(c) Cambridge, Trinity College, B.10.5, fol. 6^v

(d) Cambridge, Trinity College, B.10.5, fol. 53^v

(e) Cambridge, Trinity College, B.10.5, fol. 5^r

Plate II

From Gloss to Lexicon East and West:

a comparison of the relationship between glossing and lexicography in medieval East Asia and Europe, with a translation of the preface to the *Shinsen jikyō* 新撰字鏡（898-901）[1]

John Whitman

1. Background

Recent research on the glossed text in medieval Europe (e.g. Cinato 2015, Blom 2017) has focused on glossing as paratextual system, independent of what a specific set of glosses tell us about a particular text, or its authors, readers, or copyists, or the language of the glossator. Questions at issue in this research include the validity of gloss typologies (lexical gloss vs. syntactic gloss or construal mark, commentary gloss vs. textual gloss), the transmission of glossing techniques across regions and periods, and what glossing systems tell us about how a text was read and taught. Most recently, researchers have begun to explore the possibility of comparisons between glossing systems in the medieval West and the systems of annotation known as *kunten* (訓点 'reading marks) in Japan and the closely related system known as *kugyŏl*

1) My research for this project was supported by the East-West Center of Kansai University and the Laboratory Program for Korean Studies through the Ministry of Education of the Republic of Korea and the Korean Studies Promotion Service of the Academy of Korean Studies (AKS-2016-LAB-2250004).I am grateful to Pádraic Moran, Patrick O'Neill, and Michelle Troberg for invaluable comments. All errors are of course my own.

口訣 in Korea.[2]

In this paper, I introduce another dimension of the comparison between medieval Western and Japanese glossing systems: the relationship between glossing and the development of glossaries or dictionaries. It is well known in both traditions that glosses were a major source of material for early glossaries (as suggested by the relation between the terms "gloss" and "glossary") and similar lexicographic compendia. In a medieval context, glossed texts were a ready-made knowledge resource. Whether the glosses were in the same language as the lemmata (Latin or Classical Chinese) or the vernacular of the glossator (Old Irish, Anglo-Saxon, Old High German or Early Middle Japanese), the textually proximate relation between lemma and gloss immediately sets up the structure of what we would think of as a dictionary entry, with lemma as headword, lexical gloss as definition, phonological glosses as pronunciation or spelling, and vernacular glosses as translation. The lexicographic exploitation of glossed texts shows remarkable parallels in the medieval West and Japan, as well as some differences. This paper is intended as a preliminary exploration of these similarities and differences. The paper is structured as follows. Section 2 introduces the relation between gloss, *glossae collectae*, and glossary or dictionary as described in scholarship on medieval Europe. Section 3 presents the parallels between *glossae collectae* and *yinyi/ongi* 音義 glossaries in the medieval Sinosphere. Section 4 looks at the relation between *kunten* glosses and *ongi* in the case of two Japanese Heian period dictionaries. Section 5 is a translation of the preface to one of them, the *Shinsen jikyō* 新撰字鏡 (898–901). This text provides a rare, perhaps unique statement directly from the lexicographer of the reasons that might motivate developing a *glossae collectae* into a dictionary.

---

2) See for example the sources cited in Blom 2017: 9, footnote 8, in particular the papers collected in Whitman and Cinato 2014.

2. Gloss — *glossae collectae* — **glossary**

It is convenient to begin with some terminology. The term "gloss" has been given broader and narrower definitions; here I adopt the rather broad definition proposed by Cinato (2015: 198) of "manuscript gloss" (*glose manuscrite*): "all additions outside a principal text that make precise or diversify the information it contains".[3] Under this definition, the annotations associated with *kundoku* (訓読 vernacular reading of Chinese texts) in Japan and *kugyŏl* in Korea, including *kunten* (訓点 ·reading marks) in the former and *t'o* (吐/토, marks functioning like Japanese *kunten*) in the latter, fall into the realm of glosses (see Whitman et al 2010 for application of the term "gloss" and various glossing typologies to these annotations).

The term *glossae collectae* refers to a collection of glosses extracted from a single text or set of texts for the purpose of aiding readers of that specific material. In accordance with this purpose, the entries in a *glossae collectae* are typically arranged in the order that they appear in the source text, so that the reader may follow along with this reference source as s/he reads the text. In terms of their structure and purpose, *glossae collectae* might be thought of (with a shudder) as medieval counterparts of modern study aids like *CliffsNotes* in the United States, or their predecessor, *Coles Notes* in Canada: annotations intended to help the reader through a prestige text, structured as short consecutive entries arranged by order of appearance of the content they annotate. The main difference is in the manner of collection: *glossae collectae* were typically compiled from pre-existing marginal or interlinear manuscript glosses.

We can see the relationship between *glossae collectae* and their source

---

3) "toute augmentation péritextuelle qui précise ou diversifie l'information contenue dans un texte principal (Cinato 2015: 198).

texts in the well-known *Leiden Glossary*, a collection of 48 chapters, each *glossae collectae*, nineteen made up of headwords based on glosses on the Bible, and the remainder from ancient classical and patristic texts (Lapidge 2006: 33). The surviving text was compiled around 800 in the Abbey of St. Gall, based on an original brought to the continent from England. As a simple demonstration of congruity of the order of entries in the *glossae collectae* and their order in the source text, consider the following three entries from Chapter 19, collecting glosses on *Job*, matched up with the occurrence of the lemmata in the Vulgate:

Table 1   Example of Lemmata and glosses in the Leiden Glossary (from Hessels 1906: 18)

No.	Headword (from Hessels 1906)	Gloss	Passage in Job
15	**Tigris**	genus leonis uario colore uelocissimus	4:11 **tigris** periit eo quod non haberet praedam et catuli leonis dissipati sunt
16	**Carectum** 'reed bed'	hreod OE 'reed'	8:11 numquid vivere potest scirpus absque humore aut crescet **carectum** sine aqua
17	**Oriona** 'Orion'	ebirdhring[4] OE 'boar hunter'	9:9 qui facit Arcturum et **Oriona** et Hyadas et interiora austri

Most of the glosses in the *Leiden Glossary* are in Latin, like (15) in Table 1, but some 250 are in Old English like (16) and (17). Table 1 gives an idea of the sequencing and density of the glosses: not every chapter in the target book has a gloss extracted from it.

Western scholarship recognizes the central role of *glossae collectae* in

---

4) Patrick O'Neill points out that Hessels' translation of OE *ebirdhring* is problematic. O'Neill suggests that this word is a scribal error for *ebir+thring* (lit. 'boar confiner/oppressor'). He also observes that *ebir* for later OE *eofor* is archaic, attesting to the antiquity of *glossae collectae* in England. These were already being produced by the late seventh century, as evidenced by the Erfurt-Epinal glossary dated to that period.

the composition of glossaries, texts closer to the modern conception of a dictionary. Lapidge (1986) describes this role as a three-step process:

> ... we should bear in mind the various stages in the compilation of a glossary: first, various (perhaps random) interpretations *or interpretamenta* are copied into a manuscript above or alongside particular difficult words (or: *lemmata*) secondly, the various *lemmata* and their accompanying *interpretamenta* are collected and copied out separately in the order in which they occur in the text (we refer to these as *glossae collectae*); thirdly, the various *glossae collectae* are sorted roughly into alphabetical order, with all items beginning with the same letter being grouped together (*a*-order); finally, the entries under each letter are re-sorted into more precise alphabetical order, taking account of the first two letters of each lemma (*ab*-order). A surviving glossary may (and usually does) include materials or batches of words treated in any of these ways, though it will be obvious that when one is trying to identify the text on which the glosses were based, *glossae collectae* offer the clearest evidence. (Lapidge 1986: 53–4)

Russell (1998) describes a similar three-step process in his study of Old Irish legal glossaries. I have summarized the stages identified by Russell in Table 2.

Table 2   Gloss to Glossae Collectae to Glossary in Old Irish Legal Texts (Russell 1998)

(a)	**1ˢᵗ stage:** addition to text of interlinear or marginal glosses.
(b)	**2ⁿᵈ stage:** creation of ancillary document collecting lemmata and glosses. These remain in textual order as *glossae collectae*.
(b)	**3ʳᵈ stage:** Either (i) *glossae collectae* from one text are alphabeticized and merged with others from the same text, or (ii) with glossae collectae from other texts.

It would be a mistake to conclude that all medieval glossaries are products of this three-step process. Moran (2019) argues that the text known as *O'Mulconry's Glossary* (properly titled *De Origine Scoticae Linguae*), compiled between the seventh and the late ninth or early tenth century, does not fit into the three-step paradigm. This text was compiled as an etymological glossary, with purported etymologies from Latin, Greek and Hebrew supplied for Irish entries. Moran points out that the three-step model would require supposing that words in Irish texts were commonly glossed in these languages, which is surely not the case. He suggests the more plausible explanation that the Irish headwords were in some cases themselves glosses on Latin or Greek texts. We see in the section 4 that although a three-step model is also a useful framework for understanding the process of lexicon construction in Japan, scholars have recognized that the actual process was more complex.

3. Gloss — *yinyi/ongi* 音義 — dictionary

Chinese lexicography has a history of well over two millenia, but the tradition relevant for this study can be traced back to the *Ěryǎ yīnyì* 爾雅音義 *Sounds and meanings of the Ěryǎ* by the Three Kingdoms scholar Sun Yan 孫炎 in the late third century CE. The *Ěryǎ* 爾雅 (3rd century BCE) itself is often identified as the first Chinese dictionary. It consists of over two thousand entries made up of citations from classical literature. The entries are organized by encyclopedic category, e.g. 'words', 'music', 'heaven' etc. By the third century CE, the readings and meanings of many of the entries in the *Ěryǎ* had become obscure. The *Ěryǎ yīnyì* applied what was at the time an innovative spelling technique, so-called *fanqie* (半切 J. *hansetsu*) 'cutting and turning' spellings, which uses two characters to specify the pronunciation of a third, one for the onset and a second for the rhyme (vowel, coda, and tone) of the target character. To take an example of *fanqie/hansetsu* spelling from the *Shinsen jikyō* 新撰字鏡, the Japanese dictionary we discuss in sections 4 and

5, the first character in the dictionary, 天 Ch. *tiān*, Middle Chinese *t^hen*, Sino-Japanese *ten* 'heaven', is spelled 他 Ch. *tā*, MC *t<u>h</u>a*, SJ *ta*, and 前 Ch. *qián*, MC *dzen*, SJ *zen*. The underlined portions of the pronunciation of the two characters used in the *fanqie* spelling specify exactly the MC pronunciation of the target character and the SJ reading derived from it.

By the sixth century, the *yīnyì* 'sound and meaning' format was well established, providing a pronunciation for each headword character using *fanqie* or a single homophone (*zhíyīn* 直音 'direct sound' spellings), a concise definition, and sometimes a source for the information. Lù Démíng's *Jīngdiǎn shìwén* (經典釋文, c. 582–589) sets up this format as well as the practice of listing entries in the order they appear in the text. This format is obviously parallel to the consecutive ordering in Western *glossae collectae*, but order of entries is not criterial in defining a lexicographic text as an *yīnyì* or *ongi* (Sino-Japanese for 音義 *yīnyì*). In the Japanese tradition, two subcategories are distinguished: *maki ongi* 巻音義 'scroll *ongi*', whose entries are ordered by order of occurrence in the target text, and *bushu ongi* 部首音義 'radical *ongi*', whose entries are ordered by radical. The criterial property of *yīnyì*/*ongi* is that they target the vocabulary of a specific text or body of texts.

At the next stage in Chinese lexicography are Buddhist *yīnyì*, beginning with the *Yīqièjīng yīnyì* 一切經音義 *Sounds and meanings of the complete Tripitaka* or *Zhòngjīng yīnyì* 眾經音義 *Sounds and meanings of the entire canon* in the mid 7th century.[5] Compiled by Xuányīng 玄應 in 25 *juan* (scrolls) beginning with the *Huáyánjīng* (華嚴經 *Avataṃsaka sūtra*), this glossary is also known as the 玄應音義 *Xuányīng yīnyì*, to distinguish it from later *yīnyì* of the Tripitaka. It contains ca. 400,000 characters and over 9,000 entries from 458 Buddhist texts. Yong, Ping, and Tian (2008: 370) explicitly point out the structural parallel between the *Yīqièjīng yīnyì* and the *Leiden*

5) Ikeda (1980: 73) dates Xuányīng's death to between 656 and 663.

Glossary: like Western medieval *glossae collectae*, headwords are arranged in the order in which they appear in the source text.[6] There are further parallels as well. Both are monastic productions; Xuányīng is said to have been a monk at Da Ci'en-si 大慈恩寺, an imperially sponsored monastery in the Tang capital, Chang'an. Although Chinese tradition attributes authorship to a single individual, it is likely that compilation of the *Yīqièjīng yīnyì* was a group enterprise. A final parallel is that the entries in *yīnyì/ongi*, like those in *glossae collectae*, can be understood in terms of Blom's (2017) gloss typology, as we see in the sample entry from the Japanese *Shin'yaku Kegonkyō ongi shiki* discussed below.

A second major *yīnyì* of the Mahayana Tripitaka, also properly titled the *Yīqièjīng yīnyì* 一切經音義 but distinguished from Xuányīng's work as the 慧琳音義 *Huìlín yīnyì* or the *Dàzàng yīnyì* 大藏音義, was compiled by the monk Huilin 慧琳 in 783–807. It consists of 100 scrolls beginning with the *Mahāprajñāpāramitā sutra* (*Dà bōrĕ jīng* 大般若經). The *Huìlín yīnyì* contains ca. 600,000 characters and over 31,000 headword entries from over 1,300 Buddhist texts. Huilin was from Kashgar and knew Sanskrit. He cites heavily from the secular classics and commentary literature as well as Buddhist commentaries.

---

6) Chien and Creamer (1986: 36) describe the structure of the *Yīqièjīng yīnyì* in greater detail: "(Xuányīng)'s purpose in compiling the dictionary was to define difficult words, both Sanskrit and Chinese, that appeared in the Chinese translations of the sutras. At the beginning of each chapter is a listing from which the headwords are selected. The headwords are then arranged and numbered according to the chapter of the sutra in which they appear. The basic structure of each definition is first to give and variant renderings of the headword, then the definition, the pronunciation of difficult characters in the headword combination, and an explanation of any unusual character that appears in the definition." The Sanskrit words referred to by Chien and Creamer are actually Chinese transliterations of Sanskrit Buddhist terms, which occur in the Chinese Mahayana Tripitaka together which Chinese translations; no Sanskrit writing occurs in the *Yīqièjīng yīnyì*.

The *Xuányīng yīnyì* was transmitted to Japan in the 8th century.[7] Its transmission marks the beginning of lexicographic production in Japan, beginning in the second half of the 8th century with the annotation and subsequently the production of *ongi*. Both of the Japanese Heian period dictionaries discussed in the next section, the *Shinsen jikyō* and the *Ruiju myōgishō*, draw heavily from the *Xuányīng yīnyì*. As we see below, the same is true of the first three *ongi* compiled in Japan, prior to the end of the 8th century.

Chronologically, these three *ongi* precede the composition of the first dictionary in Japan. The *Shin Kegonkyō ongi* 新華厳経音義 was compiled in the second half of the 8th century by an unknown author.[8] The oldest surviving version, the Daiji-bon ms., is at the end of the first scroll of a copy of the *Xuányīng yīnyì* made in 1128. It contains 304 entries keyed to the "new" (80 scroll) translation of the *Avataṃsaka sūtra*), the *Dà fāng guǎng Fó Huáyánjīng* (大方廣佛華嚴經), completed in China during 695–699. This translation has its own Chinese *yīnyì*, completed by Huiyuan 慧苑 around 722, but the *Shin Kegonkyō ongi* seems instead to rely on the first scroll of the *Xuányīng yīnyì* treating the "old" (60 scroll) translation produced in the early fifth century (Ikeda 1980: 65). Ikeda shows that the great majority of entries are taken from either the *Xuányīng yīnyì* or the 6th century Chinese character dictionary *Yùpiān* 玉篇. He concludes that the author of the *Shin Kegonkyō ongi* used the *Xuányīng yīnyì* as a primary source, supplementing it with material from the *Yùpiān* 玉篇. What is important here is that the compiler could not merely mechanically copy entries from the *Xuányīng yīnyì*,

---

7) Ishida (1930), cited in Ikeda (1980), reports that the *Xuányīng yīnyì* was recorded as having been copied in Japan during the Tenpyō era (729–749) according to documents in the Shōsōin imperial treasury.

8) Miho (1974), cited in Ikeda 1980, speculates that the author was a scholar monk at Tōdaiji working during the Tenpyō Shōhō era (749–757).

because that text did not cover the specific translation that was the target text. Instead, the compiler relied on Xuányīng's glossary as a **general** reference, extracting information on the "new" translation from glosses on the "old" translation and other texts.

The *Daihannyakyō ongi* 大般若経音義 is thought to have been compiled in the late 8th century by Shingyō 信行, an historical monk of Gangōji 元興寺 temple in Nara, although neither compiler nor date of compilation are recorded in the surviving mss.[9] There are two primary mss, the Ishiyamadera-bon, thought to have been copied at the end of the 8th century, and the Raigei-in-bon, thought to have been copied in the Insei period (late 11th–late 12th c.). Between them, these mss. contain 255 entries drawn from the *Daihannyakyō ongi* 大般若經音義 (Ch. *Dà bōrě jīng*), the translation of the *Mahā-prajñāpāramitā-sūtra* completed in 660–663 (Ikeda 1980: 69–70). Ikeda surveys the entries in these two oldest mss. and shows that, like the *Shin Kegonkyō ongi*, the great majority (90%) are taken from either the *Xuányīng yīnyì* or the *Yùpiān*. He concludes that the method of compilation was the same, and depended almost entirely on these two sources. Once again, the compiler must have relied on Xuányīng's glossary not as source for glosses on the specific target text, but as a general reference, because the *Xuányīng yīnyì* did not contain a section on the *Daihannyakyō/Dà bōrě jīng*, as the Chinese translation of this sutra was not completed until 663, after Xuányīng's death (see footnote 4).

Ikeda (1980) discusses why the *Xuányīng yīnyì* was used as a primary reference for both Japanese *ongi*. He points out that both were Buddhist glossaries, and the *Xuányīng yīnyì* was the primary lexical reference in the Sinocentric Buddhist world at the time, while the *Yùpiān* dictionary and

---

9) Miho (1974), cited in Ikeda 1980, speculates that compilation of the *Daihannyakyō ongi* took place some time before Tenpyō Shingo 4 (754).

earlier lexical resources were based on classical secular sources. The *yīnyì/ ongi* headwords were also typically two-character compounds, while headwords in the *Yùpiān* are single characters; Buddhist doctrinal terms, which required precise exegesis, were very often two-character compounds. Most important, Nara period Buddhism, focused on the Kegon (Huayan/*Avataṃsaka*) and Hossō (Fǎxiàng/Yogācāra) sects, placed a premium on the new translations of Mahayana sutras associated with these sects in China and Korea. Where the *Xuányīng yīnyì* did not include these new translations, Japanese clerics were compelled to produce their own *ongi* using the *Xuányīng yīnyì* as a general reference.

The third surviving 8th century Japanese *ongi* is the *Shin'yaku Kegonkyō ongi shiki* 新訳華厳経音義私記 *Private annotations on the Sounds and Meanings of the new translation of the* Avataṃsaka sūtra in two volumes, late 8th century, compiler unknown. It draws from four sources: like the two *ongi* discussed above, it draws on the *Xuányīng yīnyì* and the *Yùpiān* dictionary, but also on the Japanese *Shin Kegonkyō ongi* introduced above. Finally, it draws on a Chinese *yīnyì* devoted to the new translation, the *Xīnyì dà fāng guǎng fó Huáyánjīng yīnyì* 新譯大方廣佛華嚴經音義 *Sounds and Meanings of the* Avataṃsaka sūtra *(New Translation)*, compiled by the Huayan monk Huìyuàn 慧苑 (674–743). As with other *yīnyì*, this work is also known by the name of its author, the *Huìyuàn yīnyì* 慧苑音義. Because of its connection with this pre-existing glossary on the same target text, the Japanese *Shin'yaku Kegonkyō ongi shiki* is labelled "private annotations" on the *Huìyuàn yīnyì*, but in fact, as Ikeda (1986, 1987) shows, as it draws on the three other sources as well, includes some Japanese vernacular glosses, and adds entries not in the Chinese glossary, the Japanese text is better regarded as an independent glossary in its own right.

The *Shin'yaku Kegonkyō ongi shiki* lists approximately 1,800 headwords.

Of these, 1,225 are taken from either the *Huìyuàn yīnyì*, or the *Shin Kegonkyō ongi*, or both (Ikeda 1986). The *Shin'yaku Kegonkyō ongi shiki* often truncates these cited entries, sometimes to the point of unintelligibility. The example below, taken from the reproduction edited by Tsukishima (1978), shows the structure of entries with Japanese glosses.

簫笛　　　　上照、訓布穎、下音天寂
　　　　　　反、七孔也、倭云布延

The headword is 簫笛 *xiāodí* (MC *seudek*, SJ *shōteki*) 'vertical and transverse flutes'.[10] The first line provides a direct spelling of the first character in the headword with the SJ homophone 照 *xiào* (MC tɕiɐu^H, SJ *shō*). This appears to be a Sino-Japanese spelling devised by the compiler of the *Shin'yaku Kegonkyō ongi shiki*, as the characters are not homophones in Middle Chinese. (The *Huìlín yīnyì* spells 簫 MC *seu* accurately with *fanqie* 蘇彫 *suo+teu*). The Japanese *ongi* then gives a Japanese vernacular reading (*kun*) for the first character 簫 in *man'yōgana* phonograms, 布穎 *puye* 'flute', showing that this character already had an established vernacular reading. The line ends with the *fanqie* spelling 天+寂 *tiān+jì* (MC *then+dzek*, SJ *ten+zyaku* or *seki*) for the second character 笛 *dí* (MC *dek*, SJ *tyaku* or *teki*). Once again, we see that the spelling, this time a *fanqie*, is accurate for Sino-Japanese but not for Middle Chinese. The second line gives a definition, "has seven holes", and provides the same Japanese vernacular reading for the whole compound as for the first character, *puye* 'flute' with the expression 倭云布延, which Tsukishima (1978) reads as vernacular Japanese: *Yamato=ni puye to ipu* 'In

10)　簫笛 *xiāodí* 'vertical and transverse flutes' occurs in scroll 7 of the old (60 scroll) translation of the *Avataṃsaka sūtra* and in the same passage in scroll 15 of the new (80 scroll) translation; it also occurs in scrolls 38 and 51 of the new translation. The word does not occur in the *Huìlín yīnyì*.

Yamato they say *puye'*.

The components of this entry may be understood in terms of Blom's (2017) gloss typology. The *fanqie* and direct spelling fit into an expanded understanding of his SUP(plement) 1 glosses, elucidating the phonology of the lemma. The vernacular Japanese glosses are what Blom calls SUB(stitution) 1 glosses. The explanation in terms of seven holes is a COM(mentary) gloss.

This entry gives an idea of the method and intent of the compilers of the late 8th century *ongi*. Like Xuányīng and other compilers of *yīnyì* on the continent, the compiler of the Japanese *ongi* designed his text to help a specific readership, Japanese clerics, understand difficult terms in this complex sutra. One of the needs of this readership was to read, and probably in some contexts vocalize the text in Japanese, that is, engage in so-called *kundoku* 訓読 (vernacular reading). A term such as 簫笛 *xiāodí/shōteki* would raise immediate questions, since it combines two terms each understood and read as 'flute'. The vernacular Japanese gloss reassures the readership that the two-character term can be read and understood as the same single-word Japanese vernacular reading used for each of the characters separately.

The focus of this section has been on the development first Chinese and subsequently Japanese Buddhist *yīnyì/ongi* in the seventh and eighth century. We have seen that like Western medieval *glossae collectae*, they were compiled for the readers of specific texts or sets, and typically (although not always) arranged entries in the order they appear in the target text. One thing that we do not know at the present stage of research is whether or how the glosses compiled in *yīnyì/ongi* were extracted from specific manuscript glosses. In theory, it should be possible to compare headwords and entries to glossed manuscript versions of the sutras from repositories such as Dunhuang in China and *kunten* glossed materials in Japan. For example, multiple annotated or glossed mss. of both translations of the *Avataṃsaka sutra/*

Huáyánjīng yīnyì/Kegonkyō exist. Although parts of the entries in the three Japanese *ongi* were taken from other lexical sources, material such as the vernacular Japanese *man'yōgana* glosses might be compared with such glossed manuscripts of the target texts, but this work remains to be done.

4. Gloss to glossary in the *Shinsen jikyō* and the Zushoryō-bon *Ruiju myōgishō*

This section discusses the two best known dictionaries of the Heian era, which bracket this period, the *Shinsen jikyō* (新撰字鏡 898–901) and the Zushoryō-bon *Ruiju myōgishō* (図書寮本類聚名義抄 1081–1100). Both of these dictionaries have been introduced in Western scholarship (Bailey 1960, Habein 1984, Seely 1991), but here I would like to focus on a specific aspect of their compilation, their relationship to previous *ongi* and to *kunten* glossed texts.

The earliest surviving Japanese dictionary is the *Tenrei banshō meigi* (篆隷万象名義 830–835) compiled by Kūkai, the founder of Japanese esoteric Buddhism, after his sojourn in China. Kūkai's dictionary is an abridgement of the Chinese *Yùpiān* 玉篇; in fact, since copies of the complete *Yùpiān* do not survive, the *Tenrei banshō meigi* is one of the primary sources for the original text. Like its source, the *Tenrei banshō meigi* is a Chinese character dictionary. Given the derivative nature of the *Tenrei banshō meigi*, the *Shinsen jikyō* is arguably the first truly Japanese dictionary. It is followed later in the 10th century by the *Wamyō ruijushō* (倭名類聚抄 931–938). Both of these dictionaries arrange characters by a combination of radical and meaning, and give some Japanese vernacular readings in *man'yōgana*.

The *Shinsen jikyō* was compiled by the cleric Shōju 昌住, who is otherwise unknown. It contains entries for some 21,300 characters in 12 scrolls. Each entry gives the Chinese pronunciation, usually a definition, and often one of 3,700+ Japanese vernacular readings (*wakun* 和訓) in *man'yōgana*. It arranges entry characters by its own inventory of 160 radicals (部), e.g. 天・日・月・肉・雨・气・風. Some sections, in particular the *Shōgakuhen* 小学篇 section mentioned in the preface translated below, and the sections in scroll 12, are arranged by semantic category such as *shataku* 舎宅 'dwellings'. Sadakari 1962/1998 shows that one such section, the *Rinji zatsuyō ji* 臨時雑用字 *Temporary and miscellaneous characters*, draws on the same kind of eighth century practical Chinese character dictionaries used in the compilation of the *Wamyō ruijushō* thirty years later.

In contrast, the *Tenrei banshō meigi* used 534 radicals closely modeled on the 540 *Shuowen Jiezi* radicals, following the practice of the *Yùpian*. In the preface to the *Shinsen jikyō*, Shōju states that he originally based the dictionary on the *Xuányīng yīnyì*, completing a preliminary three-scroll version (which does not survive) in 892. He goes on to express his frustration with using the *Xuányīng yīnyì* to look up characters and compounds outside of the limited scope of its target texts, that is, outside of its original purpose as an *yīnyì/ongi* or *glossae collectae*. In other words, Shōju tells us that he ran up against the limitations of using an *yīnyì/ongi* as a general lexicographic reference, something that Japanese lexicographers were already doing in the late eighth century, as we saw in the previous section.

Expanding his project beyond the scope of the *Xuányīng yīnyì*, in compiling the twelve scroll work that survives, Shōju tells us that he drew on the *Yùpiān* and the seventh century *Qièyùn* 切韻 rhyme tables. Textual evidence tells us that he also drew on Japanese sources such as the early ninth century *Nihon Ryōiki* 日本霊異記. By examining the order and structure of the entries, Sadakari (1959/1998) was able to distinguish between their sources. Citations from the *Qièyùn* are grouped by their Middle Chinese tone. In one such section, Shōju explicitly cites the *Qièyùn*, and in general entries grouped by tone follow the order level — rising — departing — entering tone order found in surviving texts of the *Qièyùn* or rhyme tables derived from it (Sadakari 1959/1998: 24–5).

From this discovery, Sadakari determined that Shōju's citations from the *Qièyùn* tended to be grouped in clusters. He identifies a similar tendency with citations from the the *Yùpiān*, while citations from the *Xuányīng yīnyì* are more evenly distributed. The *Xuányīng yīnyì* is the largest single source for entries in the *Shinsen jikyō* and the only source for its original three scroll precursor mentioned in Shōju's preface. Ikeda (1982) estimates that roughly half (51%) of the entries in the *Shinsen jikyō* come from the *Xuányīng yīnyì*, 18% from the *Qièyùn* and *Yùpiān*, and the remainder from indeterminate sources. Ikeda also points out that the *Shinsen jikyō*'s citations from the *Xuányīng yīnyì* draw mainly from just a few specific scrolls of that text. He concludes that the Shōju's original three volume lexicon was composed almost entirely from those scrolls, and had much the characteristics of an *yīnyì*/*ongi* itself.

The process of compiling the *Shinsen jikyō* shows parallels with the third stage of glossary compilation described by Lapidge. Shōju's main source was a consecutively ordered *yīnyì*, the Chinese counterpart of a *glossae collectae*. On this material he imposed a nonconsecutive ordering based on radicals, the Sinospheric counterpart to alphabetical order, but the ordering is not completely used throughout the dictionary. He added material from additional sources; the result is that cited material is treated in a variety of ways, reflecting how they were treated in the source.

If the compilation of the *Shinsen jikyō* shows parallels with the compilation of glossaries based on *glossae collectae*, the compilation of the *Ruiju myōgishō* 類聚名義抄 shows parallels with the process of composing lexical references directly from glossed texts. The original edition (*gensenbon*

原撰本) of this dictionary was compiled around 1100 by monks of the Shingon (真言 esoteric) school. Subsequent revised edition were produced by monks of the Hossō (法相宗 Yogācāra) school from the twelfth through the thirteenth century. The original edition was organized into three sections, representing the Buddhist triad: Butsu (仏 Buddha), Hō (法 Dharma) and Sō (僧 Sangha), although this organization is modified in later editions. The surviving ms. of the original edition is known as the Zushoryō-bon *Ruiju myōgishō* 図書寮本類聚名義抄, conventionally dated 1081-1100 and held by the Archives and Mausoleum Department of the Imperial Household Agency. It contains only the last part of the Hō section. My discussion here focuses on this ms. and in particular the groundbreaking study of its sources by Tsukishima (1959).

The Zushoryō-bon *Ruiju myōgishō* includes both single character and two-character compound entries, while later editions have mainly single character entries. The Zushoryō-bon cites its sources, while these citations are mainly eliminated from later editions. The typical Zushoryō-bon entry gives the Chinese character heading, a source, often a *fanqie* spelling for single character entries, and a Japanese meaning equivalent in *man'yōgana* (Chinese characters used as phonograms) or *katakana* (a Japanese syllabary derived from abbreviated characters used as sound glosses). The Japanese equivalents in *katakana* are drawn from glosses on Chinese classics used widely in East Asia for pedagogical purposes or as models of writing: the *Wénxuǎn* (J. *Monzen* 文選 *Selections of Refined Literature*), the *Báishì wénjí* (J. *Hakushi monjū* 白氏文集 *Collected Works of Bái Jūyì*), the *Shǐjì* (J. *Shiki* 史記 *Records of the Grand Historian*), and the *Yóuxiānkū* (J. *Yūsenkutu* 遊仙窟 *Journey to the Fairy Grotto*). It tells us a great deal about Heian period monastic education that in a dictionary compiled by monks with a Buddhist overall structure, the main references were secular classics. Japanese equivalents in *man'yōgana* phonograms were drawn mainly from glosses on Japanese texts written in classical Chinese such as the *Nihongi shiki* (*Private notes on the* Nihongi 日本紀私記), as well as Japanese and Chinese dictionaries and *yīnyì*/*ongi*.

Tsukishima (1959) showed that the source of the entry was largely predictable from its orthography and form. The orthography is faithful to the source: if the source is an older Japanese dictionary with Japanese equivalents in *man'yōgana*, the Zushoryō-bon copies the *man'yōgana*, typically preserving orthographic distinctions present in the source even when they are lost in the language of the eleventh century. Japanese equivalents in *katakana* are essentially all from *kunten* glossed texts; this is because the *katakana* syllabary was devised from abbreviated *man'yōgana*, less than three centuries earlier, for the specific purpose of glossing Chinese texts in order to read them in the vernacular. The structure of the entry also correlates with the type of source. If the source is another dictionary or *yīnyì*/*ongi*, the Zushoryō-bon cites the source first (Tsukishima 1959: 38), as in the following example:

Zushoryō-bon *Ruiju myōgishō*　　Source: Kūkai, *Kongōchōkyō ichiji chōrinnō giki ongi*

洽　弘　　云　阿万子久　　　　洽　阿万子久
<u>Kūkai</u>　says　*amaneku*　　　　　*amaneku*
　　　　　　'widely, completely'　　(cited from Tsukishima 1959: 41)

This entry is cited directly from a 9th century *ongi* by Kūkai, the *Kongōchōkyō ichiji chōrinnō giki ongi* 金剛頂経一字頂輪王儀軌音義, a source giving vernacular Japanese readings for a Chinese manual of rituals associated with the Vajraśekhara sutra. 洽 *qià*, SJ *kō*, vernacular Japanese reading *amanesi* 'wide, extensive', here adverbial *amaneku* 'widely, extensively' is the headword.

弘、Kō (underlined above) in the Zushoryō-bon entry is the attribution to Kōbō daishi 弘法大師, Kūkai's title. The Zushoryō-bon uses the exact same *man'yōgana* that Kūkai used to spell the Japanese vernacular equivalent.

Tsukishima shows, in contrast, that Zushoryō-bon entries copied from *kunten* glosses cite their source at the end of the entry, after the Japanese equivalent. The following two entries are cited from glosses on the *Hakushi monjū* 白氏文集:

Zushoryō-bon *Ruiju myōgishō*   Source: *Hakushi monjū* 白氏文集
(1113 glossed ms.)

誚 ソシル	白	誚 ソシレリ
sosir-u	*Haku*	sosir-er-i
'criticize-CONC'	*Bái Jūyì*	criticize-STAT-CONC (cited from Tsukishima 1959: 46)

Zushoryō-bon *Ruiju myōgishō*   Source: *Hakushi monjū* 白氏文集
(1113 glossed ms.)

経 ワタル	集	経 ワタル
watar-u	*Shū*	watar-u
'cross-CONC'	*Collected*	cross-CONC (cited from Tsukishima 1959: 46)

For purposes of comparison, Tsukishima uses a manuscript with *kunten* glosses in *katakana* dated to 1113, consisting of scrolls 3 and 4 of the *Hakushi monjū*. The glosses date from a few years after the compilation of the Zushoryō-bon, but they almost certainly draw on an older exemplar that would have been the same or similar to the one used by the compilers. This is confirmed by the striking match between the Zushoryō-bon *katakana* entries attributed to the *Hakushi monjū* and the glosses, as well as their quantity: Tsukishima finds 35 entries like those above replicating glosses in the 1113 ms. out of a total of 188 entries cited from the *Hakushi monjū*; that ms. preserves two out of a total of 11 scrolls in the complete work (1959: 47), so that 35 identifiable glosses is exactly the number we would predict from the 18% of the text surviving. Note that in these gloss citations, the source is cited at the end of the entry: 白 SJ *Haku* for Bái Jūyì or 集 *Shū* 'Collected' for *Collected Works*. Observe also that the Zushoryō-bon citation normalizes the morphological shape of the gloss: while the original manuscript gloss for 経 *wataru* 'cross' is in the past stative *water-e-ri* in the *Hakushi monjū* gloss, the Zushoryō-bon converts it to the conclusive form used as the citation form for verbs in that dictionary.

Tsukishima's findings are well known among Japanese *kunten* scholars, but they have never been put in a broader comparative context. They show us that compilation of the Zushoryō-bon *Ruiju myōgishō* exemplifies stages 2 and 3 in the process of gloss to glossary attested in the medieval west. The *katakana* glosses such as those we saw above from the *Hakushi monjū* exemplify stage 2: glosses are collected from an authoritative glossed text and arranged in a lexicon. In a sense, the *katakana* glosses conflate stages 2 and 3, since we have no evidence that they were first collected in a consecutively ordered *glossae collectae*, that is an *ongi* for the *Hakushi monjū*, although such an intermediate text might have existed. Instead, to the best of our knowledge, the compilers inserted them directly in their dictionary, which was arranged by radical. The *man'yōgana* equivalents from Kūkai's *ongi* represent stage 3, from *glossae collectae* to glossary.

In this section we have seen that the relationship between *kunten* gloss, *yīnyì/ongi*, and glossary or dictionary shows parallels with the three-step model identified by scholars studying the development from gloss to glossary in the medieval West. The relationship between these three stages has not gone unnoticed by Japanese scholars. Yoshida (1955/2013) observes that traditional Japanese scholarship has seen *yīnyì/ongi* as a stage prior to the compilation of dictionaries, and *kunten* glosses and other annotations as a primary source for both, but argues that the actual relation is more complex: "Logically speaking, these develop in the order primary textual annotation, *yīnyì/ongi*, dictionary; but in actuality in Japan, where these materials exist in a complex relation with their Chinese counterparts, apart from those which developed independently within the limits of their genre, there was a relationship of mutual influence between all three (1955/2013: 326).[11] Yoshida illustrates this complex relationship with a tripolar diagram showing the bidirectional relationship between primary annotations (glosses), *yīnyì/ongi*, and dictionaries:

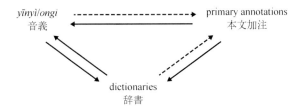

Fig. 1   The relation between annotation, *yīnyì/ongi*, and dictionary (Yoshida 1955/2013)

The solid lines in the figure represent the "normal" or "regular" directions of influence, while the dotted lines represent reciprocating influence, as when a subsequent glossator cites a *yīnyì/ongi* or dictionary. As an example of a dictionary influencing a *yīnyì/ongi*, Yoshida mentions the case of a fourteenth century *ongi* which drew its Japanese vernacular equivalents from an edition of the *Ruiju myōgishō*.

---

11)　理論的には本文加注、音義、辞書の順に発展するものであるが、シナのそれらと交錯した我が国における実際では、夫々独自にその限界内で発展するものの外に、三者間には影響の相互関係が存在している。

Surely such complex or "reversed" directions of influence exist in the Western relationship between gloss, *glossae collectae*, and glossary as well. Yoshida's perception that the three-stage model is the "logical" or normal progression conforms to what appears to be the underlying bias in both traditions of scholarship: that forms of transmitting knowledge about language closest to modern modes, that is, dictionaries, represent the apex of the development of medieval lexicography. In the context of more recent research on glossing, we should keep in mind that all three modes represent highly structured systems of knowledge transmission.

5. Translation of the preface (*jo* 序) to the *Shinsen jikyō* by Shōju, 898–901

Consider this carefully.[12] At the beginning of the Supreme Ultimate and the Primordial Qi, the Three Brilliances (the moon, the sun, and the stars) were still hidden; after the time of Fuxi and Shennong, the Eight Trigrams came into being.[13],[14] Thereupon, as benevolence and justice gradually spread, the designs of dragons were borrowed to give rise to writing; when the Great

---

12) The first three lines of the preface are cited verbatim from the beginning lines of the preface by Li Huailin 李懷琳 to the *Tang hufashamen Falin biezhuan* 唐護法沙門法琳別傳 (*The Independent Biography of the Monk Falin, Defender of the Dharma in the Tang*), compiled by the monk Yancong 顔悰 ca. 645. I am indebted to Yung-chang Tung for this observation. The quotation continues until the sentence 因鳥迹以成書(->字) 'letters ('writing' 書 in the original) were created based on the foot marks of birds' and resumes to include the passage referring to Sima Qian 史遷綴史記之文 and the phrase "heroic worthies and venerable recluses".

13) Two of the mythological Three Augusts or sovereigns of prehistoric China. Fuxi is sometimes credited with the invention of the Eight Trigrams, and Shennong with squaring them to create the Sixty-Four Trigrams.

14) The Eight Trigrams (八卦 *Bagua*) are symbols made up of combinations of three parallel solid or broken lines, basic to Daoist cosmology.

Dao was abandoned, letters were created based on the foot marks of birds.[15] Thus we arrive at Cangjie seeing the foot marks left by birds and being inspired to make letters, and proceed on to Sima Qian's composition of the text of the *Shiji*. It has been a long while now since characters have been passed down from heroic worthies and venerable recluses. The present foolish monk was born in a humble house and had difficulty finding a brilliant teacher; I lived for a long time in a bramble hut and was unacquainted with instruction. Hence books and letters were closed to my heart, and characters were obscure to my mind. All the more so when I took up brush and contemplated characters; I was in darkness as if sitting in the middle of clouds and fog; when I faced the paper and wrote text, I was clueless, as if gazing at the sky with a bowl over my head.[16] Only while scratching my head and sighing and sobbing could I hope for some slight success.

The *Yīqièjīng yīnyì* "Pronunciation and meanings of the complete Tripitaka" (25 scrolls in one slipcase) discusses pronunciation and meaning for each character and is readily understood. But when one uses it to search for pronunciations and meanings in other texts, it is very easy to get lost; it is confusing and difficult to understand. The reason for this is that there are many scrolls, and radicals are not listed, so that one can spend the whole day

---

15) This section quotes the beginning of Chapter 18 of the *Daodejing* of Laozi: 大道廢, 有仁義 "When the Great Dao is abandoned, there is humanity and justice" (Takahashi and Takahasi 2006: 9, fn 4). 龍圖 "tracings of dragons" refers to the pattern on the back of the mythical dragon horse that is supposed to have inspired Fuxi's creation of the eight trigrams, as well as, perhaps to the Yellow River Map 河圖, a scheme representing the Luo and He (Yellow) rivers from which the trigrams are also said to have been derived. 鳥迹 "bird footprints" alludes to the legend of Cang Jie referenced in the next sentence.

16) The Tenji-bon reads 如日月窺天 here. 日月 is evidently a copyists' error for 冒, 'cover', with a *kun* (vernacular) reading as *opop-* 'cover' or *kabur-* 'wear' on head. The Kyōwa-bon and Gunsho ruijū-bon have merely 月 (Takahashi and Takahasi 2006: 10, fn 12).

leafing through it to look something up. In order to make things easy to understand for beginners, I compiled the pronunciations and meanings of a very substantial quantity of the characters, and selected and recorded the vernacular Japanese readings (*wakun* 和訓) for many of those characters from a variety of texts. I set up sections in the text, so characters can be searched by radical. The draft was completed in the summer of the fourth year of Kanpyō (892). I called it the *Shinsen jikyō* 新撰字鏡 and compiled it into a single book. I found it solidly put together, and divided it into three volumes.

However after that I did not set aside my brush and did not cease to collect materials.[17)] Thus during the years of Shōtai (昌泰, 898-901), I was able to consult the *Yùpiān* 玉篇 and the *Qièyùn* 切韻 and added material from private annotations as well as characters previously omitted, further enhancing the whole.[18),19)] I also selected and inserted the characters in the *Shōgakuhen* 小学篇 and *Honzō* 本草 parts, not among the main characters, and without

---

17) The Tenji-bon reads 筆陓不捨. The second character (Chinese *yū*, Sino-Japanese *u*) denotes an ancient toponym and makes no sense in this context. The Kyōwa-bon and Gunsho ruijū-bon have 筆幹不捨 "(I) did not discard the shaft of my brush."

18) The *Qièyùn* 切韻 rhyme dictionary was completed in the 601 by Lu Fayan 陸法言. It became the standard for character pronunciation (particularly for the purpose of verse composition) in the Tang Period and became an exemplar for later rhyme tables. It provides pronunciations for over 12,000 characters using *fanqie* spellings, divided into five volumes by tonal category (two volumes for level tone, one each for the remaining three). The *Qièyùn* appears not to have been based on any particular regional variety, but rather represents a compendium of "standard" readings compiled by Lu Fayan from northern and southern sources.

19) "Private annotations" 私記 here refers to annotations (prominently, character readings) added to representative texts by authoritative individuals. Prominent examples from the this period include the *Shin'yaku Kegonkyō ongi shiki* from the late eighth century discussed in Section 3, and the *Nihon shoki siki* 日本書紀私記 compiled on the basis of various official readings of the *Nihon shoki* during the Heian period (Takahashi and Takahasi 2006: 10, fn 27).

any deep intent. Including the beauty of tones, I checked and supplemented, revised and expanded, until it became a work of twelve scrolls. Radicals number 160, excluding characters not classified into sections (*bu* 部).[20] The text includes over 20,940 characters (in addition there are over 400 *Shōgakuhen* 小学篇 characters). Apart from these, two-character compounds and characters doubled with the reduplication mark are not counted in the total.[21] Because it would be complicated to do so, I did not specify *fanqie* spellings for the characters in these two chapters (*fanqie* for each character are provided only in the sections for specific radicals). Furthermore, among the characters, some have Japanese pronunciations and meanings; these are private annotations on

---

20) Commentators have found this sentence, 片數壱佰陸披 'Parts (=radicals) number 160,' difficult to interpret (e.g. Takahashi and Takahasi 2006: 10, fn 35). The *Shinsen jikyō* is divided into 170 parts. However only a subset of these are *bu* 部'sections' associated with specific radicals (or characters used as semantic classifiers, such as the *Ten-bu* 天部 '"Heaven" section', Nin-bu 人部 '"Person" section', etc. Other characters are listed in numbered and titled chapters not classified as *bu* 部, such as Chapter 69, *Sōmoku imyō* (草木異名 'Variant names for plants and trees'). These chapters are not associated with specific radicals: Chapter 69 follows the chapter (=section) for the tree radical, and precedes the chapter (=section) for the grass radical, and includes a variety of characters not included in either. Sixteen chapters are not listed as *bu* 部 and have no single classifying radical, so the number of 160 radicals nearly corresponds to the result of subtracting these from the total of 170. It is remains unclear what the six additional radicals lacking an associated section would be. The parenthetical statement following, 末在部字等 lit. 'characters not yet in *bu* etc.' is cryptic and probably truncated.

21) Chapter 158, *Jūten dai hyaku roku jū hachi* (重点第一六八 'Chapter 158 reduplication marks') lists reduplicated characters linked with the repetition mark 𞀌, precursor of the modern typeface character 々 indicating a character to be read twice. See Galambos 2104 for discussion of this mark in medieval Chinese manuscripts. I am indebted to Galambos' paper for the image of this mark. The explicit label *jūten* 重点 'repetition mark' is noteworthy in this early source. Part 159 lists two-character compounds. These appear to have been excluded from Shōju's count. (Takahashi and Takahasi 2006: 11, fn 37). Some two-character compounds are included in the regular sections classified by character; it is not clear if (or how) these are included in the count.

various texts. Some have Chinese pronunciations and meanings; this is text from numerous commentaries and dictionaries.[22] Some have their Chinese tonal category (level, rising, departing, or entering) added, while for others this is completely omitted. For the most part this is because I created this by taking the text from numerous dictionaries and private annotations, assembling it together and mixing it up.

In general, the characters in the ancient classics have many mistakes, and the reason that *hakase* are able to teach them well is that each scholar leaves the interpretation entirely up to his own preference. They may take standard characters and argue that they are vulgar, or take acceptable characters and claim that they are standard.[23] Adding to the complications, characters may have any of the three forms, standard, acceptable, or vulgar, and their readings may have any of the four tones, as well as a vast number of meanings.[24] In some cases, a character has different shapes, while remaining the same character. Thus 崧 Chinese *song* / Sino-Japanese *shū* (variant form of the following character) and 嵩 *song/shū* 'high, lofty'; 流 *liu/ryū* 'flow' and 沭 *liu/ryū* (ancient form of preceding character); 坤 *kun/kon* 'flow' and 巛 *kun/kon* (variant form of preceding character); 憐 *lian/ren* 'flow' and 怜 *lian/ren* (simplified form of preceding character); 参 *can/san* (alternative spelling of next character) and 三 *san/san* 'three'; 予 *yu/yo* (alternative form of next character) and 余 yu/yo 'I, me'; 姦 *jian/kan* 'wicked' and 奸 *jian/kan*

---

22) 'Japanese' here are indicated as Tō-i (東夷 'Eastern barbarians), 'Chinese' as Sei-kan (西漢 'Western Han').

23) The three-way classification of characters by form as "standard" (正 Chinese *zheng*/Sino-Japanese *sei*), acceptable or conventional (通 *tong/tsū*) or "vulgar" (俗 *su/zoku*) is based on the Tang period orthographic dictionary *Ganlu Zishu* 干祿字書 by Yan Yuan-sun 顏元孫 (Takahashi and Takahasi 2006: 11, fn 46).

24) I have translated 巨多訓 *juduo xun/koda (=no) kun* here as 'vast number of meanings', rather than 'vast number of *kun*' (in the sense of vernacular Japanese readings. Shōju appears to distinguish the latter as *wakun* (和訓, 'Japanese readings').

(variant form of preceding character); 呬 *za*/*sō* (variant form of 咂 *za*/*sō* 'sip') and 嗜 *za*/*sō* 'peck, eat, speak evil'); 飜 *fan*/*hon* 'fly' and 翻 *fan*/*hon* (simplified form of preceding character); examples such as these are extremely numerous, and can be seen in the *Zhenming yaolu* 正名要録.[25] These characters have different shapes, but their pronunciation and meaning and *fanqie* spelling are both the same. There are also characters whose shape resembles one another but whose sounds and meanings are both different. 専 *zhuan*/*sen* 'exclusive' and 専 *fu*/*fu* (alternative form of 敷 *fu*/*fu* 'spread'); 傳 *chuan*/*den* 'transmit' and 傅 *fu*/*fu* 'teacher'; 崇 *chong*/*zū* 'majestic' and 崇 *sui*/*sui* 'evil spirit'; 傳 *chuan*/*den* 'transmit' and 傅 *fu*/*fu* 'teacher'; 孟 *meng*/*mō* 'great, eminent' and 盂 *yu*/*u* 'basin'; 軽 *qing*/*kei* 'light, slight' and 軽 *zhi*/*chi* 'rear of cart'; examples such as these are extremely numerous, and can be seen in the *Zhenming yaolu* 正名要録. These characters have similar shapes, but their pronunciation, meaning and *fanqie* spelling are all different. There are also characters whose radicals look the same but in fact are different. 忄 Chinese *xin* / Japanese *risshinben*, the heart radical and 巾 *jin*/*kin*, the cloth radical; 王 *wang*/*ō*, the king radical, 玉 *yu*/*gyoku*, the jade radical, and 壬 *ren*/*jin*, the ninth heavenly stem; 月 *yue*/*getsu*, the moon radical, and 肉 *rou*/*niku*, the meat radical; 丹 *dan*/*tan*, the cinnabar radical, and 舟 *zhou*/*shu*, the boat radical; 角 *jiao*/*kaku*, the horn radical, and 甬 *yong*/*yō*; characters distinguished by these radicals are distinct characters, although their radicals resemble one another. There are also characters whose stroke composition resembles one another but which are nonetheless distinct. 馬 *ma*/*ma* 'horse', 魚 *yu*/*gyo*, 'fish', and 為 *wei*/*i*, 'be, because' all have four strokes at the bottom as a basic component; the characters 鳥 *niao*/*chō* 'bird', 烏 *wu*/*u*, 'crow', and 与 *yu*/*yo* '(simplified form of 與 *yu*/*yo* 'give') all have the single stroke 一 as a basic component, while such characters as 觀 *guan*/*kan* 'watch' and 舊

---

25) The identity of this text is unclear.

jiu/kyū 'old' have the basic component 少 *shao/shō* 'few'.[26] In general it is like this, to the point that every writer who composes his/her own text makes mistakes, and only judging by the content may one comprehend it. Having said this, in the sections of the dictionary organized by radical, I have not attempted to exhaustively seek out and include variant characters.

Should it prove to be of the slightest usefulness, I would hope that future experts might add their emendations and improvements, and that it might be distributed to later generations. I have indulged the will of my brush a bit in compiling this dictionary. For the benefit of young scholars just starting out, I have made so bold as to compose these ramblings by way of a preface.

---

26) It is not clear exactly what component of the characters 觀 *guan/kan* 'watch' and 舊 *jiu/kyū* 'old' Shōju is referring to (Takahashi and Takahasi 2006: 11, fn 56). The Tenji-bon appears to use the variant shape character 観 for 觀. It is possible that Shōju identifies the left top component 艹 and the first stroke of the left bottom component 隹 with 少, although this is odd from the standpoint of stroke order.

References

Bailey, Don Clifford. 1960. Early Japanese lexicography. *Monumenta Nipponica* 16.1/2, 1–52.

Blom, Alderik. 2017. *Glossing the Psalms*: The emergence of the written vernaculars in Western Europe from the seventh to the twelfth centuries. Berlin and Boston: Water de Gruyter.

Cinato, Franck. 2015. *Priscien glosé: L'Ars grammatica de Priscien vue a travers les gloses carolingiennes* (Studia Artistarum. Études sur la Faculté des arts dans les Universités médivales 41). Turnhout: Brepols.

Chien, David and Thomas Creamer. 1986. A brief history of Chinese bilingual lexicography, in Hartmann, R.R.K (ed.) *The History of Lexicography: Papers from the Dictionary Research Centre Seminar at Exeter, March 1986*, 35–47. Amsterdam: John Benjamins.

Galambos, Imre. 2014. Punctuation marks in medieval Chinese manuscripts. In Jörg Quenzer and Jan-Ulrich Sobisch, eds., *Manuscript Cultures: Mapping the Field*. Berlin, New York: de Gruyter, 341–357.

Habein, Yaeko Sato. 1984. *The History of the Japanese Written Language*. Tokyo: University of Tokyo Press.

Hessels. John. 1906. *A Late Eighth-century Latin-Anglo-Saxon Glossary: Preserved in the Library of the Leiden University* (Ms. Voss. Q0 Lat. N0. 69). Cambridge: Cambridge University Press.

Ikeda, Shōju 池田証寿. 1980. Jōdai butten ongi to Gennō Issaikyō ongi: Daiji-bon *Shin Kegonkyō ongi* to *Shingyō Daihannyakyō ongi* no baai [Old Japanese Buddhist ongi and Xuányīn's *Yīqièjīng yīnyì*: The case of the Daiji-bon *Shin Kegonkyō ongi* and Shingyō's *Daihannyakyō ongi* 上代仏典音義と玄応一切経音義：大治本新華嚴経音義と信行大般若経音義の場合]. *Kokugo kokubun kenkyū* 64: 64-77.

Ikeda, Shōju 池田証寿. 1982. *Gennō ongi to Shinsen jikyō* [Xuányīn's *Yīqièjīng yīnyì* and the *Shinsen jikyō* 玄応音義と新撰字鏡]. *Kokugogaku* 130: 1-18.

Ikeda, Shōju 池田証寿. 1986. *Shin'yaku Kegonkyō ongi shiki* no seikaku [Characteristics of the *Shin'yaku Kegonkyō ongi shiki* 新譯華嚴經音義私記の性格]. *Kokugokokubun kenkyū* 75.

Ikeda, Shōju. 池田証寿. 1987. *Shin'yaku Kegonkyō ongi shiki* seiritsu no igi: Erin ongi o inyō suru hōhō no kentō o chūsin ni [The significance of creation of the *Shin'yaku Kegonkyō ongi shiki*: Focusing on the method citing the *Huìlín yīnyì* 新訳華厳経音義私記成立の意義：慧苑音義を引用する方法の検討を中心に]. *Kuntengo to Kunten shiryō* 77.

Ikeda, Mosaku 池田茂作. 1930. Nara chō kenzai Issaikyōso mokuroku [Catalogue of Nara period Tripitaka sutras and commentaries 奈良朝見在一切経疏目録]. In *Shakyō yori mitaru Nara chō Bukkyō no kenkyū* [Research on Nara period Buddhism as seen from sutra copying 写経より見たる奈良朝仏教の研究]. Tōyō bunko ronsho 11.

Lapidge, Michael. 1986. *The school of Theodore and Hadrian. Anglo-Saxon England* 15, 45-72.

Lapidge, Michael. 2006. *The Anglo-Saxon Library.* Oxford and New York: Oxford University Press.

Miho, Tadao. 三保忠夫. 1974. Daiji-bon *Shin Kegonkyō ongi* no senjutsu to haikei [The compilation and background of the Daiji-bon *Shin Kegonkyō ongi* 大治本新華嚴経音義の撰述と背景]. *Nanto Bukkyō* 33.

Moran, Pádraic. 2019. *De Origine Scoticae Linguae* (O'Mulconry's Glossary): An early Irish linguistic tract, edited with a related glossary, Irsan. Turnhout: Brepols.

Sadakari, Itoku. 貞苅伊徳. 1959/1998. *Shinsen jikyō no kaibō (yōshi)* — sono shutten o tazunete [『新撰字鏡』の解剖（要旨）——その出典を尋ねて—— A dissection of the *Shinsen jikyō* (summary): In search of its sources]. In Sadakari 1998, 20-48.

Sadakari, Itoku. 貞苅伊徳. 1962/1998. *Shinsen jikyō rinji zatsuyō ji to Kango-shō* [『新撰字鏡』「臨時雑用字」と漢語抄 The *Rinji zatsuyō ji* (Temporary miscellaneous characters) section of the *Shinsen jikyō* and *Kango-shō*]. Reprinted in Sadakari 1998, 110-143.

Russell, Paul. 1998. Laws, glossaries and legal glossaries. *Zeitschrift für celtische Philologie* 51, 85-115.

Seely, Christopher, 1991. *A history of Japanese writing*. Leiden and New York: Brill.

Sadakari, Itoku. 貞苅伊徳. 1998. *Shinsen jikyō no kenkyū* [『新撰字鏡』の研究 Research on the *Shinsen jikyō*]. Tokyo: Kyūko shoin.

Takahashi, Tadahiko 高橋忠彦 and Hisako Takahashi 高橋久子. 2006. *Nihon no kojisho: Jobun·batsubun o yomu* [Japanese old dictionaries: reading the prefaces and afterwords 日本の古辞書＝序文・跋文を読む]. Tokyo: Taishukan shoten.

Tsukishima, Hiroshi. 1959. Kundoku shijō no Zushoryō-bon *Ruiju myōgishō* [訓読史上の図書寮本類聚名義抄 The Zushoryō-bon *Ruiju myōgishō* from the standpoint of the history of *kundoku*]. *Kokugogaku* 37, 35–53.

Tsukishima, Hiroshi (chief editor). 1978. *Shin'yaku Kegonkyō ongi* 新訳華厳経音義 *Kojisho ongi shūsei* 1. Tokyo: Kyūko shoin.

Whitman, John and Franck Cinato (eds.). 2015. Lecture vernaculaire ds textes classiques chinois/Reading Chinese Classical Texts in the Vernacular. Paris: *Dossiers Histoire Épistémologie Langage* 7. http://htl.linguist.univ-paris-diderot.fr/hel/dossiers/numero7/explaining_what_kundoku.

Whitman, John, Miyoung Oh, Jinho Park, Valerio Luigi Alberizzi, Masayuki Tsukimoto, Teiji Kosukegawa, and Tomokazu Takada. 2010. Toward an international vocabulary for research on vernacular reading of Chinese texts (漢文訓讀 *Hanwen xundu*). 2010. *Scripta* 2, 61–84.

Yong, Heming, Jing Peng and Bing Tian. 2008. *Chinese Lexicography: A History from 1046 BC to AD 1911*. Oxford and New York: Oxford University Press.

Yoshida, Kanehiko 吉田金彦. 1955/2013. Kokugogaku ni okeru kojisho kenkyū no tachiba [国語学における古辞書研究の立場 The standpoint of research on old dictionaries in Japanese linguistics]. *Kokugogaku* 23. Revised 2011, reprinted in Yoshida 2013: 318–332 as Kojisho e no kaigan [古辞書への開眼 The rise of awareness of old dictionaries].

Yoshida, Kanehiko 吉田金彦. 2013. Kojisho to kokugogaku [古辞書と国語学 Old dictionaries and Japanese linguistics]. Kyoto: Rinsen shoten.

Hero or Villain?
— an Anglo-Norman context for the poem *Piers of Bermingham* in London, British Library, MS Harley 913

Yoko WADA

London, British Library, MS Harley 913, written in Ireland around 1330,[1] contains a variety of works such as religious verse, records pertaining to the Franciscan order and several political or social satires in Latin, English and French.[2] This paper will investigate the poem *Piers of Bermingham* (so entitled by a modern editor)[3] to determine whether it is a satire or a eulogy praising the great achievements of its subject, the Anglo-Irish second lord of Athenry who died in 1308.[1]

Before taking up the main subject, I should like to provide an overview

---

1) Alan J. Fletcher, "The date of London, British Library, Harley 913 (The Kildare Poems)", *Medium Ævum* 79 (2010), pp. 306–10.

2) Neil Cartlidge, 'Festivity, Order, and Community in Fourteenth-Century Ireland: The Composition and Context of BL MS Harley 913,' *Yearbook of English Studies* 33 (2003), pp. 33–52; A.G. Little (ed.), *Materials for the History of the Franciscan Province of Ireland A.D. 1230–1450* (Manchester: Manchester University Press 1920), pp. 122–6; Angela Lucas (ed.), *Anglo-Irish Poems of the Middle Ages* (Dublin: The Columba Press 1995), pp. 14–21; Thorlac Turville-Petre, *Poems from BL MS Harley 913 "The Kildare Manuscript"*, EETS o.s. 345 (Oxford: Oxford University Press 2015), pp. liii–iv.

3) Lucas, *Anglo-Irish Poems*, pp. 150–57. The text used in this paper is based on the edition by Turvill-Petre (*Poems*, pp. 69–73).

4) Little, *Materials*, pp. 88–9; John Thomas Gilbert, *Cartularies of St. Mary's Abbey, Dublin: with the Register of its House at Dunbrody, and Annals of Ireland* (London: Longman & Co. 1884), vol. 2, pp. 281 and 336.

of the historical background of this poem.[5] Medieval Ireland was not united as one nation but divided into many kingdoms (*túath* in Irish). In the twelfth century, one king, Diarmait Mac Murchada of Leinster whose kingdom had been taken from him asked Henry II for support to retrieve his land. Henry complied with Diarmait's request and dispatched his Norman, English, Welsh and Scottish vassals to Ireland. Diarmait also managed to make a strong ally of Richard Fitz Gilbert de Clare, who was on bad terms with King Henry at that time. Once Diarmait regained Leinster, Richard and his Norman noblemen gradually began to exercise their influence in southeast Ireland. When the ambitious King Henry became so uneasy about the situation that he himself went to Ireland, Richard handed over Leinster to him without any resistance. The king eventually placed much of Ireland under his control, but he found it very difficult to wipe out the fierce resistance of the O'Connors who ruled the midwest of Ireland. To solve this problem, Henry entered into a treaty in 1175 with Ruaidrí Ua Conchobair or Rory O'Connor, who had ousted Diarmait Mac Murchada, so that Henry was acknowledged as overlord of Leinster, Meath and Munster while Rory was allowed to rule the rest of Ireland. When King Henry's son acceded to the throne as King John in 1199, he also became Lord of Ireland and governed all Ireland. He then violated the treaty which his father had concluded, confiscating the local Irish people's property to distribute it among the Norman nobles. After that, conflicts between the king and the Gaelic Irish people continued for well over a century.

Now that Ireland had become a colony of England, a greater number of

5) Art Cosgrove (ed.), *A New History of Ireland; vol. 2, Medieval Ireland 1169–1534* (Oxford: Oxford University Press 1987; Goddard Henry Orpen, *Ireland under the Normans 1169–1333* with an Introduction by Seán Duffy (Dublin: Four Courts Press 2005); Annette Jocelyn Otway-Ruthven, *A History of Medieval Ireland* (London, 2nd edn, 1980); James F. Lydon, *The Lordship of Ireland in the Middle Ages* (Dublin: Gill and Macmillan 1972).

Anglo-Normans immigrated to Ireland. Concomitantly, in the thirteenth century, Augustinians, Dominicans, Franciscans, Carmelites and other religious orders arrived in Ireland to preach all over the country. In the middle of the thirteenth century, however, the number of the immigrants began to decrease and the Norman population got smaller except in Leinster and Munster. As England began to attach more importance to the war with France than to governing Ireland, the English crown let the local Norman nobles handle Irish administration. While Irish people were antagonistic toward the Normans, some Normans who got land in Ireland married women of the Irish royal families and acquired Irish manners and language. Those people tended to renounce their allegiance to England, and become Anglo-Irish. To make the Irish political situation still more complicated, however, they were often involved in conflicts with the native Irish, that is, the Gaelic Irish, who extended their power so much that England could hardly control them. In this fashion, vehement power struggles characterized much of thirteenth-century Ireland.

The poem, *Piers of Bermingham*, was composed during this time of disturbance in medieval Ireland, as a eulogy to Piers of Bermingham who died in April, 1308. It consists of 132 lines, which constitute a tribute to his three great achievements: (1) he intimidated thieves, (2) he harassed and captured the Gaelic Irish to whom he was the enemy and (3) he massacred the Gaelic Irish O'Connors brutally in his Carbury Castle on Trinity Sunday in 1305. On the face of it, the work appears to do honor to Bermingham's memory. Scholars such as J. E. Wells,[6]

---

6) "In 132 three-stress verses aabccb, rude and without any artistic merit, the balladist laments the death on April 20, 1308, of Peter of Birmingham, the really ruthless champion of the English settlers in Ireland, and extols his suppression of thieves and his relentless pursuit of the Irish." (J. E. Wells, *A Manual of the Writings in Middle English*, 1050–1400 (New Haven, CT: Yale University Press 1916), p.215).

A. G. Little,[7] St John D. Symour,[8] James Lyndon,[9] Alan Bliss and Joseph Long[10] agreed that the poem is a eulogy praising his extermination of the Irish. However, Michael Benskin proposed (in 1989)[11] that it is a satire on his cruel deeds against the Irish, an opinion shared by Angela Lucas.[12] In 2010, John Scattergood rejected Benskin's interpretation, maintaining that it is nothing other than a eulogy.[13] I should like to re-examine this question

---

7) "... the poem is largely devoted to praises of his attacks on the Irish" (Little, *Materials*, p. 89).

8) "Its unknown author was intensely, nay, savagely, hostile to the native Irish. He laments the death of one who was so unwearying in his persecution of them, and closes his poem with an allusion to what he must have conceived to have been his hero's best effort, namely, the murder of the O'Conors in 1305." (St John D. Symour, *Anglo-Irish Literature, 1200–1582* (Cambridge: Cambridge University Press 1929), pp. 81–2).

9) "In a poem eulogizing de Bermingham after his death he is praised for being an inveterate foe to the Irish...". (James Lydon, "A Land of War" in Cosgrove, *A New History*, pp. 267–8).

10) "Whoever the patron may have been, he was motivated by intense hostility towards the Irish." (Alan Bliss and Joseph Long, "Literature in Norman French and English to 1534" in Cosgrove, *A New History*, p. 729).

11) "Hitherto, it seems, the moderns have ignored the cultural context, and merely glanced at the surface of what they supposed to be there. For the poem is not incompetent heroic, but *mock*-heroic contrived, not a eulogy, but a satirical indictment". (Michael Benskin, "The Style and Authorship of the Kildare Poems — (I) *Pers of Bermingham*" in J. Lachlan Mackenzie and Richard Todd (edd), *In Other Words* (Dordrecht: Foris Publications 1989), p. 61).

12) "It is inherently unlikely that all Ireland would have lamented Piers's death as the author claims, and the overstatement points to the correctness of Benskin's interpretation. The poem is the work of someone not lamenting nor praising his subject, but seeking to expose him to ridicule and loathing." (Lucas, *Anglo-Irish Poems*, p. 209).

13) "It [*Piers of Bermingham*] ostensibly celebrates a dangerous man, a prototypical fourteenth-century gentry thug, who happens in this case to be Anglo-Irish, a racialist, a murderer, a bounty-hunter, who was unapologetic about his atrocities." (John Scattergood, "Elegy for a Dangerous Man: *Piers of Bermingham*" in *Occasions for Writing: Essays on Medieval and Renaissance Literature, Politics and Society* (Dublin: Four Courts Press 2010), p. 105).

with special reference to the arguments of Benskin and Scattergood, in an effort to determine the nature of the poem.

Piers of Bermingham begins by establishing the chronology on Gabriel's Annunciation to the Virgin Mary.

Sith Gabriel gan grete
Vre Leuedi Mari swete
Þat Godde wold in hir liȝte,
A þousand ȝer hit isse
Þre hundred ful i-wisse
And ouer ȝeris eiȝte.

Þan of þe eiȝt ȝere
Tak twies° ten ifere°,   twice   together
Þat wol be tuenti fulle;
Apan þe tuentieþ dai
Of Aueril bifor Mai,
So deþ vs gan to pulle°.   rob
(ll. 1–12)

The first stanza gives the year of the subject's death, using *Anno Domini* dating; the second stanza, applying the dating system of the Roman calendar, indicates the date. The combination gives us 11 or 12 April, 1308. Stylistically there seems to be a discrepancy between the religious emphasis of the first and the secular reckoning of the second. Another discrepancy is actually the date of the subject's death which is most likely to be 13 April according to the chroniclers. One wonders if the poet deliberately contrived to make the date of his death Good Friday (Easter fell on 14 April in 1308) to insinuate a comparison between the subject Piers and Christ. One also wonders why it takes the first two whole stanzas to specify the date. Another interesting thing is that the identity of the subject of this poem is not disclosed until the fifth line of the third stanza, which Benskin took as an anticlimax of bitter irony.[14] He may be right: when readers who expected that the poem would offer a dignified elegy about the death of some personage in the first two stanzas arrived at stanza three, their sudden realization that the subject was Piers Bermingham would have created a sense of bathos. After all Piers was notorious for having slaughtered many Gaelic Irish on the occasion of Trinity Sunday of all days. By contrast, Scattergood argued that the beginning pays respect to Piers as a hero among Anglo Normans.[15] He added, moreover, that the mention of the Annunciation was nothing particular since it was simply one of many ways of establishing a historical date in the middle ages, just like the first day of January or the day of enthronement of a king or a pope.[16]

The first line of the third stanza reveals something about the author's background: He was probably Anglo-Norman, since he writes, "He plucked one

---

14) Benskin, "The Style," pp. 61-2. The date of his death is recorded in several documents, of which Cartularies of St. Mary's Abbey gives the date, 13 of April, in "....Petrus de Brymingham in vigilia Pasche, et sepultus cum Minoribus apud Kyldare" (*Cartularies of St. Mary's Abbey, Dublin with the Register of its House at Dunbrody and Annals of Ireland,* vol. 2, edited by John T. Gilbert (London: Longman, 1884), p. 281). Annals of Ireland also records that "1308. Idibus April, obiit Petrus Bremingham" nobilis Hibernorum domator" (On the 13th of April died Peter Birmingham, the noble tamer of the Irish.) (Jacobi Grace, Kilkenniensis, *Annales Hiberniae* edited and translated by Richard Butler (Dublin: Irish Archaeological Society 1842), pp. 50-1). However, Dominican Christopher Pembridge's *Annales Hiberniae* in Dublin, Trinity College, MS 585, gives the date, 12 April, in "Secundo idus Aprilis, obit Dominus Petrus de Bermingham, nobilis debellator Hibernicorum" (*Cartularies of St. Mary's Abbey,* edited by Gilbert, p. 336).
15) Scattergood, "Elegy," p. 98.
16) Scattergood, "Elegy," p. 98.

of us", thus identifying with Bermingham who was also Anglo-Norman. In the fifth line, the poem mentions the name of the hero for the first time, and thereafter continues to express how much he had been admired by everyone.

He pullid us of on,	
Al Irlond makiþ mon°,	lamentation
Engelon ek° as welle,	also
Ful wel ye witte° his nam:	know
Sire Pers þe Brimgham,	
Non nede hit is to telle.	
(ll. 13–18)	

The praise of Piers' strength as a knight whom nobody can excel in fighting continues all the way until the eighth stanza. However, in stanza five, it is cunning thieves, not strong warriors, who are identified as the objects of intimidation by this noble, heroic knight, evidence which Benskin interpreted as intended sarcastically:[17]

Noble werrure° he was	warrior
And gode castel in place,	
On stede° þer he wold ride,	horse
Wiþ his sper and scheld,	
In hard wodde and feld	
No þef him durst abide.	
(ll. 25–30)	

In the seventh stanza, the author exhorts all Englishmen to weep over

---

17) Benskin, "The Style," p. 62.

his death. The audience of this poem, evidently, is English living either in Ireland or in England. It is interesting that the Anglo-Irish still identified themselves as English after all their time living in Ireland.

Al Englismen þat beþ
Sore mow wep is° deþ   his
Þat such a kniȝt ssold falle;
Þos kniȝtis euchone
Of him mai make mone,
As peruink° of ham alle.   flower
(ll. 37–42)

Next Bermingham's three feats are described, beginning with the eighth stanza. The first one is that he let no thief have any rest wherever he came: "He ne leet no thef hab rest / In no stid ther he come." (ll. 47–8) It is to be noted that thieves are again referred to in connection with the first of his three achievements. The second feat was that he chased and caught the Irish over a wide region as if he were hunting the hare, so that he became an enemy to Irishmen.

Anoþer þing also:
To Yrismen he was fo°,   enemy
Þat wel widewhare,
Euer he rode aboute
Wiþ streinþ° to hunt ham vte,   armed force
As hunter doþ þe hare.
(ll. 49–54)

Bermingham also surprised the Irish in sleep when they hid themselves in the wilderness. Again, the scene is described in terms of hunting. When Piers stormed Irish people's homes, they ran away in fear because he took their heads as security for a loan to them to buy their own beds — if they wanted to sleep without being disturbed by him. At line 54, the author compares the Irish to hares — said to be a symbol of sexual promiscuity — a reference which may imply Anglo-Irish contempt for Irish people.[18] Hunting hares also reminds us of their natural enemy, the ferret which was employed by hunters to catch rabbits or hares. The ferret would search into holes where hares were hiding and when the hares emerged above ground, hunters netted them and knocked their heads with sticks. This fits the description of how Piers caught the Irish and took their heads. If hares be equated with the Irish, then the hunter, Piers, is the ferret. The comparison is possibly also ironic since the etymology of "ferret" is the Latin *furittus*, that is, "a little thief," which made them symbols of ferocity and slyness. At the same time, ermine pelts were made from ferret hides, which only the wealthy could wear; so this might suggest another association with a rich aristocrat like Piers.

For whan hi wend° best	thought
In wildernis hab rest,	
Þat no man ssold° ham see,	should
Þan he wold driue a quest°	search
Anon° to har° nest,	at once their
In stid° þer hi wold be.	place

18) A riddle in Latin in the same manuscript seems to ridicule incest committed by the Irish (fol 49v).

81

Of slep he wold ham wake;

For ferdnis° hi wold quak   fear

And fond° to sculk awai.   attempt

For þe hire° of har bedde   hire

He tok har heuid° to wedde°,   head   surety

And so he taȝt ham plai.

(ll. 55-66)

Commenting on these stanzas, Benskin argued that Piers' deeds were not appropriate at all for a knight: in this poem he threatens only thieves, attacks sleepers and takes their heads as a deposit for the payment of their beds. Benskin found it likely that Piers is being depicted as a greedy hunter for monetary rewards since it is known that he received a lot of bounties in exchange for Irish heads.[19] Scattergood rejected his opinion by saying that it was acceptable for knights to play the role of policemen in maintaining peace and public order; they arrested criminals including thieves.[20] Certainly, the legislation passed by the 1297 parliament implies that many Gaelic Irish thieves stole possessions from the Anglo Irish, especially in the troubled period from the later thirteenth century to the early fourteenth century: "....when thieves or robbers shall come into any country to take spoils or to do any other mischief, all the country people, as soon as their approach can come to their knowledge, rise together and effectively pursue them".[21] Scattergood maintained that what Piers did was not only part of the duties of the knight,

---

19) Benskin, "The Style," p. 63.
20) Scattergood, "Elegy," p. 98.
21) Philomena Connolly, "The enactments of the 1297 parliament" in James Lydon (ed), *Law and Disorder in Thirteenth-century Ireland: The Dublin Parliament of 1297* (Dublin: Four Courts Press 1997), p. 153.

but was also in conformity with the law.[22] It should be noted that Piers served in fact as a *custos* of peace in Offaly from June 1303 to October 1305.[23]

However, the Irish whom Bermingham is described as catching and killing in the poem are not identified as criminals; in other words, he indiscriminately murdered Irish men whenever he found them. This is reflected in line 50, "To Yrismen he was fo" and corroborated by *The Annals of Inisfallen* of 1305:[24]

....he [Piers of Bermingham] was not aware that there was a foreigner in Ireland who had not undertaken to slay his Gaelic neighbor, and he knew that they would slay, as he had slain....

It is likely that Piers' deeds violated the law because the legislation of 1297 specified that the Anglo-Irish should not provoke the Gaelic Irish into war by ambushing or making night raids on them while relations were stable or a truce had been agreed; otherwise, they would be severely punished by the king.[25] Evidently, similarly cruel treatment was meted out by the Anglo-Irish to the Gaelic Irish as documented in a letter written by Domhnall O'Neill, who represented the chiefs of the Gaelic-Irish tribes, sent to Pope John XXII (1244–1334) in 1317:[26]

22) Scattergood, "Elegy," pp. 98–9.
23) Open, *Ireland*, p. 452. Piers and Thomas were, however, defeated by Calvagh O'Conor, whom Piers would murder 17 years later in the massacre depicted in this poem.
24) Seán Mac Airt (ed. and trans.), *The Annals of Inisfallen* (Dublin: The Dublin Institute for Advanced Studies 1951), pp. 395–7.
25) Philomena Connolly, "The enactments of the 1297 parliament" in Lydon, *Law*, p. 153.
26) Edmund Curtis and R. B. McDowell (edd), *Irish Historical Documents* 1172–1922. (New York NY: Barnes & Noble 1943), p. 41.

Also, as usually happens for the most part when by perfidy and guile some Englishman kills an Irishman, however noble and inoffensive, whether cleric or lay, regular or secular, even if an Irish prelate should be killed, no punishment or correction is inflicted by the said court on such a nefarious murderer; nay more, the better the murdered man was and the greater the place be held among his people, the more his murderer is honoured and rewarded by the English, not merely by the populace but even by English religious and bishops, and most of all by those to whom it falls through their positions to inflict just punishment and due correction on such evil-doers.

In addition to the information above, the letter also discloses that some Anglo-Irish clergymen declared that they should not be precluded from saying Mass after killing an Irishman because it did not count as a sin.[27]

Stanza twelve narrates the story of the massacre of Gaelic-Irish lords planned and carried out by Piers of Bermingham. It first explains how Irishmen began to threaten the Anglo-Irish with death. This seems to justify the massacre as a necessary retaliation against the Gaelic Irish in self-defense, and evidently, reflects an Anglo-Irish perspective. Certainly, there is evidence that some Gaelic Irish chieftains maneuvered to murder Anglo-Irish lords whom they hated. The names of their targets are listed in the thirteenth stanza: the Earl of Ulster (or Richard de Burgh), Sir Edmund de Butler, Sir John Fitzthomas (or Lord of Offaly, a.k.a. MacMuiris) and Sir Piers de Bermingham. The plot, however, came to light, causing the Anglo Irish to swear revenge on the conspirators. As time went by, however, they forgot their resolution, except for Piers Bermingham, who was constantly watching for a chance to retaliate:

---

27) Curtis and McDowell, *Irish Historical Documents*, p. 41.

Sire Pers þe Brimgham,

On ernist and agam°,   in jest

Þis dai was in is° þoȝt;   his

He þoȝt ordres to mak,

What time he miȝt ham tak;

Of trauail° nas him noȝt.   hard work

(ll. 97–102)

Scattergood interpreted "to make orders" in line 100 as meaning "to ordain" rather than "to issue command". He plausibly explained that the phrase originally meant "to give a blow to the head" in Middle English because a bishop puts his hand on the head of a new priest at ordination.[28] Incidentally, *Middle English Dictionary* cites this line for a figurative use of the phrase. The expression, in its sacerdotal meaning, fits what Piers did because, as I will discuss later, he struck off the heads of the guests at his castle.

The day to gain revenge came; it was "Riȝt at þe Trinite, / Whan hodes sold best be" (precisely on the feast of the Holy Trinity when hoods had best be worn) (ll. 106–7). Stanzas 18 and 19 describe Piers watching the Gaelic-Irish King O'Conchobhair accompanied by Captain Gilla Buidhe and foot soldiers coming toward his castle in Tethmoy. He thought that it was a matter of life and death — a perfect opportunity to take revenge, so that he received all of them and caused hoods to be made for them.

Sire Pers sei° ham com,   saw

He receiuid al and som,

Noȝt on iwernd° nas;   rejected

Siþ hoodis he let mak,

---

28) Scattergood, "Elegy," pp. 102–3.

No3t on nas forsak°,   omitted

Bot al he did ham grace,

(ll. 115–20)

Interestingly, no line explicitly states that "Piers slaughtered them all", but the stanza cited above tells in veiled language all about the terrible incident. The poem was probably written for locals in a small circle who knew the details of what had happened.   Benskin and Scattergood agree on the interpretation of hoods which had best be worn on Trinity Sunday mentioned in the sixth and seventh lines: they were the leather bags in which the murderers put the heads of the Gaelic Irish to carry to Dublin, where they received large rewards in exchange for the heads.[29]   We know that Piers in fact got a hundred pounds from the government for his work.   Several chronicles record this massacre.   One of the most detailed description is found in *The Annals of Inisfallen* under the year 1305:[30]

> Muirchertach Ó Conchobuir Fhailgi and In Calbach his brother, were slain by Sir Piers Bermingham, after he had deceitfully and shamefully invited them and acted as god-father to [the child of] the latter and as co-sponsor with the other.   Masir, the little child who was a son of the latter, and whom Piers himself had sponsored at confirmation, was thrown over [the battlements of] the castle, and it was thus it died.   And twenty-three or twenty-four of the followers of those men mentioned above, were

---

29) Benskin, "The Style," p. 65; Scattergood, "Elegy," p. 102.

30) Mac Airt (ed. with translation and indexes), *The Annals*, pp. 394–5.   See also Williams, The Annals, pp. 156–7, Séamus Ó hInnse (ed with translation and indexes), *Miscellaneous Irish Annals (A.D. 1114–1437)* (Dublin: The Dublin Institute for Advanced Studies 1947), pp. 130–1, and A. Martin Freeman (ed.), *Annála Connacht, The Annals of Connacht* (A.D. 1224–1544) (Dublin: The Dublin Institute for Advanced Studies 1970), pp. 206–7.

slain, for In Gaillsech Shacsanach (she was the wife of the same Piers) used to give warning from the top of the castle of any who went into hiding, so that many were slain as a result of those warnings. And woe to the Gaedel who puts trust in a king's peace or in foreigners after that! For, although they had [the assurance of] their king's peace, their heads were brought to Áth Cliath [Dublin], and much wealth was obtained for them from the foreigners. And when Piers was reproached with that, he said that he was not aware that there was a foreigner in Ireland who had not undertaken to slay his Gaelic neighbor, and he knew that they would slay, as he had slain; and that it was no wonder the foreigners harboured that evil resolution concerning them, for they (the Gaedil) had avenged themselves thoroughly before they were slain.

Clearly this record from the Gaelic side gives us more information than the poem. If its information is correct, Piers invited these Gaelic Irish to a celebration on Trinity Sunday and became godfather to a niece of Ó Conchobuir. Piers had even attended the confirmation of the child as a co-sponsor with that king. Pretending to be a good friend of the king on that Trinity Sunday, Piers caused the child to be thrown from the top of the castle.

The letter of remonstrance mentioned above of the Gaelic Irish addressed to Pope John XXII also refers to this incident:[31]

Also of the same and the banquets of the English. For the English inhabiting our land, who call themselves of the middle nation, are so different in character from the English of England and from other nations that with the greatest propriety they may be called a nation not of middle (*medium*), but of utmost, perfidy. For, from of old they have had this

---

31) Curtis and McDowell, *Irish Historical Documents*, p. 41.

wicked unnatural custom, which even yet has not ceased among them but every day becomes stronger and more established, viz. when they invite noblemen of our nation to a banquet, during the very feast or in the time of sleep they mercilessly shed the blood of their unsuspicious guests, and in this way bring their horrible banquet to an end. When this has been thus done they have cut off the heads of the slain and sold them for money to their enemies, as did the baron Peter Brunechehame (Bermingham), a recognized and regular betrayer, in the case of his gossip Maurice de S. (*sic*) and his brother Caluache, men of high birth and great name among us. Inviting them to a banquet on Trinity Sunday, on that same day when the repast was finished, as soon as they had risen from the table he cruelly murdered them with twenty four of their following and sold their heads dear to their enemies. And when he was afterwards accused to the king of England, the present king's father, of this crime, the king inflicted no punishment on so nefarious a traitor.

The mention that King Edward III let Piers go unpunished clearly shows the indifference of the Crown towards the Irish.

The penultimate stanza of the poem sounds puzzling to the modern reader.

Saue° o° wreche þat þer was,	Except one
He cuþe° noȝt red in place	was able to
No sing whar he com.	
He was Caymis kinne°,	Cain's race
And he refusid him;	
He wend vnhodid° hom.	unhooded
(ll. 121-6)	

One man who could not read or sing when he should at the ceremony of mass was rejected for a hood by Piers; in other words, he was not beheaded and "went home unhooded". He was the only Irishman who survived the massacre. He is also described as of the race of Cain, which makes sense in the context of this poem because Cain was punished by God to wander alone forever for his fratricide.[32] As mentioned above, Scattergood regarded the portrayal of the slaughter as a parody of ordination. We could say that is why this one man was not admitted to ordination and was let go, because as someone who could not read or sing properly he was not qualified to be "ordained." Benskin took note of "unhodid" and interpreted it as "not hooded" and therefore "not consecrated".[33] Another possibility of a double meaning is the word's association with falconry. When the hawker takes off the hawk's hood and lets it go and catch its prey, the bird flies away at a furious speed.

One wonders why and how this one man got away. The survivor might have been simply a nobody whose head was not worth taking. Scattergood surmised that one of the O'Connors must have escaped although we have no record to indicate it,[34] and that the author referenced Cain to suggest that the single survivor, like Cain, was protected from being killed.[35] However, it is also possible that the author might have made one person survive as a witness to tell others of the massacre in order to lend credibility to his account. The mention that the man who was spared was Cain's descendant may also be a sly reminder that in the eyes of the Anglo-Irish such Irish people are Cain's descendants, in other words, wicked savages, or outlaws.

The last stanza neatly rounds off the narrative which began with the complicated chronology of the first stanza mentioning the Annunciation: first,

32) Genesis 4:1–16.
33) Benskin, "The Style," p. 65.
34) Scattergood, "Elegy," p. 105.
35) Scattergood, "Elegy," p. 105.

it states that the author was commissioned to compose the verse as if some notable person had commissioned it; and secondly, that the author took the trouble of visiting many churches to gain a "good" indulgence of "two hundred days and more" for Piers of Bermingham.

He þat þis sang let mak
For Sir Persis sake,
Wel wid haþ igo,
Widwhar° isoȝt   far and wild
And god pardon iboȝt,
Two hundrid daies and mo.

Explicit.
(ll. 126–33)

Scattergood concluded that the poem was an epic praising a great, tragic hero on the grounds that it came together as an elegy, and that Piers was buried in an Anglo-Irish Franciscan cemetery and thus was regarded as a good Christian.[36] However, as we have seen above, many insinuations about Piers' cruel deeds are evident in the lines. Assuming that the poem was a satire, the author might have tried to pretend that he did not take it upon himself to compose it — he did it only upon request ("He that this sang let mak for Sir Pers is sake..." on lines 127–8). The good pardon which the patron/author gained (mentioned in the last two lines) was a very ordinary indulgence for the dead of "two hundrid daies and mo," which seems paltry for a great hero. One might even be tempted to interpret "god pardon iboght" as "he bought a good indulgence (with money)" — which could not have cost much for that

36) Scattergood, "Elegy," p. 105.

number of days — rather than by means of prayers or other religious acts, for a thug who treacherously killed his Irish enemies on Trinity Sunday to sell their heads for a high price.

The author was probably an Anglo-Irish religious who knew about ordination and other ecclesiastical matters. As Benskin argued, he seems to have shaped this poem as a satire, but very cautiously: to start with, he mentions the Annunciation to indicate the date of death of Piers of Bermingham and describes him as a great knight who intimidated thieves. For Piers to take Irish heads as security to lend them their beds (which should be theirs and not his) is not heroic but evil and even sounds incongruous for the great hero of a poem which begins with a lofty mention of the Annunciation. Then, as the summation of Piers' achievements, the author describes a massacre conducted on a sacred day when blood was not supposed to be shed. Finally, for the sake of Piers, an indulgence was gained after extensive travel, but the number of days so acquired appears quite small for such a renowned knight. In style and form, the poem reads as a good elegy, as Scattergood argues, but that makes the poem all the more ironic. Turville-Petre notes that "the poet neither expresses unease nor is moved to offer any justification"[37] and thereby seems to suggest that one should suspend judgement. Cartlidge, however, opines as follows:[38]

> Benskin is certainly right to point out the uneasy tone of 'Pers de Bermingham', but quite where its sarcasm is directed (at Pers, at the Irish, or at both together) still seems to me a matter of uncertainty. I remain open-minded about the exact purpose and significance of this

---

37) Turville-Petre, *England*, p. 158.
38) Cartlidge, "Festivity,", p. 43.

poem, but I think that it can be taken at least as a warning against assuming that anti-Irish sentiment in this period was simple or unquestioned within the Anglo-Irish community.

In Cartlidge's question about whether the sarcasm is directed at Piers or at the Irish lies the key to solve our problem. In this poem, the Irish are constantly trying to wriggle their way out of danger all the time and are compared to hares, which is not a compliment; it conveys a weak, timid and skulking image of them. The author was obviously not a supporter of the Irish, but he was not an ally of Piers, either. Although the author was Anglo-Irish, it is probable that he was repelled by Piers' atrocities. There is a poem in the same manuscript called "Song of the Times"[39] about contempt of the world which is obviously about an Ireland without law and order. Although we do not know whether it was composed by the same author that wrote *Piers of Bermingham*, it tells much about contemporary society: "Hate and anger is very widespread there, and faithful love is completely lacking in vigour. Men who are in the highest positon in life are most loaded with sin. This land is false and wicked, as we can see all the time" (ll. 5–10). Some lines remind one of Piers: "And those light-armed horsemen namely, who deprive the timid husbandman of compensation for his piece of land, one ought not to bury them in any church, but cast them out like a dog." (ll. 29–32) The verse also relates, "Truth is absent from stranger and from kin, as far and wide as this whole country," and at the end the author concludes, "I advise thee, have trust in no man, nor in anyone else, but take action with your own fist. Trust neither sister nor brother" (ll. 189–92). The author of *Piers of Bermingham* lived in this state of continuing conflict, where one could not trust anyone regardless of ethnicity.

---

39) Lucas, *Anglo-Irish Poems*, pp. 128–39; Turville-Petre, *Poems*, pp. 62–8. The translation cited here is by Lucas.

He was probably the kind of person who did not necessarily support the Anglo Irish just because they were his kin. This may be one of the reasons why, as Cartlidge says, anti-Irish sentiment in this period was not simple or unquestioned within the Anglo-Irish community. *Piers of Bermingham* is a parody of a eulogy whose subject was intended to be a villan.[40]

Select bibliography

Michael Benskin, 'The Style and Authorship of the Kildare Poems (1) *Pers of Bermingham*' in J. Lachlan Mackenzie and Richard Todd (edd), *In Other Words* (Dordrecht: Foris Publications 1989), pp. 57–75 and pp. 68–71.

John Burrow, *The Poetry of Praise* (Cambridge: Cambridge University Press 2008).

Neil Cartlidge, 'Festivity, Order, and Community in Fourteenth-Century Ireland: The Composition and Context of BL MS Harley 913,' *Yearbook of English Studies* 33 (2003), pp. 33–52.

Philomena Connolly, "The enactments of the 1297 parliament" in James Lydon (ed), *Law and Disorder in Thirteenth-century Ireland: The Dublin Parliament of 1297* (Dublin: Four Courts Press 1997), pp. 139–61.

Art Cosgrove (ed.), *A New History of Ireland; ii, Medieval Ireland 1169–1534* (Oxford: Oxford University Press 1987).

Edmund Curtis and R. B. McDowell (edd), *Irish Historical Documents 1172–1922.* (New York NY: Barnes & Noble 1943).

Alan J. Fletcher, "The date of London, British Library, Harley 913 (The Kildare Poems)", *Medium Ævum* 79 (2010), pp. 306–10.

A. Martin Freeman (ed., *Annála Connacht, The Annals of Connacht (A.D. 1224–1544)* (Dublin: The Dublin Institute for Advanced Studies 1970).

John Thomas Gilbert (ed.), *Cartularies of St. Mary's Abbey, Dublin: with the Register of its House at Dunbrody, and Annals of Ireland... Published by the authority of the lords commissioners of Her Majesty's Treasury, under the direction of the master of the rolls* 2 vols (London: Longman & co. 1884).

Wilhelm Heuser, *Die Kildare-Gedichte. Die ältesten mittelenglischen Denkmäler in anglo-irischer Überlieferung. Bonner Beiträge zur Anglistik* 14 (Bonn, 1904), pp. 158–64.

A.G. Little (ed.), *Materials for the History of the Franciscan Province of Ireland A.D.*

40) The present article is a substantially revised version of a paper which I read at the 27th national congress of The English Literary Society held in December, 2011. This research was financially supported by MEXT (the Grant-in-Age for Scientific Research or KAKENHI: 00123547 for 2019).

1230–1450 (Manchester: Manchester University Press 1920).

Angela Lucas (ed.), *Anglo-Irish Poems of the Middle Ages* (Dublin: The Columba Press 1995), pp. 150–7 and pp. 207–9.

James F. Lydon (ed.), *Law and Disorder in Thirteenth-century Ireland: The Dublin Parliament of 1297* (Dublin: Four Courts Press 1997).

James F. Lydon, *The Lordship of Ireland in the Middle Ages* (Dublin: Gill and Macmillan 1972).

Seán Mac Airt (ed. and trans.), *The Annals of Inisfallen* (Dublin: The Dublin Institute for Advanced Studies 1951).

Deborah L. Moore, *Medieval Anglo-Irish Troubles: A Cultural Study of BL MS Harley 913* (Turnhout: Brepols 2017).

Denis Murphy (ed.) and Conell Mageoghagan (trans. in 1627), *The Annals of Clonmacnoise being Annals of Ireland from The Earliest Period to A.D. 1408* (Dublin: The University Press for The Royal Society of Antiquaries of Ireland 1896).

Cormac Ó Cléirigh, "The Problems of Defence: A Regional Case-Study" in James Lydon (ed.), *Law and Disorder in Thirteenth-century Ireland: The Dublin Parliament of 1297* (Dublin: Four Courts Press 1997), pp. 25–56.

Séamus Ó hInnse (ed. and trans.), *Miscellaneous Irish Annals (A.D. 1114–1437)* (Dublin: The Dublin Institute for Advanced Studies 1947).

Goddard Henry Orpen, *Ireland under the Normans 1169–1333* with an Introduction by Seán Duffy (Dublin: Four Courts Press 2005).

Annette Jocelyn Otway-Ruthven, *A History of Medieval Ireland* (London, 2nd edn, 1980).

John Scattergood, "Elegy for a Dangerous Man: *Piers of Bermingham*" apud *Occasions for Writing: Essays on Medieval and Renaissance Literature, Politics and Society* (Dublin: Four Courts Press 2010), pp. 85–106.

St John D. Seymour, *Anglo-Irish Literature, 1200–1582* (Cambridge: Cambridge University Press 1929.

Thorlac Turville-Petre, *England the Nation: Language, Literature and National Community, 1290–1340* (Oxford: Oxford University Press 1996).

Thorlac Turville-Petre (ed.), *Poems from BL MS Harley 913 "The Kildare Manuscript"*, EETS o.s. 345 (Oxford: Oxford University Press 2015).

J.E. Wells, *A Manual of the Writings in Middle English, 1050–1400* (New Haven, CT: Yale University Press 1916).

Bernadette Williams (ed. and trans.), *The Annals of Ireland by Friar John Clyn* (Dublin: Four Courts Press 2007).

Kalender und Jahreszeiten im Waka-Diskurs[1]
— zu einem Konflikt zwischen Kultur und Natur —

Robert F. Wittkamp

„Warum", so fragt sich der Literaturwissenschaftler Kawamura Teruo, „gibt es in der japanischen Literatur so viele Stücke, die ihr Material aus der Natur nehmen?" Seine Antwort darauf ist symptomatisch für die japanische Sicht:

> Das Landesgebiet (*kokudo* 国土) des Japan genannten Staates ist reich an den Erhebungen und Niederungen der Berge und der Flüsse, vom Meer umgeben und eingenommen von den vier Jahreszeiten. Die Erklärung, dass es daran liegt, dass die Japaner eine solche klimatisch-geologische Beschaffenheit (*fūdo* 風土) gelernt haben zu lieben, kann uns im Großen und Ganzen zufrieden stellen. (2004: iii)

Für Kawamura sind die vier Jahreszeiten natürliche Tatsachen, welche die

---

1) Der Aufsatz geht (wie auch Wittkamp 2013) auf zwei Vorträge zurück: „Jahreszeiten und kulturelles Gedächtnis in der alten Dichtung Japans" (Tagung des Internationalen Kollegs Morphomata, Thema: Morphome der Zeit — Die Jahreszeiten im Wandel der Kulturen und Zeiten, Köln, 13. bis 15 Juli 2011) sowie „Natur oder Kultur? Zur Herkunft der Jahreszeiten in der japanischen Dichtung" (Arbeitskreis für vormoderne japanische Literatur, Thema: Mensch und Natur in der vormodernen japanischen Literatur, Frankfurt, 14. bis 16. Juni 2013). Eine erste Ausarbeitung unterlag einer anonymen Begutachtung, und ich hoffe, in der vorliegenden Ausführung die monierten Stellen korrigiert zu haben. Dem Gutachter sei für die Hinweise gedankt.

Japaner „gelernt haben zu lieben" und die mit Bergen, Tälern, Flüssen und dem Meer auf einer ontologischen Stufe stehen. Diese fasst er unter dem Begriff *fūdo* (wörtlich: „Wind und Erde") zusammen, der im Gegensatz zum Naturbegriff hervorheben soll, dass die japanischen klimatisch-geologischen Bedingungen etwas Besonderes sind. Wie Ekkehard May zeigt, gilt dieses Besondere als die unmittelbare Ursache für die japanische Dichtung, und die kulturellen Aspekte wie die Übernahme der chinesischen Schrift beziehungsweise Literatur und ihr Einfluss auf die Wahrnehmung und den Ausdruck in der japanischen Dichtung und Kultur werden damit invisibilisiert:

> Der nicht schroffe, gleichwohl deutlich wahrnehmbare Jahreszeitenwechsel brachte eine enge Verbindung der Lyrik und der Prosa mit dem Rhythmus des Jahres mit, die vielleicht einmalig in der Weltliteratur ist.[2]

In den japanischen Literatur- und Kulturwissenschaften wird das gewöhnlich auch nicht weiter hinterfragt, obwohl es die Ansicht gibt, die „ästhetische Kultur der vier Jahreszeiten" unmittelbar mit der Waka-Dichtung gleichzusetzen, was die Vorstellung einer ontologischen Identität von *vier* Jahreszeiten und Natur offensichtlich untergräbt.[3] Kawamuras Beobachtung leiten die Vorbemerkungen

---

2) May zitiert nach Schönbein 2001: 4. Obwohl Schönbeins Arbeit den Titel *Jahreszeitenmotive in der japanischen Lyrik* trägt und ihre einleitenden Bemerkungen dem „Stellenwert der Jahreszeiten in Japan" gelten, führt sie (S. 4–6) in die Jahreszeitenthematik nicht nach dem Lunisolarkalender ein, der für die Lyrik ausschlaggebend war, sondern nach moderner Einteilung. Bereits diese Perspektive bestätigt, dass die vier Jahreszeiten der Literatur keine natürliche, sondern eine kulturelle Angelegenheit sind. Einige der klassischen Jahreszeitenwörter korrespondieren nicht mit dem modernen Kalender, und deren Gegenstände sind auch nicht auf die engen Rahmen der klassischen Jahreszeiten beschränkt.

3) Ishikawa Kyūyō schreibt: „Diese kulturelle Emanzipation [Japans] geschah dadurch, dass der streng politischen Kultur Chinas die ästhetische Kultur des Waka = vier Jahreszeiten gegenübergestellt wurde" (2011b: 47–48).

zu seinem Buch *Nihon bungaku kara „shizen" o yomu* („Aus der japanischen Literatur die *Natur* lesen") ein, und die Anweisungen zu dessen Lektüre bezüglich der Natur und den vier Jahreszeiten sind unmissverständlich gesetzt. Clemens Simmer definiert die Jahreszeiten wie folgt:

> Jahreszeiten sind jährlich wiederkehrende Muster im Witterungsablauf. Hauptursache dieser zyklischen Variationen ist die jährlich sich wiederholende Variation der räumlichen Verteilung der Sonneneinstrahlung durch den Lauf der Erdbahn um die Sonne verbunden mit der zur Erdbahnebene um ca. 23° geneigten Ebene der Erdrotation. (2013: 49)

Simmer führt die Erklärungen weiter aus, und für den hiesigen Zusammenhang festzuhalten bleibt zunächst, dass die Jahreszeiten in dieser Definition in der Tat zur Natur gehören. Dennoch bleibt die Frage nach der Notwendigkeit von vier Jahreszeiten. Denn für das Klima einer bestimmten Region sind Simmer zufolge noch viele andere Faktoren wie Atmosphäre, Ozeanströmungen oder die thermische Trägheit verantwortlich. Eine Definition der Jahreszeiten, die sich am Lauf der Sonne orientiert, nennt Simmer die „astronomische Definition" (S. 50). Diese postuliere „eine Trägheit des Klimasystems von einer halben Jahreszeit also ca. sechs Wochen", aber dieser Definition stehe eine „meteorologische Definition der Jahreszeiten" gegenüber, die sich an der „beobachteten jährlichen Temperaturkurve in den mittleren Breiten" orientiere und das „im Mittel wärmste Jahresviertel" dem Sommer zuordne (ebd.). In dieser Definition beginnen der Sommer der mittleren Breiten am 1. Juni und der Winter am 1. Dezember.[1] Das war allerdings im alten Japan auch nicht der Fall, sodass es im Folgenden eher um das geht, was die japanischen

---

4) Simmer (2013: 53) zeigt am Beispiel des Monsuns weiterhin, dass die Jahreszeiten auch von der Region abhängig sind und dass sie sich verschieben können.

Wissenschaften als Jahreszeitenanschauung (*kisetsukan* 季節観) beschreiben (siehe unten), welche die Jahreszeiten als einen Bereich der Kultur ausweist. Bei der Betrachtung eines prominenten Problems im frühen Waka-Diskurs, das im folgenden Abschnitt zu diskutieren ist, stellt sich daher die Frage, ob nicht das „Land" mit seiner „klimatisch-geologischen Beschaffenheit", sondern vielmehr die menschliche Wahrnehmung, mithin die Kultur von den vier Jahreszeiten „eingenommen" ist. Zusätzliche Berechtigung für die Wahl dieses Gegenstands ergibt sich aus der ebenso unhinterfragten Tatsache, dass das Waka als Kern, mitunter sogar als Ursprung der japanischen Kultur angesehen wird.[5] Ziel der folgenden Überlegungen ist daher die Festigung der Vermutung, dass die japanischen vier Jahreszeiten weniger ein Produkt der Natur, sondern der Kultur sind, das freilich mit den vier Jahreszeiten in astronomischer Definition korrespondiert.[6]

---

5) Die Beschreibungen reichen vom Verständnis der Waka-Literatur als Voraussetzung für ein profundes Verständnis der japanischen Literatur und Kultur (Inoue et al. 1993: Vorwort, Mezaki 1993: 25) bis zum Waka als „Herz der japanischen Literatur" (Prada Vicente und Ōshima 2005: passim, Ariyoshi et al. 1993: Vorwort) oder als „Rückgrat der japanischen Kultur" (Katano 1975: 4–5). Die Ansicht, dass sich die „japanische Kultur" erst mit der *hiragana*-Schrift, das heißt mit der Literatur der Heian-Zeit entfalten konnte, ist dagegen nicht so geläufig. So sieht Ishikawa den Beginn einer selbständigen japanischen, „sich aus der Ästhetik der vier Jahreszeiten im *Kokin wakashū* 古今和歌集 und der Ästhetik der zwischengeschlechtlichen Liebe (*seiai* 性愛) im *Genji monogatari* 源氏物語 zusammensetzenden" Kultur erst um das Jahr 900 mit dem *hiragana*-Schriftsystem; vgl. Ishikawa 2011b: 48 sowie 2011a, passim. Auch Komatsu Hideo (2012, passim) bindet die mit dem *Kokin wakashū* beginnende Waka-Dichtung nahezu exklusiv an die Entwicklung der *kana*-Schrift und beschreibt beides zusammen als japanische Kultur: „Die Formung der *kana*-Schriftkunst (*kana shodō* 仮名書道), welche die in Japan geformte *kana*-Literatur [*kana* sind die *hiragana*-Zeichen — inklusive *ye*, *wi* etc. — der frühen Heian-Zeit, die noch nicht zwischen getrübt und ungetrübt unterschieden] zum Gegenstand hatte, ist es wert, als Entwicklungsbeginn einer originellen japanischen Kultur besonders erwähnt zu werden" (ebd. S. 79; zu *kana* auch S. 80).
6) Die Ausführungen geschehen weiterhin im Sinne einer Ergänzung zu Haruo

Dazu ist zunächst der im Waka-Diskurs aufscheinende Konflikt mit den Jahreszeiten zu skizzieren und als eine mögliche Ursache gewisse Schwierigkeiten im Umgang mit chinesischen Kalendern und ihren Ordnungssystemen aufzuzeigen. Die letzten beiden Abschnitte sind wieder den vier Jahreszeiten angedacht und führen den Bogen anhand des spezifischen Problems zurück zur Waka- und Haiku-Dichtung. Die im Folgenden vorgestellte Problematik, die in den als Beispiel ausgewählten Waka auf verschiedene Arten und Weisen Thematisierung findet, lässt sich dadurch präzisieren. Dabei deutet sich auch an, dass die vier Jahreszeiten ein zentrales Moment in der nachhaltigen Konstruktion der japanischen kulturellen Identität beziehungsweise japanischer Selbstbeschreibungen sind.[7] Weiterhin geht es in den folgenden Ausführungen zwar um den Kalender und die damit verbundene Herkunft der japanischen vier Jahreszeiten, aber es ist vorweg darauf hinzuweisen, dass in der dortigen Kultur bis zur Moderne die Begriffe „Landschaft" und „Jahreszeiten" als Quasisynonyme austauschbar sind.[8]

Shiranes Buch *Japan and the Culture of the Four Seasons. Nature, Literature, and the Arts* (2012), das bei der Planung für das Treffen des Arbeitskreises Vormoderne Japanische Literatur im Jahr 2013 eine Rolle spielte. Denn, so erhellend und weiterführend die Beobachtungen des US-amerikanischen Japanologen für das Gesamtverstehen der japanischen Kultur auch sind, hält er doch eine grundlegende Herleitung der vier Jahreszeiten nicht für nötig. Sie fallen bei ihm gewissermaßen vom Himmel, womit er jene Linie stützt, die wie Kawamura um eine Darstellung der vier Jahreszeiten als natürliche Entitäten bemüht ist. Ein weiterer, in diesem Zusammenhang zu erwähnender Kritikpunkt ist sein Konzept der „zweiten Natur", das aus der Sicht der Landschaftsphilosophie lediglich eine Neuformulierung des Landschaftsbegriffes — wenn auch mit „ecocriticism" eventuell unter anderen Voraussetzungen — und damit redundant zu sein scheint; die Diskussion darüber muss allerdings an anderer Stelle geschehen.

7) Das ist eines der zentralen Themen in Wittkamp 2014a/b.

8) Vgl. Wittkamp 2014a und zu einem konstruktivistischen Landschaftsbegriff Wittkamp 2004.

Jahreszeiten als Konflikt

Das erste der beiden folgenden Gedichten stammt unter dem Vermerk „aus unbekannter Hand" aus dem *Shinkokin wakashū* 新古今和歌集 („Neue Sammlung von Gedichten aus alter und heutiger Zeit"). Dabei handelt es sich um die achte der insgesamt einundzwanzig offiziellen, das heißt auf Geheiß des Tennō kompilierten Waka-Sammlungen (*chokusen wakashū* 勅撰和歌集). Das *Shinkokin wakashū* wurde im Jahr 1205 fertiggestellt und gilt in vielerlei Hinsicht als der Höhepunkt der offiziellen Waka-Sammlungen. Das Gedicht lautet wie folgt:

Mit dem Wind vermischt	風まぜに　雪は降りつつ
Der Schnee, er fällt und fällt	しかすがに　霞たなびき
Das ist so und doch	春は来にけり
Lauer Dunst zieht sich dahin	
Der Frühling, nun ist er da!⁹⁾	

kaze maze ni · yuki ha furitsutsu · shikasuga ni
kasumi tanabiki · haru ha kinikeri

Das zweite Beispiel ist das berühmte Eröffnungsgedicht zum *Kokin wakashū* 古今和歌集 („Sammlung von Gedichten aus alter und jetziger Zeit"), der ersten offiziellen Waka-Sammlung aus dem Jahr 905. Es stammt von Ariwara no Motokata 在原元方, dessen Lebensdaten unbekannt sind, und lautet mit Überschrift und Namensangabe wie folgt:

---

9) *Shinkokin wakashū*, Gedicht Nr. 8, Notation nach Minemura 1995: 25. Die Verdeutschungen stammen vom Verfasser und sind als interlineare Arbeitsübersetzungen zu verstehen.

An einem Tag gedichtet, als der Frühling ins

alte Jahr kam

furu toshi ni haru tachikeru hi yomeru

Ins alte Jahr der

Frühling, er ist gekommen —

Soll ich dieses Jahr

Denn nun das letzte nennen,

Soll ich es dieses nennen?[10]

去年とやいはむ　今年とやいはむ　年のうちに　春は来にけり　ひととせを　ふる年に春立ちける日よめる　在原元方

toshi no uchi ni · haru ha kinikeri

hitotose wo · kozo to ya ihamu · kotoshi to ya ihamu

So unterschiedlich die beiden Waka auf den ersten Blick auch wirken, handeln sie doch ein und dasselbe Thema ab, nämlich die Diskrepanz zwischen den phänomenologischen Jahreszeiten und gewisse Schwierigkeiten im Umgang mit dem Kalender. Der Unterschied zu dem vorangehenden Beispiel besteht darin, dass Motokata sich in seinem vieldiskutierten Gedicht, das Masaoka Shiki 正岡子規 Ende des neunzehnten Jahrhunderts als „dumpf und nichtssagend" niederschmetterte,[11] auf eine abstrakte Ebene begibt und

---

10) *Kokin wakashū*, Gedicht Nr. 1, Notation nach Ozawa und Matsuda 2000: 31. Vermutlich war das Gedicht original nur mit *hiragana*-Zeichen notiert; eine aktuelle und umfassende Diskussion zu diesem oftmals missverstandenen Waka bietet Komatsu 2012: 89–106.

11) Vgl. Watanabe 2009: 6–8, der freilich Shikis Kritik zurückweist und das Waka einleitend als Beispiel für das Performative (*engi* 演技) und damit als zentralen Bestandteil seiner Waka-Theorie präsentiert. Freilich wäre bei einem solchen Ansatz die Wahrnehmung der nicht-japanischen Diskurse zur Performativität wünschenswert gewesen, die vielleicht aber auch den Rahmen einer *shinsho*-Ausgabe, das heißt den populärwissenschaftlichen Rahmen gesprengt hätten.

das Thema ohne konkreten Bezug zur Außenwelt abhandelt, wogegen das Gedicht aus unbekannter Hand zwei verschiedene Jahreszeiten anhand von Jahreszeitenphänomenen unmittelbar gegeneinander ausspielt: Schnee versus Frühlingsdunst (*kasumi*).[12] Das geschieht aber ebenfalls reflexiv, was der dritte Vers *shikasuga ni* („Das ist so und doch") belegt, der für eine adversative Satzverbindung (*gyakusetsu* 逆説) steht. Dass hier das Gedicht aus der dreihundert Jahre später verfassten Sammlung zuerst genannt wird, ist in seiner Entstehungszeit begründet, da es der vermutlich im späteren achten Jahrhundert abgeschlossenen Sammlung *Man'yōshū* 萬葉集 (万葉集)[13] entnommen wurde und somit zur Entstehung von Motokatas Waka beitrug.[14] Denn im *Man'yōshū* finden sich mehrere Belege, in denen auf dieser Art und Weise zwei verschiedene Jahreszeiten miteinander — oder sollte man sagen „gegeneinander" — ausgespielt werden. Wie eng der Zusammenhang beider Waka tatsächlich ist, demonstriert beispielsweise das *Man'yōshū*-Gedicht 10: 1843. Es stammt aus dem zehnten *maki* („Rolle, Band"), das wie der achte Band nach den vier Jahreszeiten geordnet ist, aber im Gegensatz zu jenem ausschließlich Gedichte aus unbekannter Hand enthält. Es sind die beiden einzigen Bände im *Man'yōshū*, die einer Ordnung nach den vier Jahreszeiten unterliegen:

---

12) Der Herbstnebel *kiri* 霧 und der Frühlingsdunst *kasumi* 霞 sind in der Waka-Dichtung etablierte Indikatoren für die beiden Jahreszeiten, aber das war selbstverständlich nicht immer schon so. Die Wörter für bestimmte Jahreszeiten bilden sich erst mit dem Voranschreiten der schriftlichen Dichtung aus; vgl. Wittkamp 2014a: 175–210.

13) Zu Titel, Aufbau und Inhalt der Sammlung vgl. Wittkamp 2014b.

14) Das Gedicht findet sich im zehnten Band als 10: 1836; für die Aufnahme ins *Shinkokin wakashū* wurde es leicht modifiziert.

Den milden Dunst bedichten *kasumi wo yomu*

Gerade erst Gestern

Ging das Jahr vorbei, und doch

Milder Frühlingsdunst

An den Bergen von Kasuga

Stieg er schon früh empor [15)]

春昨詠
日日霞
山社
尔年
者
速極
立之
尔賀
来
春
霞

kinofu koso · toshi ha hate-shi-ka

haru-kasumi · Kasuga no yama ni · haya tachi-ni-keri

Die Überschrift bezieht sich auf drei Gedichte, aber hier soll es nur um dieses Stück gehen. Das zur unteren zweistufigen Flexion gehörende Verb *hatsu* bedeutet „zu Ende gehen, enden", und die adversative Übersetzung mit „und doch" berücksichtigt die postpositionelle Korrelation (*kakari musubi* 係り結び) von *koso* und *-shika*, der erforderlichen Indefinitform (*izenkei*) des Verbalsuffixes *-ki*, das für allgemeine Vergangenheit steht. Das Verbalsuffix *-keri* im letzten Vers,[16)] dessen Lesung sich zum einen aus semantischen

---

15) *Man'yōshū*, Gedicht 10: 1843, Notation nach Kojima, Kinoshita und Tōno 2006a: 33; die Freistellen zwischen den einzelnen Versen des Originaltextes dienen der besseren Lesbarkeit. In modernen Ausgaben werden die Gedichte in *hiragana* „entfaltet", wodurch jedoch unter Umständen mögliche „Restsemantiken" bei den sogenannten *man'yōgana*-Lautzeichen verloren gehen können. Die Umschrift berücksichtigt die Schriftzeichenverwendung der Originalnotationen nach Wittkamp 2014a/b.

16) Das Verbalsuffix *-keri* ist an die Aspektmarkierung *-nu* angeschlossen. Lewin zufolge dient diese Verbindung (*-nikeri*) dem Ausdruck des Geschehensabschlusses „in der weiteren Vergangenheit" (1975: 167), was dem Plusquamperfekt entspräche. Die Formulierung betont jedoch vielmehr das plötzliche Gewahrwerden von etwas, das bereits eine gewisse Zeit lang vorhanden ist. In dem *Shinkokin wakashū*-Gedicht ließe sich *-kinikeri* eventuell noch als „war gekommen" (und ist jetzt da) übersetzen, aber *tachinikeri* in MYS 10: 1843 eben nicht als „war aufgestiegen".

Implikationen und zum anderen aus der erforderlichen Morenzahl für den letzten Vers ergibt, bedeutet demgegenüber ein plötzliches Bemerken von etwas, das bereits eine gewisse Zeit lang da ist (*kizuki no keri* 気づきのけり), hier also das frühe Aufsteigen des Frühlingsdunstes. Das -*keri* in der Formulierung *haru ha kinikeri* aus dem oben zitierten *Shinkokin wakashū*-Gedicht steht ebenfalls für dieses plötzliche Gewahrwerden. Das Verb *tatsu* in MYS 10: 1843 bezieht sich auch auf den Frühling, der aufsteigt, und in der späteren Dichtung zieht der *kasumi*-Dunst gewöhnlich seitwärts daher (*kasumi tanabiku*). Entweder enthält das Gedicht Elemente aus älterer Dichtung, oder es wird darin geschickt mit diesen gespielt.

Warum kann der Frühling schon „im alten Jahr" beginnen, und warum kann an einem bestimmten Tag das Jahr zu Ende gehen? Die Antwort hierauf lautet natürlich: Weil es der Kalender so will. In Motokatas Gedicht geht es um den Widerspruch von Frühlingsbeginn als *risshun* 立春, dem aufsteigenden Frühling, und dem für Neujahr plädierenden Kalender, in MYS 10: 1843 darum, dass sich der Frühling durch den an den Bergen aufsteigenden Frühlingsdunst schon früher zeigte, als es dem Kalender Recht war. Die Gedichte belegen eine eigentümliche Topik, welche die gesamte offizielle Waka-Literatur wie auch die private Dichtung hindurch bis in die *haikai*-Literatur der Frühmoderne zu verfolgen ist.

Die Aufdeckung der Herkunft dieser Topik erfordert allerdings ein weiteres Ausholen, und es ist zu zeigen, wie sich die japanische Auseinandersetzung mit dem Kalender und den vier Jahreszeiten entwickelte. Denn die Jahreszeiten sind nicht nur ein zentrales Moment im japanischen kulturellen Gedächtnis — hier ist der Singular erlaubt —, sondern, und das wird sich ebenfalls noch zeigen, die diskursive Abhandlung dieses Themas war mit den Gedichten noch lange nicht beendet.

Mond- und Lunisolarkalender

Wie nicht zuletzt die Bronzescheibe aus Nebra („Der geschmiedete Himmel")
mit ihrem geschätzten Alter von 3600 Jahren zeigt,[17] sind Mondkalender die
vermutlich ältesten Belege der Erfassung von längeren Zeitzyklen. Dabei
werden die Mondphasen beobachtet und angesichts anderer klimatischer und
astronomischer Bedingungen als Zwölferset zu einer Einheit zusammengefasst.
Aufgrund der Tatsache, dass es von Neumond zu Neumond beziehungsweise
von Vollmond zu Vollmond — diese Phasen sind im Japanischen mit
sakubōgetsu 朔望月 (auch: *tai'ingetsu* 太陰月) benannt — durchschnittlich
29,5 Tage dauert und das Jahr damit nur 354 Tage besäße, müssen in einem
bestimmten Abstand Schaltmonate (jap.: *uruuzuki* 閏月) eingefügt werden.
Genau zu dieser Berechnung diente offenbar die Himmelsscheibe von Nebra,
wenn sie auch im Laufe ihrer Verwendungsgeschichte noch andere Zwecke
erfüllte. Jedenfalls, und das scheint wichtig zu sein, „passt der Mondkalender
nicht zu den Jahreszeiten", wie es beispielsweise in dem enzyklopädischen
Wörterbuch *Daijisen* 大辞泉 (Eintrag: *tai'inreki* 太陰暦 [Mondkalender],
digital) heißt.

Seit wann die Mondphasen auf den japanischen Inseln für die Berechnung
der Zeit zum Tragen kamen, scheint sich der genaueren Kenntnis zu entziehen,
aber es gibt Einritzungen in einer Gefäßwand, die ein frühes Beobachten der
verschiedenen Sonnenpositionen belegen. Sie zeigen eine Bergsilhouette, die
vermutlich vom Fundort des Gefäßes gesehen in westlicher Richtung liegt,
mit den Sonnenpositionen für die Solstitien und Äquinoktien. Das Gefäß
wurde in einer Grabanlage im Gebiet der Stadt Ehime (Präfektur Hyōgo)

---

17) Harald Meller geht diesem Thema in verschiedenen Büchern nach; vgl. Meller
2008 oder 2018.

gefunden und stammt aus der Yayoi-Zeit.[18]

Die Faktoren, die letztendlich zu den Reformationsprozessen führten, deren Ergebnis in Japan unter dem Namen *tai'in-tai'yōreki* 太陰太陽暦, also Lunisolarkalender, bekannt ist und bis 1873 im Dienst war,[19] scheinen komplex gewesen zu sein, aber ein Zusammenhang mit politischer Herrschaft — und damit auch mit der Schrift — dürfte zu vermuten sein. Wie die Schrift kam auch der Kalender (暦, chin.: *li*, jap.: *reki, koyomi*) von China über die koreanische Halbinsel nach Japan, und mit Bezug auf das Anfang des achten Jahrhunderts fertiggestellte *Nihon shoki* 日本書紀, das als die „erste der offiziellen korrekten Geschichtsschreibungen Japans" (*Kōjien* 広辞苑, Eintrag: *Nihon Shoki*) gilt, verortet die japanische Forschung seine „Ankunft" gegen Mitte des sechsten Jahrhunderts. Im *Zhoushu* 周書, das als eine der vierundzwanzig Geschichtsschreibungen Chinas die Geschichte der Nördlichen Zhou (557 bis 581) erzählt und 636 eingereicht wurde,[20] heißt es bei den Beschreibungen zu Paekche, dass dort der *yuanjia*-Kalender der Song 宋 (5. Jahrhundert) in Gebrauch sei.[21] Dabei handelt es sich um den Kalender *yuanjiali* 元嘉暦 (jap.: *genka-reki*), der in China im Jahr Yuanjia 20, das heißt im Jahr 443, entwickelt wurde und dem *Nihon shoki* zufolge in Japan offiziell ab dem elften Tag im 11. Monat im 4. Regierungsjahr (595) der Suiko Tennō 推古天皇 (554–628) in Gebrauch war.[22] Unter Jitō Tennō 持統天皇

18) Vgl. Naruse 1988: 9 (mit Abbildungen).

19) Seit 1685 war landesweit nur ein gedruckter Kalender zugelassen, „ehe ein Erlaß gegen Ende des fünften Jahres Meiji (1872) die Einführung des westlichen Zeitrechnungswesens verkündet und damit die Ära staatlich herausgegebener Lunisolarkalender chinesischer Herkunft in Japan beendet" (Leinss 2006: 7, historisches Präsens original).

20) Vgl. Wilkinson 2016: 626.

21) Vgl. Kojima et al. 2: 429, Anmerkung 16, die mit dem *Nihon shoki*-Eintrag auf die Bedeutung Paekches für die Vermittlung des chinesischen Kalenders andeuten (siehe unten, Anmerkung 49).

22) Kojima et al. 2: 538–539 (Suiko 10. Jahr, 10. Monat).

(645–702) wurde dieser Kalender 690 durch den Mitte des siebten Jahrhunderts am Tang-Hof entwickelten *lindeli* 麟徳暦 ergänzt.[23] Vermutlich aufgrund der Tatsache, Japan zwischen den Jahren 672 bis 679 erreicht zu haben, die in China unter Yifeng 義鳳 bekannt waren, ist er in Japan unter dem Namen *gihō-reki* 義鳳暦 bekannt.[24] Bei beiden Zeitberechnungen handelt es sich um Lunisolarkalender (*tai'in-tai'yō-reki*, auch: *kyūreki* 旧暦, „alter Kalender"), also nicht um „Sonnenkalender" im modernen Sinn. In dem *Nihon shoki*-Eintrag „Jitō, 4. Jahr, 11. Monat, elfter Tag" ist verzeichnet, dass von nun an beide Kalender zu gebrauchen seien, aber unter Monmu Tennō 文武天応 (683–707) wurde 697 der *gihō-reki* exklusiv verbindlich und war bis 763 in Gebrauch. Die damalige *ritsuryō*-Verfassung orientierte sich am Kalender und sah festgelegte Zeremonien an bestimmten Tagen im Jahr (*sechinichi* 節日, *sechi'e* 節会) vor, wie das Neujahr (*shōgatsu* 正月) am ersten Tag im ersten Monat. Im chinesischen Kalender wird das Jahr in vierundzwanzig „Stationen" geteilt, die auf Japanisch *nijūshi-sekki* 二十四節気 heißen und in Verbindung mit dem Sonnenjahr und den vier Jahreszeiten stehen. Jede Jahreszeit hat sechs Stationen. Sie fangen mit dem Frühlingsbeginn 立春 (chin.: *lichun*, jap. *risshun*) um den vierten Februar (im modernen Kalender) an und sind mit der „Großen Kälte" (大寒 *daikan*) um den zwanzigsten Januar beendet.[25] Allerdings haben die vierundzwanzig Stationen wenig mit dem Gregorianischen

---

23) Vgl. Kojima et al. 3: 510–511 (Jitō 4. Jahr, 11. Monat, elfter Tag).

24) Vgl. Hashimoto 1993: 27, Aso 1993: 20–21, Itō 2000: 173–175, Aoki 2001: 472. Das *Kōjien* (Eintrag: *gihōreki*) führt diesen Kalender unpräzise als *tai'inreki* („Mondkalender"). Leinss weist auf einen *mokkan*-Fund hin, der aus dem Jahr 689 stamme und das älteste Fragment eines Kalenders sei. Das runde Holzstück zeige einen sogenannten *guchūreki* 具注暦, das heißt einen „Ausführlich annotierten Kalender" (2006: 5), aber ob es sich um den *genka*- oder *gihō-reki* handelt, bleibt offen. Leinss Aufsatz beschäftigt sich mit dem letzten Lunisolarkalender, der bis 1873 in Gebrauch war.

25) Vgl. die Tabelle in Wilkinson 2015: 495.

Sonnenjahr gemein, da beispielsweise der um den vierten Februar liegende Frühlingsbeginn *lichun*, bei dem die ekliptikale Länge (黄経 *kōkei*) der Sonne 315° beträgt,[26] und das Frühlings- oder Primäräquinoktikum um mehrere Wochen auseinander liegen.

Die eingangs genannten Schwierigkeiten resultieren wie gesehen aus der Differenz von Mondphasen, Kalender und Phänomenen der Natur, wenn also, wie in Motokatas Gedicht, „ins alte Jahr schon der Frühling gekommen ist". Wie ebenfalls bereits bemerkt, ist der Lunisolarkalender eng mit den vier Jahreszeiten verbunden, was — und das ist zu betonen — zwar logisch erscheint, auf phänomenologischer Ebene jedoch nicht zwingend erforderlich ist. Wie der Kunsthistoriker Paul von Naredi-Rainer im Zusammenhang mit den vier Jahreszeiten und der Entwicklung europäischer Städte zeigt, spielt die Vier eine grundlegende Rolle. Zwar spricht er von den „Universalien der Stadtbaukunst" (2013: 21), bezieht sich aber auf die europäische Kulturgeschichte. Chinesische Städte bestätigen jedoch die „Universalität" für den ostasiatischen Raum, denn ab dem frühen achten Jahrhundert dienten sie als Modell für die Konzipierung der ersten japanischen Großstädte Fujiwarakyō, Heijōkyō (Nara) und Heiankyō (Kyōto). Diese Anlagen folgten genau jenen Vorgaben, die auch für „die Städte römischen Ursprungs" (S. 19) relevant waren, wenn auch die Umsetzung vermutlich unterschiedlich verlief.[27]

---

26) Vgl. *Kōjien*, Eintrag *risshun*.

27) Eine Abbildung der Stadt Turin aus dem Jahr 1577 zeigt einen quadratischen Aufbau mit „Gitternetz (Schachbrettanordnung)"; vgl. Naredi-Rainer 2013: 20. Japanischen Hauptstädte wurden bis zur Errichtung von Kamakura und Edo (Tōkyō) nach chinesischem Muster gebaut. Im Norden lagen die nach Süden gerichteten Inneren und Äußeren Palastanlagen (*daidairi* 大内裏), zu denen vom Suzakumon-Tor 朱雀門 aus nach Süden die Hauptstraße (*suzaku ōji* 朱雀大路) zum Rajōmon-Tor 羅城門 führte. Das Stadtzentrum war gitternetzförmig zu beiden Seiten der Hauptstraße und um die Palastanlagen angeordnet. Dieses „Schachbrettmuster" heißt im Japanischen *jōbō* 条坊; *jō* steht für die großen Straßen in ostwestlicher Richtung, *bō* für die nordsüdlichen. Naredi-Rainer (S. 18–19) zeigt auch, wie die vier Jahreszeiten und

Das Zusammenfallen der in den *Man'yōshū*-Bänden Acht und Zehn für die prospektive Memoria und das kulturelle Gedächtnis wichtigen Instrumentalisierung der Jahreszeiten mit dem Beginn der Stadt nach chinesischem Muster dürfte kein Zufall sein.

Der Lunisolarkalender, der in Japan die längste Nachhaltigkeit besaß, war der 861 eingeführte *senmyō-reki* 宣明暦.[28] Er wurde erst im 2. Jahr Jōkyō (1685) vom *jōkyō-reki* 貞享暦 abgelöst, der Gerhard Leinss zufolge vier Kalenderreformen durchlief und somit auf verschiedenen „Ausgangskalendern" (*genreki* 元暦) beruht.[29] Im Wikipedia-Eintrag zu *reki/koyomi* gilt dieser Kalender im Gegensatz zu den vorangehenden Kalendern nach chinesischen Vorbildern als „kalendarische Berechnung, die durch die Hände der Japaner anfertigt wurde". Offenbar orientierte sich dieser aber zunächst am chinesischen *shoushili* 授時暦 (jap.: *juji-reki*), der das Jahr in 365, 2425 Tage einteilt und in China von 1281 bis 1644 in Gebrauch war,[30] wurde aber rasch von dem von Shibukawa Harumi 渋川春海 (1639–1715) vervollständigten *jōkyō-*

---

28) Vgl. Leinss 2006: 38, der mit „Kalender umfassender Klarheit" übersetzt. Leinss (ebd.) zufolge lag diesem ein Wert von 365, 2446 Tagen zugrunde, sodass sich nach „823 Jahren ein Überschuß von 1,9752 Tagen ergeben mußte" (ebd.).

29) Vgl. Leinss 2006: 19, der auch zeigt, dass der Kalender für das neue Jahr niemals die Angabe „1. Jahr" (*gannen* 元年) tragen konnte. Der Eintrag zum Kalender (*reki/ koyomi* 暦) in ja.wikipedia.org zeigt eine Abbildung der ersten Seite des Kalenders für das Jahr 1729 (Kyōho 14), der auf dem Jōkyōreki beruht, der Leinss (ebd.) zufolge bis 1753 gültig war. Leinss (S. 9–37) erläutert die einzelnen Spalten der Abbildung des Kalenders zum Jahr 1779, aber die Wikipedia-Abbildung ist wesentlich schärfer abgebildet (als in der PDF-Datei) und steht zum Vergleich bereit.

30) Zum Vergleich: Simmer zufolge hat ein Jahr „derzeit astronomisch gesehen die Länge von 356,24219052 Tagen" (2013: 52). Das entspreche einer Länge von 365, Tagen, 6 Stunden, 48 Minuten und circa 45 Sekunden, was alle vier Jahre ein Schaltjahr notwendig mache, das aber alle 100 Jahre ausfallen müsse und alle 400 Jahre nicht ausfallen dürfe.

die vier Himmelsrichtungen in engem Zusammenhang stehen, was für Ostasien freilich ebenso gilt. Kalender, Tageszeit und Himmelsrichtungen folgen einem gemeinsamen Beschreibungsmuster.

Kalender abgelöst. Der *jōkyō-reki* fand bis 1873 Verwendung, als er vom Kalender vom westlichen Zeitrechnungswesen abgelöst wurde.

Zu den kulturellen Wurzeln der vier Jahreszeiten in Japan

Der früheste historische Vermerk zu Jahreszeiten auf den japanischen Inseln findet sich in dem chinesischen Geschichtswerk *Wei zhi* 魏志 aus dem späten dritten Jahrhundert;[31] dort heißt es über die *woren* 倭人 (jap.: *wajin*) genannten Einwohner der japanischen Inseln mit einem Zitat wie folgt:

> Das *Wei-lüeh* sagt: „Nach ihrer Sitte wissen sie nicht um den ersten Monat [des Jahres] und die vier Jahreszeiten [四節]. Nur die Feldbestellungen im Frühling und die Ernten im Herbst zählend machen sie die Jahresberechnung.
>
> 魏略曰其俗不知正歲四節但計春耕秋收爲年紀[32]

In China selbst gab es einem Orakelknochen zufolge zunächst ebenfalls nur eine Einteilung in Frühling und Herbst, und Edymion Wilkinson vermutet die Teilung in vier Jahreszeiten (*sishi* 四時) als eine Entwicklung der „Chunqiu 春秋 period [722–476], if not in the Western Zhou [1046–771]". Er verbindet direkt mit den beiden Solstitien und Äquinoktien und zitiert einen Passus aus dem *Liji* 禮記, dem „Buch der Riten", der die vier Jahreszeiten auflistet.[33]

---

31) Zu den „Beschreibungen der Ostbarbaren im *Wei zhi*" („Wei-chih Tung-i-chuan") vgl. Seyock 2004: 15–19 („1.1 Textbeschreibung und Textkritik"), zum Titel ebd. S. 15.

32) Zitiert nach Seyock 2004: 55. Das originale Zitat ist mit kleineren Schriftzeichen und einer Doppelzeile in den Text eingefügt; vgl. ebd. S. 348.

33) Vgl. Wilkinson 2015: 494–495, dort auch mit Erklärungen zu weiteren Entwicklungen und der chinesischen Kalenderterminologie, und S. 3 zu den Jahresangaben der genannten Perioden.

Die chinesische Terminologie gelang mit der Schrift auf die japanischen Inseln, und Anfang des achten Jahrhunderts entstanden in Japan mit dem *Kojiki* 古事記 und dem *Nihon shoki* zwei Geschichtswerke, die mit Entstehungsmythen beginnen und mit der Chronologie der Tennō-Linie in Historiographie übergehen, im Falle das *Kojiki* sogar ohne ontologischen Bruch.[34] Obwohl Schrift und Kalenderterminologie ohne Zweifel vom Kontinent stammen, gibt es bezüglich der Jahreszeiten doch Hinweise auf autochthone Selbstbeschreibungen. So handelt eine Mythe aus dem *Kojiki*-Buch „Ōjin Tennō" von zwei Brüdern namens Akiyama no Shitahi Wotoko 秋山之下氷壮夫 und Haruyama no Kasumi Wotoko 春山之霞壮夫, die um die Gunst der Izushi Wotome no Kami 伊豆志袁登売神 buhlten.[35] Als Namenszusatz für „Herbstberg" steht das Wort 下氷 (*shitahi, shitapi*), das sich von dem Verb *shitafu* (*shitapu*) ableitet, dem Sich-Verfärben der Blätter im Herbst. Als Attribut für den „Frühlingsberg" steht der Frühlingsdunst *kasumi* 霞, der allerdings wie gesehen seine feste Verbindung mit dieser Jahreszeit erst später bekam. Bekanntlich widerfährt in der *Man'yōshū*-Dichtung dem Herbst eine eindeutige Präferenz,[36] aber im *Kojiki*-Mythos trägt den Sieg der jüngere Frühlingsberggott davon. Unter Hinzunahme anderer früher Texte, wie des aus dem späteren siebten Jahrhundert stammenden *Man'yōshū*-Gedichts 1: 16, das einen Wettstreit um die Qualitäten von Frühling und Herbst thematisiert,[37] deutet sich an, warum die japanische Forschung für die Mythen sowie die frühe Dichtung den Frühling und den

---

34) Zum *Kojiki* vgl. Wittkamp 2018. Beim *Nihon shoki* schließt sich nach den ersten beiden Bänden mit Mythenerzählungen eine Geschichtsschreibung im chinesischen Stil (jap.: *hennentai* 編年体) an.

35) Vgl. Yamaguchi und Kōnoshi 1997: 278–282 und für die Übersetzung ins Deutsche Antoni 2012: 190–191, 727 (Kommentar).

36) Vgl. die Anzahl der Gedichte in den Abteilungen zu den vier Jahreszeiten im achten und zehnten Buch.

37) Vgl. Wittkamp 2014b: 183–184.

Herbst im Zentrum der Jahreszeitenanschauung (*kisetsukan*) sehen. Das entspricht auch der frühen Fremdbeschreibung im *Wei zhi*. Das genannte Gedicht von Nukata no Ōkimi 額田王, die in der zweiten Hälfte des siebten Jahrhunderts lebte, zeigt jedoch deutlich die Spuren der chinesischen Dichtung und ist wohl eher als ein Produkt der Schrift zu sehen. So ist freilich auch bei den Namen der beiden Brüder Haruyama und Akiyama eine gewisse Skepsis angebracht.

Nebenbei bemerkt sei, dass die Forschung seit Ogyū Sorai 荻生徂徠 (1666– 1728), dem konfuzianischen Gelehrten aus der mittleren Edo-Zeit, bei der Etymologie der Wortes *haru* 春 (Frühling) wie auch beim Herbst *aki* 秋 gewöhnlich auf die Landwirtschaft verweist. Der oben zitierte Passus aus dem *Wei zhi* spricht ebenfalls dafür. Allerdings lässt die frühe *Man'yōshū*-Dichtung diesen Zusammenhang vollkommen außer Acht. Es gibt zwar Lieder mit Hinweisen auf die Landwirtschaft, die Jahreszeiten selbst dagegen tauchen aber gerade dort nicht auf. Auch in den alten Liedern (*kayō* 歌謡) aus dem *Kojiki* oder *Nihon Shoki*, die zum großen Teil identisch sind, spielen sie ebenfalls keine Rolle.

In der erwähnten *Kojiki*-Mythe deutet allerdings ein Detail darauf hin, dass der sogenannte Frühling vor der Einführung chinesischer Lunisolarkalender eher dem heutigen Frühling entsprach. Die Mutter von Haruyama hatte diesem nämlich ein Hemd und eine Hose aus Glyzinienranken (*fuji-tsura*; *fuji* auch: Wisteria, Blauregen etc.) genäht. Das war in der damaligen Zeit offenbar nichts Ungewöhnliches, aber als Haruyama bei der Izushi Wotome no Kami ankam, verwandelte sich die Kleidung in Glyzinienblüten (*fuji no hana*). Diese Verbindung von Frühling und blühenden Glyzinien sieht Watase Masatada als Indiz dafür, dass der „alte Frühling im alten Kalender (*kyūreki*) mit dem dritten Monat" begann, was im modernen Sonnenkalender ungefähr dem Anfang Mai entspricht, also der Zeit, wenn die japanischen Glyzinien auch heutzutage noch zu blühen beginnen.[38] Die blühende Glyzinie der Jahreszeitendichtung im *Man'yōshū* in den beiden Bänden Acht und Zehn ist bis auf eine Ausnahme, in der sie als Kopfkissenwort dient, dem Sommer, also der „kalenderkorrekten" Jahreszeit zugeordnet.

Die vier Jahreszeiten

Die Schaffenszeit des Hofdichters (*kyūtei kajin* 宮廷歌人) Kakinomoto no Hitomaro 柿本人麻呂 begann vermutlich Ende des siebten Jahrhunderts und hielt bis Anfang des achten Jahrhunderts an.[39] In seiner Dichtung, die zu den älteren, aber nicht den ganz alten Teilen der Sammlung *Man'yōshū* zählt, tauchen wiederholt Begriffe wie *haru tatsu* 春立つ oder *aki tatsu* 秋立つ auf (hier mit *hiragana*-Umschrift), die auf die vierundzwanzig Stationen (*nijūshi sekki*) des chinesischen Kalenders verweisen, in dem der Frühlings- und Herbstanfang mit *lichun* 立春 respektive *liqiu* 立秋 bezeichnet sind. Seit der einflussreichen Untersuchung „Überlegungen zur Jahreszeitenanschauung im *Man'yōshū* — der chinesische Begriff »*lichun* [jap.: *risshun*]« und der japanische Begriff »*harutatsu*«" von Arai Eizō aus dem Jahr 1976 geht die Forschung allerdings davon aus, dass es sich bei den beiden Begriffen um unterschiedliche Konzeptionen und Wahrnehmungen handelt. Arai zufolge stellten in der chinesischen Sicht der Himmelssohn auf der Grundlage des himmlischen Mandats und in seinem Auftrag die „Beamten der Vier Zeiten" die Jahreszeiten künstlich auf, wodurch es an genau festgelegten Tagen zum

---

38) Watase (1993: 10–11) führt noch weitere Belege an. Die blühende Glyzinie, bei Watase *fuji no hana*, taucht im *Man'yōshū* wie folgt auf: *fuji* vier Belege, *fuji-nami* sechzehn Belege (ohne Kopfkissenwort), *fuji no hana* ein Beleg, *fuji-hara* drei Belege; fünf davon finden sich in den beiden Jahreszeiten-*maki* (ein Beleg für *fuji*, drei für *fuji-nami* sowie eine Verwendung als Kopfkissenwort *fuji-nami no*).

39) Alfred Lorenzen legte 1927 zu Hitomaro eine Dissertation vor.

Wechsel der Jahreszeit gekommen sei.[40] Dagegen „werden" und „wandeln sich" in japanischem Verständnis die Jahreszeiten und folgen kontinuierlich auf- und auseinander. In der Diktion Arais heißt das: „Sie formen sich an sich [und aus sich])".[41] Aoki Shūhei zählt „zusammenfassend und ergänzend" noch zwei weitere Merkmale auf, nämlich den „Punkt, dass [die vier Jahreszeiten] deutlich in der Natur selbst (*shizen sono mono*) wie Frühlingsdunst, Schnee, Pflaume, Buschsänger etc. in Erscheinung treten", sowie den „Punkt, dass [die vier Jahreszeiten in Formulierungen] wie »ankommend« (*kitsutsu aru*) oder »vorüberziehend« (*sugitsutsu aru*) durch die fortschreitende Zeit und Schritt für Schritt ablaufend dahinziehen".[42] Den Wortschatz, der in der Dichtung diese Bewegung zum Ausdruck bringt, bezeichnet Arai als „stilistische Merkmale für die Sichtweise der dahinziehenden Jahreszeiten" (移行的季節観の文体的徴表 *ikōteki kisetsukan no buntaiteki chōhyō*).[43] Dazu gehöre beispielsweise auch das präsumptive Verbalsuffix *-rashi* in Verbindungen wie *haru sugite natsu kitaru rashi* („Frühling scheint vorüber, Sommer gekommen zu sein") aus dem *Man'yōshū*-Gedicht 1: 28 der jungen Jitō Tennō, das heutzutage eher als Nr. 2 der Sammlung *Hyakunin isshu* 百人

40) Arai (1976: 76–77) spricht von *tenkan* 天館 und *shiji no kan* 四時の館, den amtlichen Astronomen.

41) Arai (1976: 77) bemüht die Notation *sokujiteki ni* »*nari-sadamari*« 即自的に「生り定まる」, die Hashimoto (1993: 27) jedoch in 即自的に成り定まる mit gleicher Lesung überführt. Im Falle Chinas benutzt Arai die transitive Wendung *jin'i toshite* »*tate-sadameru*«, das künstliche Aufstellen. Der Begriff *sokujiteki* mit der Bedeutung „an sich" (jap. *an jihhi*) scheint auf Hegels Dialektik zurückzugehen.

42) Aoki (1996: 51) drückt das wie folgt aus: 経過的な時期を経て漸移的に推移するもの *keikateki na jiki o hete zen'iteki ni sui'i suru mono*. Diese Formulierung besteht aus vier Ausdrücken für zeitliche Ver- oder Abläufe, Wandlungen etc. und deutet damit die Relevanz an, den dieser Aspekt der kulturellen Identität in der japanischen Wahrnehmung eingenommen hat. Es wäre freilich interessant zu wissen, ob die Originalformulierungen nur für die beiden Übergangsjahreszeiten Frühling und Herbst gelten oder auch bei Phänomenen des Sommers und Winters vorkommen.

43) Arai 1976: 81.

一首 („Hundert Menschen ein Gedicht") bekannt ist.

In dieser Argumentation stehen die chinesischen vier Zeiten *sishi* 四時 (jap.: *shiji*) im Gegensatz zu den japanischen vier Jahreszeiten *shiki* 四季, und dieser Gegensatz wird auch dementsprechend ausformuliert. Bei der kontinentalen Variante handele es sich nämlich um eine diskontinuierliche Jahreszeitenanschauung (*danzokuteki kisetsukan* 断続的季節観, ebd. S. 78, 87), bei der Inselvariante dagegen um eine kontinuierliche Jahreszeitenanschauung (*renzokuteki kisetsukan* 連続的季節観, ebd. S. 88). Somit stünden die Begriffe zwar im „Bewusstsein des chinesischen Kalenders", aber Arai und mit ihm die Forschung unterscheiden eine

> [...] davon abweichende, unserem Land eigene, aus alter Zeit stammende Jahreszeitenanschauung (*kisetsukan*). [Bei der] Konzeption (*hassō*), Vermutungen aus den Beobachtungen der Naturphänomene zu ziehen, handelt es sich nicht um die chinesische Konzeption, von außen in scharfer Trennung die Jahreszeiten voneinander abzugrenzen.[44]

Bei der Formulierung „aus alter Zeit kommende Jahreszeitenanschauung" (*korai no kisetsukan* 古来の季節観) kann es sich jedoch kaum um die „vier" Jahreszeiten handeln, sondern höchstens um Frühling und Herbst. Und auch daran dürften Zweifel angebracht sein, zumal in dem oben angeführten Zitat aus dem *Wei zhi* die Begriffe „Frühling" und „Herbst" keine japanischen Wörter sind, sondern zur chinesischen Fremdbeschreibung gehören. Anders gesagt: Sie sind kein Beleg dafür, dass die Bedeutungen der beiden Schriftzeichen auf den japanischen Inseln als die Bedeutungen, die sie im *Man'yōshū* besitzen, bekannt waren. Es lässt sich lediglich vermuten, dass die autochthonen Vorstellungen, Wahrnehmungen und vielleicht auch Wörter mit

---

44) Hashimoto 1993: 27.

Hilfe der chinesischen Schriftzeichen konkretisiert wurden.

Hashimoto Tatsuo (1993: 27) jedenfalls sieht mit der weiteren Entwicklung der Dichtung eine Anpassung der japanischen Jahreszeitenanschauung an das chinesische Denken und bei Ōtomo no Yakamochi 大伴家持 (718–785), der als Hauptkompilator des *Man'yōshū* gilt, und seinen Dichterfreunden, die mit Yakamochi für die spätere *Man'yōshū*-Dichtung der ersten Hälfte im achten Jahrhundert stehen, die Realisierung der „chinesischen Jahreszeitenanschauung". Zur Argumentation führt er die drei *Man'yōshū*-Gedichte 20: 4488 bis 4490 an, die auf einem Bankett am achtzehnten Tag (*setsubun* 節分) im zwölften Monat entstanden, das heißt einen Tag vor dem „offiziellen" Frühlingsanfang *risshun*, der in jenem Jahr auf den neunzehnten Tag und somit noch „ins alte Jahr" fiel.[15] Dieser *risshun*-Tag entsprach im modernen Sonnenkalender dem vierten Februar des Jahres 758. In den drei Gedichten kommt die Hoffnung zum Ausdruck, dass der heutige Tag der letzte im alten Jahr ist und morgen der Frühling kommt, wobei das erste Gedicht sogar den fallenden Schnee und den Winter auf diesen letzten Tag beschränkt. Bei solchen Gelegenheiten sei es immer wieder zu „Verschiebung" (*zure* ずれ) gekommen, die etwa durch Phrasen wie *shikasuga ni* („das ist so, und doch") deutlich werden.

Einige Tage später, am dreiundzwanzigsten Tag des zwölften Monats, verfasste Yakamochi, der vermutlich ebenfalls an dem Bankett teilgenommen hatte, ein Kurzgedicht (*tanka* 短歌), das große Ähnlichkeiten mit dem eingangs zitierten und später ins *Shinkokin wakashū* aufgenommenen Waka-Gedicht aufweist. Name und Beamtenstellung des Dichters gehen aus der Nachbemerkung hervor:

---

45) Vgl. auch Aso 2015: 568 oder Inaoka 2015: 566, die sich beide auf das *Nihon rekijitsu genten* 日本暦日原典 von Uchida Masao (1975) beziehen.

Ein Gedicht vom Bankett, das am 23. Tag in der Villa des Chibu no Shōfu Ōhara no Imamaki Mahito [verfasst wurde]

Nijūsannichi ni Chibu no Shōfu […] no ihe ni shite utage suru uta isshu

Zählt man die Monde

Ist es immer noch Winter

So ist es und doch

Ein milder Dunst zieht dahin

Ob der Frühling schon begann?!⁴⁶⁾

tsu-ki yo-me-ba · i-ma-da fuyu na-ri · shi-ka-su-ga ni

kasumi ta-na-bi-ku · ha-ru ta-chi-nu to ka

右
一
首
右
中
弁
大
伴
宿
祢
家
持
作

尓
霞
多
奈
婢
久
　
波
流
多
知
奴
等
可

都
奇
餘
米
婆
　
伊
麻
太
冬
奈
里
　
之
可
須
我

宅
宴
歌
一
首

廿
三
日
於
治
部
少
輔
大
原
今
城
真
人
之

Die drei oben genannten Gedichte artikulieren lediglich die Hoffnung auf den kommenden Frühling, aber in diesem Gedicht ist es so, als ob sich dieser nur wenige Tage später tatsächlich konkret zeigt. Aso Mizue（2015: 572）zufolge kommt der Ausdruck *tsuki yomeba* 都奇 餘米婆（„zählt man die Monde“）nur in diesem Gedicht vor,⁴⁷⁾ und sie umschreibt die ersten beiden Verse mit „auf dem Kalender ist es noch Winter“. Das Gedicht zeigt eine Reflexion über den Konflikt von Monden als Indikatoren eines Kalenders und den diesem widersprechenden natürlichen Gegebenheiten. Es scheint den Kalender

---

46) *Man'yōshū*, Gedicht 20: 4492, Notation nach Kojima, Kinoshita und Tōno 2006b: 450, die *tsuki yomeba* (wörtlich: „die Monde lesen“) als „mit lauter Stimme zählen“ (ebd.) auslegen.

47) Das spräche gegen das Mondzählen als alten Brauch der Zeitrechnung, aber in den *Kojiki*-Mythen gibt es die Gottheit Tsukuyomi, den Mondzählenden Gott, einen Bruder von Amaterasu Ōmikami und Susa no Wo; vgl. Wittkamp 2018: 140.

zu hinterfragen, demzufolge der Frühlingsbeginn mit dem ersten Tag im ersten Monat (*shōgatsu*) beginnen müsste, der in jenem Jahr 758 auf den siebzehnten Februar fiel. Laut Vorwort verfasste Yakamochi das Gedicht am dreiundzwanzigsten Tag (im zwölften Monat), was dem neunten Februar entsprach, aber wie oben gesehen lag der Frühlingsbeginn *risshun* dieses Jahres bereits zwei Wochen zuvor.[48]

Wie auch Aoki Shūhei darlegt, bezieht sich das „Lesen der Monde" in diesem Gedicht auf den Kalender im Sinne von „Monde zählen".[49] Was er jedoch als *zure*, als „Reibung" zwischen der kontinuierlichen und diskontinuierlichen Jahreszeitenanschauung beschreibt, für die das Stereotyp *shikasuga ni* „ein wichtiger Ausdruck" (ebd.) sei, kann sich kaum auf die „indigene", vorschriftliche Jahreszeitenanschauung der Japaner beziehen. Denn wie beim *Kojiki*-Mythos der beiden Brüder Herbstberg und Frühlingsberg gesehen, entsprach der Frühling vor der Einführung des chinesischen Kalenders vielleicht eher dem heutigen Kalender, begann also circa sechs Wochen bis zwei Monate später.[50] Was hier als „Index für die Natur an sich" stehe, nämlich das Stereotyp *kasumi tanabiku/haru*, der dahinziehende Dunst, verdankt sich selbst schon dem Kalender und der Schrift. Dass ab dem Frühling bis in den Sommer, also über mehrere Monate hinweg, die Berge dunstverhangen sind, lässt sich trotz Erderwärmung noch heute jedes Jahr beobachten.

Der in den zitierten Gedichten ausgedrückte Konflikt lässt sich somit als

---

48) Vgl. Kojima, Kinoshita und Tōno 2006b: 450 und weiterhin Inaoka, der *tsuki yomeba* mit „den Mond als Kalender zählen" (2015: 567) erläutert.

49) Aoki 2001: 52. Die japanische Lesung von 暦 mit *koyomi* für „Kalender" geht eventuell auf das Zählen der „Tage [*ke*] als Einheit der Zeit" (*Jidaibetsu kokugo daijiten jōdaihen*, Eintrag *ke* [= Omodaka 1983: 279]) zurück (*ke yomi → koyomi?*). Im *Nihon shoki* kommt 暦 das erste Mal in einem Eintrag zum 15. Regierungsjahr von Kinmei Tennō vor, aber die Lesung lautet dort *reki*; vgl. Kojima et al. 2: 428–429.

50) Simmer (2013: 50), der wie gesehen bei den Jahreszeiten eine astronomische von einer meteorologischen (klimatologischen) Definition unterscheidet, macht weiterhin

Diskrepanzen zwischen den Mondphasen und dem Lunisolarkalender einerseits sowie den Wahrnehmungen der Jahreszeiten andererseits bestätigen. Zum letzten Punkt ist allerdings zu bemerken, dass rein der Quellenlage zufolge die Wahrnehmung als vier Jahreszeiten selbst der Rezeption und reflexiven Auseinandersetzung mit der chinesischen Kultur geschuldet ist. Denn „natürlicherweise" besteht keine Notwendigkeit einer Einteilung in vier Jahreszeiten. Beispielsweise ließen sich ein Zyklus aus nur zwei Hälften wie „Langwerden" und „Kurzwerden" denken — eben *haru* und *aki*. Der astronomischen Definition von Jahreszeiten als „jährlich wiederkehrende Muster im Witterungsablauf" zufolge wären auch die Regen- und die Taifunzeit als klimatologisch markante und jeweils eigene Abschnitte, eben als Jahreszeiten denkbar. Im Sinne der Kulturwissenschaften ist die japanische Dichtung kontingent: Sie ist, wie sie ist, aber ohne den Kontakt mit der chinesischen Kultur wäre sie vermutlich ganz anders gewesen.

Abschließend bleibt festzuhalten, dass die Jahreszeitentopik als Thema der japanischen Dichtung noch bis ins siebzehnte Jahrhundert hinein Nachhaltigkeit besaß. Das belegt ein Gedicht, das heute als das älteste Haiku von Matsuo Bashō 松尾芭蕉 (1644–1694) gilt. Damals war er vermutlich neunzehn Jahre alt, und mit Überschrift und einer deutlich vernehmbaren Anspielung auf das Eingangsgedicht zum *Kokin wakashū* heißt es darin wie folgt:

---

darauf aufmerksam, dass aufgrund der elliptischen Sonnenumkreisung, bei der sich die Erde den Keppler'schen Gesetzen zufolge im Sommer etwas langsamer bewege, der „Nordsommer [derzeit] um ca. 3 Tage länger als der Nordwinter" (S. 51) ist. Simmers Beobachtungen gelten für die mittleren und hohen Breiten oberhalb des nördlichen Wendekreises, wozu auch China und Japan gehören. „Wäre die Erdbahn um die Sonne ein Kreis", schreibt er, „so wären die vier Jahreszeiten exakt gleichlang". Damit deuten sich weitere Schwierigkeiten bei der Kalenderberechnung an, zumal sich die Bahn der Erde um die Sonne und die Neigung der Erdrotationsebene ständig ändern (ebd.).

Da am 29. Tag der Frühling aufstand

nijūkyū nichi risshun nareba

Ist der Frühling gekommen,

Oder will das Jahr schon gehen?

Am letzten Tag im Winter[51]

haru ya koshi toshi ya yukiken ko-tsugomori

二十九日立春なれば
春や来し年や
行きけん小晦日

Der letzte Tag im zwölften Monat war ein *ko-tsugomori*, wenn es ein „kleiner Monat" (*shō no tsuki* 小の月) war, das heißt ein Monat mit neunundzwanzig Tagen.[52] Nach Monden gerechnet ist das noch Winter, worauf das der Umgangssprache entnommene Jahreszeitenwort *ko-tsugomori* hindeutet. Der *risshun*, der offizielle Frühlingsanfang, fiel in diesem Jahr jedoch auf diesen Tag. Dass der *risshun* noch in das alte Jahr fällt, kommt wie gesehen öfters vor, und anhand gewisser Umstände wurde bei diesem Haiku konkret das Jahr 1662 (Kanbun 2. Jahr) ausgemacht.[53] Allerdings dürften Bashō zu diesem

---

51) Notation nach Kon 1989: 13.

52) Komatsu zufolge, der das *Kokin wakashū* Gedicht Nr. 312 von Ki no Tsurayuki diskutiert, sei dem Wort *tsugomori* ein „zerstörerischer Wandel" aus *tsuki-gomori* widerfahren. Das liege daran, dass die ursprüngliche Bedeutung als das „Sich-Verbergen des Mondes" aufgrund der Verschiebungen zwischen Mond- und Sonnenkalender, die zum Ausgleich alle drei Jahre den Schaltmonat *uruuzuki* 閏月 erforderlich machten, hinfällig geworden sei, da unter Umständen in dieser Nacht der Mond eben nicht verborgen war. Um daher den in *tsuki-gomori* enthaltenen Verweis auf den verborgenen Mond zu invisibilisieren, habe sich das Wort *tsukigomori* „zerstörerisch" zu *tsugomori* gewandelt. Das gelte ebenfalls für das Wort *tsuitachi* („erster Tag im neuen Monat"), das sich aus *tsuki-tachi* („der Mond tritt wieder hervor") herleite; vgl. Komatsu 2008: 39–42.

53) Da jedoch Zweifel an diesem Jahr aufgekommen sind, führen Imoto und Hori (1999: 84), wenn auch nicht ganz überzeugt, das Haiku als Nr. 149 und verorten es in dem wesentlich größeren Entstehungszeitraum zwischen 1661 und 1681; die Notation weicht bei Imoto und Hori leicht von Kon 1989: 13 ab.

Thema kaum irgendwelche Schwierigkeiten mit dem Kalender motiviert haben, denn für seine Haiku in dieser frühen Phase waren eher die Tradition und Topik, kurz das kulturelle Gedächtnis ausschlaggebend. Soweit dem Verfasser bekannt, war der Topos allerdings mit Bashōs Aktualisierung — spätestens aber mit Einführung des modernen Kalenders — ausgereizt, wenn auch die Jahreszeiten selbst ihren zentralen Platz innerhalb japanischer kultureller Gedächtnisse bis heute ungebrochen behaupten können.[54]

54) Vgl. Wittkamp 2013.

Literatur:

Antoni, Klaus (2012): *Kojiki: Aufzeichnung alter Begebenheiten*. Berlin: Insel, Verlag der Weltreligionen.

Aoki Shūhei 青木周平 (2001): Kisetsu 季節, in: Aoki Takako 青木生子 / Hashimoto Tatsuo 橋本達夫 (Hg.): *Man'yō kotoba jiten* 万葉ことば事典 [Wörterbuch *Man'yōshū*]. Tōkyō: Yamato Shobō, S. 472–479.

Arai Eizō 新井栄蔵 (1976): *Man'yōshū* kisetsukan-kō — kango »risshun« to wago »harutatsu« 万葉集季節観攷 —— 漢語〈立春〉と和語〈ハルタツ〉 —— [Überlegungen zur Jahreszeitenanschauung im *Man'yōshū* — der chinesische Begriff »*lichun* [jap.: *risshun*]« und der japanische Begriff »*harutatsu*«]. In: *Man'yōshū kenkyū* 万葉集研究 5, S. 73–99.

Ariyoshi Tamotsu 有吉保 et al. (Hg.): *Waka no honshitsu to hyōgen* 和歌の本質と表現 [Zum Wesen und Ausdruck des Waka]. Tōkyō: Benseisha (Waka bungaku kōza; Bd. 1).

Aso Mizue 阿蘇瑞枝 (1993): Natsu 夏. In: Inaoka Kōji 稲岡耕二 (Hg.): *Man'yōshū jiten* 万葉集辞典 [*Man'yōshū*-Lexikon]. *Kokubungaku* 国文学 (Gakutōsha, Sonderband) 46, S. 17–24.

———— (2015): *Man'yōshū zenka kōgi* 萬葉集全歌講義 [*Man'yōshū* — Vorlesungen zu allen Gedichten, Bd. 10]. Tōkyō: Kasama Shoin.

Hashimoto Tatsuo 橋本達雄 (1993): Aki 秋. In: Inaoka Kōji 稲岡耕二 (Hg.): *Man'yōshū jiten* 万葉集辞典 [*Man'yōshū*-Lexikon]. *Kokubungaku* 国文学 (Gakutōsha, Sonderband) 46, S. 24–32.

Imoto Nōichi 井本農一 / Hori Nobuo 堀信夫 (²1999): *Matsuo Bashō shū* 松尾芭蕉集 [Sammlung Matsuo Bashō]. Tōkyō: Shōgakukan (Erstauflage 1995, Shinpen Nihon koten bungaku zenshū, Bd. 70).

Inaoka Kōji 稲岡耕二 (2015): *Man'yōshū* 萬葉集 Bd. 4. Tōkyō: Meiji Shoin (Waka bungaku taikei, Bd. 4).

Inoue Muneo 井上宗雄 et al. (1993): Shogen 緒言. In: ders. et al. (Hg.): *Uta no hassei to man'yō waka* うたの発生と万葉和歌 [Entstehung des *uta* und das *man'yō-waka*]. Tōkyō: Kazama Shobō, ohne Seitenangabe (Waka bungaku ronshū, Bd. 1).

Ishikawa Kyūyō 石川九楊 (2011a): *Man'yōgana de yomu Man'yōshū* 万葉仮名でよむ 『万葉集』 [Das *Man'yōshū* mit *man'yōgana* gelesen]. Tōkyō: Iwanami Shoten.

Ishikawa Kyūyō (2011b): *Tokigatari Nihon shoshi* 説き語り 日本書史 [Erläutert: Geschichte der japanischen Schrift]. Tōkyō: Shinchōsha.

Itō Takao 伊藤高雄 (2000): Kisetsu to gyōji to matsuri 季節と行事と祭り. In: Sakurai Mitsuru 櫻井満 (Hg.) unter Mitarbeit von Ozaki Tomiyoshi 尾崎富義 / Kikuchi Yoshihiro 菊池義裕 / ders.: *Man'yōshū o shiru jiten* 万葉集を知る辞典 [Lexikon zum Kennenlernen des *Man'yōshū*]. Tōkyō: Tōkyōdō Shuppan, S. 172–192.

Katano Tatsurō 片野達郎 (1975): *Nihon bungei to kaiga no sōkansei no kenkyū* 日本 文芸と絵画の相関性の研究 [Forschung zum Verhältnis von japanischer Literatur und Malerei]. Tōkyō: Kasama Shoin.

Kawamura Teruo 川村晃生 (2004): *Nihon bungaku kara „shizen" o yomu* 日本文学か ら「自然」を読む [Die „Natur" aus der japanischen Literatur lesen]. Tōkyō: Bensei Shuppan.

Kojima Noriyuki 小島憲之 / Kinoshita Masatoshi 木下正俊 / Tōno Haruyuki 東野治之 (⁶2006a): *Man'yōshū* 万葉集. Tōkyō: Shōgakukan (Erstauflage 1995, Shinpen Nihon koten bungaku zenshū, Bd. 6 bis 9, hier Bd. 8).

————— (⁶2006b): *Man'yōshū*. Tōkyō: Shōgakukan (Erstauflage 1996, Shinpen Nihon koten bungaku zenshū, Bd. 6 bis 9, hier Bd. 9).

Komatsu Hideo 小松英雄 (2008): *Teinei ni yomu koten* 丁寧に読む古典 [Klassische Literatur sorgfältig lesen]. Tōkyō: Kasama Shoin.

————— (2012): *Misohito moji no jojōshi —* Kokin wakashū *no waka hyōgen o tokihogusu* みそひと文字の抒情詩 —— 古今和歌集の和歌表現を解きほぐす [Das lyrische Gedicht mit 31 Schriftzeichen: den Waka-Ausdruck im *Kokin Wakashū* entwirren]. Tōkyō: Kasama Shoin (Neuauflage, original 2004).

Kon Eizō 今栄蔵 (³1989): *Bashō kushū* 芭蕉句集 [Bashō Haiku-Sammlung]. Tōkyō: Shinchōsha (Erstauflage 1982, Shinchō Nihon koten shūsei, Bd. 51).

Leinss, Gerhard (2006): Japanische Lunisolarkalender der Jahre Jōkyō 2 (1685) bis Meiji 6 (1873). In: *Japonica Humboldtiana* 10 (2006), S. 5–89.

Lewin, Bruno (1975): *Abriss der japanischen Grammatik* (zweite verbesserte Auflage). Wiesbaden: Otto Harrassowitz (Erstauflage 1959).

Lorenzen, Alfred (1927): *Die Gedichte Hitomaro's aus dem Manyōshū — in Text und Übersetzung mit Erläuterung.* Hamburg: Kommissionsverlag L. Friedrichsen & Co.

Meller, Harald (2008): *Der geschmiedete Himmel. Die weite Welt im Herzen Europas vor 3600 Jahren.* Stuttgart: Theiss in Wissenschaftliche Buchgesellschaft.

————— (2018): *Die Himmelsscheibe von Nebra. Der Schlüssel zu einer untergegangenen*

Kultur im Herzen Europas. Berlin: Ullstein Verlage.

Mezaki Tokue 目崎徳衛 (1993): Nihon bunkashi ni okeru waka 日本文化史における和歌. In: Ariyoshi Tamotsu 有吉保 et al. (Hg.): *Waka no honshitsu to hyōgen* 和歌の本質と表現 [Das Wesen und der Ausdruck des Waka]. Tōkyō: Benseisha, S. 25–40 (Waka bungaku kōza, Bd. 1).

Minemura Fumito 峯村文人 (1995): *Shinkokin wakashū* 新古今和歌集 [Neue Sammlung von Gedichten aus alter und jetziger Zeit]. Tōkyō: Shōgakukan (Shinpen Nihon koten bungaku zenshū, Bd. 43).

Naredi-Rainer, Paul von (2013): Die Zahl 4 in Kunst, Architektur und Weltvorstellung. In: Greub, Thierry (Hg.): *Das Bild der Jahreszeiten im Wandel der Kulturen und Zeiten*. München: Wilhelm Fink, S. 17–48.

Naruse Fujio 成瀬不二雄 (1988): *Nihon kaiga no fūkei hyōgen — genshi kara bakumatsu made* 日本絵画の風景表現 ―― 原始から幕末まで [Landschaftsausdruck in der japanischen Malerei — von den Anfängen bis zum Ende der Tokugawa-Zeit]. Tōkyō: Chūōkōron Bijutsu Shuppan.

Ozawa Masao 小沢正夫 / Matsuda Shigeho 松田成穂 (²2000): *Kokin wakashū* 古今和歌集 [Sammlung von Gedichten aus alter und jetziger Zeit]. Tōkyō: Shōgakukan (Erstauflage 1994, Shinpen Nihon koten bungaku zenshū, Bd. 11).

Prada Vicente, Maria Jesus De / Ōshima Hitoshi 大島仁 (2005): *Yuragi to zure no nihon Bungakushi* ゆらぎとずれの日本文学史 [Geschichte der japanischen Literatur zwischen Erschütterung und Verschiebung]. Kyōto: Mineruba Shobō.

Schönbein, Martina (2001): *Jahreszeitenmotive in der japanischen Lyrik — Zur Kanonisierung der kidai in der formativen Phase des* haikai *im 17. Jahrhundert*. Wiesbaden: Harrassowitz (Bunken. Bd. 6).

Seyock, Barbara (2004): *Auf den Spuren der Ostbarbaren. Zur Archäologie protohistorischer Kulturen in Südkorea und Westjapan*. Münster et al.: LIT-Verlag (BUNKA — Tübinger interkulturelle und linguistische Japanstudien, Bd. 8).

Shirane Haruo (2012): *Japan and the Culture of the Four Seasons. Nature, Literature, and the Arts*. New York: Columbia University.

Simmer, Clemens (2013): Warum vier Jahreszeiten? Die klimatologische Perspektive. In: Greub, Thierry (Hg.): *Das Bild der Jahreszeiten im Wandel der Kulturen und Zeiten*. München: Wilhelm Fink, S. 49–55.

Watanabe Yasuaki 渡部泰明 (²2009): Waka to ha nani ka 和歌とは何か [Was ist das Waka?]. Tōkyō: Iwanami (Erstauflage 2009).

Wilkinson, Endymion (2015): *Chinese History — A New Manual Fourth Edition*. Cambridge und London: Harvard University.

Wittkamp, Robert F. (2004): Konstruktivismus, Wahrnehmung und Gedächtnis: Ein Plädoyer für einen konstruktivistischen Landschaftsdiskurs. In: Moerke, Andreas / Andrea Germer (Hg.): *Grenzgänge: De-Konstruktion kollektiver Identitäten in*

Japan. München: Iudicium, S. 239–256 (Japanstudien, Bd. 16).

————— (2013): Jahreszeiten und kulturelles Gedächtnis in Japan — vom *Man'yōshū* zur Gegenwart. In: Greub, Thierry (Hg.): *Das Bild der Jahreszeiten im Wandel der Kulturen und Zeiten.* München: Wilhelm Fink, S. 99–115 (Abbildungen in „Tafeln" S. 8–10).

————— (2014a): *Altjapanische Erinnerungsdichtung — Landschaft, Schrift und kulturelles Gedächtnis.* Band 1: *Prolegomenon: Landschaft im Werden der Waka-Dichtung.* Würzburg: Ergon (Beiträge zu kulturwissenschaftlichen Süd- und Ostasienforschung, Bd. 5a).

————— (2014b): *Altjapanische Erinnerungsdichtung — Landschaft, Schrift und kulturelles Gedächtnis.* Band 2: *Schriftspiele und Erinnerungsdichtung.* Würzburg: Ergon (Beiträge zu kulturwissenschaftlichen Süd- und Ostasienforschung, Bd. 5b).

————— (2018): *Arbeit am Text – Zur postmodernen Erforschung der Kojiki-Mythen.* Gossenberg: Ostasienverlag (Deutsche Ostasienstudien, Bd. 34).

Yamaguchi Yoshinori 山口佳紀 / Kōnoshi Takamitsu 神野志隆光 ([7]2007): *Kojiki* 古事記. Tōkyō: Shōgakukan (Erstauflage 1997, Shinpen Nihon koten bungaku zenshū Bd. 1).

『貧しき人々』と『ペテルブルク年代記』

近 藤 昌 夫

はじめに

　ペテルブルク中央工兵士官学校で製図・設計を学ぶために、16 才で
モスクワから上京したドストエフスキーは、およそ 30 編の小説を残し
たが、そのうちの 20 編近くがペテルブルクを舞台にしている[1]。作品
数ひとつをとっても、ドストエフスキーが都市の作家であることに異論
の余地はないであろう。

　もちろん、ドストエフスキーばかりがペテルブルクを舞台に作品を書
いたわけではない。ことに 1840 年代後半は、多くの作家がこぞってペ
テルブルクと庶民を描いた「都市ルポルタージュ」の時代であった。

　40 年代前半にゴーゴリの影響下に成立した自然派文学は、1845 年か
ら 1848 年にかけて「祖国雑記」、「同時代人」「ペテルブルクの生理学」、
「ペテルブルク文集」などの雑誌を大いに賑わせた。I・ツルゲーネフ、D・
グリゴローヴィチ、A・ゲルツェン、I・ゴンチャローフ、N・ネクラー
ソフ、そしてドストエフスキー兄弟らが、虐げられた様々な弱者・余計
者たち、すなわち都会で貧困に喘ぐ不幸な人々や、物静かで慎ましい人々
あるいは有能だが意志薄弱な人々（たとえば水運び屋、小役人、屋敷番、
元教師、料理女、売春婦など）の日常を、ペテルブルクの薄汚れた闇の
風景——汚物まみれの裏階段、霧や雨で濡れた古びた建物、埃や泥だら

---

1) Анциферов Н. Душа Петербурга. М. 2014. С. 204.

けの路地、黒ずんだ木造のあばら屋など——とともに事細かに観察し、描写することで、ペテルブルク社会の病を明るみに出していたのである。それら、いわゆる「生理学的スケッチ」の中から物語の主人公が誕生する。ゴーゴリの『外套』（1842）の万年九等官アカーキィ・アカーキエヴィチにはじまる、「文士連中からなぶりものにされ、からかわれる」貧しい小役人たちである。

　ドストエフスキーも、「生理学的スケッチ」の集大成のひとつであるネクラーソフの『ペテルブルク文集』に『貧しき人々』（1846）を発表し、ペテルブルクの貧民窟と貧しい下級官吏の生態を解剖してみせたが、ドストエフスキーのペテルブルクとの向き合い方は、他の自然派の作家たちのそれとは異なるものだった。

　『貧しき人々』の翌年に発表された「新聞連載フェリエトン」集『ペテルブルク年代記』（1847）が、作家と都市の関係について教えてくれる。

　フェリエトンとはフランスで誕生した文学ジャンルのことである。そもそも近代都市の発展とともに生じた出来事や世相を扱う新聞雑誌の囲み、雑報欄あるいは備忘録を指す言葉であったのが、本国フランスで「都会という試薬品の作用を受けて」異化され、さらにバルザックの『幻滅』やウージェーヌ・シューの『パリの秘密』などによって文学に近づきはじめたのであった。この進化型のフェリエトンはロシアに入ると、自然派の「生理学的スケッチ」の影響を受け、ペテルブルクの「世態風俗的題材を作品に仕上げる独特な方法」へと変質していった。若きドストエフスキーもこのジャンルに関心をもち、帝都ペテルブルクの「都会風俗、都会風景を自分の好きなように観察してまわり、それに付随して自分自身の気持までも考察の対象とする」脱備忘録型フェリエトンを目指したのであった[2]。その結果誕生したのが、「サンクト・ペテルブルク通報」紙に連載された、4編のフェリエトンからなる『ペテルブルク年代記』

　2）コマローヴィチ『ドストエフスキーの青春』中村健之介訳、みすず書房、1978年、164～165頁。

であり[3]、そこには「人の像をとった生きている都会のイメージ」があ
りありと描かれている[4]。

　みずから建築への愛着を明らかにしているドストエフスキーが[5]、製
図設計を学び、40年代後半に都市と都市住民の生態を描くフェリエト
ンに手を染めたのは、生活圏としてのペテルブルクに強い関心を抱いて
いたからであって、当時の流行ばかりではなかったのである。

　「ペテルブルクは散歩しながら、考えをまとめるのである」[6]とはフェ
リエトンの特徴をよく表したA・プレシチェーエフの言葉だが、ドス
トエフスキーも、たとえばセナーヤ広場を散策しながらペテルブルクを
擬人化し（「ペテルブルクはむくれていた」）[7]、春を迎えて様変わりす
る帝都の描写に、芝居、雑誌、社会、文学、漫画、街の事件など、様々
な時事的出来事の批評を織り交ぜて、モスクワとは正反対の理念に基づ
いて創設された北の人工都市から[8]、ロシアの歴史・文化・風土、ロシ
ア人の民俗性や気質、ものの見方を説き起こしている。

　フェリエトン作家ドストエフスキーは、ロシア人の国民性が良くも悪
くも活きいきとあらわれる場所はペテルブルクを措いてほかにないと考
え、気儘な散策者あるいは傍観者としてではなく、1個の生活者として
ペテルブルクとその住人を、いわばマクロコスモスとミクロコスモスの

3）『ペテルブルク年代記』は、1847年4月27日、5月11日、6月1日、そし
　て6月15日の4編のフェリエトンからなる。
4）コマローヴィチ前掲書、171頁。
5）同書、192頁。
6）1847年4月13日のフェリエトン（『ドストエフスキー全集』第24巻、新潮社、
　1979年15頁）。
7）1847年4月27日のフェリエトン。同じフェリエトンの別の箇所にも「寝起
　きのペテルブルクは機嫌が悪くて怒りっぽく、まるで昨日の舞踏会に腹を立て
　て顔が土気色になり、いら立っている社交界の女のようだ。頭のてっぺんから
　足のつま先まで怒っていた」、あるいはペテルブルクの灰色の巨大な壁、大理
　石などが「悪い天気に腹を立てているみたいで、ぶるぶる、湿気で歯をがくが
　くさせていた」等の擬人化表現が散見される。
8）ドストエフスキー『作家の日記2』小沼文彦訳、筑摩書房、1997年、405頁。

照応関係の中でとらえていたのである。

　たとえば、「悪名高い一ツーリスト」すなわちフランスの文人で『1839年のロシア』の著者アストルフ・ド・キュスティーヌ批判に耳を傾けてみよう。

　『ペテルブルク年代記』の 1847 年 6 月 1 日のフェリエトンは、ロシアの後進性、劣等意識をあげつらうキュスティーヌの偏見 —— ペテルブルクは西欧の珍妙な模倣に過ぎないし、ロシア民族の誇りであるモスクワも族長時代の伝統を否定している —— を紹介し、次のように反論している。

　「町の研究」に勤しみ、ペテルブルクの建築様式に「思想の統一と躍動の統一」を読み取るドストエフスキーによれば、「ロシアの頭であり心臓」であるペテルブルクの混沌は、「すべてが生きて躍動し」続け、いまだ創造過程にあるからだという。ピョートル大帝の偉大な理念は、様々な領域で「具現化され、成長し」、「ペテルブルクの沼地においてだけでなく、もっぱらペテルブルクを生命とする全ロシアにおいて日ごとに根を下ろしつつある。」これはひとえに、すべての階層が偉大な思想を実現する共同事業に呼び寄せられ、新しい生活に生き生きと邁進しているからにほかならない。ロシアの民族性がヨーロッパの影響によってたやすく滅び去るはずがない。なぜなら「自己の現在の瞬間、生きている瞬間を積極的に愛している国民は健全であって、その瞬間を理解することができるはず」だし、「その生命力と源泉はその国民が永遠に生きるに足りる」からだという[9]。

　このように『ペテルブルク年代記』は、ペテルブルクの「生理学的スケッチ」でも備忘録型フェリエトンでもなく、ペテルブルクという顔をしたロシアとロシア人を描いた新しいフェリエトンだったのであり、40年代後半のドストエフスキーに新境地をもたらした肥沃な文学的土壌といってもよいものだったのである。V・コマローヴィチはいう。

9）6 月 1 日のフェリエトン。

『ペテルブルク年代記』に収められたフェリエトンは、なんらかの
かたちで『女あるじ』をも、『かよわい心』をも、『白夜』をも、そ
してまた 1848 年の小作品群（『ポルズンコフ』『他人の女房』『やき
もちやきの亭主』『クリスマス・ツリーと結婚式』）をも、予告して
いる。ひと言で言えば、『ネートチカ・ネズワーノワ』を除いて、
1847 年後半から 1849 年の逮捕に至るまでの間にドストエフスキー
の発表した作品のすべてが、ここに予告されているのである[10]。

コマローヴィチはこれらの小説を、その後の 1 人称小説に連なる「告
白の性質を帯びた文学作品」と特徴づけ[11]、『ペテルブルク年代記』以
前の『貧しき人々』については、『分身』や『プロハルチン氏』とともに、
ゴーゴリに学んだコミカルな手法を駆使した旧来の作品とみなして一線
を画している[12]。しかしながら『貧しき人々』の書簡体は告白以外の何
ものでもないし、先述した脱備忘録的フェリエトンの特徴――「都会風
俗、都会風景を自分の好きなように観察してまわり、それに付随して自
分自身の気持までも考察の対象とする」――も指摘できる。
　たとえば 9 月 5 日のジェーヴシキンの手紙を読んでみよう。
　役所に出勤するジェーヴシキンが、1 日の活動を開始した起き抜けの
町に惹かれ、自然派作家のように住人の様子を覗き見ようとすると、「目
を覚まし、動き出し、煙を吐いて、湯を沸かし、ガチャガチャ音をたて
る」町からしっぺ返しをくらい、疎外感を覚える。けれどもジェーヴシ
キンは、そこで退散することなく内省する。同じアパートの異なる階に
暮らす、貧しい靴職人と大金持ちの、靴をめぐる夢の例え話を持ち出し
て、社会主義的な思想と絡ませながら自己卑下は無用と自分の気持ちを
綴っているのである。

10）コマローヴィチ前掲書、178〜179 頁。
11）同書、169 頁。
12）同書、184 頁。

『貧しき人々』にもフェリエトン作家ドストエフスキーが浸潤しており、『貧しき人々』のドストエフスキーは、ペテルブルクを自然派小説のペテルブルクのような舞台背景ではなく、『ペテルブルク年代記』のペテルブルクすなわち擬人化される生命体とみなしていたのではないだろうか。

小論は、『ペテルブルク年代記』を『貧しき人々』のメタ・テクストに用い、物語に内在化されたペテルブルクの文学的意義を明らかにすることで、ドストエフスキーのデビュー作に新たな解釈を提示するものである。

1 『貧しき人々』のメタ・テクスト 『ペテルブルク年代記』

1-1 貧民窟

『貧しき人々』は、47才の貧しい小役人マカール・ジェーヴシキンと、孤児で10代後半の病弱な娘ワルワーラ・ドブロショーロワの往復書簡である。書簡体小説であることで、読者は自然派小説の特徴のひとつであったセンチメンタリズムを期待し、作品もまたそれに応えてドストエフスキーは「新しいゴーゴリ」として迎えられ、一躍文壇の寵児となった。

物語は、ワルワーラへの愛情を恋人気取りで有頂天になって綴る、ジェーヴシキンの幸福な手紙にはじまる。ワルワーラの手紙にも次第に打ち解けた表現が増えてくるが、結局彼女はブイコフという田舎地主に嫁ぎ、残されたジェーヴシキンは「貧民窟」で宛名のない手紙に悲痛な想いを書き綴るのだった。

『貧しき人々』にもペテルブルクが縦横に描かれている。

　閣下から百ルーブルを下賜されたジェーヴシキンは、幸福な気分でネフスキー大通りを散歩する。気分転換にフォンタンカ河岸からゴローホワヤ通りを歩いている。また、ワルワーラとふたりで市内北西部の島々を訪れたり、借金のためにヴォスクレセンスキー（現リテイヌィ）橋を渡って北東部のヴィボルク通りまで足を伸ばしたりもしている。いっぽう、T県の片田舎から家族でペテルブルク区に越してきたワルワーラは、父の死をきっかけにワシーリエフ島に転居。母の病没後はジェーヴシキンの住む貧民窟に移り住み、追悼ミサの祈りにはヴォルコヴォ墓地に足を運んでいる。

　ペテルブルクの各所がそれぞれの手紙に内在化され、ふたりの女中の手を介して行ったり来たりするのだが、『貧しき人々』の主なペテルブルクは「とんでもないおんぼろの貧民窟」である。

　ジェーヴシキンの手紙によると、かれらの貧民窟には、肩を寄せ合う棟続きの安アパートが、中庭（ドヴォール）と呼ばれる、暗くて狭い共有スペースを作っている。ジェーヴシキンのアパートのように、出入り口が2箇所──表通りに面した、鋳鉄とマホガニー製の玄関（パラードナヤ）と、中庭に面した、ありとあらゆる汚物にまみれた裏階段──ある建物もあれば、ワルワーラのアパートのように中庭に面した裏階段がひとつあるだけで、表通りに出るには中庭に降りてスクヴォズニークといわれる、建物1階部分に穿たれた、アーチのような共有通路を利用しなければならない建物もある。

　この「貧民窟」にあるジェーヴシキンの貸間は、アパートの共同炊事場の片隅を衝立で仕切っただけの空間で、臭気と湿気でマヒワがつぎつぎと死んでいくという。

　アパートや劣悪な貸間（「台所」）の描写は事細かに描かれているが、「貧民窟」の所在はテクストに明記されていない。「貧民窟」や「長屋」などと訳されているтрущобаには、「貧しく薄汚い、老朽建物密集地、スラム街、またその薄汚れた暗い廃屋、住居」のほかに「難所、僻地、片

田舎」などの意味もある。ペテルブルクのどの辺りだろう。まずはジェーヴシキンの散歩の道筋から所在を推測してみよう。

1-2　散歩の経路

　9月5日の夕方、ジェーヴシキンは気分転換に散歩に出かける。雨雲が空を覆い、足下にはフォンタンカの川霧が漂っていた。河岸通りを歩くジェーヴシキンの目に入ってくるのは、酔っ払い、職人、御者、貧しい小役人、復員兵など大勢の貧しい人々の姿であった。さらにジェーヴシキンが歩いて行くと、フォンタンカ川に架かる「橋の上」で、薄汚れた身なりの年配の女性達が、霧に濡れたまま座り込んで店開きしている。通行人相手に、湿気た糖蜜菓子や腐りかけたリンゴを売っていたのである。足下の石畳は河岸通りの霧で湿り、背の高い、煤だらけの家にも霧がかかり、ジェーヴシキンは侘しい気分になる。

　ゴローホワヤ通りに曲がる頃には辺りは暗くなり、ガス灯に明かりがともりはじめた。ゴローホワヤ通りはうってかわって富裕層の賑やかな街である。公爵令嬢や伯爵夫人を乗せたピカピカの馬車が行き交い、高級洋品店やパン屋が軒を連ね、ショーウインドウがきらきら輝いていた。

　たとえばこうして街を見ながら歩いているうちに、ジェーヴシキンの脳裡に自由思想すなわち理不尽な貧富の差にたいする疑問が湧きはじめ、ペテルブルクが内在化されていくのであった。

　この日のジェーヴシキンは、フォンタンカを下流から上流へ河岸通り伝いに歩き、ゴローホワヤ通りまでやってくると左折して、人通りの多い市内に向かっている。そうであれば、「その辺のどうしようもない屑みたいな飲んだくれが、ワルワーラを馬鹿にする」貧民窟の所在は、フォンタンカ下流域のコロムナ地区すなわちポクロフ広場界隈の可能性が高い。また異なる視点から、すなわち物語に内在化されたペテルブルクにも目を向けて「貧民窟」の所在を絞り込んでいこう。

1-3　マカール・ジェーヴシキンという九等官

　ペテルブルクの「土着民」（ベリンスキー）ジェーヴシキンの性格は、最初の手紙すなわち４月８日付けの２通の手紙からおよその輪郭をつかむことができる。

　４月８日の朝、ジェーヴシキンはワルワーラの部屋の窓辺に置かれたホウセンカの植木鉢をみて驚喜する。カーテンの端が折り曲げられて植木鉢に留めてあったのだ。偶然の悪戯を、ジェーヴシキンは自分への好意のしるしと独り合点して舞い上がり、これからは毎日カーテンで気持ちを伝え合おうと恋人気取りでワルワーラに書き送っている。

　日常の些末な出来事に敏感に反応してしまう感受性の強さと[13]ロマンチックな空想癖は、ジェーヴシキン本人も認めるところであり、何か短い引き写しひとつあれば空想はそれこそ限りなく羽ばたいていくという。

　鉢植えのホウセンカはジェーヴシキンの贈り物である。

　ジェーヴシキンの困窮を知るワルワーラは、贈り物をやめるよう再三頼んでいるがいっこうに伝わらない。その後もジェーヴシキンは花、お菓子、葡萄、下着、刺繍用の絹糸などを贈り続ける。金銭を都合することもある。

　なにも下心があったわけではない。同じアパートの住人ゴルシコフに無心されると、ジェーヴシキンは、自分よりも貧しいという理由でなけなしの20カペイカを渡している。この性格は、ワルワーラが手紙で繰り返し呼びかけるとおりである（「優しいマカールさん」８月４日、「ほんとうにあなたはなんて善良なかたなの」６月11日）。ワルワーラに頼まれ、早起きしてはるばるヴィボルク通りまで足を運ぶのも（８月５日）、役所を休み、風邪を押してまでワルワーラの嫁入り準備に奔走するのも（９月27日）、持ち前の善良さ、優しさからなのである。

13）８月21日の手紙にも「実は私自身も、何でもかんでも敏感に感じてしまうほうでしてね」とある。

感受性が強く、善良で優しい空想家は、気が変わりやすいのも特徴である。4月8日、朝はカーテンの1件で晴れ晴れと伊達男気取りでいたジェーヴシキンであったが、役所にいる間に何ひとつ変化のない現実に空しさを覚え、午後にはすっかり気が滅入ってしまうのであった。同じ日の2通目の手紙で、ジェーヴシキンは、心の赴くままに「気取った文章で馬鹿みたいなことを」書いてしまったと何度もひどく悔しがり、自分の気持は父親の愛なのだと弁解している[11]。

変節の背景にあるのは自分自身への強い関心である。

4月8日の2通の手紙の違いは、1通目が部屋の様子や住人など、身の回りの描写が多いのにたいし、2通目は自己分析や自己主張に終始していることである（「私は決して清潔でも、えり好みが激しいわけでもありません」「私は坊ちゃん育ちとは違います」）。また、ワルワーラの言葉を冷やかしと受け取る自尊心や、ワルワーラの言葉を素直に受け取らない懐疑的な一面も垣間見られる（「私の感情の吐露を、全然見当違いに受け取っています」）。

2通目の手紙からは過剰な自意識も読み取れる。

たがいの部屋の窓が真向かいに面している、ジェーヴシキンとワルワーラのアパートは、述べたような小さな中庭を挟んでいる。この狭い中庭が、ジェーヴシキンには意地悪でそら恐ろしい世間に思えてならない。ワルワーラに招かれても気軽に訪問できないのは、いくら自分はワルワーラの「庇護者」で、父親の愛で接していると公言しても、ワルワーラの家に行くには必ずこの中庭を通らなければならず、通れば間違いなく誰かに目撃され、口さがない連中に「根掘り葉掘り尋ねられたあげく、ありとあらゆるゴシップやデマが飛び交い、ありもしないことを勘ぐら

14）同様の変節はその後も繰り返される。たとえば9月5日の手紙で格差のない、平等な社会の実現が必要だと熱く説いたジェーヴシキンは、4日後に役所で陛下に100ルーブルを下賜されるとブルガーリンの主催する保守系の新聞「北方の蜜蜂」を読み、陛下の寛大さを方々で喧伝し、ワルワーラにも陛下のために祈るよう力説している。

れてしまう」からなのである。恐怖と敵意を抱くほど風聞や世間体を気にするのもジェーヴシキンなのである[15]。

　風采の上がらぬ、50がらみの貧しい小役人の複雑多様な性格は、読み進むうちに輪郭が絞られていく。ジェーヴシキンは、感受性の強い、優しい空想家で、気が変わりやすく懐疑的なところがあり、自己分析に熱心で、落ち込んだかと追うと怪気炎をあげる、躁鬱の差の激しい、自意識過剰な人物として造形されているのである。

　これら複雑で多様な性格は、ドストエフスキーがフェリエトン『ペテルブルク年代記』の中で、ペテルブルクの産物だという、ある種の変わった住人すなわち夢想家のそれと多くの点で一致している。

1-4　夢想家

　『ペテルブルク年代記』の6月15日のフェリエトンによれば、北の町ペテルブルクに自然が必要なように、仕事には愛情と人格のすべてが求められる。しかしながら、愛情を注ぐことのできる仕事に就ける例はごく希である。すると、「活動を望み、直接的実生活を欲し、現実を渇望しているが、弱い、<u>女性的でやさしい性格</u>の人びとの心中には、徐々に謂うところの夢想癖が生じてきて、人はついに人間ではなくて、なにか奇妙な<u>中性的存在物</u>──夢想家になる（傍線引用者）」という。そしてこの「ペテルブルクの悪夢であり、罪の権化であり、悲劇、あらゆる惨劇、あらゆる破局、変転、発端、大団円を見せる、無言の、神秘的な、陰鬱な、野蛮な悲劇」である夢想家には、次のような外見的特徴と性格が備わっているという。

　外見はというと、辛い深刻な仕事を抱えているわけでもないのに、蒼

15）その後もたとえば、「生理学的スケッチ」の対象にされて衣食住にわたって日々の生活が細々と詮索されることに怒りをぶつけ（7月8日）、手紙の下書きをうっかり落としてしまったときにはもう破滅だとわめき立てている（8月11日）。

白い、疲れ切った表情を湛えている。目はとろんとして生気がない。性格のほうは極端に移り気で、躁鬱が激しく、無礼になったり、親切で優しくなったり、エゴイストかと思いきや気高さを示したり、形式主義を嫌う自分がおとなしい形式主義者だったりする。このように、夢想家というのは気分にムラがあり、概して気むずかしい質なので付き合いにくい相手だという。

家ではどうかというと、かれらはふだん隠者のようにひきこもり、感覚を研ぎ澄ませながら書物の「毒」で空想世界を肥大化させている。それもほんの数頁の「毒」さえあれば、まるで熱病に罹ったかのように、精根尽きるまで自分の空想世界に没頭できるという。

空想世界や非現実的な人生に楽しみや幸福を見いだす感受性の強い夢想家にとって現実は往々にして非友好的であり、敵対的ですらある。したがって夢想家はおのずと人を避け、世事に無関心になっていく。この「誤った考え」の結果、夢想家は夢と現実を取り違え、「人生というものは自然と日々の現実における絶えざる自己観照であることを知ろうとしなく」なり、目の前の幸福をつかみ損なって無気力無関心に陥ってしまうのである。

ペテルブルクの夢想家を以上のように説明した後、ドストエフスキーは、次のような独白で締めくくる。「こんな生活が悲劇でないと言えるのか！罪でもなければ、おそろしく困ったことでもないと言えるのか！カリカチュアでないと言えるのか！われわれみんな多少とも夢想家ではないのか！」。

夢想家の、精彩を欠いた風貌も、気難しい性格も、悲劇的運命も、すべて『貧しき人々』の主人公ジェーヴシキンを彷彿とさせる。

ジェーヴシキンも頭の薄い、吹けば飛ぶような風体で、述べたように感受性が強く、やはり書物の引き写しひとつで空想世界に羽ばたく夢想家である。ワルワーラが手紙で呼びかけるように、「誰よりも優しい」人で、「不思議な性質」（8月5日）の持ち主である。「娘」を意味する「ジ

ェーヴシカ」に由来する苗字も「中性的存在物」を思わせる。また移り気で、世間の干渉にたいして、たとえば「意地の悪い毒舌家」どもと敵意をあらわにし（8月5日）、最後は独り「貧民窟」で宛名のない手紙に「ひたすらあなたに書きたい、愛しいワーレンカ」と悲痛な気持を綴って破滅していく。ジェーヴシキンは、まさしく「ペテルブルクの悪夢」の権化といってもよい主人公なのである。

　最初の手紙のジェーヴシキンが幸福の絶頂にいるのも、破局が運命づけられているからにほかならない。

1-5　夢想家に効く薬

　毎日のように役所でからかわれ、虐められ、おどおどしていた夢想家が、「昨日、私は幸せでした」（4月8日）とあふれる歓喜をつたえる相手ワルワーラ・ドブロショーロワは、ジェーヴシキンにいわせると「それはそれは良い影響」（7月1日）を与える相手だという。具体的にみてみよう。

　本来ジェーヴシキンは、「小さな部屋でそっと静かに暮らしていく」（7月8日）のを好む、孤独を愛する内向的性格なのだが、4月8日のジェーヴシキンは、驚くべきことに、みずから進んでアパートの住人たちと交わろうとしたり、窓を開けて春の日差しと香りを楽しんだりしている。ワルワーラがジェーヴシキンの劣悪な住まい（「台所」）を気の毒がると、明るくて「便利で快適そのもの」であるばかりか、家賃が浮いたおかげで砂糖を入れてお茶を飲む余裕もできたと強がり、こうみえても自分は強かで剛毅な男なのだと虚勢を張っている。

　ジェーヴシキンは、ワルワーラに心配をかけまいとして空威張りするだけではない。自己卑下もするが（「私は愚鈍です」7月1日）、みずから自分の価値を認め、自分の内面に目を向け、自分自身を知ろうとし、自分なりに自分自身を理解しているのである。

ジェーヴシキンがみせる、自分自身への強い関心は、これも夢想家とともにドストエフスキーがペテルブルクの観察から得た、同時代のペテルブルク住人の特徴である。6月1日のフェリエトンでドストエフスキーは、同時代を「万人の懺悔の時」と呼び、「人は語り書き、世間の前で己自身を、しばしば心痛と苦悩をもって、分析している」と述べているが、ジェーヴシキンもワルワーラとの出会いによって世間並みに懺悔し、自己分析しながら世の中と張り合っているのである（「私は今ようやく世の中に出たのです」6月21日）。

　清書屋風情がと世間から蔑まれようが、自分はこの仕事に誇りをもっていると胸を張るジェーヴシキンは、「自分は必要不可欠な存在である」（6月12日）とみずから自分の価値を認め、「少しおちついて自分の心をのぞいてみたら、自分が正しかったこと、まったく間違っていなかったことがわかり」（7月28日）、「あなたと知り合ってから、私はまずじぶんというものがよりよくわかるようになり、それからあなたを愛するようになりました」と書いている。このようにジェーヴシキンに、自分が「一人の人間であり、心もあれば頭もある立派な人間なのだと気づいたのです」（8月21日）といわせることが、つまり夢想家ジェーヴシキンが自分自身を肯定的に評価するようになったことが、ワルワーラがもたらした「良い影響」のひとつだったのである。

　自尊心を示し、自己分析に勤しむジェーヴシキンは、女優に熱を上げた昔語りをしたり（7月7日）、感情的になって我を忘れたり、酒で憂さ晴らしをしたり、生きいきと情熱的に自分を表現している。ワーレンカに求婚者があらわれたと聞けば、ワルワーラと自分を侮辱したと大いに憤慨し、酒の力を借りて相手の家に押しかける（7月28日）。ひ弱なジェーヴシキンはたちまち放り出されるが、勇気と男気をみせているのである。

　良いことは良い、悪いことは悪いと正直にいう道徳意識も働くし、良心の呵責を感じれば、嘘をついてしまったことを反省し、謝罪もする。

ワルワーラが落ち込むと「くよくよすることは恥ずかしいことですよ」と励ましと慰めの言葉を書き（6月28日）、相手に同情もすれば、「人の振る舞いの細やかな配慮というもの」に気を配る美徳もみせる（6月26日）。

　このように、20年間も家主の老婆とその孫娘と3人でひっそりと暮らしていた夢想家ジェーヴシキンが、ワルワーラの「良い影響」によって「中性的存在」から、述べたような、道徳意識と美徳をそなえた、情熱的で男性的な1個の人間へと劇的に変化することも、『ペテルブルク年代記』の夢想家の特徴に符号する。

　6月15日のフェリエトンによれば、「病気で変人で陰鬱なペテルブルク」あるいは夢想家にはよく効く「有益なもの」があるという。すなわち夏の別荘生活、自然、運動、太陽、緑の樹木そして「善良な女性」である。これらは、夢想家に道徳感覚を呼び覚まし、現実の幸福をもたらし、無気力無関心から救い出し、人生とは「自然と日々の現実における絶えざる自己観照」であることを教えてくれるのだという。

　なるほどジェーヴシキンとワルワーラの手紙のやりとりは、あらゆる自然がよみがえり、万事快調な春、4月にはじまり、白夜の初夏と別荘生活の夏を経て秋、9月に終わる。そして秋の訪れとともに、「善良さ」と「強情な性分」を象徴する「ロバ」からなる苗字すなわちドブロショーワをもつワルワーラもジェーヴシキンの側から去って行く。ポクロフスキー親子との思い出を綴った手帳で読者の涙を誘う、善良で「意地っ張り」（4月8日）な少女ワルワーラは、自然とともに、ペテルブルクとペテルブルクでうまれる悲劇的タイプに効く「有益なもの」のひとつだったのである。

　このように、ジェーヴシキンには『ペテルブルク年代記』の夢想家の性格や生態が顕著にあてはまるが、それ以外にもまだ当てはまるタイプがある。

　懐疑主義者もそのひとつである。ジェーヴシキンの懐疑的な一面につ

いてはワルワーラとの関係ですでに触れたが、ほかにもたとえばゴルシコフの幼い息子の死に臨み、深い同情を示しながらも口減らしができて両親は喜んでいるかもしれないと邪推するし（6月22日）、知人のエメーリヤが同僚達から受けた十カペイカのカンパを、持てる者の慈善ではなく、見物代とみなす冷めた眼差しがある（8月1日）。

　さらに、過剰な自意識が昂じて被害妄想に陥るタイプも指摘できる。

　述べたように、ドストエフスキーは当時を「万人の懺悔の時」と呼んでいたが、当代のほとんどの人は「分析は分析している者たち自身をも容赦しないこと」を承知していたし、「実におとなしい連中ばかりで、誰を怒らせるつもりもない文士に対して腹を立てるよりも自分自身を知るほうがよいということ」も納得していたという。ところが疑心暗鬼や被害妄想に陥る人々もまだいて、その中の「たいへん興味を引くタイプ」を次のように紹介している。

　　彼らのうちのある者は、事は自分に関することではなく、他の誰かに関することであるにしても、それにしても、なんのために活字にするのか、どうして活字にすることを許すのか、という特別な原理を盾にして、世上人身の退廃と礼儀作法の忘却を声を大にしてあげつらった。またある者は、そんなことをしなくても現に美徳は存在しているではないか、（中略）したがってなんのために美徳の心配をし、それを探し求めるのか、そんなことはただ神聖な美徳の名をむだに用いることに過ぎない、と言った。（6月1日のフェリエトン）

　これは、プーシキンの『駅長』を読んで「自分の人生がそっくりそのまま手に取るように描かれていると感極まり（7月1日）、ゴーゴリの『外套』に激しく憤るジェーヴシキンそのひとである（7月8日）。

　ワルワーラから『外套』を借りたジェーヴシキンは、自分の私生活が「あの男」すなわちゴーゴリに覗き見され、何から何まで暴き立てられ

140

たと憤慨し、いったい「何のために書くのか」と激しく息巻く。

> いったい何のためにこんなことを書くんでしょう？こんなことが何
> のために必要なのか？こんなことを書けば、読者の誰かが外套を作っ
> てくれるとでも言うのでしょうか？いいえワーレンカ、これを読ん
> だら、またその続きを読みたがるだけです。誰でもときには身を
> 潜め、自分の至らなかった点を隠そうとして小さくなり、どこであ
> れ出かけることにもびくびくすることがあるものです。中傷を恐れ
> るからです。世の中の何であれ、あらゆることから怪文書はでっち
> 上げられますからね。それから今や、こちらの市民生活から家庭生
> 活までが洗いざらい文書になって出廻り、何もかもが印刷され、人
> に読まれ、嗤われ、陰口を叩かれているじゃありませんか！これじ
> ゃあ表に顔を出すこともできやしません。なにしろ今では、歩き方
> ひとつ見ただけで、我々小役人だとわかることがすっかり証明され
> てしまったのですからね。（7月8日）

大いに憤ったジェーヴシキンは、自分なら結末で美徳の勝利を訴える
という。

> いちばんいいのは、あの可哀想な主人公を死なせたりせずに、こん
> なふうにすることです――外套は見つかり、彼の美徳の詳細を知っ
> た例の将軍は彼を自分の役所に配置転換させ、官位を上げて給料も
> たっぷり出してやる――こうすれば、いいですか、悪は罰せられ、
> 美徳は勝利し、役所の同僚たちは皆、何ひとつよいことはなかった
> ということになるのです。私だったら、そんなふうにしたでしょう。

ジェーヴシキンは、夢想家を中心として『ペテルブルク年代記』に描
かれている複数の否定的なタイプから複合的に造形された主人公なので

ある。『ペテルブルク年代記』のドストエフスキーが、ペテルブルクを
しばしば擬人化していることを考慮すれば、ジェーヴシキンを、病んだ
ペテルブルクとその住人たちの比喩と考えてもいいだろう。

　実際、優しい「中性的存在物」ジェーヴシキンに起きた変化がもたら
す驚きは、『ペテルブルク年代記』のドストエフスキーが驚く、花咲き
乱れる初夏のペテルブルクの変化にきわめてよく似ている。6月15日
のフェリエトンでドストエフスキーはペテルブルクを「痩せた病身の若
い娘」に喩えていう。

　　わがペテルブルクの自然が、なんだか思いがけず、不意に、その力
　　強さ、そのあらゆる勢力を発揮し、緑を装い、柳絮の芽を出し、着
　　飾って花が咲き乱れるとき、その自然にはなにか説明しがたいナイ
　　ーヴなところ、なにか心を動かすところさえある……どういうわけ
　　かわからないが、こういう自然はわたしに痩せた病身の若い娘を思
　　わせる。その娘をあなたは、時に気の毒に思いながら、時にはなに
　　か同情の愛情をもって眺め、時にはぜんぜん目もくれないのだが、
　　それが突如、一瞬の間だけ、しかもなんとなくわれにもあらず、奇
　　蹟的に、説明しがたく美しくなり、あなたは驚きあきれて、われ知
　　らず自分に尋ねる――いかなる力があのいつも悲しげな、物思いに
　　沈んだ瞳をあのように火のごとく輝かしたのか、何があの蒼ざめた
　　頬に血をのぼせたのか、何があのやさしい顔に情熱と熱望を注いだ
　　のか、なぜ胸があんなに高まるのか、何があの女性の顔に力と活気
　　と美しさをもたらし、その顔をあんな微笑で輝かし、あんなまばゆ
　　いばかりの、火花がはじけるような笑いで生気を取りもどさせたの
　　か？と。あなたは自分のまわりを見まわし、なにかを探す、あなた
　　は気がつく……だが、その一瞬はすぎてしまう、そしてもしかする
　　と、その翌日にはあなたは例の悲しげな物思いに沈んだ、そしてぼ
　　んやりした目付き、例の蒼ざめた顔、例のいつものおとなしい、お

142

　　ずおずした動作、疲労、無力、うつろな哀愁、そして一瞬熱に浮か
　　されたことに対するなにか無益有害な遺憾の念の痕跡にさえ出会う。
　　それにしてもいまさら比喩でもなかろう！（傍線引用者）

　一瞬の驚異的な変化が過ぎ去った「娘」の「例のいつもの」様子は、
先に述べたような、しょぼついた目をした移り気な夢想家の外貌や性格
と同じであり、４月８日のジェーヴシキンにあらわれる、躁鬱の極端な
落差とも重なる。一瞬の高揚ののち、ジェーヴシキンは舞い上がってし
まったことを即座に悔やみ、落ち込んでしまうのであった。
　ペテルブルクを「痩せた病身の若い娘」にたとえたドストエフスキー
は、「娘」を意味するロシア語「ジェーヴシカ」をもとに、自然派の文
士連中の批評の的になっていた「脅しをかけられないと、何ひとつしよ
うとしない」（７月８日）貧しい小役人の名前をつくり、ペテルブルク
から生まれ落ちた優しい夢想家、懐疑主義者、過剰な自意識と被害妄想
の人を描いたのである。

２　『貧しき人々』のペテルブルクあるいはコロムナ

　秋、ペテルブルクが不機嫌な表情を浮かべはじめる頃、まだ夏の名残
があるステップにワルワーラが「あっさり」去って行くと（「どうして
またこんなに急な話なんでしょう」９月23日）、夢想家ジェーヴシキン
に悲劇的幕切れが訪れる。
　ワルワーラがみずから去って行くのは、ジェーヴシキンを造形する、
内在化されたペテルブルクのまた別のタイプが作用したのである。４月
27日のフェリエトンによれば、ペテルブルクという巨大な生体の細胞
を成す、貧しい人々の「小さなサークル」から「我慢のならぬタイプ」
すなわち「善良な心のほかは何ももたない主人公」がうまれるという。

この主人公は未来永劫満ち足りて幸福であるためには自分の善良な心だけで十分だと確信し切って世間に出現するのである。成功疑いなしと信じている彼は世間に打って出るに当って、他のいっさいの手段を蔑視する。彼は、例えば、何事においても控え目にしたり抑えたりすることを知らない。すべてがむき出しで、あけっ放しである。

　この男はいきなり人が好きになって親しくなるという傾向がはなはだしく、しかも誰でもすぐさまそのお返しに、彼が誰でもを好きになったというその事実だけで、みんなが彼を好きになると確信しているのである。

　「この主人公」の片鱗は、ジェーヴシキンの最初の手紙にすでにあらわれている。みたようにジェーヴシキンは一方的に好意を書き連ね、ワルワーラがいくら頼んでも贈り物をやめようとしない。これは善意の押し売りである。自分の赤裸々な思いを手紙に綿々と吐き出し続けるジェーヴシキンには、優しい夢想家、自尊心の強い、自意識過剰な懐疑主義者に加えて無邪気で自分本位な善人も同居しているのである。

　4月8日、贈り物に恐縮したワルワーラは、苦痛を覚えながらもカーテンの端を折り、ホウセンカの鉢にひっかけて謝意を表した。その後もワルワーラは自分のためにお金を使わないようにとたびたび釘を刺し、6月20日の手紙では「金輪際、おやめになって」とはっきり書いている。それでもやめないジェーヴシキンに、「何もしてあげられない」（7月1日）と苦しい胸の内を綴るワルワーラは、ジェーヴシキンの無償の善意が重荷になってくる。借金までして贈り物をしていたことを隠していたジェーヴシキンにワルワーラはつぎのようにいう。

　ああ、マカールさん！　最初のうちのご好意、私に対する共苦のお気持ちや肉親に対するような温かい愛情で留めて、その後の要りも

しないものへの無駄遣いをなさってはいけなかったのです。あなたは私たちの友情を裏切ったのですよ、マカールさん。だって私に隠し立てをなさっていたのですから。（中略）あなたが私に満足感をもたらそうと思ってしてくださったことが何もかも、今や私にとっては悲しみとなり、ただ、今となっては何の役にもたたない悔恨の情を残すばかりです。（7月27日）

　苦痛は募り、とうとうワルワーラのほうからジェーヴシキンに金を工面し、ジェーヴシキンにとってもっとも大切な自尊心を傷つけるに至る（8月13日、8月14日）。それでもジェーヴシキンは、自分がワルワーラを侮辱していることに思い至らない。

　4月27日のフェリエトンによると、この無邪気きわまりないタイプが女性を好きになるとその女性は「彼の愛が原因でやせ細り、ついには彼といっしょにいるのが彼女にはいやでいやで」たまらなくなるという。行き過ぎた善意が相手を侮辱していることに気づかないジェーヴシキンの無邪気さが、ワルワーラの病気の一因となった可能性は否定できない。

　ジェーヴシキンは道徳観も美徳も持ちあわせているが、やはり病気がちのワルワーラには過剰すぎる人なのである。ジェーヴシキンの善意が心に重くのしかかり、苦痛になったワルワーラは、これ以上ふたりが不幸にならないように「お互いに敬遠しなければなりません」（7月27日）と書く。

　こうして物語は、ワルワーラがジェーヴシキンから逃れる手引きをしはじめる。

　アンナの回し者がアパートにあらわれ、恐ろしくなったワルワーラは、ジェーヴシキンに引っ越しのための借金を依頼する。ジェーヴシキンは追い詰められる。借金がうまくいかなければ「死も同然」だし、うまくいって「助けたら助けたで、あなたは私のもとから飛び去ってしまう」（8月4日）からである。

結局ジェーヴシキンは借金に失敗するが、最も恐れることが待っていた。ワルワーラ宛ての手紙の下書きをうっかり落としてしまい、ふたりの関係がアパート中のうわさになるのである。ワルワーラまでが物笑いの種になり、「酔っ払いとくっついている」女と指さされる始末であった。（8月14日）

　ワルワーラの名前はギリシア語の「バルバロイ」に由来するが、自然豊かな田舎から不毛なペテルブルクにやってきた「余所者」ワルワーラは、「私はここを出て行きます」（8月14日）と書き、幸福だった子供時代の田舎の秋に思いを馳せると「ここでこのまま死にたくありません――この土地に埋葬されるのは嫌なのです」（9月3日）といって、ブイコフのプロポーズを受け入れる（「お嫁に行きます」9月23日）。「意地っ張り」のワルワーラに二言はない。しかもジェーヴシキンが驚くほど急に（9月23日）、まるで足早に去ってゆくペテルブルクの夏のように結婚話は進んでいく。

　こうしてジェーヴシキンは、貧民窟で宛名のない便箋にひとり悲しい思いを書き続けることになるのである。

　『ペテルブルク年代記』によれば、この悲劇的な主人公は、世間を避けて「ひどく寂しい、難所（неприступный уголок）」に住んでいる。ジェーヴシキンの住む「とんでもないおんぼろの貧民窟」すなわちтрущобаにも「難所」という意味があることはすでに述べた。

　『貧しき人々』に内在化されたペテルブルクを、『ペテルブルク年代記』をメタ・テクストにして考察してきたが、『貧しき人々』の「貧民窟」の所在は、『ペテルブルク年代記』からうまれた作品に照らしてみてもコロムナの一隅と考えるのが妥当であろう。『かよわい心』のワーシャの婚約者リーザが暮らすのも、『白夜』の夢想家が住む「奇妙な一隅」も、『家主の妻』のオルドィノフが家探しをする、「町の中心部を遠く離れたペテルブルクの町外れ」もコロムナである。先に述べた、ジェーヴシキンの散歩の道筋とも一致する。

　『貧しき人々』のペテルブルクすなわち「貧民窟」をコロムナとする
根拠はもうひとつある。コロムナが、プーシキンやゴーゴリにとっても
特別な場所だったからである。

3　ペテルブルク文学の聖地コロムナ

　プーシキンは、ペテルブルクの最初の住居から目と鼻の間にあったポ
クロフ教会とその界隈を舞台にして『コロムナの家』（1830）を書いた。

> 　後家さんは日曜日には　夏であろうと冬であろうと
> 　娘をつれてポクローフ教会へ行き
> 　会衆の最前列の左側　詠隊席の
> 　かたわらにたたずむのだった。ぼくはいま
> 　あそこには住んでいないが　たしかな夢想の
> 　助けをかりて　目ざめつつ幻の世界にあそび
> 　コロームナへ　ポクローフへと思いをはせ──日曜日には
> 　あの教会のロシアふう公祈祷に出るのが好きだ。　（木村彰一訳）

　『コロムナの家』は次のような物語である。
　コロムナにある年老いた信心深い老母と美しい娘の家で、料理女が降
誕祭前夜に天に召された。娘パラーシャが連れてきた新しい料理女は、
マーヴラという名で、女装した恋人の将校であった。日曜日、マーヴラ
をひとり家に残してパラーシャとポクロフ教会のミサに出かけた老母は、
祈りの途中でマーヴラのことが気になりはじめた。何かくすめたりしな
いだろうか。居ても立っても居られなくなった老母が、パラーシャを教
会においてひとり家に戻ってみると、なんとマーヴラが鏡の前で髭を剃
っている。料理女は、腰を抜かした女主人をひょいとまたいでそれっき

り姿を消してしまった。

　『コロムナの家』は喜劇的小品とされているが、降誕祭をきっかに男女が入れ替わるのは、ロシアの縁日（グリャーニェ）で観られる仮装やペトルーシカ人形芝居などと同じように、「死と再生のパトス」が根底にある「カーニヴァルの笑い」[16]あるいは対称性の社会を再認させる祝祭日の原理が指摘できる。バレエ音楽『ペトルーシカ』で民衆劇の「あべこべの世界」がもたらす生命の再生を表現したストラヴィンスキーが、『コロムナの家』をもとにオペラ・ブッファ『マヴラ』を創作したのも、ロシアの詩情ばかりでなく同様のロシア文化の特徴を見いだしたからであろう[17]。実際『コロムナの家』の語り手は、古めかしい文学を嗤い、祝祭日や定期市の広場で見物人の笑いを呼ぶ道化のように、権威の失墜を目論む叛徒精神を隠さない。

　　　競走馬とぼくは言う！こいつならパルナッソスの
　　　跑馬だって追い抜けまいよ。もっとも天馬ペガソスも
　　　寄る年波でもう歯がないし　ひづめで掘ったれいの泉も
　　　水涸れだ。パルナッソスはいらくさはびこり
　　　アポロンおやじも隠居の身。婆さんミューズの輪踊りなんぞは
　　　ぼくらにとっちゃ興ざめもいいところ。
　　　そこでぼくらは陣営を古典の山の頂から
　　　のみの市へとうつしたしだいだ。（木村彰一訳）

　当時、コロムナのポクロフ（現ツルゲーネフ）広場には聖堂があり、市が立った。人でごった返す「のみの市」や縁日の広場は、王と道化の地位がひっくり返るたびに笑いの渦に包まれ、広場を見護る聖堂では、

16）バフチン『ドストエフスキーの詩学』望月哲男・鈴木淳一訳、筑摩書房、1995年、251頁。
17）拙著『ペテルブルク・ロシア』未知谷、2014年、143頁を参照されたい。

降誕祭や復活祭に天と地が入れ替わった。『青銅の騎士』でピョートル
大帝の騎馬像に挑み、再生神話の儀礼を遂行したエヴゲーニィがコロム
ナの住人であることも考慮すると[18]、プーシキンのコロムナは、ピョー
トル大帝の人工都市の周縁にあって自然が秩序を刷新する神話的境界域
とみていいだろう。

その『コロムナの家』についてゴーゴリは、「プーシキンには八行詩
の物語がある。料理女の物語だが、彼女にはコロムナ全体とペテルブル
クの自然が溌剌としている」[19]と述べ、一連の「ペテルブルク小説」に『コ
ロムナの家』の反転の原理を関連付けた。

降誕祭の反転劇ヴェルテープを物語構造にもつ『ネフスキー大通り』
では、ピロゴーフ中尉が、コロムナのメシチャンスカヤ通りで身分が下
の職人にこっぴどく痛めつけられる。『鼻』ではコロムナに住む床屋の
イワンが、「大地開きの日」の早朝にパンを切り割ると、中から八等官
コワリョフの鼻があらわれる。イワンがネヴァ川に捨てた鼻は、五等官
の制服に身を包み、カザン聖堂にあらわれて官等が下の主人を一蹴する。
『狂人日記』では、コロムナのコクーシキン橋のたもとにある「でかい家」
で、犬のメッジィがポプリーシチンを「道化人形」と嘲笑する。ポプリー
シチンは、最後はみずからスペイン国王を名乗り、癲狂院に送られる。
『肖像画』第1部は、1枚の肖像画に魅入られた貧しい画家チャルトー
フが、金で画壇の頂点に上り詰めるものの、真の才能を目の当たりにし
て自害する物語である。1831年から1年間コロムナに住んでいたゴー
ゴリは、『肖像画』第2部で画家Bの口を借りて、コロムナを次のよう
に紹介している。

　　「みなさんもご存じのように、この市にはコロームナと呼ばれてい
　　る区域があります」と、彼は語りはじめた。「あのあたりはペテル

18）同書、101頁を参照されたい。
19）1831年11月2日、A・S・ダニレーフスキイ宛書簡。

ブルクのほかの区域とはまるきりちがっていて、都でもなければ田舎でもなく、コロームナの通りへ足を踏みいれると、どうしたことか、わかわかしい希望も情熱もみんなどこかへきえてしまうのが自分でもわかるようなところです。あそこには未来というものがなく、なにもかもひっそりと静まりかえり、浮世ばなれしていて、すべてが都会の動きからはなれて澱んでいます。（横田瑞穂訳）

　肖像画のモデルは、エカチェリーナ2世の御代にコロムナに住んでいた冷酷な高利貸しで、死の間際に自分の魂を肖像画に宿して永遠の命を手に入れたのであった。チャルトコーフを含め、肖像画に取り憑かれた人々は誰も彼も悲劇に見舞われた。その肖像画の前で、これは亡父の作品で、見つけ次第破り捨てるようにと生前父に頼まれたとBが来歴を語っている間に、肖像画は忽然と姿を消していた。
　「『外套』の主人公アカーキィ・アカーキエヴィチはコロムナにある自宅に急ぐ」[20]。だがその夜、木造のあばら屋が建ち並ぶ人気のない道を出て、目の前にひらけた「恐ろしい荒野のような場所」すなわちポクロフ広場に足を踏み入れたアカーキィは、仕立て下ろしの外套を強奪されてしまうのであった[21]。アカーキィは長官に直訴するが、頭ごなしに怒鳴り散らされ、ショックのあまり気が触れて昇天する。だがその後アカーキィは、亡霊となって長官の外套を奪い去り、一矢を報いるのだった。
　このように、プーシキンのコロムナを継承したゴーゴリは、社会を笑いで浄化する反転の至芸を繰り広げてみせたのであった。
　反転の原理は、コロムナを内在化した『貧しき人々』にも働いているだろうか。
　『貧しき人々』でドストエフスキーが、ジェーヴシキンにプーシキン

20) Беляева Г. Прогулки по старой Коломне. М.:Центрполиграф. 2009. С. 143.
21) Беневоленская Н. Образ Петербурга в русской литературе XIX века. СПб. 2003. С. 20.

の『駅長』をセンチメンタリズムの小説と誤読させ[22]、また、ゴーゴリの『外套』を世間という恐怖を描いた小説と誤読させたのは、先述した「たいへん興味を引くタイプ」の内在化であると同時に、自然派の伝統——センチメンタリズムと恐怖小説——にたいする立場を明確にしたのであり、それゆえ結末でカラムジンの『哀れなリーザ』（1793）が暗示されるのである。

　カラムジンの『哀れなリーザ』は、ロシアセンチメンタリズムの金字塔といわれる作品である。

　貧しい農民の娘リーザは老母とモスクワ郊外で暮らしている。病弱な母親の面倒を見るため、リーザは町で花を売り歩いている。ある日、エラストという貴族の青年があらわれ、ふたりは深い仲になる。リーザに飽きたエラストは、招集を理由にリーザのもとを去っていく。別れの愁嘆場でリーザは縋るようにいう。「忘れないで、忘れないでねあなたの哀れなリーザを」。それから2ヶ月ほどたったある日のこと、リーザはモスクワの町で商人の後家さんと馬車に乗るエラストを見かける。エラストを訪ねると、事情が変わったと手切れ金を渡される。絶望のあまりリーザは修道院の池に身を投じた。

　ジェーヴシキンは、ワルワーラと家庭を築けなければ「モスクワの後家さんと一緒になったほうがいい」といったブイコフの言葉尻をとらえて何度も繰り返す。「モスクワの後家さんと一緒になったらいい」と。するとワルワーラは、別れの手紙（「明日、私たちは出発します」9月30日）を「忘れないでください、忘れないでくださいあなたのあわれなワーレンカのことを」と結ぶ。これは江川卓が指摘したように、エラストを見送るリーザの愁嘆場を彷彿とさせずにはおかない[23]。

　自分の書簡体小説で、「センチメント」と「センシビリティ」では夢想家という、「ペテルブルクの悪夢であり、罪の権化であり、悲劇、あ

22）江川卓『ドストエフスキー』岩波書店、1984年、43〜45頁。
23）同書、31〜32頁。

らゆる惨劇、あらゆる破局、変転、発端、大団円を見せる、無言の、神秘的な、陰鬱な、野蛮な悲劇」の恐怖から免れることはできないと明言したドストエフスキーは、自然派文学の伝統を次のように転倒する。

　ジェーヴシキンの不幸の原因のひとつは、『駅長』のサムソン・ヴィリンにしろ、『外套』のアカーキィ・アカーキエヴィチにしろ、自分を他者とすり替え、型にはめて自分を理解していることにある。ワルワーラもジェーヴシキンに、「私の人生を通してのみ生きようとなさっている」、それでは不幸になるばかりだと書き送っている（8月5日）。

　『外套』を読み、自分の貧しさが覗き見られ、生活が暴露されたと激しく憤るジェーヴシキンは、バフチンの言葉を借りれば「自分があらかじめ絶望的なまでに決定され、まるでもう死んでしまった人間のように、おしまいにされてしまっているのを感じた」のである[24]。だが、死ぬ前から死んでしまっているジェーヴシキンは憤る。憤るのは、「同時にそのような仕打ちが間違っていること」も感じたからである。「文学的に完結されてしまった自らの像に対する主人公」のこの憤りを、バフチンは「風変わりな《叛逆》」と呼んでいるが、先述の「たいへん興味を引くタイプ」を念頭に置いてのことだろう。ジェーヴシキンは、たとえ「風変わり」でも、「死人扱いするような他者の評言の枠を打ち破ってやろう」[25]とする「《叛逆》」児なのである。この善良な夢想家である「風変わりな《叛逆》」児に、『貧しき人々』のメタ・テクスト『ペテルブルク年代記』は生きる力のベクトルを示している。

　　生きるとは、自分自身を素材にして芸術作品を作ることであるということを忘れている、いや、夢にも考えていないのである。彼の宝であり、彼の資本である善良な心は、社会の大衆が目に入らない半睡状態、無関心状態、孤独の中においてではなく、広い関心、社会

24）バフチン前掲書、120～121頁。
25）同書、122頁。

152

の大衆とその直接的要求に対する共感の中においてはじめて磨かれて、貴重な、贋物でない本物の輝くダイヤモンドとなるのだということを忘れているのである！（4月27日のフェリエトン）

　ベケートフ兄弟及びペトラシェフスキーのサークルに接近し、キリスト教的社会主義に傾倒していたドストエフスキーは、ジェーヴシキンのような善良な心が真価を発揮できる新しい社会の到来をペテルブルクの営みの中で予感しており、同じフェリエトンで「明るい喜ばしげな光線」に喩えている。

　「濃い紫色のもやの中から一瞬だけ元気よく飛び出してきて」、不機嫌で仏頂面のペテルブルクの「陰気なじめじめした壁にちらつき、雨の雫の一滴一滴の中でくだけて千の火花」となるこの「明るい喜ばしげな光線」は、『ペテルブルク年代記』からうまれた『かよわい心』（1848）では、凍てつく夕映えのネヴァ河岸に輝く「幾千万とも知れぬ細かい火花」となって、無邪気な善人アルカージィに、「ネワの幻想」とも「消え去るペテルブルク」ともいわれる「新しい黄金時代」の暗示をもたらす。

　このように、コロムナを内在化した『貧しき人々』には、自然派を転倒して、「貧民窟」という「難所」がやはり「難所」であるユートピアに変転する予感が秘められているのである。

おわりに

　ペテルブルクとペテルブルク住民のフェリエトン集『ペテルブルク年代記』をメタテクストとして『貧しき人々』を検討した結果、ジェーヴシキンが夢想家をはじめとする病んだペテルブルクの比喩の集合体であること、ドストエフスキーが反転のトポスであるコロムナを継承して、

躍動するペテルブルクで夢想家のロシアを変容させようとしていたことが明らかになった。

　ジェーヴシキンは、ゴーゴリをはじめとする自然派小説の小役人たちのように、不遇を託つばかりではなかった。たとえ一時的ではあれ、自然やワルワーラから良い影響を受けて自分を生き生きと肯定的に受け入れ、自由思想を口にする「風変わりな《叛逆》」児であった。

　ドストエフスキーは「風変わりな《叛逆》」児ジェーヴシキンに形象化された、悲劇的に自己完結してしまうペテルブルクの生きる力を、社会全体の営みの中で変容できると考えたので『貧しき人々』の舞台をコロムナに設定したのである。

　『かよわい心』で「幾千万とも知れぬ細かい火花」となった「明るい喜ばしげな光線」は、シベリア流刑後のフェリエトン『ペテルブルクの夢』（1861）では「限りない億万の針のような霜の火花」となり、さらに『未成年』（1875）のアルカージィには、疲れ切った青銅の馬が吐く「火のような息」となって「新しい黄金時代」の幻あるいは雲散霧消するペテルブルクのイメージが繰り返されていく。

　『貧しき人々』はゴーゴリ時代の旧来の手法にとどまらず、『ペテルブルク年代記』にも、またその後の作品にもアーチを架けていたのである。

注
ドストエフスキーの作品からの引用は以下に拠った。記して謝意を表す。
• ドストエフスキー『貧しき人々』安岡治子訳、光文社、2010 年
• ドストエフスキー『ペテルブルク年代記』染谷茂訳（『ドストエフスキー全集』第 24 巻、新潮社、1979 年所収）

文献一覧
江川卓『ドストエフスキー』岩波書店、1984 年
近藤昌夫『ペテルブルク・ロシア』未知谷、2014 年
コマローヴィチ『ドストエフスキーの青春』中村健之介訳、みすず書房、1978 年
バフチン『ドストエフスキーの詩学』望月哲男・鈴木淳一訳、筑摩書房、1995 年

Анциферов Н. Душа Петербурга. М. 2014.

Беляева Г. Прогулки по старой Коломне. М.:Центрполиграф, 2009.

Беневоленская Н. Образ Петербурга в русской литературе XIX века. СПб. 2003.

付記
本研究は JSPS 科研費 JP17K02631 の助成を受けたものです。

『歴史的なもの』と『歴史主義』の懸隔

ベルジャーエフ、サルトル、カミュ、ポンティ、アロン

川　神　傳　弘

1　客観的真理から主体的内面への移動

　ニコライ・ベルジャーエフは 1900 年代初頭から 1930 年代のロシアで、特に進歩の観念に潜む危険性について深い洞察を展開した実存哲学者である。その哲学思想は形而上学的文明批評の趣を濃厚に示しているが、基底に宗教的かつ神秘主義的啓示を契機とする実存的体験が横たわっている点で特異である。実存的と称される思想家であったが、第二次大戦後フランスで流行したサルトルの無神論的実存主義の趨勢のためにベルジャーエフは霞んでしまったかに見えるが、その遠因は 18 世紀のヴォルテールに代表される啓蒙主義思想に求められるべきであろう。

　18 世紀はヴォルテールの世紀と称され、「光明の世紀」siècle des lumières とも言われるが、光は理性を意味する言葉で、悟性、認識、精神の明晰や精神が獲得する知識を意味することもあった。彼ら 18 世紀の文人たちは〈光明の人＝哲学者〉呼ばれる科学の探求者であり、彼らには一様に宗教の軛を脱して、一切を理性の立場から批判しようとする精神態度が窺える。その批判精神は時として直接行動に結びつくこともあり、その意味でヴォルテールは文学者の政治・社会参加の草分け的な存在でもある。批判精神は言い換えれば自由検討の精神であり、理性がいわば活動の自由を得て、あらゆる分野に懐疑と批判の目を向ける時代が到来したのである。理性を普遍的審判者とする点では 17 世紀と符

号を一にするが、伝統的権威を否定し、政治問題や社会問題をも批判対象とした点において若干異なる。

ルネッサンス以前のヨーロッパではキリスト教の教義が客観的真理であり、人々はその教義に則って生活した。だから中世人の生活は宗教による縛り故に、自由を奪われた抑圧社会であったという見方もできるが、それは逆に言えば、自分たちは神によって守られているという安堵を感じる社会でもあったということもできる。

ところで、17世紀では、地政学的に見て全ヨーロッパの三分の二が教会領であり、頂点に達した教会権力の腐敗が始まる。こうした状況は否応なく教会の伝統的権威の失墜に繋がる。キリスト教会の赫々たる権威が衰えるのに比例して人々は神への信頼を失う。こうしたベクトルは彼ら信徒たちをして個人的主体への着目に赴かしめるのである。つまり頼るべき支柱を失った個人は、必然的に頼れる対象を自己自身に向け始めたのである。こうして"自分以外に頼るものはない"という想いが、その後ルターやカルヴァンによる宗教改革や宗教戦争を経て、人々はそれまでの神中心の枠を超えた人間個人の、即ち自分自身の精神生活の重視を招来する方向に仕向けたということになる。つまり人間は徐々に宗教の軛を逃れて人間的実存の主体的内面に目を向けるようになってゆく。神を想う以前に、また神を思う以上に「生きている自分がまずある」という認識は「実存」の認識と言える。

しかし、人々は一挙に無神論に奔るほどの勇気を持ち合わせなかった。かくて神の存在を人間理性が説明し、神を理論的に解釈する時代が訪れた。その時点で神は崇められるべき対象の地位から滑り落ちた。このような考え方を理神論 déisme と言い、無神論に到る前段階として18世紀啓蒙主義時代に生まれたが、それは自然宗教 religion naturelle とも言いうる神学で、それまでの護教的イデオロギーに対抗する有力な武器となった。ヴォルテールが推し進めた啓蒙主義はこういう性格のもので、理性と理論に根差す信仰を重んじる宗教観である。人間は啓示や聖書に

拠らなくても被造物や自然を通して善を知ることができ、そもそも神は
人間を合理的存在として創造されたとする考えである。この考え方は結
局フランス革命につながるのであり、フランス革命の思想は、その時代
の信仰の中に既に非宗教的性格を宿していたと言える。

2　主体的内面の重視

　個人の内面を重視する、実存的内面の吐露がそれ以前に無かったわけ
では勿論ない。ポール・ヴァレリーは自著『精神の危機』の序章におい
て「内面生活を西欧の人間に教えたのはキリスト教である」と語り、「キ
リスト教は人間の精神にこの上なく微妙な、この上なく重要かつ豊饒な
問題を提起した」としてその例をいくつも挙げているが、なかでも「知
識の拠ってきたる源泉・確実性とか、理性と信仰の間に起こる対立とか、
信仰と行為・奉仕の間の矛盾とか、自由・隷属・恩寵」などの項目はそ
のまま主体的内面・内省に繋がるものと思われる。

　17世紀のデカルトが理性の尊重を唱えて以降、それ以前には「神」
に遠慮して後塵を拝していた個人主体という考えが前面に躍り出て、主
体的内面が公言されるようになったということは、いわばキリスト教精
神から個人的主体の分離が始まった事実を物語っている。それでもやは
り18世紀における人間存在の在り方に関する考え方は理性尊重、理性
信仰などの客観的真理を拠り所とする本質論的人間観であったと言える。
大っぴらに個人的実存の主体的内面表現が跳梁するには、果たして20
世紀の無神論的実存主義の到来を俟たねばならない。人間は如何なる存
在？人間の存在の在り方はどのようなものであろうか？

　20世紀になって存在論の哲学で華々しく登場したのがサルトルである。
しかしながらサルトルは、あれほど精力を傾けて執筆した『存在と無』
において、広範なスペースを割いて披歴した「絶望」論や「不安」論を

簡単に否定してしまうのである。それはまた、『嘔吐』の時代を彼が乗り越えた事実を意味するものでもあった。『嘔吐』の主人公ロカンタンが、モノを凝視するたびに催していた嘔吐感や不安、絶望の時代が去ったのだ。それは「即自存在と対話する対自存在」という図式からの解放をも意味していた。1980年3月ヌーヴェル・オプセルヴァトゥール紙上で三度にわたって連載されたベニ・レヴィーとの対談でも繰り返して述べているし、ヌーヴェル・オプセルヴァトゥール紙上でもはっきり述べている。

　　絶望について語りはしたが、あれはでたらめだ。[1]

と語り、戦後になって"新たな状況の中で新たな選択をなす自由"に目覚めたことを告白している。過去の言説が現状に合わないとなれば、新たな状況・situation に取り組まなければならない。かくしてサルトルは躊躇うことなく過去の自説を翻すようになる。その言説は状況の推移に応じてメアンダーを余儀なくされる性格のものとなる。それはサルトル特有の恒常的自己超越・dépassement とも言えるもので、彼は自分の過去に対しても自由であることを、自らの言動を通じてわれわれに提示したと言えよう。かくてサルトル思想の特質は<u>超越・生成</u>となり、彼は時代と状況によって前言撤回 revenir sur ～することを躊躇しなくなる。このやり方は一部読者を白けさせ、センセーショナルな議論を呼び起こすものであったが、主体的人間や人間存在の在り方への関心や拘泥以上に価値ある思想を彼が見出したからであろう。平たく言えば彼は自分の気持ちに正直な人間なのだ。

1）サルトル、『いま　希望とは』「朝日ジャーナル」海老坂武訳、1980, 4, 18, 13頁.

（1）「私は不安といったことを随分語ったが、実は自分が不安などを覚
　　えたことは一度もない。あれはただのモードの問題に過ぎなかった」[2]

（2）飢えて死ぬ子供を前にして『嘔吐』は無力である”“作家たるものは、
　　今日飢えている二十億の人間の側に立たねばならず、そのためには
　　文学を一時放棄することもやむを得ない。

　この時点でサルトルの哲学は超越と生成の哲学・philosophie du
dépassement et du devenir へと舵を切るのである。1964年ル・モンド
紙のインタビューに応えて彼が発した回答は、言わば彼自身の過去の生
きざまを否定するものであっただけにかなりの反響を巻き起こした。

　以上二件の表明は要するに、それまでの主体性と主観性の実存主義、
つまり作品『嘔吐』の示す無力性から人救い主義宣言への移行表明であ
り、それは価値判断として個人の“内的現実”を重視する感覚的実存体
験の表現から、より客観的で主知主義的なものへの変貌を示すものであ
る。つまりサルトルの視点が〈個〉から〈全体〉を俯瞰するポイントに
移動したのである。それは美しくない美意識から救済・人救いの観念へ
と重点が移動したとも言えよう。ある意味でそれは宗教的範疇に属する
ものとなり、かくしてサルトルは戦後急速に神なき宗教とも言うべきマ
ルクス主義に接近することになる。
　実は、第二次大戦後の無神論的実存主義者の泰斗であったサルトルが
フランス共産主義に急接近する切掛けを作ったのはメルロ＝ポンティで
あった。ポンティの『ヒューマニズムと恐怖政治』[3]は当時右傾化しつ
つあったフランス知識人を呼び戻す効果を狙ったものであったが、その

　2）サルトル追悼、「アンドレ・グリュックスマンに聴く」、『海』中央公論、
　　1980, 7月号　328頁〜、西永良成訳.
　3）メルロ＝ポンティの『ヒューマニズムと恐怖政治』.

論考の根底にはヘーゲルの歴史哲学・歴史主義が横たわっているのである。つまり、ヘーゲルの歴史観がサルトルの歴史観となり、更にそれがメルロ＝ポンティに受け継がれた。その歴史観を端的にメルロ＝ポンティは次のように語る。

　「歴史は本質的に闘争である。主人と奴隷の闘争であり、階級の闘争である。人間の条件の必然性によってそのようになるのである。それはまた、人間の精神と肉体、つまり無限と有限が分かちがたいものであるという根源的パラドクスによるものである。具体的な人間存在のシステムとして、各人は他者を客体として扱うことによってしか自分を肯定することができない」。[4]

　かくして、ヘーゲルの歴史主義はマルクス主義におけるプロレタリア革命の理想的目標に変わり、やがてロシアにおける『スターリンの大テロル』[5]に代表される大恐怖政治、すなわち密告制度や強制収容所送り、拷問、暴力、虐殺などによる人民の抑圧体制を生みだす原因となったのである。拙稿は、左翼思想の理想的な目標が如何なるものであったのかを、ベルジャーエフの言う「歴史的なもの」とヘーゲル的「歴史主義」の相違を比較することによって、そのイメージを明らかにする試みである。

3　時代のエートス ethos

　エートス ethos とは、一時期ある国民や社会に蔓延する雰囲気と理解してもらいたい。ヘーゲルの「歴史哲学」が運用されるべき時代のエートスがまずあった。1950 年前後においては〈全体主義〉なる語彙や概

4）Merleau-Ponty, *Humanisme et Terreur*, Gallimard, 1947, *Le Yogi et le Prolétair*, p.110.
5）O. フレヴニューク、『スターリンの大テロル』、富田武士訳、岩波書店、1997. 3-4 頁.

念は未だ人口に膾炙したものではなかった。知識人たちにしても、それがファシズム的かつネガティヴな概念であると承知していても、一知半解の域を超えるものではなかった。全体主義という語彙は 1920 年頃イタリアのファシズムを対象にロンドンタイムスが使用したとされるが、大方のフランス知識人の理解では、この語彙の向かう矛先は、ナチス・ドイツのファシズムであった。なぜなら、知識人世論は「ソ連は社会主義の祖国であるから、その共産党の政治指導の在り方を直截的に非難することはタブー」とするのが一般的であったからだ。いわばそのようなエートスがフランス社会に定着していた。

　フランスでは大戦終了前後から、ロシアのスターリン体制下において民衆の自由や人権が抑圧されているという報告が洩れ伝わり始めていた。しかし、ソ連に《均質的で普遍的な社会》という〈理想郷〉実現の夢を託していた大半の知識人らにとって、そのような報告は単なる噂の域に止まるものでしかなかった。例えば 1936 年ソヴィエト連邦から帰国したアンドレ・ジッドの著した『ソヴィエト紀行』 *Retour de l'U.R.S.S.* は既にしてソ連の強制収容所の存在を示唆するものであったが、ロマン・ロランやアンリ・バルビュスなどフランス知識人の要求を容れて、ジッドは『ソヴィエト紀行修正』を出さざるを得なかった事実が、当時のフランスの思想的雰囲気を表している。

　しかしながら、ソ連の恐怖政治は着々と進行していた。1936 年 7 月第一次モスクワ裁判の開廷以降、スターリンの〈大粛清〉が始まる。裁判はその後 1937 年 1 月、3 月の計三回に及ぶ反革命分子に対する公開裁判であった。実際にはソ連経済の混乱と国民生活の貧窮を被告人の陰謀のせいにし、指導者の執政の失敗を糊塗するために行われたのである。大テロルとも称される大粛清では、一旦〈人民の敵〉の嫌疑をかけられると、被告の同僚、友人、親族にまで同様の疑いがかけられた。また、密告の奨励と相互的監視体制が強化される。拘禁所の拷問による自白の強要による犠牲者は 1937-8 年だけで数百万人と言われる。一般に粛清

purge は、本来政治的意味合いで党からの除名を意味するものであったが、以上のような経緯で大量抑圧を強調するためにテロルとよばれるようになったのである。

　モスクワ裁判は見せしめであると同時に、見せかけの裁判であった。スターリンはこの裁判で反対派のみならず、自分に忠実であった人間をも粛清し犠牲者にした。この時代、でっち上げの無実の判決で命を落とした人は、裁判によって処刑された者100万人、強制収容所で死亡した者2,000万人と言われるが、ロベール・コンケストは1970年刊行の『大恐怖政治』[6]において、1936-50年強制収容所での死亡者に3,000万人という数字を計上している。

　O. プレヴニュークの『スターリンの大テロル』では1937-38年に概数ながら700万人が逮捕され100万人が銃殺され、200万人が強制収容所で死亡したとされる。1938年末では監獄に約100万人、強制収容所には約800万人の囚人がいた。この二年間だけの数字は、スターリン（「鋼鉄の人」の意で、本名ではない）の時代全体に想いを馳せるとき、それ以上の数字を想像させるに充分であろう。彼の独裁体制は1929-50年にかけて実に20年間に及ぶものであるからだ。またハンナ・アーレントは自著『全体主義の起源』[7]において2,600万人という数字を挙げているが、いずれも正確な数字ではない。その著でアーレントは「ナチ政権が犠牲者をまことに正確に把握していたのに反し、ロシア体制では消耗した数百万の人々については信頼できる根拠に立つ数字が全く存在しないからだ」と述べている。当初数多の犠牲者が増加し続けるソ連内部の状況にフランスが動じる気配がなかった理由の一つは、自国がドイツ占領下にあったためであろう。

　大戦終了後フランス人は数年前までナチス・ドイツが設置していたア

6）Robert Conquest, *La Grande Terreur*, Paris, 1970.
7）ハンナ・アーレント、『全体主義の起源3』、大久保和郎訳、みすず書房、2003年、7-8頁.

164

ウシュビッツ、トレブリンカ、ブッヘンバルトなどの強制収容所からの
生還者がもたらす手記に敏感な反応を見せた。具体的には、1943 年ド
イツ占領下でドイツ国防軍兵士に対する政治活動の廉で逮捕され、拷問、
監禁の後ブッヘンバルト強制収容所に送られた困苦の体験者ダヴィッド・
ルッセの報告である。ルッセはソ連にもドイツと同様の収容所 camp
de concentration が存在することを知らしめると同時に、かつての収容
所仲間に呼びかけて〈ソヴィエト連邦収容所に反対する国際委員会〉を
立ち上げた。因みに、ラーゲリ goulag という言葉によって初めてソ連
の収容所のシステムを紹介したのもルッセであった。

　ソ連国内の凄まじい抑圧体制に関して陸続ともたらされる報告は徐々
にフランスの知識人の牢固とした認識の隙間に浸み込んでいった。分け
ても、革命的暴力の象徴ともいえる強制収容所の存在が露呈するに至り、
知識人らはロシアの抑圧体制とマルクス主義理論のはざまに整合性を見
出しうるのか否かを模索しつつも、コミュニズムへの信頼は揺るぎ始め
る。全体主義の非道な体制はファシズムにのみ限定されるものと信じて
いた彼らにとって、人民の理想を追求するコミュニズムの祖国が、実は
一党独裁支配、密告、追放、強制収容所送り、拷問、暴力、虐殺などの
手段を駆使する過酷な抑圧体制であり、要は恐怖政治 terreur 体制であ
るとは信じがたいことであった。かくして、様々な情報故に知識人は、
全体主義はファシズムであれコミュニズムであれ、いわば左右どちら側
にも発生し得る現象なのだという可能性に目覚めたと言えよう。

4　知識人の動揺

　こうした状況は《均質的で普遍的な国家》État hommogène et universel
実現の夢を共産主義体制に託していたフランス知識人を動揺させること
になった。それまでナチス Nationalsozialist ドイツに象徴されるファシ

ズムの対蹠的位置にあって、180度異なる“理想の体制”と仰ぎ見てき
た共産主義国家の実情報告によって、共産主義とファシズムに対する見
方の変更を余儀なくされるのである。これら二項を同一視する人々が現
れ、ついには反共産主義anti-communismeに傾く者が徐々に増えてゆく。
また、時宜を得てこの動向に拍車をかける小説が生まれた。ハンガリー
生まれの作家アーサー・ケストラーによる『真昼の暗黒』である。「モ
スクワ裁判」に取材したこの作品は1945年フランス語訳されている（フ
ランス語訳は『ゼロと無限』）。とはいえ、アメリカとソ連がリーダーと
なって対峙する資本主義と社会主義という世界観の二極構造においては、
大方の知識人は社会主義陣営支持であり、ソヴィエト贔屓であることに
変わりはなかった。それが知識人社会の常識であり、ある意味で社会主
義的であることが知識人の資格とするエートスが醸成されていたとも言
えよう。かく常識として定着する要因となったのは1916年にレーニン
の書いた『帝国主義論』によるというのが通説である。

　ところで、一般にヘーゲルによる歴史の段階的発展論に具体的なイメ
ージを与えたのはマルクス主義ということになっている。しかし、レイ
モン・アロンは、On a guère lu,en France, le Capital, et les écrivains
s'y réfèrent rarement.[8]「フランスでは『資本論』はほとんど読まれな
いし、著作家はめったにこれに言及しない」と語っている。したがって、
マルクスの『資本論』よりもむしろ資本主義経済の最高の発展段階に到
達した帝国主義について「資本主義は死滅しつつあり、現在は社会主義
革命の前夜である」とするレーニンの『帝国主義論』の主張の方が感覚
的かつ直接的に知識人を魅了したと思われる。〈弱者＝プロレタリアー
トの救済〉という煌きを放つ大義名分が1940-50年代の知識人を魅了し、
共産主義志向に奔らせたという推測が可能である。「マルクス主義の宣
伝活動は常に資本主義の根本的不正の認識を培い、搾取の原理でこれを

8）Raymond Aron, l, *Opium des Intellectuels*, Calmann-Lévy, 1955, p.85.

補強し続けていたからである」[9]というアロンの言葉からも、それを窺い知ることができる。

5　平等主義的・共産主義的幻想の源流

　現代共産主義の理想郷の源流は、ノーマン・コーンの『千年王国の追究』によれば、キリスト教宗教思想のなかに漂っていた幻想的信仰にあったようだ。信仰の根底にあったのは〈ヨハネの黙示録〉を拠り所とする貧民たちの間に生じたメシア（救世主）待望論であり、8世紀から16世紀にかけて中世ヨーロッパの各地で起きた宗教的異議申し立ての無政府主義的な運動の総称のようである。なお、「千年王国説」は「至福千年説」とも称されるものであることを予めお断わりしておく。

　ノーマン・コーンの『千年王国の追究』によると、キリスト教は〈終わりの時〉〈終わりの日〉〈この世の終わりの姿〉に関する教理という意味で、常に一種の〈終末論〉を内包してきた。千年王国主義はキリスト教的終末論の変形にすぎない。そのセクトや運動が描く救世観の特徴は共同体的であること、彼岸でなくこの地上で実現されるという意味で現世的であること、単なる現状改善でなく完璧を期す意味では絶対的であること、ほどなく忽然と現れるという意味で緊迫的であること、超自然的な力によって完成されるという意味では奇跡的であることなどであるが、この幻想的信仰にたいする現世的宗教を奉じるセクト集団の境遇は悲惨で不安定であり、彼らは狂暴で無秩序、時には文字通り革命的であった。[10]

　「千年王国主義高揚の世界と社会不安の世界とは、当時ぴったりと重なり合っていたのではなく、部分的に重なっていた。生活の物質的条件

9）ibid., p.84.
10）ノーマン・コーン、『千年王国の追究』、江川徹訳、紀伊国屋書店より。

を改善したいという貧民通有の願望が、最後の黙示録的大虐殺世界を通して無垢へと再生した世界の幻想と混じり合っていた。悪人たちは皆殺しにされ、そのあと聖徒たちすなわち当の貧民たちが、彼らの王国、苦しみも罪もない国土を築くことになるというものであった。このような幻想に駆り立てられてあまたの貧民たちが果敢な行動に走ったが、それは一揆とは全く異質なものであった。ある意味において、今世紀の幾つかの大きな革命運動の真の先駆を示唆するものであった」。[11]

更に、コーンはヨーロッパの平等主義的共産主義の起源について次のような見解も付け加えている。

「ヨーロッパの革命的終末論を形成するに至った様々な中世の幻想と同様に、その起源は古代世界にまで遡ることができる。中世ヨーロッパが、身分・財産の平等や、なにびとからも抑圧や搾取を受けることなき状態、普遍的信頼と同胞愛、財産と配偶者を完全に共有することを特色とする状態、つまり〈自然状態〉なる観念を継承したのはギリシャ・ローマ人からであった。ギリシャ・ローマの文学では、〈自然状態〉は遠い昔に失われた黄金時代に地上に存在したものとして描かれている。オヴィディウスの『転身物語』にあるその神話表現は、後世の文学の中で反復して表現され、中世時代の共産主義思想に著しい影響を及ぼすことになった」。[11]

このように、当時のソ連のプロレタリア革命が目指した《均質的で普遍的な国家》や平等主義の観念の基盤は、幻想的信仰や文学が養い育てた、ある意味で神話と言ってよいものであるが、その幻想的神話の根は深い。

11）ibid., p.5.

6　サルトルと、先鋒メルロ＝ポンティによる進歩的暴力理論

　第二次大戦の終戦前後からすでに兆候はあったが、戦後になってソ連国内の凄まじい抑圧体制の存在について陸続ともたらされる報告が徐々にフランス知識人の、ソ連贔屓の牢固たる認識を揺るがし始める。就中、革命的暴力の象徴とも言うべき強制収容所の存在が隠しようもなく露呈するに至り、知識人らはロシア国内の抑圧体制とマルクス主義理論の間に整合性を見出すことの可否を模索し、コミュニズムに対する信頼継続を逡巡せざるを得なくなるのである。かくして一部フランス知識人のコミュニズムを支える信念も揺らぐことになった。

　前述したことだが、全体主義の非道な体制はファシズム社会にのみ限定されるものと信じていた彼らにとって、人民の理想を追求するコミュニズムの祖国が、実は一党独裁の支配体制で、密告の奨励、追放、強制収容所送り、拷問、暴力、虐殺などを駆使する過酷で抑圧的な体制であって、その実態が恐怖政治 terreur であることなど到底信じられなかったのである。聞こえてくる様々な情報は、全体主義がファシズム、コミュニズム左右いずれの側にも発生しうる現象である可能性を否定しがたいものにしてゆく。ナチス Nationalsozialist ドイツがその先鋒であるファシズムと対蹠的位置にあって、180 度異なる "理想の体制" とみなされてきた共産主義国家の実情報告によって、共産主義とファシズムを同一視する人々が現れてくる。こうして反共産主義 anti-communisme に傾倒する人々が増えてゆくことになった。時宜を得てハンガリー生まれの作家アーサー・ケストラーによる『真昼の暗黒』が出版されて反共的動向に拍車がかかった。"モスクワ裁判" に取材したこの小説作品は1945 年フランス語訳されている（フランス語訳では『ゼロと無限』）。

　1947 年このような反共産主義的気運が醸成されつつあった情況に大

きく揺さぶりをかける一書が刊行された。メルロ＝ポンティの『ヒューマニズムと恐怖政治』Humanisme et Terreur[12] である。あらかじめ『ヨガ行者とプロレタリア』le Yogi et le prolétaire のタイトルでサルトル主幹の『現代』誌上に掲載されたこの論考は、先のアーサー・ケストラーの『真昼の暗黒』に対する批判的考察を試みた本であるが、左翼陣営からすれば右傾化しつつある世論に歯止めをかける目論見によって出されるべくして出た論文であった。その主張を鮮明に特徴づける見解をいくつか紹介する。

L'histoire est donc essentiellement lutte, — lutte de maître et de l'esclave, lutte des classes, — et cela par une nécessité de la condition humaine et en raison de ce paradoxe fondamentale que l'homme est indivisiblement conscience et corps, infini et fini. Dans le système des incarnées, chacun ne peut s'affirmer qu'en réduisant les autres en objets.[13]

「歴史は本質的に闘争である。主人と奴隷の闘争であり、階級の闘争である。人間の条件の必然性ゆえにそのようになるのである。それはまた、人間の精神と肉体、つまり無限と有限が分かちがたいものであるという根源的なパラドクスによるものである。具体的な人間存在のシステムとして、各人は他者を客体として扱うことでしか自分を肯定することができない」。

Une révolution, même fondé sur une philosophie de l'histoire est une révolution forcée, est violence.[14]

「革命は、それが仮令歴史哲学に基づくものであっても強制された革命であり、暴力である」。

---

12) Merleau-Ponty, *Humanisme et Terreur*, Gallimard, 1974, *Le Yogi et le Prolétaire*, p.110.
13) Merleau-Ponty, *Humanisme et Terreur*, Gallimard, 1974, *Le Yogi et le Prolétaire*.
14) ibid., p.110.

La terreur historique culmine dans la révolition et l'histoire est
terreur.[15]

「歴史上恐怖政治は革命において絶頂に達する。歴史とは恐怖政治で
ある」

こうした文言が示唆するように、彼は未来のヒューマニズムのために
暴力を伴う革命の必要性を説く。かくして有名な《進歩的暴力理論》
violence progressive の登場となる。その骨子となる内容はほぼ次のよ
うなものだ。

メルロ＝ポンティは「非暴力というリベラルな原則は政治的な弁別基
準としてはまったく役に立たない。なぜなら、万一この点でコミュニズ
ムがファシズムと同一視されるとしても、それはリベラリズムについて
も同じことが言えるからである」と前置きした上でこう続ける。

La révolution assume et dirige une violence que la société
bourgeoise tolère dans le chômage et dans la guerre et camoufle
sous le nom de fatalité. Mais toutes les révolutions réunies n'ont pas
versé plus de sang que les empires. Il n'y a que des violences, et la
violence révolitionnaire doit être préférée parce qu'elle a un avenir d'
humanisme.[16]

「革命は、ブルジョワ社会が失業や戦争を許容し、運命の名において
カムフラージュした暴力に責任を持ち、指揮を執る。しかしすべての革
命を束にしても、様々な帝国が流してきた血の量を超えることはない。
暴力しかないのである。革命の暴力は、ヒューマニズムの未来あるがゆ
えに、より好ましいものであるはずだ」。

次に彼は《普遍的階級》の暴力とファシズムの暴力の違いに言及する。

Car si prorétariat est la force sur laquelle repose la société
révolutionnaire, et si le prolétariat est cette《classe universelle》que

---

15）ibid., p.99.

16）ibid., p.98.

nous avons décrite d'après Marx, alors les intéréts de cette classe portent dans l'histoire les valeurs humaines, et le pouvoir du prolétariat est le pouvoir de l'humanité. La violence fasciste, au contraire, n'est pas celle d'une classe universelle, c'est celle d'une 《race》 ou d'une nation tard venue.[17]

　「万一プロレタリアートが革命社会の力であるとすれば、またプロレタリアートがマルクスの言うような《普遍的階級》であるとすれば、その時この階級の利益は歴史的ヒューマニズムの価値をもたらす。プロレタリアートの力はヒューマニズムの力であるからだ。逆にファシストの暴力は普遍的階級の暴力ではない。それは《人種》の暴力もしくは後進国の暴力である」。

　また多方面からの批判に晒された〈革命の目的と手段〉の齟齬について次のような弁明を試みる。スターリンの〈恐怖政治〉に対する論拠としてリベラリストたちは〈ヒューマニズム〉を引き合いに出す。彼らは、人間は単なる手段としてではなく、目的として扱われなければならぬとするカントに準拠している。しかしスターリン問題に関するこのような取り組み方は〈理想主義〉に過ぎる。現在、人間が目的として扱われているようなところはどこにもない。そして論旨は次のように展開する。

Depuis que *Darkness at noon* a paru, il n'est pas un homme cultivé dans les pays anglo-saxon ou en France qui ne se déclare d'accord avec les fins d'une révolution marxiste, regrettant seulement aille à des fins si honorables par des moyens est avec le marxisme. Il faudrait d'abord observer que les catégories memes de 《fins》 et de 《moyens》 lui sont tout à fait étrangères.[18]

　「『真昼の暗黒』が発刊された後、アングロ―サクソンの国々やフランスでは、マルクス主義革命の目的は是認するが、かくも恥ずべき手段で

---

17) ibid., pp.115-116.
18) ibid., p.133.

172

立派な目的に邁進するのはまことに遺憾と表明しない教養人は一人もいない。実際、《手段を選ばず》という楽天的シニズムはマルクス主義とはいかなる共通点もない。もともと《目的》とか《手段》とかの範疇そのものがマルクス主義と無縁であることに気付くべきだ」と語り、さらに、

En réalité, il n'y a pas la fin et les moyens, il n'y a que des moyens ou que des fins, comme on voudra dire en d'autres termes il y a un processsus révolutionnaire dont chaque moment est aussi indispensable, aussi valable donc que l'utopique moment final. Le matérialisme dialectique ne sépare pas la fin des moyens. La fin se déduit tout naturellement du devenir histrique. Les moyens sont organiquement subordonnés à la fin ultérieur.[19]

「実際には、目的とか手段とかいうものはない、敢えて言うなら目的しか、手段しかない。言い換えれば、革命のプロセスは一瞬一瞬が《究極の》ユートピアの瞬間と同じくらい不可欠で価値あるものだ。弁証法的唯物論は手段と目的を切り離すことはない。目的は必然的に歴史の生成から演繹される。手段は有機的に目的に従属する。差し迫った目的はそれ以降の目的の手段となる」。

ここでわれわれはポンティが「歴史の生成」を重要視している事実に注目しておく必要がある。「歴史の生成」という観念の意味内容を見守って行かねばならないが、彼の言い分はさらに続く。

世界中どこにも"主人と奴隷""死刑執行人と犠牲者"は存在する。だから、〈リベラリズム〉の方が〈スターリン主義〉より価値があるとは言えない。カント的態度表明の裏には人間による人間の搾取や植民地、帝国主義がある。それは避けがたいものとして受け入れなければならない。政治というのは常にそういうものだ。ヒューマニズムは精々のところ、現実との接触を持たぬ哲学者のもたらす心地よい夢でしかなかった。非暴力？万一それをまともに取り上げるのであれば、われわれはヨガ行

19）Tzvetant Todorov, *l'Homme dépaysé*, Seuil, p.140.

者にならなければなるまい。そのようなことができるだろうか。人間は本質的に〈社会に組み込まれ、位置付けられた存在〉un être engagé, situé である。人間は自分が自分を作ると同時に他人が作るものである。われわれはこの歴史から逃れることはできない。

　メルロ＝ポンティは〈未来のヒューマニズム〉実現のために、現今の〈恐怖政治〉はやむを得ないと考える。

　ソ連は目下のところ社会主義経済を推し進める世界で唯一の国だから、ソヴィエトの計画にはある程度特権が認められなければならない。特権の一つが暴力である。ファシズム体制であれリベラリズム体制であれ、その歴史の創成時には暴力がまずあった。したがって、現在の共産主義の暴力は恐らく、新たな歴史の創造に伴う小児疾患（はしか）である。未来のヒューマニズムに到達するために辿らなければならぬ迂回 détour なのだ。

　既にフランスにおいても、1936-38 年のモスクワ裁判がでっち上げの裁判であり、ソ連の現行のシステムが多くの点でファシズムの典型的特徴を示していることを認めざるを得ない情況になっていた。が、それでも一般的基準によってソ連を判断するに躊躇する気分が色濃く残っていた。ポンティの迫力あるソ連擁護は、反共産主義の勢いを再び反―反共産主義に靡かせるに充分な効果をもたらした。

　ソヴィエト政府は資本主義の包囲、ナチスの脅威などに対処しながら資本の基本的蓄積を実現しなければならなかった。強制的な手段に頼る以外になにができるだろうか。結局われわれが忘れてならないのは〈歴史の特性は迂回すること〉なのである。共産主義は息の長い計画であり、うまく着地させるためには、ある程度の犠牲はやむを得ない。「手を汚す」ことを受け入れなければならず、暴力的手段も必要なのだ。

　以上がメルロ＝ポンティの恐怖政治的専制政治擁護論の概要である。因みに「手を汚す」という表現はサルトルの劇作『汚れた手』Les Main sales となり、「迂回」détour はサルトルの『スターリンの亡霊』

においてソ連擁護のキーワードとして使われている。

7　楽天的進歩史観の源泉

　ところで、サルトルやメルロ＝ポンティなどの進歩主義者たちが、暴力と強制収容所の世界であるスターリンの全体主義体制を擁護し続けた理由は何であったか。『国替えを余儀なくされた人』[20]においてツヴェタン・トドロフが指摘しているのだが、一つにはサルトルは事実確認に関心を持たなかったので、ソ連国内の過酷な状況が充分見えていなかった。次にマニ教的善悪二元論に嵌ってしまい、サルトルはドグマに盲目的に執着する信者の姿勢を取り続けた可能性も考えられる。が、いずれにせよこうした進歩主義者の態度は、当時フランス知識人の間に浸透し始めた「歴史は段階的に発展する」とするヘーゲルの歴史哲学の観念に乗っかった風潮であった。段階的にとは、資本主義の次代を担う新たなステップは共産主義communismeであると、彼らは漠然と予想していた事実を意味している。密着することは無かったにせよ、サルトルがcommunismeと常に並行関係の行動をとり続け、全体主義思想を擁護した裏に、フランス社会に蔓延するこうした思想的背景があったことは否めない。

　それはいわば「進歩史観」とも称されるべきもので、それは彼らの頭の中では信仰対象の観念にまで純化凝縮されていたのではないだろうか。つまり、スターリン主義という新たな信仰が育まれていたと言えよう。L'Opium des Intellectuesからレイモン・アロンの言を借用するならば、その信仰は"革命と暴力による救済の神話"であり、"選ばれた階級としてのプロレタリアートの神話"、また"左翼の神話と歴史崇拝の神話"[21]

20）Tzvetant Todorov, *l'Homme dépaysé*, Seuil, 1996, p.142.
21）レイモン・アロン、『知識人の阿片』、Calmann-Lévy, 2004. より。

であり、こうした神話が新たな信奉の対象となったのである。〈支配・隷従の二重性・dualité maîtrise-servitude〉に〈均質的で普遍的な国家〉がとって代わること、つまりキリスト教の神秘体の地上における実現である。

歴史崇拝についてさらに捕捉すると、『全体主義の起源』（1951年）の著者ハンナ・アーレントは、マルクスとヨーロッパ政治思想の伝統について次のように記している。

> ヘーゲルの哲学は全体として歴史哲学であり、彼はあらゆる哲学思想を他のすべての思想とともに歴史の中に解消した。ヘーゲルが論理さえも歴史化し、さらにダーウィンが発展の観念によって自然さえも歴史化して以降は、歴史的概念に対する激しい攻撃に抵抗し得るものは何も残されていないように見えた。[22]

こうして、ダーウィンの進化論という追い風を受けて進化論的歴史尊重主義は圧倒的なものとなった。歴史の動因をあらゆるものの中に内在する矛盾に見るヘーゲルの弁証法においては、例えばAという現象は自然にBになるのではなく、Aが否定されてBが生まれる構図になっている。AB間の対立があらゆる現象の変化運動の原動力となっている（「一般に世界を動かしているのは矛盾である」『エンチクロペディア』119節）のだが、現象の変化・運動の過程はその矛盾を内包したまま全体として総合されてゆくのである。それがいわゆる弁証法の総体性であり完結性なのである。そういうわけで、矛盾と対立を抱える近代社会も、腐敗と堕落に満ちた時代も歴史の発展過程に過ぎないとヘーゲルは考えたのである。

こうした進歩史観を敷衍すると、革命による暴力や虐殺、また強制収容所の存在でさえ歴史の発展過程の一コマとなり、〈絶対者〉が自己の本質を実現する過程でしかないということになる。ヘーゲルは絶対的な

22）ハンナ・アーレント、『カール・マルクスと西欧政治思想の伝統』、佐藤和夫訳、大月書店、2002年、12頁.

理性が世界を支配しており、世界の発展を支配するものは世界精神（神）であり、世界史は神の摂理によって目的論的に決定されていると考えた。よってナポレオンのような英雄も、目標実現のためにある段階で利用された操り人形（道具）に過ぎない。闘争と矛盾の継続と見える世界の歴史も理性的に、つまり必然的に進展してきたということになる。

　かくして"手放しの"というのは言い過ぎであろうが、いささか楽天的な"進歩史観"が識者の間に蔓延したことは想像に難くない。この歴史認識では、個人は歴史の奴隷・道具である。付言すると、この思考方法はハイデッガーが疎んじたところの人間を〈道具存在〉とみなすものでもある。

8　ベルジャーエフの「歴史の意味」

　ベルジャーエフの神的実在や信仰に対する考えは若干パスカルのそれに似ている。彼は何より「信仰」と「理性」の関係を整理しようとした人であった。そのことは、「真理は論証によって導き出せるか」という問いに表れている。

　「真理とは導き出されるものでも、論証されるものでもなく、出会われ看取されるものだとしたらどうだろう」[23] という問いが表明しているように、彼は神的実在（真理）の理性による捕捉は疑わしいと考えている。

　「啓示とは何か。現代人はこの言葉を聞くとぎょっとする。この言葉は、合理主義的実証主義に感染したすべての人々にとって、無縁であり敵対的である。信仰心を容認し、これへの心理的要求を感ずるこの上なく繊細な人々も、啓示を認めることには決して同意しない」[24] と、啓示に関

23）ニコライ・ベルジャーエフ、青山太郎訳、ベルジャーエフ著作集II「新たな宗教意識と社会性」、行路社、1994 年、7 頁.

24）ibid., p.228.

する人々の無思慮を指摘した上で、

　「現代世界は神秘体験を軽視している。神秘体験は、われわれの世界がそれによって生きている現実的理解からはほど遠く、また、われわれの時代がかくも心砕いている社会機構の整備を、神秘体験と結びつけることはむずかしい。この世の支配的意識が神秘的体験の内に見るものは、精神異常か、個人的な奇行かであり、この領域に踏み込んだものを、人は救い難いものと見做して、真面目には相手にしなくなる。現代の「意識的な」人々が神秘体験に対してとる態度とはこうしたものであり、彼らにとって神秘体験の問題は存在しない。宗教の真理が粗野な迷信と、神秘体験がオカルト的・降神術的いかさまと混同されている。人々は、合理性の陽光が神秘思想の月光に最終的に打ち勝ったと信じた。しかし、合理主義の病を病む人々には、陽光は見えない」[25]と彼は語る。

　ベルジャーエフは啓示信仰、神秘体験などによって、人間存在の在り方そのものの持つ神秘性を軽視することの危険性を示唆している。しかしそれ以上に彼の注意を惹きつけていたのは、理性と合理主義から派生した〈歴史哲学〉の問題であり、世界のどの民族もが体験することになった啓蒙主義の功罪である。

　彼は「啓蒙時代は聖なるものと、有機的な伝統と歴史的な伝統を破壊したのであった。およそ一切の人間文化と地上の民族の命を流出させる根源であるあの生の神的秘儀から抜け出して、自己を向上させる時代である。この啓蒙時代において、あの直接的な生の秘儀の外に、あるは上に、人間理性の僭越が始まる」[26]と述べて人間理性の跳梁跋扈する危うさを指摘した。また、

　「啓蒙時代は《歴史的なもの》を否定する」[27]と述べ、彼の目指す《歴史的なもの》と啓蒙時代に始まった〈歴史主義〉には大きな隔たりがあ

25）ibid., p.30.

26）ibid., p.30.

27）ibid., p.13.

ると、ベルジャーエフは見る。爾来一方に『歴史的なもの』、他方に認識する自分という分離した対立が生じる。つまり啓蒙時代に始まる分裂と反省が問題なのである。それは、

「啓蒙時代に始まった歴史哲学には宿命的に深淵が欠け、歴史の神秘への突入がなされない」[28]からなのだ。ベルジャーエフの言う《歴史的なもの》とは、先に紹介したように「存在と生の秘儀、生の神的秘儀」である。啓蒙的歴史主義は、自己を理性的かつ客観的に捉えるがゆえにその歴史観は有機性に欠ける。論理的表現は、いわば、血肉を具えた生身の人間存在を捉えるに適さないのである。18世紀ヴォルテールは狂信に由来する不寛容を寛容に導くために理性の効用を説いた。しかしベルジャーエフの考えでは、やがて人間理性の僭越が始まり合理主義の病がはびこって神聖な伝統の破壊工作がはじまり、それは聖書そのものの破壊にいたった。宗教改革の時代に始まったこの伝統破壊は啓蒙時代に勢いを得て〈歴史主義〉の思想となり、ヘーゲルにおいて発展を遂げ、マルクス主義のプロレタリアート革命をもたらすことになったこと言を俟たない。

ベルジャーエフは「マルクスの経済的唯物論は歴史哲学の領域における最も興味ある動向の一つであるが、その大きな貢献は、あの歴史の聖物と伝統の裸形化の過程を最後の結論にまでつきつめたところにある」[29]として、「一切の歴史的聖物と歴史的伝統をとことんまで情け容赦なく破壊し殺戮すること、マルクス主義の歴史観以上のものを私は知らない」[30]と語り、18世紀に始まった啓蒙理論が人間存在の在り方を無機的な経済理論に変えてしまった事実を嘆くのである。

その結果「歴史的過程における唯一本来的な実在としては、ただ唯物的経済的生産の過程だけがあることになり、これが生み出す経済的諸形

28）ニコライ・ベルジャーエフ、『歴史の意味』、氷上英廣訳、1998 年、14-15 頁.
29）ibid., p.14.
30）ibid., p.14.

態が、唯一の存在論的、真に第一義的、実在的なそれとして出現するに至る。その他一切のものは単なる第二義的なもの、単なる反映、単なる上部構造に過ぎない。宗教、精神、文化、芸術、人生そのものが単なる反映であって、本来の実在性を欠いている」[31]ということになるのだが、マルクス主義の主張する啓蒙理性はそこに留まらなかった。それはメシア的要求を満たす最後の光として突き進むことになった。それが「進行する歴史」という考え方である。つまり「歴史には方向性 sens がある」とする考えであり、歴史は一定の方向に向かって進歩することになるのである。

　時期的にも〈ダーウィンの進化論〉という追い風を受けて、進化論的歴史尊重主義が圧倒的なものとなっていた。そこでベルジャーエフは「進化論」と人間社会の「進歩の観念」の明らかな違いについての自説を展開する。

　「進歩の観念は進化の観念と混同されてはならない。進歩の観念は歴史的過程の目標を設定し、この目標の光に照らして歴史的過程の意味をわれわれが発見することを要請する。進歩の観念は、歴史の中に存在していないような、いかなる時代、過去・現在・未来のいかなる時期にも結び付けられず、むしろ時代を超えているような目標を要請する」[32]

　また「進歩の理論は過去と現在を犠牲にして未来を神格化するのであり、科学的見地からも哲学的ないし道徳的見地からもこれを正当化することはできない。進歩の理論は一個の宗教的帰依、一個の信仰を示す。進歩の理論は、人間世界の歴史の諸課題が未来において、人類の運命において、高次の完全な状態が到達される瞬間が到来するであろうということを前提としている。人類の歴史の運命を満たすあらゆる矛盾が解消され、あらゆる問題が解決されることを前提としている。これはコントとヘーゲルとスペンサーとマルクスの信仰であった。この仮定は正しい

31）ibid., p.14.
32）ibid., p.14.

のだろうか」。[33]

　進化の観念と進歩の観念の混同が招く危険についてベルジャーエフはさらに分析を進める。

　「進歩の観念の古い根源は宗教的・メシア的な根源である。それはメシア的解決の観念、つまり歴史の運命の理念、地上的解決の観念という古いユダヤ主義的観念である」。[34]それはまた「神の国の到来の観念、いつの日か実現すべき完全の国、真理と正義の国の到来という観念である。このメシア的至福千年説の観念が進歩の理論において世俗化されたのである。19世紀の人々は進歩の宗教に帰依したのであり、それがキリスト教の代用品となったと言っても言い過ぎではない」[35]とも語っている。

　結果として進歩の観念はソヴィエトにおいて、キリスト教の「千年王国説」と結びつき、平等主義的・共産主義的幻想である「プロレタリア革命思想」となり、ロシアのスターリン体制下で、強制収容所における2000万人とも3000万人とも言われる大量の犠牲者を生み出すことになった。ベルジャーエフがこうした警告とも言える文書を著したのは、スターリンによる恐怖政治が始まるはるか以前であったのであり、彼の慧眼が同胞の災厄を予言することになったのは誠に不幸なことであった。

9　『反抗的人間』が惹き起こした
カミュ・サルトル論争

　1951年こうした状況を背景にして登場したのがアルベール・カミュの『反抗的人間』である。「激情による犯罪と論理による犯罪がある」[36]という鮮烈な書き出しで始まるこの評論は、端的に言って「論理による

33）ibid., p.18.
34）ibid., p.18.
35）ibid., p.228.
36）ibid., p.229.

悪の系譜学」généalogie du mal であるが、たちまちサルトルをはじめ
とする進歩的左翼陣の攻撃にさらされた。その内容を一言でいえば「歴
史の発展のために人の血が流され、《進歩的暴力》の名のもとに暴力が
容認される」ことに疑問を提示するものであった。カミュは発作的犯罪
とは別の、用意周到な「論理的整合性」の衣装をまとう犯罪、すなわち
"論理の悪"の存在することを訴え、過激と中庸を比較する思考の重要
性を強調するのである。言い換えればそれは、狂信に対して寛容を求め
ることに他ならない。

　その著作において、「"死刑執行人"と"奴隷"は世界中どこにでもいる」
とするメルロ＝ポンティの主張に呼応してカミュは『犠牲者も否、死刑
執行人も否』*Ni victime ni bourreau* を著し、〈目的は手段を正当化する〉
la fin justifie les moyens という社会主義者の主張に待ったをかける。
要するに、理想の未来を実現するという目的は、いかなる残虐非道も許
容しうるのかと。当作品の基調は〈人の命を救うことこそが大切なこと〉
l'essentiel est sauvetage des vies であり、それは作中ライトモチーフ
のように反復して現れる。「できるだけ流血と苦痛を避けなければなら
ない」[37] は宗教戦争の時代のモンテーニュの想いに似ている。そしてこ
の『反抗的人間』が発端となってカミュとサルトルの論争が始まる。

　論争の中心的な論点は "進歩的と称される暴力" を特別に優遇するこ
とは許されるか否か、ということにあった。カミュは一貫して人命尊重
の立場を崩さず、大量殺人の不当性を訴える。論理的犯罪 crime logique
とは理論づけられた犯罪 crime qui se raisonne のことで、あらかじめ
計画された犯罪 crime prémédité である。カミュは、Nous sommes au
tepmps de la préméditation et du crime parfait.[38]「われわれは予謀の
時代、完全犯罪の時代に生きており」、それを可能にするものは C'est la
philosophie qui peut sérvir à tout, même à changer les meurtriers

---

37）Albert Camus, *l'Homme Révolté*, Gallimard, 119ᵉ édition. p.13.
38）Albert Camus, *Ni victime ni boureau*, O. C. t. II. p.336.

en juge.「あらゆることに役立ち、殺人者を裁判官にさえしてしまう哲学である」と語る。このように『反抗的人間』のテーマは哲学の体系や思想の教義が暴力を正当化し、暴力を招来する危うさを問題にするものであった。

　カミュは、プロレタリアートによる《均質的で普遍的な国家の実現》という彼らにとって〈絶対的なもの〉への到達は不可能なことと考えていた。元来宗教嫌いのカミュは、マルクス主義的なメシア思想を拒んだのである。『反抗的人間』で述べているように、彼の目には、歴史に関するマルクスの理論はユートピアもしくは欺瞞と映っていた。

　論争のきっかけは 1952 年 5 月サルトル主幹の『現代誌』79 号に掲載されたフランシス・ジャンソンの『反抗的人間評に対する――A. カミュあるいは反抗心』である。カミュが 1951 年に著した『反抗的人間』の反響は絶大であった。[39] ジャンソンは自筆の冒頭部分 9 頁から 10 頁にかけて、カミュの著書に左右両翼から高い評価が寄せられた事実を皮肉交じりで次のように紹介している。

　「本書は一挙に思想界の各方面の賛同を得ている。「非常に重要な書」「大作」「近年の大収穫、世紀の半ばに現れた偉大なる書」「西欧思想の転換点」「〈人間にならいて〉ともいいうる、気高く、人間的な作品」「かくも価値ある書は、戦後フランスに現れたことがない」――こうした賛辞はいくぶんの差はあれすべての批評家のうちに見られた。『モンド』紙のエミール・アンリオ氏からジャン・ラクロア氏まで、またクロード・ブルデ氏（『オブセルヴァトゥール』誌）から、『生ける神』誌のマルセル・モネ氏を経てアンリ・プティ氏（『解放されたパリ人』誌）にいたるまですべてしかりである。右翼の方へと万古不易のフランスの高嶺を襲った熱狂的旋風が決定的だと思わぬにしても、カミュの立場に立ったら、僕ならどうにも不安でかなわないことだろう。彼の著書が、多種多様の

39）フランシス・ジャンソン、『革命か反抗か――カミュ＝サルトル論争』、佐藤朔訳、新潮文庫、平成 22 年、9-10 頁.

精神の持ち主を有頂天にさせたのは、不思議な力によるものか。みんなが欣喜雀躍して迎えた「福音」とはなんだろうか」。このような書き出しで始まるジャンソンの『A．カミュ　あるいは反抗心』はカミュ批判の書であり、これに応えてカミュも同誌8月号に「『現代』誌主筆への手紙」を書く。同号ではサルトルも、カミュの反抗の理論を激しく弾劾する『アルベール・カミュに応える』*Réponse à Albert Camus* を発表した。当然ながらコミュニストやシュールレアリストの側からはカミュに対する反対の声が上がっていたが、右翼や中立左派の多くがカミュを支持したので、反発的にサルトルの舌鋒はすさまじいものとなった。カミュの言い分は、サルトルやジャンソンがソ連の強制収容所について多くを語らない事実を指摘するものであった。この問題についてサルトルは次のように応じる。

　「あなたが、私の本のいかなる批評もロシアの強制収容所をなおざりにしては成立しないと書いたとき、あなたは彼の論文がそのことに触れなかったことで彼を責めている。それについては恐らくあなたが正しい」と、一先ずカミュの言い分を認めた上で、「あなたは、ジャンソンが自分の権利であるかの如く、あなたの本の中のソヴィエトの強制収容所のことについて触れなかったという否定しえない事実を利用して、社会参加を主張する雑誌の編集長の私がこの問題に取り組まないだろうと示唆しているが、それは公正に対する重大な過ちであり、偽りである」[40] と反論し、弁明を展開する。

　「ルッセの声明の数日後われわれは強制収容所に関する数本の論文を発表した。日付を調べれば、その号はルッセの介入以前に作成されたことがわかる」。[41]

　しかしサルトルは直後に自らの偽らざる本音を吐露する。

40）Jean-Paul Sartre, *Réponse à Albert Camus*, in Situations IV, Gallimard, 1993, pp.103-104.
41）ibid., p.103.

「そうだカミュ、わたしもあなたと同じように強制収容所は許しがたいものだと思う。ただし、いわゆるブルジョワ新聞がそれを毎日書き立てるやりかたも同様に許しがたい」。[12]

サルトルも強制収容所の存在を非難するが、論点の比重はむしろ後半部の〈ブルジョワ新聞に対する非難〉の方に比重の懸かった態度表明と言えよう。いわばサルトルにとって〈絶対的なもの〉l, absolu は現在を犠牲する価値を有する〈未来〉futur である。対してカミュのそれは、後に詳述するが〈ここ・今〉hic et nunc なのだ。カミュにとっては現在こそが絶対的なものなのであり、「ここ・今」を享受する、その喜びを味わうことこそ重要なのである。サルトルは逆に〈ここ・今〉を相対化するのである。サルトル的意識は今の瞬間を味わうというより、現在を超える意識であり、未だないものを志向し続ける意識であり、それは現状に対する恒常的な不満の源泉とも言えるものだ。

そしてサルトルの意識の志向する未来の内容は、プロレタリアートによる〈均質的で普遍的な社会〉の実現した社会の実現した姿ということになる。強制を伴いながらも、その理想に向かって革命は進行するはずであり、そうであらねばならない。それがサルトル側の歴史認識であった。要するに、サルトルは現状否定の未来志向派であり、彼の実存哲学の基底にはヘーゲルの弁証法に由来する「否定性」Négativité がある。根底に否定性を秘めた進歩主義の哲学である。

10　カミュ　〈現実への忠実〉と〈大地への同意〉

一方カミュは〈現実への忠実〉と〈大地への同意〉を表明して憚らない。現状否定の未来志向であるサルトルとは対蹠的である。『シジフの神話』『裏と表』『結婚』の一部をすでに少部数公刊していたが、彼の作

42）ibid., p.104.

家としての出発点はやはり『異邦人』であるとしたい。構想から5年後の1942年に刊行された当作品は絶大な評価と反響を呼んだ。因みにこの作品が構想された1937年カミュは共産党を離党している。

ところで、極力接続詞を避け、細切れのフレーズを並べ、もっぱら複合過去形を用いたこの作品が、それでも"みずみずしい文体"と称される理由はどこにあるのだろう。要因の一つは主人公が自然を享受する姿に求められる。享受の対象は主人公ムルソーが恋人マリーと戯れる「海」であり、夕方勤務から解放されたムルソーが帰途岸壁を歩きながら感じる「さわやかな空気と新鮮な息吹」であり、J'avais tout le ciel dans les yeux et il était bleu et doré.[43]「目いっぱいに空がひろがり、それは青くまた黄金色であった」ような「空」、また小説『異邦人』の主役とも言える「太陽」でもある。かくして初期の書きものが示しているように、カミュには〈自然への同意〉consentement à la《physis》が明瞭に見て取れる。それは1939年刊行の自伝的随筆『結婚』のなかで、フィレンツェのピッチ美術館裏手にある16世紀のイタリア式庭園ボボリの高台から見下ろしながら観想するカミュが感じた「大地への同意」《consentement à la terre》でもある。カミュはいくつかの著書で倦むことなく繰り返す。Le monde est beau, et hors de lui, point de salut.[44]「世界は美しい、世界の外に救いはない」と。カミュの場合、大地への同意は人間を幸福に導くためのキーワードである。つまりカミュは自然naureを、大地terreを、また世界mondeを愛する人であり、physis〈ものごとの自然の形〉を肯定する姿勢が彼の根底にある。ここでサルトルとカミュの対比を整理しておくと「反自然」antiphysisのサルトルに対して「自然」physisのカミュ、以下「行動」actionに対して「観想」contemplation、「自己投企」projet 対「郷愁」nostalgie、「自己超越」transcendence 対「大地に根を張ること」enracinement、「義務存在」

43）Camus, *lÉtranger*, folio, p.34.

44）Camus, *lÉtranger*, folio, p.34.

devoir-être 対「存在」être …という形で平行線をたどることになる。

　『異邦人』の主人公ムルソーについて言えば、確かに母の棺を前にしてタバコをくゆらせ、葬儀の翌日マリーと海で戯れる行為は社会の慣習にそぐわない。また、彼は事務所のトイレの湿ったタオルに我慢できなかったり、後方から来て追い抜いてゆくトラックを突然友人と一緒に追いかけて飛び乗ったり、自己の欲求に素直で正直であり、それゆえ世辞を含め世間的な儀礼に対応できないなど、彼は幼児性を宿した、言い換えれば五感の要求や本能の誘惑のままに行動する青年として描かれている。いわば社会的なお芝居 théâtre sociale への配慮が欠けるために、外見上刹那的に見えるのだが、それはまさに「ここ・今」hic et nunc に生きる青年の姿そのものである。また、社長がムルソーにパリ行きを打診する場面がある。

　「『君は若い。気に入ってもらえる生活になるはずだ』僕は、そうですね、でも結局どちらでもいいのです、と言った」[45]。

　主人公の言葉は、彼が野心家でないこと、出世や進歩・発展とは縁遠いタイプであることを示している。つまり彼は未来志向でない、生成の観念とも無縁な"ここ・今"を享受する人間なのだ。エリック・ヴェルネールが《カミュ的享楽》frui camusien と呼ぶものがこれである。

　「不条理の壁は乗り越えがたいという意識が人をして悲劇的であるが、それゆえ精神的な高揚をもたらすここ・今に追い込む。逆に言えば、カミュ的享楽は不条理の苦い体験である」[46]ということはある意味で不条理が「ここ・今」に人を誘うとヴェルネールは解釈しているようだ。確かに一方でその解釈も可能だが、それだけでは利那主義を超えることはできないだろう。もちろん、ムルソーはカミュの分身であるから、一面でカミュにそうした傾向はあるかもしれないが、ムルソーはカミュ自身ではない。先に述べたように不条理の苦い体験であるカミュ的享楽は実

45）Camus, ibid., p.68.
46）Eric Werner, *de la Violence au Totalitarisme*, Calmann-Lévy, 1972, p.73.

は、絶望の裏返しの顔なのである。

享楽「その喜びはカミュにあっては、世界の外に救いはないという確信のなかに源泉を見出す、絶望の裏返しでしかない」[17]

カミュは今ある世界を享受する人間であり、宗教的来世を希求することもなければ、サルトル的生成 devenir に興味を示すこともない。世界を肯定するその姿は現実を超える transcender le réel ことを拒むものである。暴力による革命よりも、不完全であってもこの世界との調和 s'accorder au monde を選ぶのだが、実はそれは中庸というカミュの「反抗」の思想そのものなのだ。

『反抗的人間』の第五章「正午の思想」において彼は、「反抗自体は相対的正義しか願わず…世界は相対の世界である」「絶対視された歴史では、暴力は正当化される」「現代の熱狂的信徒は、中庸を軽蔑する」と語り、暴力を伴う革命よりも反抗することを勧める。その意味で、つまり狂信を避け寛容を説く点で、彼はモンテーニュの衣鉢を継いでいるとも言えるだろう。

11 レイモン・アロンの『知識人の阿片』

1955年レイモン・アロンは『知識人の阿片』*l'Opium des Intellectuels* を発表した。アロンはカミュ、サルトルらとともに1930年代アレクサンドル・コジェーヴの『精神現象学講義』を受けた一人であったが、その後は反—反共主義（共産主義）に対抗する論客となっていた。その著書の巻頭にカール・マルクスとシモーヌ・ヴェイユの興味深い対をなす銘句二つが併記されているので紹介しておきたい（但し、英語版には掲載がない）。

47）Eric Werner, ibid., p.73.

〈宗教は不幸に打ちひしがれた人間の嘆き、精神なき時代の精神であると同時に、愛なき世界の魂である。それは人民の阿片である〉カール・マルクス[48]

〈マルクス主義はその語彙の最も背徳的意味合いで完全に宗教である。それはとりわけ宗教生活として、またマルクスの正鵠を得た言葉に従うならば、絶えず人民の阿片として使用されてきた事実を共有している〉シモーヌ・ヴェイユ[49]

宗教は阿片であろうか。マルクスは宗教を阿片と規定して否定し、他方ヴェイユはマルクス主義こそが宗教であり、よって阿片であると切り返したのである。上記の対句表現はアロンが当著書に込めた意図を明確に示唆する指標である。

結局、古いユダヤ主義的観念であるメシア的解決の観念がマルクスによって進歩の観念になり、歴史の運命の理念となって、地上的解決の観念になったのである。それは神の国・完全な国の到来の観念で、メシア的千年王国説が進歩の理論によって世俗化されたものであった。ベルジャーエフの言うように、19世紀の人々は進歩の宗教に帰依したのであり、それがキリスト教の代用品になったのである。

アロンはその本の第9章で〈宗教を探し求める知識人〉Intellectuels en quête d'une Religion というタイトルを付して、当時の知識人の心的傾向について次のような批判的推察を試みている。

「われわれが見てきたようにマルクス主義の予言は、ユダヤ・キリスト教の予言の典型的図式と一致する。予言はすべて現状を非難し、かくあらねばならぬもののイメージを描き、輝ける未来と忌まわしい現在を隔てる壁を乗り越えるための個人やグループを選ぶ。政治革命なしに社

48）Raymond Aron, *l'Opium des Intellectuels*, 2004, p.53.
49）ibid., p.53.

会の進歩を可能にする階級なき社会は、理想国家を待望する人々が夢見たキリスト教の千年王国に匹敵するものであり、共産党は《教会》である。この教会に対して、福音に耳を傾けようとしない異教徒＝ブルジョワや、長年月その到来を予告してきた革命を認めようとしないユダヤ人＝社会主義者が反対している」。[50]

　また「マルクス主義者らの言う革命が実現しなかったのは、観念そのものが神話的であったからと語り、次のように結論づける。

　「すべての過去の革命と同様、プロレタリアートを引き合いに出す革命も、エリートから他のエリートへの暴力の交代を示すものである」[51]と。革命思想は組織と機構の維持を優先するあまり、否応なしに恐怖政治的全体主義 caractère terroriste-totalitaire の性格を帯びてしまうのであろうか。

　こうした革命思想は神話的であるという考えをカミュも『反抗的人間』のなかで述べている。時代の中にキリスト教の理想を導入することは可能であろうか。カミュは疑問を提示する。彼にとってもそれは神話でしかない。しかも危険な神話である。二世紀にわたって人類は世界のあちこちで革命的希望に根拠を与えようとしてきたが、試みはすべて失敗によって清算された。「革命家たちは不可能なことに挑戦していた」とカミュは言う。ニーチェ同様カミュがキリスト教的・ヘーゲル主義の否定性を拒否するのはそのためである。世界（この世）をなおざりにした彼方の幸福の可能性はまことに疑わしいものであるからだ。

　ハンナ・アーレントも『カール・マルクスと西欧政治思想の伝統』の第一章で、19 世紀の二つの主要な問題は労働の問題と歴史の問題であったとして、こう語っている。

　「ユートピア社会主義の主要な欠点は、マルクス自身が考えたように非科学的であるという点にあるのではなく、労働者階級を無権利な貧し

50）ibid., p.53.

51）ibid., p.53.

190

い集団とみなし、彼らの解放のための闘いだとみなした点にあった。キリスト教的な隣人愛という昔からの信念が社会的正義の激しい情念へと発展した」[52]。

こうしてプロレタリア革命が始まり、社会正義の名のもとに不寛容が始まった。それは宗教改革の時代モンテーニュが心を痛めた狂信と不寛容の時代の再来である。18世紀ヴォルテールは、狂信と宗教人による不寛容をデカルト以来の理性と合理論によって乗り越えようとした。しかし、その合理主義（理性）は無神論的唯物史観になったが、それはある方向に向かって進歩する歴史主義という名の進歩史観であった。ベルジャーエフやアロンが考えたように、人々はキリスト教の代用品である進歩の宗教に帰依し、歴史の運命の理念と地上的解決に奔走するあまり、目的のために人間を犠牲にすることを躊躇わなくなったのである。

未来志向それ自体は異常でもなんでもない。向上心の原動力でさえある。科学技術の領域の様々な発明・発見を支えているのは目標に向かって前進する未来志向である。ところが、人間の心性の領域については、この生成・進歩の観念は不都合な様相を呈する。歴史的に見て、人間の精神生活、就中倫理的心性が生成・発展しているかどうかについては、明確な解答が得られないからである。

たとえばB.C.18-17世紀バビロン第一王朝ハムラビ王の成文法「ハムラビ法典」の有名な条文「目には目、歯には歯」は復讐限定法である。それは片方の目を潰された被害者に加害者の片目のみを潰す権利を保障する法律であった。復讐は往々にして過度になる恐れがあるので、その行き過ぎを防止するための条文であり、人間の性情が本能的に有する衝動的行為は制御しがたいものであることが暗黙裡に示されている。衝動的性情を制御する能力と忍耐はわれわれ現代人にも難しい業であろう。

あるいは旧約聖書「出エジプト記」でモーゼの石板に刻まれた十戒は

52）ハンナ・アーレント、『カール・マルクスと西欧政治思想の伝統』、佐藤和夫訳、大月書店、2002年、12頁.

B.C.13世紀頃の禁令だが、殺人、姦淫、盗み、偽証、貪欲などは今なお新聞紙上を賑わせている。いずれにせよ犯罪や道徳的不品行を戒める徳目は今もって十全に守られているとは言いがたい。有史以来、いや恐らくは先史時代以来人間の道徳的心性は進歩していないのではないかと考えざるを得ない。それほど人間の欲心は限りないものなのだろう。キリスト教七つの大罪は傲慢、吝嗇、色欲、怒り、大食、妬み、怠惰だが、それらは17世紀のモラリストであるロシュ・フーコーが人間観察によって暴いた人間の業でもあった。それらは犯すべきでないと知りつつ犯してしまう衝動的行為であり、自己利益と自己愛ゆえの負の性情（心の暗黒面）に支配された衝動である。人間の自己保存の本能と直結しているがゆえに、時代に関係なく存続し続けるであろう。したがって、人間の実践道徳に生成・発展を期待することには無理がある。この領域に関する人間心性に進歩は認めがたい。ゆえに進歩という物差しで見る限り、道徳 morale は理性を駆使した論理 logique に太刀打ちできない。確かに科学的思考の世界においては論理の整合性が成立する。しかし、残念ながら人間の心性は物事を論理的に処理しうるほど単純な代物ものではない。人間は機械ではないのである。人間の心性には合理論的思考の枠組が出来る前に先ずは情が存在していたのだ。それが人間心性の宿命とも言える。

　つまり、マルクス主義革命思想のような、合理的な理想や信条を貫徹せんとする意志と行動は多分に狂信的なものになり、人間の犠牲の上に成立する論理体系の形成を可能にし、畢竟論理の整合性が人倫を踏み超えることを可能にする図式が出来上がるのではなかろうか。イデオロギーは元来人間のためにあるべきだが、そこではイデオロギーのために人間があるのであり、結局主客が転倒しているのである。

Característica internacional del movimiento dadá:

su recepción en Japón

(International Character of the Dada Movement: Its Acceptance in Japan)

Shu TSUZUMI

Carácter Internacional del movimiento dadá

El dadá, que nació en Zúrich hacia 1916, se difundió por ciudades como París, Nueva York y Berlín, entre otras. El líder del dadá en Zurich, Tristán Tzara, era rumano, mientras que otro fundador de la escuela, Hugo Ball, era de origen alemán. En el Cabaret Voltaire, que es la cuna del movimiento, se reunieron artistas cuya nacionalidad era muy variada aunque no los mencionaré aquí. Solo diré que el dadá tiene un carácter internacional desde su nacimiento. Walter Conrad Arensberg, coleccionista de arte, poeta y crítico norteamericano, que participó en el movimiento vanguardista estadounidense, dijo: "DADA est américain, DADA est russe, DADA est espagnol, DADA est suisse, DADA est allemand, DADA est français, belge, norvégien, suédois, monégasque"[1].

En España, dejando de lado la presencia de Francis Picabia, quien publicó la revista 391 en Barcelona, existió el ultraísmo, movimiento que duró desde finales de la década de los 10 hasta la de los 20. El ultraísmo surgió y fue impulsado por el creacionismo de Vicente Huidobro, poeta chileno que participó

---

1) Conrad Arensberg, Walter. "Dada est américain". Littérature en no. 13, May 1920, p. 15-16. Nishimura Yasunori menciona a este artículo en 西村靖敬. 1920年代パリの文学 ──「中心」と「周縁」のダイナミズム. 多賀出版, 2001, p. 156.

temporalmente en revistas dadá y que antes de su llegada a Europa ya había compuesto algunos poemas visuales en Chile. Mientras tanto, en Aeméica se siente su eco en el manifiesto del noísmo en Puerto Rico o el nadaísmo y en los manifiestos del estridentismo iniciado en México por Manuel Maples Arce. También en la voz individual de José Antonio Falconí Villagómez, poeta ecuatoriano.

Por otro lado, en Asia aceptaron el dadá Japón y Corea. En el segundo, no se formó ningún movimiento, pero Ko Hanyon (1903-1983), o Ko Tata[2], se dedicó a escribir obras dadaístas en su juventud. A los 17 años fue a Japón y estuvo allí casi tres años hasta que sufrió el Gran Terremoto de Kantō. Después de volver a su país recibió a los dadaístas japoneses.

Aceptación de Dadá en Japón

Dadá se puso "de moda" en Japón a finales de la era de Taishō (del 30 de julio de 1912 al 25 de diciembre de 1926). En esa época de Taishō se divulgó la denominada "democracia de Taishō", tendencia liberal y democrática, y se promovieron movimientos socialistas y obreros que durarían hasta los primeros años de la era de Shōwa (del 25 de diciembre de 1926 al 7 de enero de 1989) en la que sufrirían la represión del gobierno. Debido a la influencia de las corrientes políticas, en la esfera de la poesía el "arte popular" era una de las corrientes principlaes de la era de Taishō. Por otra parte, se encontraban escuelas simbolistas, algo parnasianas, que se mantenían apartadas de dicha corriente. Hagiwara Sakutarō (1886-1942) criticó a los grupos de poetas de *waka* (poema japonés tradicional) por ser demasiado formalistas y artificiales, y revolucionó la poesía lírica moderna con un estilo coloquial que primaba la

---

2) El sistema de pronunciación del coreano no tiene consonante sonora: "dadá" se pronuncia "tata".

emoción y el sentimiento. El grupo "Shirakaba-ha", que en 1910 publicó una revista cuyo primer número llevaba el mismo nombre, era otra de las corrientes principales de la era. Este grupo abrazaba un humanismo basado en afirmación absoluta del yo. Entre sus miembros, en su mayoría escritores o pintores como Mushanokōji Saneatsu y Shiga Naoya, se encontraba el poeta Senge Motomaro (1888–1948). Casi todos recibieron muy positivamente el nuevo arte europeo.

En aquella época no pocos poetas escribieron poemas dadaístas o cercanos a dadá, pero ¿cómo conocimos el dadá los japoneses? La primera presentación del dadá en Japón fueron dos artículos del periódico "Yorozuchōhō" escritos el 15 de agosto de 1920 por Wakatsuki Shiran, dramaturgo y Yōtōsei: "El último arte epicúreo: Dadaísmo recibido con entuasismo" y "Dadaísmo por todas partes". Aunque críticos, ambos artículos explican bien la situación del nacimiento del movimiento dadá y su idiosincracia. El 9 de agosto del mismo año, en el diario "Yomiuri-shinbun" el pintor Tōgō Seiji escribió el artículo "La ciudad del arte: dadá", y en el mismo diario, del 17 al 21 de agosto el poeta Kawaji Ryūkō publicó "Qué es el dadá?"[3]

Nakahara Chūya, poeta representantivo de la era Shōwa, muy conocido por el poema "Yogorechimatta-kanashimini (A la tristeza por estar sucio)", escribió poemas dadá como "Namu-dadá"[4]. Nació en Yamaguchi y estudió francés en Tokio Gaikokugo Gakkō (Instituto de Lenguas Extranjeras de Tokio), donde conoció las obras poéticas de Rimbeaud y Verlaine. Influido por ellos su poesía derivaría hacia el simbolismo, pero en sus años en el

---

3) Para presentar la teoría del dadá Nakayama Chiruu tradujo "Le Manifeste de M. Antipyrine" de Tzara en el número 9 de la revista de poesía "Cine" en1929. Nakano Kaichi, citando esa traducción, definió que el dadá no es locura sino el estado consciente de ser loco, como se lee en el manifiesto. (中野嘉一. モダニズム詩の時代. 宝文館出版, 1986, p.258).

4) "Namu", que precede al objeto de la creencia, normalmente como buda o sutra, significa profunda fe: "Namu-amidabutsu" o "namu-myōhōrengekyō".

colegio había leído el poemario de Takahashi Shinkichi, posiblemente el primer poeta dadá en Japón, que le atraía mucho. Aunque muchos literarios insistían que eran dadaístas y escribían obras que clasificaron como dadá, Takahashi es uno de los poetas del dadá japonés que no debemos olvidar: los otros son Tsuji Jun y Hagiwara Kyōjirō.

Poetas japoneses principales del dadá

Takahashi nació en 1901 en Yawatahama, puerto pesquero de Ehime en la isla de Shikoku. Depués de dejar la Escuela Superior de Comercio se trasladó a Tokio, la capital, pero volvió pronto al pueblo natal, donde trabajó en un diario e ingresó en un temlpo, del cual casi lo expulsan. Durante esos años leía literatura extranjera, por ejemplo a Dostoyevski, a través de traducciones. La lectura de poetas como Shimazaki Tōson (1872–1943), poeta que partió del romanticismo, y Fukushi Kōjirō (1889–1946), que escribió poesía libre y coloquial desde un punto de vista humanista, lo llevó a componer poesías, pero lo que realmente decidió su camino fueron las frases del manifiesto de Tristan Tzara que aparecieron en los artículos de Yorozuchōhō. En 1921 fue de nuevo a Tokio, donde conoció a los poetas Satō Haruo (1892–1964), Hirato Renkichi (1894–1922) y Tsuji Jun.

Este último compilaría y publiacaría sin permiso del autor *Dadaist Shinkichi-no-shi* (Poesía de Shinkichi, dadaísta), el principal poemario de Takahashi como dadaísta y el primer libro del género. Al visitar a Tsuji por primera vez, ya había publicado un artículo titulado "Dadá-butsu-mondō (Diálogo de dáda y Buda)" en un periódico regional de Shikoku, además de 60 ejemplares de *Makuwauri-shishū* (1921), el primer poemario de Makuwauri, su seudónimo como escritor de *waka*. Aunque todavía no mostraba un carácter intensamente dadá, en la cubierta del libro aparecían impresas las letras "DAI (sic)", por lo que se puede intuir su intento de seguir la tendencia dadá[5] Por último, también había publicado "Dadá-no-shi-mittsu (Tres poemas dadá)" en el número de octubre de 1922 de la revista *Kaizō* (Reorganización). En su visita a Tsuji, le dejó a este su novela "Hokuro (Lunar)" con unos apuntes.

El motivo de la visita de Takahashi a Tusji fue el interés que le causó la lectura de *Jigakyō: Yuiitsusha-to-sono-shoyū* (1921), traducción de *El único y su popiedad* de Max Stirner, filósofo alemán. Visitó al traductor en su casa de Kawasaki y le dijo que escribía poesía dadá. Tsuji, que conoció el concepto de dadá por la visita del joven poeta, empezó a estudiarlo a través de los comentarios de Katayama Koson (1879–1933), profesor de literatura alemana, Kawaguchi Ryūkō (1888–1959), poeta que había fundado la editorial Shokō-sha, en la que se publicarían obras de Hirato Renkichi, Hagiwara Kyōjirō, Murano Shirō entre otros, o Moriguchi Tari, crítico que había estudiado en París y que presentaba las últimas corrientes del arte europeo. Además leyó artículos al respecto en revistas en inglés y después se dedicó a su difusión. En agosto de 1922 publicó un importante ensayo, "Dadá-no-hanashi (Sobre dadá)".

El dadá de Tsuji no estaba fundamentado en una poética destructiva y negativa: unió el dadá con la filosofía de Stirner y consideró el dadá como "perfecto amante de la realidad" Para él, el dadá no solo consistía en unir palabras cuyas relaciones fueran extravagantes, ni en yuxtaponer cosas carentes de significado. Le gustaba la idea de que el dadá viviese tal cual es; no lo consideraba un movimirento antiarte sino una manera sincera de vivir. Para Tsuji el dadá no era la ruptura con la tradición, por lo que trataba de vivirlo al modo oriental, como un japonés, y hasta dijo que se alegraba de hallar el espíritu dadá en los libros budistas[6].

---

5) Décadas después, Takahashi dice que pensaba marcar "DA II" en el segundo poemario. (高橋新吉, 小山榮雅. ダダイズム・禅・そして詩. 流動, 1979, 11(6), p. 210.)

6) 玉川信明. ダダイスト辻潤. 論創社, 1984, p. 167-170.

A Takahashi, que por entonces estaba afectado por la muerte de su hermano menor, le desagradó el hecho de que Tsuji hiciera propaganda del dadá y que se convirtiera en una especie de gurú del movimiento. Visitó a Tsuji para reprocharle que le había robado el honor de ser el primer dadaísta en Japón. En 1923, tras las protestas de Takahashi y a modo de compensación, Tsuji publicó *Dadaist Shinkichi-no-shi*. Tsuji compiló poemas de Takahashi publicados en *Makuwauri-shishū* y otros escritos inéditos de sus cuadernos. Todo el trabajo, selección y ordenación de los poemas corrió a cargo de Tsuji. En el poremario había muchas erratas y salieron algunos poemas no definidos por el autor, lo que le provocaría su rechazo. Pese a la aversión de Takahashi, lo cierto es que Tsuji se mostró muy considerado hacia el joven poeta, diecisiete años menor que él, y para muchos lectores ese poemario no es sino la obra clave que liga a Takahashi con el dadá. De hecho, años después él mismo mostraría admiración por Tsuji, mencionando también los defectos de su benefactor.

De *Dadaist Shinkichi-no-shi* se suele citar el poema "Sara (plato)", en cuya primera línea aparece 25 veces el idiograma 皿 (sara, plato) y al que sigue una sola palabra en la siguiente línea: "kentai(hastío)" El autor, consciente de la fuerza visual de la tipografía, utiliza la repetición de ideogramas para provocar cierta sensación de realismo (el ideograma es el objeto mismo) al tiempo que niega toda búsqueda de sentido.

Hacia 1927, ya en la era Shōwa, Takahashi iba a templos y procuraba adquirir una sólida formación espiritual zen. Se decía que era un hombre loco. Fujiwara Sadamu (1905-1990), poeta y crítico, decía que era recto por naturaleza y que por eso mismo recurría a excentricidades[7]. Para mantenerse siempre fiel a su rectitud tuvo que abandonar su carrera e ingresar en el templo de la escuela Shingon.

---

7) 高橋新吉. 高橋新吉詩集. 創元社, 1952, p. 231-232.

Tsuji Jun, quien dio a conocer al público la poesía dadaísta de Takahashi, nació en Asakusa, Tokio, y estudió en Seisoku-kokumin-eigakkai, una academia privada de inglés, y en Athénée Français, la escuela de francés. Era un intelectual típico de la era Taishō, que tradujo obras extranjeras como *Genio e Follia* (1877) de Cesare Lombroso, criminólogo y médico italiano. Siempre sintió mucha antipatía hacia la autoridad y vivió como un nihilista. En 1912, antes de conocer a Takahashi, se casó con Itō Noe, su alumna de la escuela femenina de Ueno, donde él enseñaba inglés, pero en abril de 1916 se separó de ella. Itō, que escribía y actuaba radicalmente para mejorar la situación de las mujeres (negando, por ejemplo, el sistema matrimonial), tuvo una relación con Ōsugi Sakae, líder carismático del anarcosindicarismo en Japón.

Tsuji, en 1928, cuando ya había publicado *Dadaist Shinkichi-no-shi*, partió de Kobe a París como enviado especial del periódico de Yomiuri-shinbun. El 1 de enero del mismo año se celebró una reunión para despedirlo en Café Lion, entonces cafetería y ahora cervecería, en Ginza. En la fiesta interrumpió Takahashi, irritado, con un cuchillo en la mano, y Tsuji lo terminó honrando como el primero que introdujo el dadá en Japón, afirmando que no valía la pena discutir sobre quién había sido el primero[8].

Un año después volvió de París, pero en sus últimos años, después de caer en la demencia, realizó excentricidades e ingresó en varios hospitales. Algunas veces viajó vestido de "komusō", monje mendicante. Para él, este modo de vida era parte de la práctica dadá.

Otro de los poetas dadaístas más importantes es Hagiwara Kyōjirō. Se conmocionó con la muerte de Hirato Renkichi, que murió por enfermedad pulmonar con solo 27 años. Hirato no publicó ningún poemario, pero desde 1917 escribió poemas a la manera cubista y futurista yuxtaponiendo nombres directamente ligados a la civilización moderna. En 1921 difundió el folleto

8) 玉川信明 (1984), p. 203-204.

titulado *Mouvement Futuriste Japonais, Par R=Hyrato*, influido por el futurismo marinettiano, aunque en sus poemas introdujo diestramente otras formas de la vanguardia europea como dadá, imagismo, cubismo y constructivismo. Con este tabajo anunció los albores del futurismo japonés junto a los trabajos de Kanbara Tai (1898-1997), que presentó la teoría de la escuela italiana traduciendo las obras de Umberto Boccioni y Filippo Tommaso Marinetti, a quienes conoció personalmente, y Yamamura Bochō (1884-1924), quien logró renovar la poesía con su segundo poemario *Seisanryōhari* (San cristal de tres aristas) (1915). A Hagiwara le atrajo mucho la práctica futurista y cubista tras la lectura del poema "Asuka (Asuka, capital antigua del período del mismo nombre)"[9] de Hirato, que contribuyó la difusión de la poesía libre de corte coloquial.

En enero de 1923 Hagiwara fundó con Okamoto Jun (1901-1978), Tsuboi Shigeji (1897-1975) y Kawasaki Chōtarō (1901-1985) *Aka-to-kuro* (Rojo y negro), una revista de poesía muy importante en la historia de la poesía japonesa moderna que probablemente recibió una fuerte influencia del vanguardismo de Hirato. *Aka-to-kuro* contó con 4 números, con un extra de solo cuatro páginas, pese a que sufrió una interrupción a causa del Gran Terremoto de Kantō, ocurrido el 1 de septiembre del 1923. En el último número de 1924 se hizo patente su carácter de "abanderada de la negación y destrucción". Contra la corriente principal de la época, la "poesía popular" — en los primeros números Hagiwara solo pudo escribir poesía de este estilo —, se lanzó un eslogan radical: "¡La poesía es una bomba! ¡El poeta es un oscuro autor del crimen, que la echa contra el muro sólido y la recia puerta de la cárcel!". La revista adquirió de este modo un espíritu cercano al anarquismo y al nihilismo.

Después de *Aka-to-kuro*, Hagiwara participó en MAVO, el movimiento

---

9) Salió en la revista 日本詩人. 1921, 1(2), el número de noviembre.

que inició, el artista Murayama Tomoyoshi (1901-1977), buscador incansable de los nuevos caminos del arte vanguardista en exposiciones de arte y performances, en las que actuaba. MAVO publicaba una revista que llevaba el mismo nombre del grupo. Sus páginas se inspiraban en el constructivismo y eran muy tipográficas y visulaes, con fotos y dibujos. Entre sus participantes se encuentran pintores, escritores y poetas como Kitazono Katsue y Yoshiyuki Eisuke, además de Hagiwara. Las obras que aparecían en la revista eran muy modernas e innovadoras. La cubierta del número 3 de noviembre de 1924 se llevaba un petardo, por lo que el volumen fue prohibido.

En 1925 Hagiwara, ayudado por algunos miembros de MAVO, publicó *Shikei-senkoku* (Sentencia de muerte), un poemario muy gráfico que usaba técnicas como el linograbado. De este poemario, años después, Ono Tōzaburō (1903-1996) dijo: "El nombre de Hagiwara será recordado en la historia de la poesía japonesa contemporánea por haber insuflado de manera extrínseca al lirismo japonés, que por naturaleza tiende a cerrarse a pesar de la atmósfera liberal de la época, de un espíritu revolucionario semejante al de los estilos futurista y dadá en la Europa extenuada tras la Gran Guerra, aunque solo fuera temporalmente; estilos que introdujo en el mecanismo de su propia poesía, logrando en gran medida darle una apariencia igual de vanguardista." [10].

Él título provocativo de *Shikei-senkoku* (Sentencia de muerte) no representa la actitud rebelde dadaísta a un nivel abstracto, sino que se refiere a algo muy concreto. Durante el desorden causado por el Gran Terremoto de Kantō los gendarmes estrangularon al matrimonio Ōsugi Sakae e Itō Noe junto a su sobrino de 6 años. Furuta Daijirō, anarquista, planeó el asesinato del comandante de la ley marcial para vengarse de las víctimas, pero para llevar a cabo su plan necesitaba dinero, así que mató a un empleado de banco. Fue

10) 小野十三郎. 多頭の蛇. 日本未來派發行所, 1949, p.226.

arrestado y el tribunal lo condenó a muerte. Koshiyama Miki sugiere que el título *Shikei-senkoku* hace referencia a esa sentencia[11]. El poemario, con un estilo sin precedentes logró la libertad absoluta y la individualidad a la que aspiraba Hagiwara; pero la intensidad de su poesía duraría poco.

強烈な四角
鎖と鐵火と術策
軍隊と貴金と勲章と名譽
高く　高く　高く　高く　高く　高く聳える
首都中央地点 —— 日比谷
屈折した空間
　　　無限の陥穽と埋没
　　　新しい智識使役人夫の墓地
高く　高く　高く　高く　高く　より高く　より高く
　高い建築と建築の暗間
　　殺戮と虐使と囓争[12]

Cuadrado intenso

Cadena y hierro candente y artificio

Ejército y metal precioso y medalla y honor

ALTO ALTO ALTO ALTO ALTO ERGUIDO ALTO

EL CENTRO DE LA CAPITAL —— HIBIYA

Espacio torcido

　　Trampa y anonimato infinito

11）萩原恭次郎. 死刑宣告. 日本図書センター、2004, p. 193-194.

12）ibid. p. 114.

Nuevo cementerio del peón empleado del conocimiento

ALTO ALTO ALTO ALTO ALTO MÁS ALTO MÁS ALTO

Oscuridad entre construcciones altas

Matanza y maltrato y lucha mordaz

Son las primeras estrofas de "Hibiya", el poema más citado del pormario. Los poemas de *Shikei-senkoku* se encuentran en la ciudad moderna, pero no es alabada como en el futurismo italiano sino que es criticada por la situacón de angustia de los idividuos que viven en ella. Takahashi Shūichirō (o Hideichirō) afirma que no se trata de la negación total propia del dadaísmo sino la preeminencia de su espíritu — que es muy distinto a la actitud intelectual — y una voluntad de ruptura que sitúa en el centro la individualidad absoluta[13]. Obviamente, la cooperación de los artistas de MAVO fue indispensable en la formación del poemario, pero esa voluntad de ruptura individualista debió de ser precisamente, más que la novedad gráfica y visual del libro, el motivo principal que movió a otros poetas coetáneos como Tsuji.

Aunque el eslogan que llevaba en el número 1 de *Aka-to-kuro* era muy agresivo, los poemas de Hagiwara en los primeros 3 números de la revista fueron muy populares, como "Hatake-to-nōson（Campo y pueblo agrícola）" en el primero. En el número 4, finalmemte, se manifestó como dadaísta publicando "Aka-to-kuro-daiichi-sengen（el primer manifiesto de "Rojo y negro")": "¡Enciéndalo todo!", "¿Para el ideal?, o ¿para la justicia ? ¡No! ¡Para el último punto de explosión de nuestro cuerpo podrido!". Pese a la radicalización tardía de Hagiwara, *Shikei-senkoku*, en el que no hay ningún poema con el mismo título que el poemario, realizó una crítica violenta contra la sociedad y también contra sí mismo, algo que no había existido antes y que no volvería a repetirse en el futuro.

13）高橋秀一郎、破壊と幻想：萩原恭次郎私論、笠間書院、1978, p.91.

Después de *Shikei-senkoku*, Haiwara publicó poemas del mismo carácter pero en ellos la voluntad, antes sólida, era ahora algo inconsecuente, indefinida y aun dudosa. Takahashi Shūichirō encuentra este debilitamiento espiritual del revolucionario Hagiwara cuando este abandona la capital, Tokio, y regresa a su pueblo natal, Ishikura, perdiendo así el impulso de la vida en la ciudad, cuyo tema ya ha agotado[14]. Este hecho siginificativo de que la dinámica de la ciudad es la fuerza impulsora de la poesía moderna y vanguardista.

Años después de la publicación de *Shikei-senkoku* Hagiwara Kyōjirō obró en conformidad con las ideas de Ishikawa Sanshirō, anarquista, quien propuso "domin-shugi (autoctonismo)" para fomentar el desarrollo de la sociedad. Esta influencia sería más evidente en las obras posteriores tras su regreso a Ishikura. Más tarde, tanto Hagiwara como Ishikawa serían detenidos y encarcelados por sus ideas. Su último poema publicado fue "Asia-ni-kyojin-ari (Hay un gigante en Asia)", que afirmaba el "panasianismo" de carácter ultranacionalista. Siguió bebiendo con el estómago gravemente dañado y falleció por anemia hemolítica.

A pesar de la debilitación de la intensidad de sus poemas, es cierto que con solo un poemario, *Shikei-senkoku*, Hagiwara impresionó profundamente a los poetas jovenes de su era, algunos de los cuales seguirían el camino del dadá y otros la vía del anarquismo. Al fundar *Aka-to-kuro* — otro trabajo importante de Hagiwara ya mencionado — , visitó a Arishima Takeo (1878–1923), que lo desconocía, para pedirle que financiera la revista. Arishima, por entonces ya un escritor conocido y muy generoso con los jóvenes literatos, le comentó que una nueva poesía nacía en Japón y que entre los poetas de la nueva generación era notable Takahashi Shinkichi[15].

---

14) ibid. p. 110.
15) ibid. p. 190.

Conclusión

De nuevo este nombre, Takahashi. Su figura aparece una y otra vez en los albores del dadá japonés. Para terminar cito algunas de sus frases sobre el dadá. Takahashi no tenía dudas de que Tzara estudiaba el budismo zen porque su negación del valor de la lengua es muy semejante a "furitsumonji" o "furyūmonji", la concepción de que uno no debe aferrarse a las palabras o letras, porque "satori", conocimiento de la verdad absoluta, no se puede escribir a través de ellas[16]. Takahashi conoció el dadá casi un año antes de la publicaión de *Makuwauri-shishū*, gracias a las palabras de Tzara, que le emocionaron y que consideró una manifestación del zen; "Me opngo a toda fuerza universal que bulla en el interior de un sol podrido y supurante"[17]. Para Takahashi, el dadá no era motor de revolución o motivo de matanza y consideraba que su separación del surrealismo se debía a André Breton, que no entendía la generosidad budista de Tzara.

En la visión del dadá de Takahashi la semejanza entre la idea de Tzara y la del zen tiene mayor importancia que nada. Sobre todo en sus últimos años, en los que escribía poemas sublimes, únicos, basados en su religiosidad, la espiritualidad zen. En ese sentido llegó a decir que el dadá no era más que epígono del budismo, pero que su recurrencia (en los 60) provoca la resurrección del budismo. Estas plabras suyas no transmiten desprecio por el dadá; Takahashi estaba más bien orgulloso de haber sido el primero y el único que introdujo el dadá en Japón. Acerca de Tsuji, a quien debía la publicación del poemario *Dadaist Shinkichi-no-shi*, dijo que al fundar la revista dadaísta *Kyomu-shisō-kenkyū* (Estudio de ideología nihilista) cayó en el nihilismo. Por otra parte, se negó a llamar a Hagiwara Kyōjirō dadaísta,

---

16) 高橋新吉. ダダと禅. 宝文館出版, 1971, p. 45.

17) ibid. p. 45 y p. 71.

quien tampoco nunca se llamó dadaísta a sí mismo[18]. Takahashi Shinkichi fue el único que entendía el dadá correctamente y lo abandnó en el mar Genkai-nada al viajar a Corea en 1924[19].

Takahashi definió ese año como el fin del dadá en Japón. ¿Es eso cierto? Para el dadá japonés, el equivalente de la Gran Guerra Munidal, fuente del nihilismo de la época, fue el del Gran Terremoto de Kantō, un desastre nunca antes experimentado. Ese seísmo no solo trajo la sensación de nihilismo, sino también la destrucción de la tradición, creándose así una ocasión para el nacimiento de un nuevo arte. En tal ambiente japonés, lejos de los movimientos de Europa y Estados Unidos, el dadá tuvo muchas variaciones por la situación o interpretación de aquellos que lo aceptaron. Igual que se ve en el ultraísmo español, a veces se confundió o se mezcló con otras escuelas vanguardistas como el futurismo y el cubismo. Como ideología estuvo ligado al anarqusimo político, y, en consecuencia, los poetas dadaístas o "ex-dadaístas" fueron reprimidos. La tendencia nihilista del dadá conduce a algunos poetas a la religión, como en el caso de Takahashi, que llegó al conocimiento del zen y que pensó que el zen es más dadá que el dadá. La cuestión es que el dadá japonés, floreciente en la era Taishō, no fue solo una moda, sino que cambió profundamente la corriente de la poesía japonesa de las eras de Meiji y Shōwa.

En las últimas páginas de *Rittaiha-Miraiha-hyōgenha* (Cubismo-futurismo-expresionismo), escrito por Ichiuji Yoshinaga en 1924, se encuentra un breve capítulo dedicado al dadá en el que el autor define el dadá como egoísta y desesperado; la vida y expresión del instinto instantáneo. También lo considera un complemento del futurismo y del cubismo. Según él, el dadá define "todo" como "nada"; pertenece al presente y a este mundo y no piensa

---

18) Takahashi dice que *Shikei-senkoku* tiene pocos elementos dadá y solo ofrece elementos del nihilismo o del anarquismo. También reprocha la revista *Aka-to-kuro* indicando que trataron de incluirla en el dadá después de dejarla publicarse.

19) 高橋(1971), p. 68. y 高橋, 小山(1979), p. 212–213.

en el nirvana eterno. Por lo tanto, es indiferente a la conciencia de la sociedad: es individualista[20]. Esta explicación de Ichiuji se refiere al dadá europeo, pero sirve igualmente para explicar el dadá japonés.

20) 一氏義良. 立体派・未来派・表現派. 笠間書房, 1924, p.418-419.

Bibliograía

安藤元雄ほか監修. 現代詩大事典. 三省堂, 2008, 781p.

伊藤信吉編. 萩原恭次郎詩集. 彌生書房, 1973, 160p.,（世界の詩68）.

大杉栄ほか. 最初の衝撃. 學藝書林, 1968, 529p.,（全集・現代文学の発見1）.

小野十三郎. 多頭の蛇：詩論集. 日本未來派發行所, 1949, 236p.

神谷忠孝. 日本のダダ. 響文社, 1982, 247p.

神原泰, 瀧口修造ほか. 現代詩講座：第三巻. 金星堂1929, 360p.,（世界新興詩派研究）.

北川冬彦. 現代詩II. 角川書店, 1966, 210p.,（角川新書）.

ケネス・クウツ-スミス. ダダ. 柳生不二雄訳. PARCO出版局, 1976, p.170.,（PARCO Picture Backs）.

マシュー・ゲール. ダダとシュルレアリスム. 巖谷國士, 塚原史訳. 岩波書店, 2000, 446p.,（岩波世界の美術）.

古俣裕介.〈前衛詩〉の時代──日本の1920年代──. 創成社, 1992, 162p.

坂田幸子. ウルトライスモ──マドリードの前衛文学研究. 国書刊行会, 2010, 240p.

ミッシェル・サヌイエ. パリのダダ. 安藤信也ほか訳. 2007, 442p.

鈴木大拙. 禅. 工藤澄子訳. 筑摩書房, 1987, 219p.,（ちくま文庫）.

鈴木大拙. 禅と日本文化. 北川桃雄訳. 岩波書店, 1940, 196p.,（岩波新書）.

塚原史. 切断する美学；アヴァンギャルド芸術思想史. 論創社, 2013, 537p.

塚原史. ダダイズム：世界を綱ぐ芸術運動. 岩波書店, 1918, 272p.（岩波現代全書）.

辻潤. 絶望の書. R出版, 1972, 315p.

野田宇太郎. 日本近代詩事典. 青蛙房, 1961, 268p.

萩原恭二郎. 死刑宣告. ほるぷ, 1979, 159p,（特選名著復刻全集近代文学館）.

復刻版：ゲエ・ギムギガム・プルルル・ギムゲム：全十冊・別冊1. 不二出版, 2007.

馬渡憲三郎編. 現代詩の研究──成立と展開──. 南窓社, 1977, 300p.

万有百科大事典 1：文学. 小学館, 1973, 759p.

村山知義. 構成派研究・現在の芸術と未来の芸術. 本の泉社, 2002, 82p., 283p.

吉川凪. 京城のダダ、東京のダダ：高漢容と仲間たち. 平凡社, 2014, 223p.

和田博文編. 日本のアヴァンギャルド. 世界思想社, 2005, 296p.,（SEKAISHISO SEMINAR）.

Muriel Durán, Felipe. La poesía visual en España. Almar, 2000, 290p.,（Colección patio de escuelas）.

Jarillot Rodal, Cristina. Manifiesto y vanguardia: los manifiestos del futurismo italiano, dadá y el surrealismo. Servicio Editorial de la Universidad del País Vasco, 2010, 417p., (Filología y lingüística).

Rojas, Pablo (ed.). Poetas de la nada: Huellas de Dadá en España. Renacimiento, 2017, 428p., (Los cuatro vientos).

Apablaza, Claudia (ed.), Corominas I Julián, Jordi (prol.). Manifiestos vanguardistas. Barataria, 2011, 251p., (Humo hacia el sur).

フアン・パブロ・ビジャロボスの前半生と作品について
——『犬売ります』を中心に——

平　田　　　渡

1　作者の生い立ち

　フアン・パブロ・ビジャロボス Juan Pablo Villalobos は、1973 年、メキシコ中央部の、少し太平洋岸寄りに位置するハリスコ州の古都で、メキシコ・シティーに次ぐ人口をかかえ、その美しさから「西部の真珠」とたたえられる大都市、グアダラハラに生まれたが、成長したのは、同州の〈魔法のように魅力的な町〉といわれる中都市ラゴス・デ・モレーノであった。

　そののち、大航海時代にはスペインとのあいだに船が盛んにゆき来した、メキシコ湾岸の港町、ベラクルスにある同名の大学に進学。スペイン語圏の言語と文学の分野で学士号をとる。卒業論文のテーマは、〈文学ジャンルと（修道士）セルバンド・テレサ・デ・ミエル師の回想録における表現について〉であった。ちなみに、〈修道士〉セルバンド・テレサ・デ・ミエル師は、キューバの作家、レイナルド・アレナスが書いた、奇想天外な歴史小説の傑作『めくるめく世界』（1966）の主人公として天下に名声を馳せている。

　以後、数年にわたって、トイレの人間工学とか、勃起不全を改善するための医薬品の副次的な効果とか、まったく文学とはかけ離れた研究にいそしんだ時期があった。

　また、ベラクルス大学言語文学研究所の給費生として、アルゼンチン

の現代作家セサル・アイラ研究プロジェクトに参加した。

2004年、ラテンアメリカ諸国の学生のためのEUのアルバン計画の奨学金を獲得して、バルセロナ自治大学に留学。文学理論と比較文学についての博士課程の単位を修得するけれど、けっきょく博士論文は書けないままだった。

その頃から2010年までのあいだに、ブラジル人留学生アンドレイア・モローニと知りあい結婚。やがて長男マテオが生まれる。『犬売ります』*Te vendo un perro* はアンドレイアに献呈されているけれど、アンドレイアとは、いうまでもなく現ビジャロボス夫人のことにほかならない。

父親になったフアン・パブロは、子どもの視点からメキシコ社会を描くことを思いつき、『巣窟の祭典』*Fiesta en la madriguera* を書きあげた。そして、2010年、バルセロナのアナグラマ出版社から上梓し、作家としてのデビューを飾った。

後日譚によると、処女作として出したかったのは『犬売ります』の方だったらしい。けれども、十一回も書き直しているうちに十年の歳月が経ってしまい、『フツーの町で暮らしていたら』（2012）*Si viviéramos en un lugar normal* にも追いぬかれて第三作に退くことになったという。作品に登場する〈魔術師〉こと、マヌエル・ゴンサーレス・セラーノのような、世に埋もれた芸術家のことが書きたいと心底思うまでに、それだけの永い時間がかかったのである。

2011年から14年まで、サッカーのワールド・カップ（2014）と夏季オリンピック（2016）開催前の好景気にわく、"未来の大国"でアンドレイア夫人の母国、ブラジルに移住するが、政治、経済的に"ハイパー過去の国"だとわかって肩を落とす。そして、何かにつけて、暮らしやすかったバルセロナのグラシア大通り界隈のことが思い浮かぶようになり、急いで舞い戻ることにした。そこでは、何よりも、国内外からやってくる人びとが醸し出すコスモポリタン的な雰囲気を愉しみながら、安心して生活を送ることができたのである。

そのあと、2015 年、十年にわたる難産の末に『犬売ります』が出て、『巣窟の祭典』と『フツーの町で暮らしていたら』とともに、メキシコもの三部作が完成する。

さらに、2016 年には、バルセロナを舞台に、ありふれたことが狂気に変わり、奇妙なことがついには常態となり、もう笑うしかない世界を描いた悲喜劇『ぼくの話を信じてくれと誰にも頼むつもりはない』*No voy a pedirle a nadie que me crea* を世に問うた。

最新作は、『中央アメリカの子どもたちのアメリカ合衆国への旅　わたしには夢がありました』（2018）*Yo tuve un sueño El viaje de los niños centroamericanos a Estados Unidos* である。これは、いちばん傷つきやすい子どもたちを中心にすえ、その目を通して、ホンジュラス、エル・サルバドル、グアテマラからメキシコ経由でアメリカ国境をめざす移民たちの難行苦行の旅のありようを、十話に分けて捉えたノンフィクションである。

タイトルは、周知のとおり、アフリカ系アメリカ人による公民権運動の指導者、マルティン・ルーサー・キング牧師が、1963 年にワシントンのリンカーン記念堂でおこなった、有名な演説に出てくる言葉、「私には夢があります」I have a dream に由来している。

2 『犬売ります』との出会い

2016（平成 28）年、秋のある日、京都大学博士課程在学中のカタルーニャ人の親友、イヴァン・ディアスと話をしていたとき、最近、変わったことはありませんかと尋ねた。すると、じつは、スペインのアストゥーリア地方の中都市ヒホンにある、サトリという名前の出版社 Satori Ediciones から、芥川龍之介『〈羅生門〉ほか歴史もの短篇集』*Rashomon y otros relatos históricos* と泉鏡花『草迷宮』*Laberinto de hierba* の翻訳を、2015年と16年に出したところなんです、という答えが返ってきた。

そのあと、あっそれから、先ごろ、ぼくが作中人物として登場する小説が、バルセロナの出版社から出たんですよ、と恥ずかしそうに打ち明けたので、びっくりしてしまった。それは、イヴァン・ディアスが、カタルーニャの首都近郊で暮らしていた、自治大学の学生時代に親しくなったメキシコ人、フアン・パブロ・ビジャロボスが書いた『ぼくの話を信じてくれと誰にも頼むつもりはない』という前述の作品であった。なんでも、出版元のアナグラマ社が主催するその年のエラルデ小説部門賞まで受けたというのである。

デビューまもない作家の友人がいること自体、初耳だったし、何よりもイヴァン・ディアス本人が登場人物になっている作品があるというので、こちらは口をあんぐりと開けるばかりだった。

そんな自慢話めいたことは、適当に聞き流しておけばいいのに、つい、どんなふうに描かれているか気になったので、原書を取り寄せて読んでみることにした。

小説には、確かに、メキシコからバルセロナ郊外の大学に留学した〈フアン・パブロ〉と、タラゴナ出身のカタルーニャ人〈イヴァン〉が、登場するくだりがあった。〈フアン・パブロ〉が、ユングの神話学講座で知り合った友だちとして現われるのだ。そこでは、〈イヴァン〉は、学士か博士の論文を書いている〈フアン・パブロ〉に向かって、メキシコ人作家、ホルヘ・イバルグエンゴイティア（1928-83）を取りあげて、突然、パロディ論を展開しはじめる。ドイツの哲学者、ペーター・スローターダイクや、アメリカの作家、ヘンリー・デイヴィッド・ソロー『ウォールデン　森の生活』の言葉で理論武装しながら、持論をまくし立てる。それに対して、〈フアン・パブロ〉はボードレールの見解を引きあいに出して対抗するのである。

ほかならぬ畏友、イヴァン・ディアスが顔見世然として登場し、有名

な文学賞にも輝いた作品だから、読んで面白かったらぜひ翻訳してやろうという下ごころは満々であったが、全体的には、狂気を主題にしたブラック・ユーモアがかった作風で、ひとひねりしてあり、玄人受けはしても、残念ながら日本の読者には受け入れられそうにもないように思われた。

そこで手をひけばよかったのだが、乗りかかった船というやつで、すでに日本に紹介済みのフアン・パブロ・ビジャロボスの作品、『巣窟の祭典』（表題作と『フツーの町で暮らしていたら』所収。難波幸子訳。作品社。2013 年）は言うまでもなく、ほかの作品にも目を通してみたのである。

残っていたのは、2014 年のサッカーのワールド・カップ開催にちなんで、ポルトガル語で書かれ、ブラジルだけで出版された『ハリスコ州スタイルでは通用しない』*No estilo de Jalisco*、それに三冊目の小説『犬売ります』であった。前者は、文学ではないので、考慮には入れなかった。

『犬売ります』の方は、ちょうど〈隠れた怪作小説〉というふれこみで売り上げを伸ばしている三島由紀夫『命売ります』（ちくま文庫。1989 年）を読んでいたところで、タイトルが似通っていることもあって、どんな作品か興味津々、わくわくしながらひもとくことになった。そして、結果は、期待にたがわぬ出来であった。

3　作品のあらすじ

主人公は、画家になる夢やぶれて、かつて屋台のタコス屋を営んでいたテオ（ドーロ）。舞台はメキシコ・シティー、時間は 2013 年に設定されている。

テオは、御年 78 歳ながら、まだ矍鑠としており、退職者ばかり 12 人が入居している下町の古びたマンションで暮らすことになる。家賃は高

くないのだが、年金はもらっておらず、残りわずかな貯えをあてに、日々酒場でビールを飲むことに、かけがえのない老後の喜びを見出している。

　まず、年齢が筆者と同様、古稀をすぎた70代というのに親近感を抱いた。隣りの部屋の女フランチェスカとエレベーターに乗り合わせる場面から始まるけれど、滑り出しは快調である。そうなると、あとは作品の世界にじわじわ引きこまれてゆくものである。

　テオにからむ作中人物としては、マンションの玄関ホールで毎日のように、文学作品の読書会を開いているフランチェスカ（72歳）と、マンションにほど近いところにある八百屋の女将、ジュリエット（67歳）が登場する。このふたりの女性がテオとのあいだに三角関係を作り出す。フランチェスカは元英語教師で、文学に造詣が深いインテリ派、ジュリエットは反政府運動や革命シンパで、爆弾代わりの安いトマトを活動家に供給する行動派といったふうに、対照的に描かれている。

　テオは、両者を恋敵として競わせておいて、双方に言い寄るけれど、肝腎の恋の道には長けていないので空まわりするばかりである。そうした老いらくの恋の駆けひきがユーモアをこめて語られている。

　ほかに、玄関の扉が開いている隙にマンションに入りこんで、テオの部屋までやってきた、モルモン教伝道の、うぶなアメリカ人青年、ヴィレム。それにジュリエットの紹介でテオの友だちになった、非合法活動をしている毛沢東主義者の中国人マオ。この両者は、ジュリエットの孫娘で婦警の、ドロテアをめぐって恋の鞘あてをする間柄である。

　さらに、ドロテアの上司の巡査も絡んでくる。この〈パパイア頭〉は、テオが犬を殺して肉屋に売りつけたという告発を受けて、ドロテアとともにテオの家まで捜査にやってくるけれど、のちに小説を書いているという噂のあるテオに迫って、おのれひとりのために、しゃむに文学教室を開かせ、小説を書く手ほどきを受ける。

　物語は、ときどき過去にさかのぼり、テオの両親や姉といった家族の身に起こったことや、歴代の飼い犬のこと、テオの十代の頃の初恋が取

りあげられる。

　初恋の相手マリリンは、すらりとした長い脚をした、とびきりの美少女というか、いわゆる小町娘である。そんなわけで、学校帰りには、男たちが待ち受けており、あとからぞろぞろついてゆくので、そのうち長蛇の列ができる始末である。マリリンの家の近くに住むテオは、母親同士が親しかったことから、学校帰りのマリリンを家まで送ったり、彼女が壁画で有名な画家ディエゴ・リベーラのデッサンのモデルになると、邸まで送り迎えをするボディガード役をひき受けたりする。じつは、テオは、ひそかにマリリンに恋心を抱きつづけ、彼女のあとをつけまわす男たちのひとりだったのだが、そんなことはおくびにも出さない。そして近づきになったあと、同伴のつれづれに彼女の絵を描く許しはもらったものの、いつも主導権を握られたままで指一本さわらせてもらえない。どうやら、テオは若い頃から、こと恋愛に関してはすこぶる付きの奥手だったことがわかる。

　いっぽう家庭では、画家の道を志した父親は、夢が叶わず挫折したばかりか、飼い犬の死からおのれの浮気が発覚すると、家族を棄てて遠い太平洋岸の港町マンサニージョに落ち延びる。のちに成長したテオと姉は、父親のもとを訪ねるけれど、そのときの父親の様子が、生きているのか死んでいるのか判然としない、まことに幻想的で微妙な筆致で描かれており、読者を惹きつけて離さない。

4　作品の特徴について

　そうした幻想的な場面は、ほかにも見られ、この小説の特徴となっている。たとえば、しばしば舞台となるマンションのエレベーターがそうである。たった四階を昇り降りするのにやたらと手間どり、時には何時間も要するほどの不思議な代物として描かれている。

また、〈ラ・クカラーチャ〉 *La cucaracha* という歌にも歌われたメキシコ名物（？）のゴキブリが、跳梁跋扈する場面が圧倒的な迫力で捉えられている。マオが考え出した効果てきめんの駆除法によって、ゴキブリがテオの部屋からエレベーターに殺到し、折り重なるように溢れかえるくだりはおぞましいけれど、棄てがたい魅力を孕んでいる。

　そして何よりも特筆すべきは、1985年9月19日に起きたメキシコ大地震によって、革命記念碑に眠っていた、マデーロ大統領ほかの革命家の墓が、暴かれる場面であろう。

　原文から引くと、

　「二日後、原因調査を依頼された専門家」が「結果を発表すると、（中略）革命家たちの口髭は、死後もずっと伸びつづけ、下水道の装置に絡みつくまでに至っていた」

Dos días después, los peritos designados para encontrar una explicación dieron su veredicto (⋯). Eran los bigotes de los revolucionarios, que no habían parado de crecer y se habían enredado en el sistema del alcantarillado.[1]

というのである。

　そうした報告書の内容について、文学通のフランチェスカは、テオにこう述べる。

　「それにしても、革命家が亡くなったあとの口髭の話は、剽窃ですよ。たしかにガルシア・マルケスの小説にあったと思うわ。もっとも、いつまでも伸びつづけるのは口髭ではなくて、女の髪の毛だったけれど」。

　― ¡Eso es un plagio! Creo que está en una novela de García Márquez, sólo que es una cabellera de mujer la que no para de crecer en lugar de los bigotes.[2]

1）Juan Pablo Villalobos ― *Te vendo un perro*. Editorial Anagrama, Barcelona, 2015. pág.129

2）Ibid. pág.131

　これは、ガルシア・マルケスお得意の魔術的リアリズムの好例と言えるかもしれないが、植民地時代にペルー副王領で狂犬病にかかり、悪魔憑きになった侯爵令嬢の物語、『愛その他の悪霊について』（旦敬介訳、新潮社、1996 年）の冒頭で、作者によって紹介されている、物語の由来を語ったくだりを指している。なんでも、令嬢の髪の長さは 22 メートルあって、毎月 1 センチずつ、200 年間にわたって伸び続けたものだというのである。

　そういえば、日本語には、その上手（うわて）をゆく、愁（うれ）いゆえに伸びた、白髪三千丈（約三千三十メートル）という言い方があることを想い出したけれど、ともかくも、フアン・パブロ・ビジャロボスは、こんなふうにしてガルシア・マルケスに敬愛（オマージュ）の念を捧げているのかもしれない。

5　テオドール・アドルノ『美の理論』の思想

　ところで、主人公のテオは、『犬売ります』の中で、自慢げにこう述べている。

　「わたしは、どんな揉めごとや諍（いさか）いも『美の理論』からの引用を唱えて解決する悪い癖がついていた。そうやって、電話セールスの男や何人もの行商人、数十名の保険外交員、六回の月賦で墓を売りつけようとした輩（やから）を追っ払ったことがあるのだ」。

Había adquirido el mal hábito de intentar resolver todas mis querellas recitando párrafos de la *Teoría estética*. Ya me había quitado de encima a más de un agente de telemarketing, a varios vendedores ambulantes, a decenas de promotores de seguros y a uno que quiso venderme un sepulcro a seis plazos.[3]

　ドイツの哲学者で社会学者、音楽評論家でもあるテオドール・アドル

3）Ibid. pág.27

ノ（1903-69）が著わした『美の理論』は、いうまでもなく人生哲学の本などではなく、れっきとした美学の本なのだが、テオがちゃっかり自らの行動規範に取りこんでいる点が面白い。とりわけ、その中で見つけた〈探さざる者、発見に至ることなし〉Quien no busca no encuentra というオーストリアの作曲家アノルト・シェーンベルク（1874-1951）の言葉は、テオが座右の銘にしているものである。

　さて、次に引用するのは、テオがフランチェスカ主宰の読書会メンバーの頭を狂わせてやろうと考えて、自分のノートに書き写した『美の理論』の一節にほかならない。彼は、フランチェスカが何らかのかたちで自分のノートを盗み読みし、おのれの息のかかった読書会メンバーに伝えていると見ていたのだ。そして、このくだりこそ、テオが生きていく上で『美の理論』を心の支えにする源泉となった中心思想ではないだろうか。

　「芸術作品に全責任を負わせることを要求すれば、責任の重さが増大する。それゆえに、正反対の無責任さ要求して芸術作品を副次的な主題に変えなければならない。無責任さというものは、芸術に不可欠な遊びという要素を想い起こさせる。生真面目な色合いは、権力的でいかめしい行動と同様、芸術作品を滑稽なものに貶めることであろう。芸術作品において、無条件に威厳のあるものを放棄すれば、確乎とした方法論的原則となるに違いない」。

La exigencia de responsabilidad total de las obras de arte aumenta el peso de su culpa, por eso hay que contrapuntearla con la exigencia antitética de irresponsabilidad. Esta recuerda al ingrediente de juego sin el cual no se puede pensar el arte. Un tono solemne condenaría al ridículo a las obras de arte, igual que el ademán de poder y magnificencia. En la obra de arte, la renuncia sin condiciones a la dignidad puede convertirse en el órganon de su fortaleza.[4]

4）Ibid. págs.26-27

　ここでは、「生真面目な色合いは」ではじまる後半に注目したい。そこでは、「生真面目」なものはもちろん、「権力的でいかめしい」ものは、「芸術作品を滑稽なものに貶め」るとして批判され、「威厳のあるもの」を「放棄すれば」、「方法論的原則」が立てられるという指摘が見られる。

　そうした権力的なものに対する厳しい目は、『犬売ります』に通底した基本的な思想にほかならない。フアン・パブロ・ビジャロボス自身も、バルセロナの新聞、ヴァングアルディア紙に掲載された、あるインタヴューで、

　「たとえば、わたしの生まれ故郷、ラゴス・デ・モレーノ出身の画家、マヌエル・ゴンサーレス・セラーノのように、社会の底辺に埋もれているような人物が、もともと好きなのです」

　(…) quería protagonistas marginales, por ejemplo, Manuel González Serrano, pintor que nació en mi tierra, Lagos de Moreno.[5]

　と述べているとおりである。この画家は、作品では、最初は主人公が営むタコス屋に、どこか顔に見憶えがある〈魔術師〉として姿をあらわし、突然「犬売りますよ」という話を持ちかけるのだが、のちに、野良犬に囲まれて野たれ死にする。やがて回顧展が開かれたとき、テオはようやく身許を確認するに至る。どうやら作者は、野良犬をふくめた、社会の周縁にうごめいている、忘れられた人びとに共感をよせ、掘り起こそうとしているかに見える。

　さらに、ヴィレムというモルモン教の青年が、アメリカのユタ州からはるばるメキシコ・シティーまで、聖書を片手に伝道にやってくるけれど、そのとき、テオは、愛読書『美の理論』を片手に、行き当たりばったりに開けたページを朗読して、丁々発止と論戦を展開する。そうした中に以下のようなくだりがある。

　「進歩した芸術は、悲劇的なものを材料にして喜劇を書きあげる。崇

5) Una entrevista que hizo Núria Escur con Juan Pablo Villalobos, publicada con el titulo de *Escribir desde el sarcasmo* en Vanguardia.

高なものと遊びは、交わるところがある。意義深い芸術作品は、芸術に敵対するものを吸収する。幼児性という胡散くさい隠れ蓑が欠けているところでは、芸術は譲歩を見せるものである」。

— El arte avanzado escribe la comedia de lo trágico. Lo sublime y el juego convergen. Las obras de arte significativas intentan asimilar la hostilidad al arte. Donde falta esa capa sospechosa de infantilidad, el arte ha capitulado.[6]

『犬売ります』は、テオと父親、画家を夢見た親子二代の挫折の物語といっていい。これに、浮気が発覚したあと、父親が家族を棄て遠い町に行って別居するようになること、そして、母親と姉が 1985 年のメキシコ大地震で倒壊した病院で犠牲者になることを加えれば、悲劇的な色合いはいっそう濃いものとなるであろう。

物語は、作中人物の現在と過去を行きつ戻りつしながら、メキシコ革命以降のメキシコの政治と美術の流れをなぞりつつ進んでゆくが、悲劇的なものがフアン・パブロ・ビジャロボス独特の風刺とユーモアにくるまれて語られているせいか、思いの外、あっけらかんとした明るさを伴った世界が現出しているように見えるのが不思議である。

6 ヴォルフガング・イーザー〈空所の理論〉の援用

そうした風通しのよい空気を作り出しているのは、本文中に見られる空白の効用と言えるかもしれない。新人作家にありがちな、ぎゅうぎゅう詰めの、息苦しさから解放された、ゆったりとした構成になっているのである。

主人公は、酒場でビールやテキーラを飲んで家に帰ると、ノートに向

6）Ibid. pág.55

かい、絵と文章からなる、小説ではないものを書いて愉しんでいる。け
れども、フランチェスカをはじめ読書会のメンバーからは、ひそかに小
説を書いていると思われている。

　おかげで、あるとき犬の肉を売った嫌疑がかかり、動物愛護法違反の
取り調べに来た巡査〈パパイア頭〉と顔見知りになったばかりに、のち
に小説の書き方を教えてくれとせがまれる始末。しぶしぶ引きうけ、い
やいやながら相手をする腹いせに、テオは、文学理論の本をぱらぱらめ
くって、ドイツの文学研究者、ヴォルフガング・イーザーの〈空所の理
論〉を含む、次のような一節を読みあげて〈パパイア頭〉を煙に巻くの
である。

　「文学史を分析すると、空所は、物語経済学の要素、あるいは修辞学
の省略法に特徴づけられる、単なる緊張とサスペンスを生み出すものか
ら、断片的な性格をそなえた現代文学の主役に躍り出たことを示してい
る。ヴォルフガング・イーザーによれば、断片化された性格をもつ物語
形式は、空所の貢献度を高める方に向かうのである。もっとも、空所が
残されたままの組み立てになっていれば、読者はずっといら立ちをおぼ
えることになるけれど」。

*Un análisis de la historia literaria muestra el traslado de los espacios
vacíos como elementos de economía narrativa o como productores de
tensión y* suspense *— caracterizados en la figura de la elipsis — a su
papel central en la literatura moderna, de naturaleza fragmentaria,
en la que, según Wolfgang Iser, las formas narrativas de carácter
segmentado permiten acrecentar aportaciones de espacios vacíos, de
manera que los ensamblajes dejados en blanco se transformen en
una irritación permanente de la actividad representadora del lector.*[7]

　そのあと、

　「すべてを語る必要はなくて、小説にはたくさん空所を入れていいんだ」

7）Ibíd. pág.171

— (…) No tienes que contarlo todo, puedes meter muchos espacios en tu novela.[8]

と言って教えさとす。

『犬売ります』をお読みになれば分かるけれど、フアン・パブロ・ビジャロボスは、まさに本書においてヴォルフガング・イーザーの〈空所の理論〉を実行に移しているのである。ひとつひとつの話がやたら短い上に、会話の部分が目立って多いのだ。あまりにも話が短すぎて、散文詩に見間違えそうになるところもある。そんなわけで、正直な話、この理論は筆者が翻訳を決意するときに大いに効き目を発揮することになった。もともと空白の美を尊ぶ日本人として嬉しい限りだったのである。

最後に、これは、目ざとい読者ならすぐにお気づきになるに違いないが、『犬売ります』は書き出し部分と締めくくり部分がまったく同じ文章になっている。つまり、物語がくるくるまわる円環的な構造をなしているのである。これは、この小説の世界が、過去から現在、現在から未来へと直線的に流れてゆく近代的な時間とは異なり、マヤ文明やアステカ文明に見られるような、循環している神話的な時間のもとにあることを示している。そういえば、作品の舞台となっている現メキシコ・シティーは、かつてのアステカ文明の都テノティティトランの廃墟の上に建設されていることが想い起こされる。

参考文献

1. Juan Pablo Villalobos—*Te vendo un perro*. Editorial Anagrama, Barcelona, 2015.
2. Ibid. — I'LL SELL YOU A DOG. High Wycombe, Los Angeles, 2016. Translated by Rosalind Harvey.
3. フアン・パブロ・ビジャロボス『巣窟の祭典』難波幸子訳、作品社、東京、2013。
4. テオドール・アドルノ『美の理論』大久保健治訳、河出書房新社、東京、1985。

8）Ibid. pág.171

【執筆者紹介】（執筆順）

パトリック・オニール	委嘱研究員・ノースカロライナ大学チャペルヒル校 文学部教授
ジョン・ホイットマン	委嘱研究員・コーネル大学・国立国語研究所教授
和 田 葉 子	主　幹・関西大学　外国語学部教授
ローベルト・ヴィットカンプ	研　究　員・関西大学　文学部教授
近 藤 昌 夫	研　究　員・関西大学　外国語学部教授
川 神 傳 弘	客員研究員・関西大学　名誉教授
鼓　　　宗	研　究　員・関西大学　外国語学部教授
平 田　　渡	研　究　員・関西大学　名誉教授

関西大学東西学術研究所研究叢書 第11号

Trends in Eastern and Western Literature, Medieval and Modern.

令和 2 （2020）年 3 月 25 日　発行

編著者	和 田 葉 子
発行者	関 西 大 学 東 西 学 術 研 究 所 〒564-8680　大阪府吹田市山手町 3-3-35
発行所	株式会社 ユ ニ ウ ス 〒532-0012　大阪府大阪市淀川区木川東 4-17-31
印刷所	株式会社 遊 文 舎 〒532-0012　大阪府大阪市淀川区木川東 4-17-31

Trends in Eastern and Western Literature, Medieval and Modern.

Contents